Rosalind Slater was born in Northern England where she spent her first 26 years. After marrying young, she emigrated to Canada with her husband and two small daughters. One year later, a third daughter was born.

She received two degrees in Literature from the University of Guelph, Ontario and it was when she began research for her Master's thesis, studying the Condition of England Novels of Elizabeth Gaskell, that she became enthralled with her Northern roots and from where this her first novel was born. Her life since then has taken a circuitous route.

She spent many years in a local theatre company as an actor and a director of many plays. More latterly, she took on the task of full-time caregiver to her husband when he was diagnosed with A.L.S. Since his death she has been reborn as a musician taking joyfully to playing flute, and as a writer. Now the wheel has turned full circle with this the publication of her long-awaited novel *To Have and to Hold*.

For my family who have walked the long road with me, and especially the original four: Keith, Diane, Hilary and Keirsten.

Rosalind Slater

TO HAVE AND TO HOLD

AUSTIN MACAULEY PUBLISHERS™

LONDON • CAMBRIDGE • NEW YORK • SHARJAH

A CIP catalogue record for this title is available from the British Library.

ISBN 9781398441330 (Paperback)
ISBN 9781398441347 (ePub e-book)

www.austinmacauley.com

First Published 2023
Austin Macauley Publishers Ltd ®
25 Canada Square
Canary Wharf
London
E14 5LQ

Over the years, many people have helped me bring this novel to publication. I'd first like to acknowledge the writers who were on a weekend at Totley Barton in Devon in 1974 and encouraged my basic idea. This idea came from my paternal grandmother who, as a young girl, worked at Cressbrooke Mill and knew some of the mill slaves who'd spent their lives spinning cotton. They told her their stories which I have used to enhance my own fertile mind in bringing you the story of Emma and Susie.

After many years in a dark cupboard, my notes came back to life with the help of a theatre friend who showed an interest in what I was writing. His name was John LHeureux and I wish to acknowledge him in memory. He was a great thespian.

When my first draft was ready, my granddaughter, Juliet Eales, offered her expertise as she read, corrected and encouraged my rewrites. Before I sent the then-final draft to my publisher, my three daughters Hilary, Diane and Keirsten read the finished work along with three friends Marilyn Whiteley, Elizabeth Bone and Karen Albertson who all gave comprehensive and constructive criticism. Throughout the rewriting phase, I am indebted to my grandson, Iain Lamont, who has helped me enormously to overcome my computer illiteracy.

To my friends Jill and Peter Gill, Jim Ball, Jacqui Coll, Liz Poulton, Ann Stahlman Marilyn and Mark Sears and Alan Mellors and the Friday club for their continued faith in me, I say a big thank you.

This acknowledgement would not be complete without mentioning my beloved and always supportive husband, Keith, who throughout our lives together was my one and only best friend.

Now I have only one more acknowledgement, to my publisher Austin Macauley who agreed to bring my first novel into the light and from whom I'm sure I will receive all the help and guidance that I need.

Chapter One
The Kidnapping

The barge was moored in the waiting bay. Large shadows could be seen stealthily making their way towards it along the canal cutting. Each shadow seemed to reflect a deformity in its rounded back, but as the figures came into the light, these humps were proven to be wriggling sacks from which muffled sounds escaped. The night was dark but not enough to hide the shadowy figures. One stumbled on a rock and dropped what he was carrying. He let out an oath as he bent to retrieve it, discovering as he did so that the sack had stopped its wriggling. It was just then that a waif appeared in the neck, and quietly winged it down the path.

'After him, catch the whelp!' cried the man and leapt into action. Soon another had joined him and the two men gave chase. Although the child had a start on them, the two well-fed men soon caught up and grabbed the urchin by the scruff; the older man gave him a cuff to his jaw that rendered him unconscious.

'That's a lively one. We'd better watch out for him or he'll give us trouble,' said the man. The other agreed as both re-hefted their loads and made to board the barge. Six or seven men followed, bumping their sacks after them down the stairs into the hold. The wriggling had now stopped and all was quiet as the shadowy men once again set out from the barge with empty sacks that needed to be filled.

'Where's the workhouse?' asked one of them. 'We've got a large load to pick up there.'

'Aye, it's aways on the other bank, we'd better cross by the drawbridge further upstream,' the other answered.

Quietly, the shadows once again made their way to where the contraband children were housed. It was a long night but eventually, all were aboard and the barge master shook the reigns to alert old Dobbin, the drag horse, that it was time

9

to be off. The ponderous old cart horse slowly picked up the well-known route and sure-footedly began his long journey into the night, taking these urchins to start their apprenticeships in the cotton mills of the north.

One of these was little Emma, rain was falling as she came to her senses. She was cold. It was dismal. All around her in the darkness could be heard the cries of small children, 'Momma…Mom…Nursey, where are you?' But the only answer was the sound of water. She was scared, she began to cry…she was very cold…her bonnet had fallen off…she tried to replace it but her fingers wouldn't allow this small luxury of warmth. *Where am I,* she thought, *and where's Nanny?* She needed the chamber pot. Why didn't Nanny come? She began to cry again, big tears that ran down between her fingers. The two ragged girls sitting next to Emma smelled. She wrinkled her nose distastefully and covered her eyes so that they wouldn't notice her. Peeping between her fingers she saw the elder looking at her with flinty eyes. She had a snub nose and she looked like Emma's toy monkey, which brought on another deluge of tears.

'What're you crying for?' said the monkey girl.

'I miss my nursey and the man wouldn't let me bring my monkey,' said Emma plaintively.

She'd forgotten that she didn't want them to see her.

'Don't be so soft, you'll not see them again. You'd better buck up,' said the monkey child.

Emma wished she'd said nothing. She'd been right in the first place. She didn't like her. The smaller girl was holding something tightly in her fingers.

'What's that you've got, Susie?' said the monkey girl.

''s nothing,' said the little child.

'Gi' it to me, you know Ma wouldn't let you have it,' said the monkey girl.

Although the younger one held on for all she was worth, the monkey girl finally won the day, prizing open the other's hand and extracting a pendant on a chain.

'Give it to me, give it to me,' wailed little Susie as she bit the other sharply on her arm.

'Ow!' the monkey girl yelled, dropping the prize. As quick as lightning, the little girl grabbed the trinket and raced off with it down the deck with the other one following her screaming.

'No running,' called a masterful voice as a large woman with a warty face entered the fray. 'What's all this about?' she asked.

'She's taken my pendant,' said the monkey girl, 'and Ma said I had to have it.'

'That's not true!' said the other child, her fierce green eyes watering under her carroty-coloured hair. 'She stole it out of Ma's drawer and it's mine because Ma took it off me.'

'I'll have that then,' said the woman, 'if you can't agree, neither of you'll have it.'

'It's not fair, it's not fair,' both children cried.

'Silence!' yelled the big woman, the wart on her nose wobbling as she spoke. 'I'll put this somewhere safe and you can have it back when you agree.'

The small girl moved away from the monkey girl and moved back to her seat beside Emma, choking on her tears. The sobbing and choking left her gasping for breath and she was promptly sick on Emma.

As Emma looked down at her small hands where the vomit was mixing with the salt of her tears, she suddenly was reminded of the nursery window at home when raindrops formed rivulets and washed away the winter London fog... Where was Nanny? A fresh burst of grief was shared by the sickly child and, in fear, the two clung together. Oblivious to the smell, rain and the now churning canal, they fell asleep in each other's arms.

Daybreak saw no change in the weather. The rain poured down onto the boat full of children who huddled together for warmth. Their little ghost-like faces peeped out of the shadows. Cold and near clemmed, for they'd eaten little in the past twenty-four hours, they set up a thin wailing cry. Emma woke up shivering. Her thin wool coat was not warm enough in this weather. She noticed the large woman now wearing a blue apron making her way along the crowded deck.

'Don't cry, Susie,' she said to the red-headed child, 'the lady's going to feed us.'

'Don't want any,' Susie replied but was induced to take the stale crust that was plopped into her new friend's outstretched hand.

'Where's your sister gone to?' Emma asked her.

'I don't care, and she's not my sister,' Susie lisped.

Emma was secretly glad that the big monkey girl had disappeared on the crowded barge. She and Susie could be friends together, she thought, without the other one interfering. She took off her thin coat and shared it with her new friend, draping it around both of their shoulders. The gesture seemed to warm her, and her unhappiness subsided a little.

The journey finally ended and the now orphans were shoved or carried, depending on their condition. Some were exhausted and they were encouraged to hold on to a rope which had a handhold for each small child. The rain of the previous night had made the cobblestones slippery and without the rope it would have been difficult for the children to walk on them without falling. The snake of weary limbs, moved relentlessly along by the man, inched its way out of the small dock and into open fields. A large barn came into view and it was here that the children were housed until they could be divided between the two mills in the district.

The two gentlemen in top hats came into the large barn.

'Line up along that wall,' said the man. The little ones cried not knowing what was going to happen. Emma and Susie held hands tightly. They didn't want to be separated when they'd just found each other. The man came into the barn and held up his hand for quiet.

'Now,' he said, 'Mr Brierly is going to pick the children he wants, so stand tall and he'll choose.'

Emma and Susie held their breath as one and put their shoulders back trying to make a good impression on Mr Brierly. The tall thin man sniffed with his pointy nose as he surveyed the offerings. His sharp gaze seemed to see everything and it made the little girls fear the unknown. It came to rest on them, and then he lifted his black-clad arm and pointed a long finger in their direction. Happily, the two little girls let out a united breath, knowing they'd been chosen together.

Then the fat man came forward to choose and all of the children knew which way they were going. This done, they spent another day in the barn waiting until daylight evaporated and they could be brought in secret to the mills.

Mr Jones marched his workers off first and Emma was happy to see monkey girl in their midst. Seeing her retreat, Susie went off to find the woman with the wart on her nose to ask if she could have her pendant back, and Emma marvelled at such a little girl having the courage to speak up for her rights.

All the children were taken to a large brick building with tiny dirty windows climbing up and down its side, like caterpillar eyes staring down at them. The scary building was next to where they were housed, in the apprentice hall, until they were older.

The hall had wooden bunk beds and the children were paired off two to each bed. They were to find out later that shifts were worked and the beds were used almost continually turn and turn around. Although the beds were very hard, the children slept well, because they worked long hours in dreadful conditions.

That first night Emma and Susie had no idea where they were or why they were there. No one thought to enlighten them about what their lives would be like and why they'd been brought to this large scary building with caterpillar eyes that looked down on them all the time. They found out soon enough. Next morning, they were awakened early and taken to the large building with its dirty staring eyes. Each child was allotted to a worker who was labouring on the big clanking machines.

The new arrivals were scared and cried a lot but soon they were silenced by a man waving a big stick and threatening them if they were 'frabbit.' They had to watch the second-year apprentices to learn how to be scavengers. Their small bodies and tiny fingers could get into small parts of the machine to clean out blockages from the cotton fluff. This was extra scary because the machines were not stopped whilst they did their jobs.

A boy named Joe was teaching Emma and he showed her the missing place on his hand where fingers had been. 'What happened?' Emma asked.

'You have to be fast,' said Joe, 'or your fingers can get caught in the machinery and torn out, like mine were.'

'Did you cry?' said Emma.

'Not much,' Joe answered, 'you have to be tough to show them they'll not win.'

'But didn't it hurt an awful lot?' said Emma.

Joe was thoughtful before answering, 'You have to be fearless to survive. Now let's get on with showing you how to work or we'll both be punished.'

In this world where cotton was king and time meant money either gained or lost, human life meant little and was dragged along into the cotton gold rush. This then was the life that Emma and Susie had been displaced into and the two girls were forced to learn quickly.

But it was Emma's common sense that kept Susie protected many a time as the years went by. They shared everything as they grew up side by side in the dismal mill, two small lives entwined to strengthen each other. The one jolly, more carefree, the other careful not to incur the wrath of their owners.

Chapter Two
The Early Years

The dreary, difficult years dragged by with the only break in the week being Sunday when Mr Brierly, being a religious man, had the mill closed. The workers attended church on Sunday morning and following worship they had an hour of Sunday school where they were taught by Mrs Brierly and the older Misses Brierly to read their Bibles. In the school room where Sunday school took place there were pictures on the wall depicting stories from the Bible. Emma loved looking at these as she went off into her own dream world. There was one depicting the parable of the talents and another fearful one which showed Heaven and Hell.

Emma liked the Heaven part with God sitting in glory wearing white robes, but the picture of Hell was terrifying to the small child. It showed a Satan figure which resembled Mr Brierly and small devils with pitchforks dancing around him and prodding the sinners in the flames which burst forth out of the very ground. In the foreground of the picture were the newly dead who were being weighed and their twisted faces showed their agony when they were found wanting. This fearful scene made a great impression on Emma and she determined never to be found wanting.

The children sat on little stools in this room, their thin dresses making the seats extra hard, as the Brierly women swished around like butterflies in perfumed dresses of light-coloured silk.

'I think that Delilah and Jezebel would have fine clothes like theirs,' whispered Susie one day when they were old enough to begin noticing that not everyone was dressed in patched skirts of cheap calico.

'Hush,' whispered Emma glancing at Hell, 'we don't want to be in trouble for talking above our station.'

'I'd like it very well,' retorted Susie, 'if someday I didn't have to sew patches on the patches to keep my body covered.'

Just then she received a hard slap to the back of her head as Mrs Brierly, gliding silently behind her, heard what she was whispering.

'Pay attention, girl,' said Mrs Brierly. 'There is no reason to talk. You should be listening to the scripture, which is being read for you so beautifully by Miss Maud, so that you may hear and know the word of our lord.'

Susie looked at her angrily but dared say no more. She mouthed at Emma, her eyes flashing, 'Why should I know the lord, he doesn't seem to know or care for me.'

Luckily, she had the sense to lower her lids or she'd have received harsher punishment, and Emma saw no reason to answer, she knew Susie's temper would get both of them into trouble if she didn't watch out.

The two girls always shared their dreams when they were alone. This didn't happen very often, but they usually managed a short time on Sunday afternoons when they were doing their weekly washing in the steamy cellar washhouse. Even there they were not alone and had to be careful that no one heard their plans of escape.

And so the years went on and they were moved into the garret to sleep with the other women. Now fully 'trained', they had their own looms to tend, and they worked close by each other in the weaving shed.

...

'Oft in danger, oft in woe, onward Christians, onward go,' Mr Brierly sang out, his fine baritone voice in competition with the clanking of the shuttles as they flew to and fro.

'Oh, look out Emma, here comes Mr Brierly!' Susie bent her head lower over her work so that her owner would not see the remains of laughter around her mouth. Mr Brierly didn't approve of levity. He felt that it cut down on production. Susie was a merry young girl and found it very hard to conform to the dour Northerner's standards. Emma cried herself to sleep many a night because of the harsh treatment inflicted on the unflinching Susie. 'Susie, you're too proud by half,' would remark the conforming Emma. 'If you'd be more humble, they'd be kinder to you.'

15

'Maybe they have my body and that by fraud, but no one is ever going to hold me against my will.' The girls would whisper together in their own special corner of the garret. This was the only time they could have any speech. Although they worked side by side, the noise of the machinery made it impossible to talk during the day. Both of them had learned to lip read out of necessity but it was nice to have a cosy chat together.

'Come along girls, there's a time and place for everything, wipe that smile from your mouth,' roared Tom Burly. Susie's jollity soon subsided. She didn't want to be reported to Mr Brierly. The mill owner was a formidable figure; he hadn't changed much in the years since they'd been bought by him. His habitual black dress enhanced his resemblance to the devil in Susie's mind, and though his hymn singing and references to scripture in his spoken word would imply he saw himself very differently, his workers had their own ideas. Susie bent her head to better see the frame she was working on.

'I'll show him a thing or two when I'm grown up,' she mouthed at Emma. Emma was silent and thoughtful. Would they ever grow up, she was thinking. Oh, she knew they'd grow bigger. She'd noticed a bodily change in herself already on that score, but would they ever be real people and not just mill orphans? The conditions in the mill were very dangerous and many of the children had been crippled for life or even killed by the long hours and harsh treatment they had had to endure.

As they whispered together that night, Susie made a sharp statement.

'No one will keep me in t'mill once I'm grown up.' Emma was silent. She'd like to think Susie was right but wasn't sure how they could escape. A girl had tried it once saying that she would lead the way. The other orphans had been too scared to follow and the escapee, Lizzie was her name, had been held down by men while Tom Burly had cut her hair so close that he had nicked her scalp in many places. After that an opportunity had not arisen. Tom Burley had made doubly sure that no one else would try to escape. They were kept prisoner except on Sunday afternoons and even that day, once they had finished Sunday School, (which Mr Brierly insisted on for the looks of the thing) someone was always around to make sure that they did their bits of washing. Emma wondered if it would all end in the typhoid or pneumonia as was the case with many of the captives. They'd had many deaths in the cold months of each year and their work force by now was so depleted that Mr Brierly had had to bring some more apprentices over from the other mill. They were a sorry-looking lot. Mr Jones had not given his best workers, not him.

One girl, who'd had an accident with the machinery, had half of her face cut away and her temper matched the angry red whorls on her skin. She looked out of a half-closed eye, daring the world to tangle with her. But Emma didn't have the energy to fight. Most of the time she was too tired to even think. She was a dreamy girl and sometimes would go off into her own world. She was thankful for Susie's presence. Having a friend made life a lot more bearable.

'Susie, are you awake?' A grunt was the reply from the other pallet. The other garret residents were asleep also.

'What do you want, Emma?'

'I was only wondering if you were still awake.'

'Well, I am now. You are a one Emma. We'll never be able to wake up in t'morning.'

'I was just thinking about Christmas, do you think Ned will come home this year?'

'I don't know.' Susie grunted.

'It would be lovely if he gave me a sugar pig again, it tasted that sweet,' said Emma longingly.

'Emma, he only threw it to you because he didn't want it hi'self. He didn't even know who he'd thrown it to. You were just lucky to be passing at the right moment.'

'Well! I can dream, can't I, Susie Brierly?'

'Please yourself if you're daft enough to turn your head for someone who's above your station,' Susie returned.

'I wasn't turning my head, I just said it was sweet, that's all. Can't a body enjoy a bit of sweetness if she wants to. Oh, I'm going to sleep. There's no talking to you these days, you're getting so high up,' said Emma.

'Well, I like that. You're the one who's after sugar pigs from Mr Brierly's nephew and you're the one who woke me up from my sleep. I'll say good night to you,' said Susie grumpily.

Nothing more was said by the two girls, but it was a long time before either of them settled down to sleep.

What was wrong with her? Emma wondered. She had done nothing lately but quarrel with Susie, and Susie was her best friend. Oh, damn Ned Brierly and the sugar pig and Christmas and everything. She sighed, if only she could get a

Christmas present of her very own like the two Misses Brierly, but that was a dream that would never come true. She fell painfully asleep in a sober mood. At least they didn't have to work on Christmas day, and that would be a treat.

Chapter Three
Life in the Mill

The slow weeks crawled relentlessly on. The girls rose at 4:30, for their day began at 5 A.M. Emma, now fourteen, had her own looms to tend and though the job was hard, she liked it more than being skivvy for the back tenters. She was still in the same room with its cloying atmosphere, since the fluff from the raw cotton floated around, but she felt a renewed sense of pride to watch the calico pouring out of the machine as she tended it. Tom Burly rarely had to remind Emma of her responsibilities. She quietly got on with the job, her small wiry hands working effortlessly to achieve an even result. Back and forth flew the shuttle as the stream of white calico coiled into the waiting skip.

'Come on, Emma, breakfast time,' yelled Susie as she hurried past Emma. Why was Susie always so eager to enter the eating room? Always the eternal optimist, Susie dreamed of the day when their meagre breakfast might take on a better shape than gruel (optimistically called porridge by Mrs Raymond, the oversized cook) and a half slice of oat cake dished out to each girl.

'Oh Emma, it's burnt again,' the disappointed Susie whispered as the tainted smell drifted to their nostrils.

'Poor Susie, I've given up looking forward, that way I'm not hurt like you are.'

'Oh no, what about sugar pigs?'

Emma was silent. At times Susie could be that sharp with her. She wished she hadn't mentioned the sweetmeat but if you couldn't tell your innermost thoughts to your best friend, what good was friendship? Emma sipped the weak tea just passed along to her. This was one part of breakfast that she enjoyed. The scalding liquid warmed her as it trickled through her chilled body. How cold the mill was at this time of year? Well, never mind next week was Christmas and then she could look forward to spring.

'Time to go,' called Tom Burly.

'Oh, have a heart, we've only just got us tea,' said Susie.

'None of that lip from you my girl,' yelled Tom Burly. 'Now back to it.' Susie moved slowly along with the other women.

Emma hung back a bit. She hadn't forgiven her yet for her earlier taunt. Maybe if she treated her a bit cooler, Susie would watch her tongue a bit more. Emma, returning to her loom, went off into her own reverie:

On Christmas Eve Ned Brierly would arrive home and after taking tea with his family, his uncle would maybe happen to say: 'Look here lad, as you're going to take my place in t'mill someday, how'd you like to take a look at things like?'

And of course being a dutiful nephew, Ned would reply: 'Nothing I'd like better, uncle.' As the two men strode between the looms taking in the operation of the mill at a glance, suddenly Ned would notice her fine calico and: 'Who is this beauty who weaves such a fine piece of work?' he would ask.

'Why that's Emma,' his uncle would reply, 'the best worker I've had in many a day.'

'Haven't I seen you somewhere before?' Ned would say, as Emma dutiful to a sign from the owner would move away from her loom for a minute.

Trembling with shyness, Emma would answer him: 'Yes sir, 't was I as received your sugar pig last Christmas,' and, as he saw the longing in her eyes, he would put his hand in his coat pocket and produce another sweet meat similar to the previous one.

'Do you like sweets, Emma?' he'd say.

'Oh, yes sir,' she'd blushingly reply...

'Emma! Where are your thoughts going a wandering?' Susie was beside her. 'You'll do yourself a mischief one of these days if you go daydreaming like that.'

Emma came back to earth with a bang and guiltily returned her thoughts to the job at hand. She'd better forget sweets and dreams. These kinds of thoughts were not fitting for a mill orphan. The material flowed out of the loom, a sea of white foam pouring on as it carried her young life with it.

Christmas day, that long awaited festival came and went and brought no Ned with it nor sweetmeats to lighten the dismal time for Emma. Ned, it was rumoured, had gone to spend Christmas in the Midlands with a college friend and wouldn't be seen until later in the year, maybe not until Easter-time.

Chapter Four
Spring at Last

The spring flowers appeared on the bank, breaking through the hard earth in their determined way.

'See Susie, there's inspiration for us indeed,' said Emma as they walked two by two to church one cold spring morning. 'If those fragile plants can battle through the hard ground to give us a bit of pleasure in our dismal lives, there's hope for you and me to get away from t' mill.'

'Am with you there, lass, but how do you suggest we go about it? We've only Sunday to us selves, and then not for long.'

'Am not so sure,' answered her friend, 'but I'm determined to try. I know little else but t' mill and we've been in it all but twelve ye'r an all.'

'Ay it's been a long hard haul since that time we sailed along t' canal in that rickety boat. We've seen plenty a' changes in t' loft, more than half our lot has died. There must be a reason why you an' me have been saved,' remarked Susie.

'And we're not going to find it here,' returned Emma. 'I for one want to know some 'at about rest' at world.'

'Well, I'm with you, you know that,' said Susie, squeezing her hand. 'We've gone through a lot together lass and I'm game for anything you are.'

As the mill folk filed silently into the cold church, Susie and Emma were more pensive than usual. The prayers were very welcome. Emma was able to allow her mind some freedom as she knelt on the thread-bare cushion. Her thoughts drifted effortlessly away, though not, sadly, to her maker. Over the years she had got used to allowing her mind to drift, as her body would have done if she'd been free. Today her thoughts were taking her to enjoy the sunshine and the richness of the country-side surrounding the mill. And maybe her maker heard her silent cry for help. As the steward rose to read the notices, Emma's thoughts were suddenly arrested by what he was saying. It was his job to impart the secular side of church activity and his words 'A village fete with fair,' suddenly jolted her back to earth. When, when? She silently begged, but the more alert Susie had heard the full announcement and gleefully turned her full gaze on Emma.

'Next Sunday week,' she whispered, 'do you think we can escape in t' afternoon?'

'Shush,' Jessie Burns spat at them, her twisted mouth making more noise than they were. 'Do you want to get all of us in trouble?'

'Better watch out, Emma, we don't want any of them telling tales on us. Just because some of them live at home or know who their fathers are, they think they're better than us,' Susie whispered.

As the priest intoned the benediction Emma realised that at last the long service was almost over. For once it had gone on much too long. Usually she enjoyed this, her only outing of the week, but today she had more to think of and she didn't need any distractions. They left the stone building with the rest of the workers and returned to their home in the dark mill. There they shared their thoughts on the news they'd received, whispering as quietly as they could.

Susie, who was always the one with ideas, though sometimes these were so far-fetched that they were likely to get the girls in trouble, gripped Emma's hand excitedly. 'We could offer to walk over Eyam way to deliver some 'at for Mr Brierly,' she hopefully said.

'And why would we when we haven't done it afore?' retorted Emma. 'No, it's got to be something more simple than that.'

They both pondered on the subject as they washed their few small garments, rubbing them on the washboard to remove spots and stains. The cellar where they worked was a dismal place with a musty smell and no window, worse even than their weekly habitat.

'You know I don't know about you, Susie, but whenever I hear of the possibility of a change of scene, only to have it whisked away from me, I feel lower in my spirits than if I'd never heard of it.'

For once Susie had nothing to say but she hung her head in a forlorn manner showing her friend her similar feelings. They were both a bit low spirited for a few days, but finally it was Mr Brierly himself who solved the problem. On the Friday evening prior to the fair he suddenly appeared with Tom Burly, whilst they were eating a mess of greasy potato and bacon which was their supper, and announced that he needed six volunteers to work in his name for a good cause.

22

It was Tom's irascible finger which pointed out those stalwarts for him. This was similar to the time they'd 'volunteered' to go on the barge. Decisions were always made for them.

Though the girls were half dead with fatigue they followed Tom Burly as he led them to the heath. Here to their surprise, they found that they had been volunteered to help unload and erect stalls and side show tents for the Whitsun Fair, to be held for the following two days. The girls' spirits rose and their tired limbs developed a new spurt of energy. This work, though hard, was a fine change from anything they'd known before. It was good to have some part in the fair, if only as workers.

When at midnight, they felt they could go on no longer, Mr Knowles, the church warden, finally said, 'I think we'll call it a day.' The weary troupe made its way back to the mill. They were met by Tom Burly, who, opening the door for them, made way for them to climb to the garret, re-locking the door in their wake.

'I don't know how he thinks we'll escape tonight, or where he thinks we'll go,' said Susie, 'but I'll have a try one of these days you just mark my words, Emma Brierly.'

Saturday dawned bright but cold and 4:30 A.M. arrived too soon for the night workers.

'Ooo, all my joints ache,' Susie exclaimed as she rose stiffly from her pallet.

'Mine too,' said Emma, 'I expect it's all that extra work last night as 'as done it.'

'Yes it must be nice to be a lady and go to the merry fair instead of working on it like merry hell.'

'Susie, watch your language,' laughed Emma, 'or somebody'll tell Tom Burly and he'll have your tongue scrubbed with carbolic again like last time.'

'What are you two at?' said Bess Watson. 'You're getting above your station, Susie.'

'Oh what do you know of my station or anyone else's either?' retorted Susie. 'We'll show you when we run away from t' mill.'

'Where'll you go?' Bess questioned, hopefully.

'I don't know, but we'll find somewhere, I can tell you, we shan't be like you, being owned until we're old women.'

'You'll be very clever, with a big stick and a basket of eggs, but young girls 'as 'as no relations is safer being looked after in t' mill than traipsing around t' countryside on their own. You'll see, Charles Peace'll get you,' Bess retorted.

'Oh, yes,' scoffed Susie, ''an 'll have a good try.' But, as Bess made her slow way downstairs, Susie was thoughtful. 'I wonder who that is, Emma.'

'Who, Charles Peace? I don't know, I suppose it's an old wives' tale like all the rest. You know the man in the moon, old Nick, Charles Peace,' Emma replied.

'Oh yes, like that is it?' and Susie laughed as they made their way down to the mill. The workers were quiet that spring morning, as they toiled at their looms. Emma worked along with the others but the hard labour of the previous evening had a deadening effect on her control and the shuttle as it flew from side to side added a soporific effect to the general motion. Suddenly her head fell forward into the works, and though not badly hurt, she was stunned by the accident.

Susie helped her to sit down for a minute and herself tried to tend the other girl's racing machinery, but it was too much for her and as bad luck would have it, Tom Burly noticed the disturbance.

'What's going on here?' he yelled as he made his way across the greasy floor. No one spoke. They knew enough to keep quiet until questioned again. An answer at this point would probably be construed as impertinence and would be an excuse for him to use violence. Surprisingly, however, a voice spoke up in defence of the stoppage.

'Them girls has had enough, Tom Burly, working them til midnight and then expecting them to get up and work at 5-o-clock. It's not right.'

Susie looked around to see who had spoken and received a cuff for her action. She lowered her head quickly but not before Burly had seen the hatred she felt towards him shining out of her green eyes. Tom Burly was a coward and she knew that the blow he had inflicted on her was because he was too afraid to aim it at her helper.

The short break had nonetheless done Emma a great deal of good and the dizziness now having passed, both girls were able to return to their looms. A while later, Emma was aware that someone was standing behind her. This sense of a presence was verified out of the corner of her left eye. Trying not to show her discomfort, she carried on with her weaving but it was a difficult task with a stranger standing in such close proximity.

After what seemed like an eternity, the figure moved into her sight and beckoned her to leave her looms for a minute. Emma was surprised that Mr Brierly himself wanted to speak to her. She readily obeyed his command and was delighted to hear his next words. 'Emma, I have heard that you and Susie have been doing extra work to help the community and I'd like to give you something in return. The two of you may go to the fair for two hours this evening along with the others who helped erect the stalls.'

Emma was overwhelmed at what she heard. Mr Brierly could not resist a chance to teach, however, and he went on to catechize her on hard work bringing forth its own reward. Emma didn't care, her heart was singing. Never in her life before had she been given a treat of her very own, and her confused joy knew no way to react, after her stuttered thank you to her kind benefactor. She turned to share her joy with Susie, but Mr Brierly had moved on down the mill and was now addressing her friend. Emma's pent up emotion burst forth in tears of joy. Susie at last was free to share that feeling and the two girls hugged each other in their delight and for the rest of the day, with a new energy, they worked with a will.

As 8-o-clock chimed in the church tower, the small excited band gathered in the loft waiting for Tom Burly to turn the key. This was the first time they'd ever been allowed out at night, and the preparations they'd made for their treat were in line with young aristocrats getting ready for a ball. The girls wore their Sunday dresses of brown Bombazine under their shawls and had polished up their clogs as best they could. The men had trimmed each other's hair and beards so as not to look disreputable as they rubbed shoulders with wealthier folks.

'Who'd'a thought owd Brierly ud 'a come up trumps,' said a garrulous old man at the back of the small group.

'This is the first time in my living memory he's done it,' spoke up another. Bill and Ben, brothers who had been sold into apprenticeships by the poor house and lived most of their lives in the mill, were the spokesmen. And their comments spoke for the whole group. None of the workers present knew the reason for Mr Brierly's generosity, and as they didn't want him to change his mind at the last minute, they only wondered and marvelled at their good luck. As they left the mill, Emma and Susie skipped ahead, delighting in the sweet smell of an early spring evening. The other four, somewhat older members of the group, were no less joyful but were a bit more subdued. Climbing out of the mill hollow, they beheld a new crescent moon peeping over the ridge.

'A moon to wish by,' said Meg Davis as she caught up with the younger women. The three of them linked arms as they jog-danced along the cobbled street and sang a merry tune, their clogs keeping time to the words.

'As I was going to strawberry fair singing, singing, buttercups and daisies I met a man with gold in his hair fal-de-re.'

Bill caught up with the merrymakers and taking his responsibility as eldest member more seriously than need be, he chided them for their noisy revelry, his breath whistling through a gap between his misshapen teeth.

'*Whist* it's not for mill slaves to disturb worthy citizens with their noise.'

'Oh shut up your preachifying, do, Bill Brierly. Surely a body has the right to enjoy one evening in a whole lifetime!' spoke up Meg.

'Silence woman and know your place,' said Bill.

'Hush both of you or the whole time out will be ruined by your quarrelling,' said Ben. 'Listen, I can hear the music of the merry-go-round. Let's all hurry to get the most out of our break from the mill.'

As they approached the heath and came to Farmer Walker's field, they could hardly believe their eyes. It had been transformed into a very fairy land. Colour, light and sound seemed to emanate from it in one mass. The fair ground with its booths and stalls decorated with glittery objects, and the merry-go-round similarly decorated with tiny mirrors, twinkled joyfully picking up stray light from the gas lamps on the high street by the church. The mill workers stood and gazed in awe, a little fearful of so much happy abandon.

'Emma, let's get away from t' others for a while and see what we can find,' said the ever-adventurous Susie.

'Don't you be getting yourself lost,' called Bill after them, as the two girls moved off into the crowd.

'Roll up, roll up and see one of the wonders of the world.' A man dressed in a tiger skin and top boots caught the girls' attention.

'Ooo, look at him, Emma.'

'I am but I don't think we ought to,' replied her friend.

'Come along young ladies, don't be shy,' called tiger skin. 'Can I interest you in the spectacle within my tent?'

'No thank you sir,' whispered Emma, but Susie pulled her towards the tent.

'What does it cost?' She enquired.

'For you my dear, I'll strike a bargain, both of you for the price of one.'

'But we have no m…' Emma began to say money but Susie delivered a smart kick with her clog and the other girl was left gasping.

'I could let you have my shawl,' said Susie, and as she said to Emma later, he looked as if he might need it if the weather got colder, the tiger skin not covering his arms. The man's pleasant demeanour changed when he found out the girls had no money.

'Be off with you,' he scowled. Then looking at Susie he seemed to change his mind. 'You come back yourself,' he whispered to her, 'after I get off here.'

'And what would I be doing here alone, and after the show is over?' asked Susie wonderingly.

'I could show you a few wonders of my own,' laughed tiger skin, but Emma did not like the look in his eye. Even though Susie had kicked her ankle, she wasn't going to let her out of her sight. She dragged her friend unwillingly away. Susie was always ready to find out about things, but not always cautious. Just then they caught up with Meg who was watching a group of men at the shooting gallery.

'One of them men has just won a trifle bowl!' she greeted them excitedly.

'That's nothing Mrs, he won a pair of dogs last year,' broke in the man standing next to them. 'Our John's a real professional with a gun.'

Emma's eyes turned to the person under discussion. She saw that he was dark haired though pale of complexion and not extra tall but strong in his arms as he lifted the gun for another shot. As she was watching him, she noticed the little card with the picture of a rabbit move slightly to the left and the pellet fell shy.

'You moved that card!' said the marksman angrily.

'No guvnu'r I didn't, don't be a sore loser.' The smile didn't reach the eyes of the thin greasy-haired fellow who was the stall holder.

'I'm not a sore loser but I don't like sly tricks and I say I should get another shot.'

'This shot costs money. I'm not going to be giving it away,' wheedled the man.

'Well, then, don't get between a marksman and his quarry.' John was becoming red in the face, his hands were clenching, and his brother sensing a skirmish, started to push through the crowd to join him.

Emma began to follow him but was restrained by Meg. 'Don't get involved, Emma, it's none of your business!'

'But I saw the card move!' retorted the younger girl. 'And I'm going to speak up for what's right.'

'If we get into trouble, we'll not be allowed out again!' said Meg catching hold of her shawl to restrain her. Emma however, was adamant and she pulled away from Meg and followed the man through the crowd. She was just in time to see John's brother trying to persuade him to 'let it be.'

The stall holder was looking smug until Emma spoke up, 'You did move that card mister, I saw you do it.'

John turned to see who had defended him, as the stall-holder laughing maliciously, asked, 'What does a girl like you know of a shooting gallery?'

John rounded on him to defend her. His blood was up and putting the gun down, purposefully clenched his fists and administered a blow to his opponent.

'Come along, John, let's get out of here,' his brother begged him, 'none of this is worth a fight.'

John grudgingly had to agree, but he was determined before he left to speak to the girl who had stuck up for him in a difficult situation.

'My name's Emma and I work in the mill,' she answered hesitantly, in reply to his question.

'Well, I'm John Blacklock and I work in the pit at Miller's Dale,' he returned. 'So Emma, would you care to join us for a drink of something to warm you? Maybe your friends would like to come too. We've got to meet the lads over there,' he pointed to the pub in the village square. Meg was a bit apprehensive but when she saw how excited Emma and Susie were, she allowed herself to be persuaded and they all trooped across to the crowded public house.

The Whitsun Fair had brought more people than was usual into the warm interior of the 'Black Swan'. Light and pleasant chatter spilled out to welcome the newcomers as John opened the door for his party of friends. The girls were shy in all this masculine company. The evening was turning out to be more than any of them could have dreamt. The miners were a jolly bunch, well known in the Black Swan, and though rough they were polite enough to the women.

'Now what'll it be?' John invited them to join him.

'Nothing stronger than ale, I thank you,' spoke up Meg, 'these girls ain't used to strong drink.'

'Well, good home brewed ale will take a lot of beating,' said Matt. 'Let's all drink to your fair saviour John in good home brew.'

Blushingly Emma accepted the glass that was proffered to her. The light glanced off the amber liquid as she raised it to her lips carrying the warmth of the room and the company into the depth of her senses. Catching John's eye, she smiled her pleasure at the sensation of wellbeing this action had produced.

Raising his own glass in recognition, he was heard to murmur to his brother that he'd buy a glass anytime for the crooked stall holder who, by his sneaky action, had thrown Emma in his way.

Looking around her in wonder, Emma was mesmerised by the unaccustomed scene. Bright lights picked up the different coloured liquids behind the bar, splashing the tawny hue onto the faces of the patrons and washing away their usual pallor. 'I'd've never thought such a place existed,' Emma whispered to her friend.

'It's the kind of place we've always been warned against in church,' said Susie, 'but I can't see anything wrong here, can you?'

The older Meg was not so sure. 'It seems alright at present,' she said, 'but I suppose it depends who comes in here of a night.'

Just then a newcomer arrived and was made most welcome by the others. He was obviously a popular man as everyone moved over to make room for him.

'Give us a song Caleb,' shouted one of the miners. 'I thought you'd decided not to join us. We've met these young women at the fairgrounds so I'm glad you've come.'

'What'll you have me sing?' Caleb nodded to the women. Emma shook her head, she didn't know any songs.

'How about cherry ripe?' said John quietly, seeming to sense her reticence. 'That's a good song for mixed company.'

'Very well,' said the good-natured Caleb and he began to sing, his fine baritone voice swelling out joyously in the opening lines.

'Cherry ripe, cherry ripe, ripe I cry, fools and fair ones come and buy.'

Emma sat spellbound delighting in the mellow tones. 'I'll remember this night for the whole of my life,' she said and Susie agreed, adding her opinion of the light hearted song and comparing it favourably with the hymn singing of their owner.

'Though they are both baritone, Caleb's voice is so much more pleasing,' she said shyly.

'What're you women on about?' Matt said cheerily. 'We're usually in the Mucky Duck on Fridays. You can meet us here anytime you want to.'

Emma bit her lip. How easy life seemed to be for other people. These cheery miners would never believe what their lives were like if they told them. Abruptly she climbed off the stool with, 'we'd better go Susie,' thrown over her shoulder as she did so. Time was going by and they had to meet the others at the fair before returning to the mill. Though Susie protested, Meg agreed that time was going quickly.

'When'll I see you again?' John whispered to Emma.

'I don't know, maybe never,' she replied. Although he was puzzled by Emma's reply, he still insisted on seeing the women back to the fair, even though they protested.

'There are some 'rum 'uns around fair grounds,' John said, 'and I'd rather make sure you're all safe and sound than sit here drinking ale.' They walked sedately towards the fair, Matt gaining on them before they reached it. He upset their sedate promenade by catching Susie around the waist, and twirling her in his strong arms, in time to the music. Round and around they went, faster and faster until they couldn't keep on their legs and, falling to the ground, they dissolved into happy laughter.

Chapter Five
Susie Makes a Dash for It

After this taste of the outside world, Susie could not be still again. The night of freedom kept replaying over and over in her memory. Resentment for the men who had kidnapped her and forced her into a life of slavery became ever stronger as the days turned into weeks and soon a month had passed since the Whitsun Fair.

It was a Sunday afternoon and the girls were working on their laundry when Susie suddenly flicked soap suds into Emma's eye to gain her attention.

'Hey, what're you doing,' said Emma in an exasperated tone. 'You've wet me through!'

'Oh, keep your hair on,' retorted Susie, 'it's just that I've had an idea.'

'Go on then,' said Emma.

'Well, you know how the rolls of cloth are sent to the shipping room before being sent away?'

'Yes!' replied her long-suffering friend.

'How do you feel about stowing away in the middle of the roll, and making our escape that way?'

Emma was stunned at the idea, but thinking it through she thought that it might work. 'But there's not room for us both in one roll,' she pointed out, 'and the roller is too narrow, we'd have to somehow re-roll it more loosely. And when could we do that?'

'I've been thinking about that,' said Susie. 'If you were willing to try it, I'd roll you in the cloth of an evening, in fact the evening before the cart comes to fetch it. I think it comes Tuesday night, and then on Wednesday morning the fellows would come to collect it and you'd be out in the world. What do you think?'

Emma thought it was the most hair brained scheme she'd ever heard, but she didn't want to antagonise her friend so she just nodded quietly. 'But what about you.'

'Don't worry about me, I'll think of something else,' said Susie.

Another couple of weeks went by with nothing happening and the warm weather seemed to make life in the mill ever more dreary. Susie's temper became more erratic, her agile mind had jumped from one idea to another, not fastening clearly on any one plan. She could see the escape she'd planned, in the roll of cloth, working partially, but she couldn't see how she herself could follow Emma: and in addition to not wanting to be alone in the mill, she also didn't like the idea of her friend being abroad in the big world. Emma, she felt, needed a stronger presence to guide her.

One night as the women prepared for rest, Susie sat on her pallet and refused to undress.

'What's wrong with you, Susie?' Meg Watson spoke up. 'You can't take all night or we shall be blamed for wasting candles.'

'I'm not going to bed,' said the stubborn Susie.

'Well, suit yourself,' spoke up Meg, 'the morning will come soon enough for me.' And she dropped wearily onto her pallet.

'Susie, what's up with you?' Emma, though concerned, was also exasperated, she knew that Susie's volatile nature had been disturbed by their night of freedom.

'Mr Brierly had been better not to have let us out than to have you in this mood for over a month, now sharpen up or we'll all pay the price for your silliness.'

Susie looked up at her with a strange expression, her eyes burned like white hot metal in the foundry and Emma felt a similar burning of fear in her stomach.

'Emma, I'm not sleeping in this mill garret another night and that's flat so don't try to stop me, I'm making a break for it now and you can either come with me or not. It won't make any difference 'cause I'm going anyway.'

'What about our plans, Susie?' said Emma. 'Don't spoil it now by letting your temper take control of you, calm down and let's think it through quietly. Please Susie,' she begged as the other girl began to thrash about flailing her arms and screaming her wish to be released.

'Susie Stop!' and Emma made a grab for her arm as Susie became more hysterical rushing around the stifling garret. The other women added their voices

32

to Emma's but unlike her, most of them were only concerned for the consequences to themselves in Susie's wild behaviour. She began to pound on the locked door screaming her wish to be freed with Emma close behind trying to calm her.

'Susie please it's not the right time for this, we should talk about it some more and make our plans,' said Emma.

But Susie was past reason and she continued to bang and scream. The cacophony made it seem endless but only a few minutes had passed before Tom Burly's angry voice could be heard heralding his arrival on the scene and the rusty key was turned in the lock.

Emma who was still close behind Susie, trying to calm her friend down, did not realise that she had a plan and as the door opened Susie put it into practice, by instantly quieting and slipping aside. In the dark Tom grabbed the nearest limb. It was Emma's arm and as he wrenched it, he dislocated her shoulder, causing her to scream out in pain and fall backwards onto the floor. Susie, taking advantage of the commotion, slipped carefully around the door jamb and noiselessly out of the door, ending up standing on the landing outside. Now she crept downstairs silently, for she'd left her clogs behind her. And as she opened the big oak door and gingerly gained the outside, she was seized with such swinging emotions that she had to sit on the ground to control them. What joy she felt that she had reached the other side of that locked door but she was also beset by panic in being utterly alone for the first time in her life.

If only Emma were with her. If only they could have thought of a plan of escape that included them both, but Susie had realised as she puzzled constantly over the problem that it would be easier for one to make her escape than both of them. They had tried to make escape plans for much of their lives and now in the crucial hour, Susie had left Emma behind. Did she feel guilty? She wondered. She tried to rationalise that she did not. Although she'd heard Emma's cry of pain, she was not aware what had caused it and thought that it could have been because of her escape. Well, Emma had had the chance to follow her, she just didn't have the courage, Susie thought sulkily. Susie was choosing to forget that in her rush to leave she hadn't shared her plan with her friend, or given Emma time to consider. She sat forlornly on the ground for some time, feeling the pain of her loss, for though she tried to blame Emma's lack of courage, she finally had to admit that her impulsive nature was the main cause of her being alone.

Once having faced her own demons, she was ready to move on. What use was it to lose her chance of freedom, she thought, just because Emma hadn't come with her, and when she thought of her friend, she excused herself by saying that Emma had her own reason for holding back. Emma had not been the same, Susie thought, since she'd met John at the Whitsun Fair and it was because of John that she was willing to sacrifice her bid for freedom. And now Susie would show everyone that she had not been born to a life as a mill worker. Falteringly at first and then with a firmer tread, she started down the lane away from mill bottom. The clinkers on the road cut into her bare feet. But thinking that after all the hardship she'd suffered sore feet were a small problem, she strode out purposefully to a new life independent of rules and regulations forced on her by the masters of the cotton trade.

…

Meanwhile candles had been brought to the garret so that Tom Burly could 'take a look' at Emma's shoulder. Her arm hung loosely down her side and it was obvious to even the stubborn overseer that his violent action had caused damage to the girl. He was not one to admit his own faults, so he turned his anger onto the other garret dwellers and castigated them for the noise. In all the hubbub, Susie's absence was not immediately noticed. Emma's pain was obvious as she half swooned on her pallet. Burly tried, by an opposite action, to relocate the shoulder, but the scream Emma let out was enough to stop his attentions.

'I'll call for the nurse,' he said as he hastily backed downstairs. Meg ran to the swooning girl.

'I don't know how Susie could do that to all of us,' said the frightened woman. 'We'll all cop it when they find out she's gone, and you her best friend, in all that agony, oh well a day.'

Many hours passed before the local midwife, who did duty to the poor in all areas of nursing, puffed her body up the narrow stairs heralding her arrival with gasping breaths. By this time Emma was in such pain that she was nearly unconscious on her crude bed. Nurse Murgatroyd lowered her bulk down beside the suffering girl and gently took the injured limb.

Giving Emma a piece of knotted calico to chew on, she soothed the injured girl as she gently manipulated her shoulder whilst whispering to her with mother talk, 'There a day, my lovely child.' Finally she administered a dose of liquid

34

which burned as it trickled down Emma's throat, but did its job in helping her sleep, and easing her pain.

'There now, sleep my lovely,' said the nurse, knowing full well that Emma would get no time off to heal her wound. Tom Burly, maybe realising his wrong, left them alone for the rest of the short night and the errant Susie was given a few more hours to make good her escape.

...

Her first feeling of elation on leaving the cotton mill had now left her, and her spirits were low as the cold and damp struck through her thin shawl. She could not feel her bare feet and she decided to shelter under a low stone bridge. In the cold and lonely night, she could not help thinking of her life-long friend and wondering how Emma was taking her friend's actions. Taking her feet underneath her as she sat on the ground, she began to size up her situation. *Well, even though I'm alone, I'm free from t' mill. I can do anything I like and no one can stop me she thought bravely.* Cheered by this thought, the cold seemed not so bad. For a little while she fell into a restless, exhausted sleep. As first light began to creep along the horizon she slept on, troubled by nightmarish dreams of loaves of bread and hot sweet tea that were always just out of her reach. A slight sound startled her from her restless slumber.

A face too close to hers caused her to jump up and scream. The poor animal was more scared than she. As the black-faced sheep scudded out through the end of the bridge, it gave her an idea. Sheep always sheltered on the hill side and now that spring was here, be it a cold wet spring, many of the sheep would be in their folds for spring lambing. Susie decided that these lambing centres would be snug and warm during the cold nights so long as she could avoid the shepherds who would be around for emergencies.

Without more ado, she set out to climb the gentle hillside making towards a copse of trees for camouflage. The grass was soft under her sore cold feet. The mist evaporated as the sun began to rise in the sky. It would be a fine day after all, inspiring her spirits to rise with the sun and see how perfect the world looked out of the constriction of the mill walls.

Susie was not to know at this point that her hasty escape had caused more problems for her friends in Cressbrook mill. Discovering Susie's absence, Tom Burly had demanded to know her whereabouts. But as none of the garret dwellers knew anything about her after she'd tricked him into opening the door, his demands were futile. He ripped apart the small room, his surly face darkening more as his search proved useless. He would not admit his mistake however and continued to toss the small pallets around, his anger bringing out the red blotches on his face. There was no point in the workers saying that they couldn't see the events of the previous night, since they had no candle light, he still meted out punishments, and the 'Hands' were put on a fast until such time as Susie turned up again. (Like a bad penny Tom was heard to snarl.)

'What'll we do now?' spoke up Meg. 'Should we tell?'

'Can't tell what we don't know,' said Jessie Burns. 'Do you know something you're not telling?'

'No, I don't know anything,' Meg replied in a frightened voice. Emma awoke to the noises of the discord around her. She had a dull throbbing in her shoulder which was matched by the one behind her eyes. She tried to rise, but retching with the pain, fell back exhausted onto her hard pallet. Meg moved to her side and tried to help the injured girl, but it was no use. The dizziness the action of rising brought on made it impossible for Emma to so much as move.

'We'd better call Tom Burly,' said Meg.

'You do what you darn well like,' said the arrogant Jessie, 'but leave me out of it. I'm not doing without for a slip of a mill orphan who's no better than she ought to be.'

Though Meg rose to the girl's defence, it was no use. Once the other women had a spokesman in Jessie, they refused to help the injured Emma, and all insisted that dizziness or not she should get up and do her work. Helping her gently on her good side, Meg lent her own strength to the fainting girl and together they were able to get her dressed, but with one arm hanging limply inside her sleeve. Tom Burly unlocked the door with extra care and counted them as they made their slow descent into the mill.

'What's wrong with you miss?' he accosted Emma as she passed by him with Meg's help.

Neither of the women spoke. If he had forgotten his violent action during the night, they certainly hadn't.

'Answer me,' yelled Tom Burly. 'Are you shamming it again?'

The men had now joined the women and old Bill entered the fray.

'You've no cause to pick on the women, Tom Burly. They al' us does a good day's work and then some. And what's wrong with young Emma's arm?'

36

Tom Burly was so surprised to hear someone standing up to him that for once there was a short silence. Meg spoke up in answer.

'This overseer dragged her arm out of its socket last night,' she said. 'And Emma's so poorly this morning that she can hardly walk from faintness and having no food has not helped her either.'

The cowardly Burly could push the women around, but once the men were there looking with disapproval, he began to bluster his innocence in the attack.

'I just grabbed the wrong one that's all. I knew something was happening with all the noise and this girl caused a distraction so that her no good friend got by me and out into the street. She'll come to no good, you mark my words.' And he stomped out into the carding room.

The men took advantage of his absence to question Meg further and she made them aware of Susie's escape.

'Someone should go after her,' said Bill, and Ben nodding his agreement added,

'There's some bad creatures lurking around and we don't want them to harm our Susie.'

'But what'll we do?' said Ben. Ideas were scarce. The men were given little more freedom than the women and they couldn't see how the situation could be changed.

...

Susie, though hungry, was enjoying the happiest day of her life. The smell of the sweet grass, the warm wind on her face and the gentle sound of lambs baaing were balm to her senses. She lay in the verdant grass gathering clumps of it in her empty hands. How lovely just to be still for no reason except her own wish, gazing at a cloudless blue sky and hearing the sky-larks singing. She lazily began to pick daisies and fashioned a chain of them to wear on her hair. Presently she lay down and drifted off to sleep. How long she slept she could not tell but she was gently roused as she gradually became aware that the beautiful day was changing. It began to get cool and sitting up she shivered and drew her shawl around her thin shoulders. The sun had gone behind a cloud and as if they had a premonition of change the birds had stopped their joyous song.

It's funny, thought Susie, *that now the sun has gone down I'm feeling hungry and a drink of water wouldn't go amiss either.* She continued to climb to the top of the grassy knoll but hearing voices, and not being sure if at this moment she wanted to meet their flesh, she slid into an indentation in the hillside the curvature of which had sheltered many a labouring sheep.

The voices subsided and Susie peeped cautiously out of her hiding place and for the second time that day found herself gazing into deep dark eyes. This time she was able to stifle her scream so the passers-by were not aware of her presence. Susie and the animal looked at each other for some time then the sheep seemed to come to a decision and turning around in a sedate dance it came and lay down next to the now icy cold girl. 'Well, that's a thing,' Susie spoke gently to her woolly companion, 'we can keep each other warm,' and closing her eyes went happily to sleep. So ended her first day of freedom.

Chapter Six
Emma Is Given an Infirmary Order

The mill workers had passed an anxious morning without Susie. Emma half expected her friend to appear at any moment, propelled into their spinning room by Tom Burly, but when this didn't happen, she didn't know whether to be glad or sorry. She would have loved to see Susie safe and she didn't know how she would go on without her friend but Emma was not a selfish woman and deep inside she was happy for Susie to get the freedom she'd always desired.

Emma's injury was causing her distress and though it was her left shoulder that was useless, her right had also been bruised in the fall. She glanced across to the loom where Susie would normally have been working but today she received no friendly wink, for who should be there but Jessie Burns.

The very worst substitute for her friend had been moved into Susie's place in the weaving shed and Emma gained no comfort from the knowledge of how life would be from now on. Try as she might it was impossible to work all her looms as quickly as was necessary and around noon, sick and hungry, Emma collapsed onto the floor. The shuttle released, danced against the weft bringing the ends down as it smashed against the loom. Chaos reigned for some time. All the machines had to be stopped. And for some moments no-one took any notice of the prostrate Emma, but suddenly a commanding voice demanded to know the cause of the stoppage.

Mr Brierly strode into the mill and seeing Emma lying on the floor called Tom Burly for assistance. As the not too gentle Burly dragged Emma to her feet, her shoulder was wrenched again causing a second swoon. Mr Brierly could not ignore this occurrence and dispatched one of the hands to call a doctor. Meanwhile he demanded to know the whole story, which Tom Burly had attempted to keep from him.

Jack Cobb appeared and breathlessly announced that the doctor would be delayed for a few hours as he was assisting at a difficult delivery of twins. Emma was just beginning to come round but could not rise as yet. Seeing her deathly pallor, Mr Brierly commanded a cart be brought to transport her to the infirmary where a doctor could look at her damaged limb.

The farm cart drew up to the mill door and the waiting party helped the weak girl to ascend. Then followed a bumpy ride and Emma was glad of the straw-stuffed sacking which was being transported, along with herself, into Buxton. The journey was a slow one and if it hadn't been so uncomfortable, she would have taken pleasure in her unexpected outing. As it was, the journey seemed interminable. At last the cart reached town and she was dropped off at the hospital gate.

'You'll be alright, Missy,' said the kindly driver of the cart. 'I can't stay with you, I've got my straw to deliver, but I'll see you later.' Emma realised, as had Susie, the sudden freedom, but unlike her friend, Emma was filled with dread at her lone state. In her weakened condition, she sank to the ground, tears falling down her pinched cheeks and bringing with them the release that she needed.

Release from the almost unbearable tension of the last twenty-four hours. A time in which everything that she and Susie had dreamed of for so many years was suddenly within reach. She was outside the mill, but where could she go in her enfeebled state? She obviously had to go into the building and gain some help for her injured shoulder. But once inside would it be possible to escape again, she wondered. Should she forego this, her chance to live a normal life in the real world?

The decision was made for her because just then Mrs Murgatroyd came round the corner. Emma was too slow in hiding herself and the kindly woman, recognising her patient of the previous night, was delighted to see that she was being allowed medical assistance.

'Come along deary, I'll take you to outpatients. I'm going there myself,' she said.

Emma had no other course than to follow the nurse as she padded slowly through the doors of the infirmary and along a stone passageway that smelled strongly of carbolic.

'Now I'll have to revise my opinions of Tom Burly,' said the good woman, 'if he's allowed you an outpatient order, he must be better than I'd've given him credit for.'

Emma was quick to disillusion her, explaining that it was Mr Brierly himself who'd insisted on the farm cart bringing her into Buxton along with the sacks of straw.

'Oh, that's how it is, well, he can easily afford to lose you for an afternoon or even longer,' sniffed Mrs Murgatroyd. 'The goings on in that mill ought to have been stopped many a year ago, but who's to do it? No one cares for the poor and that's a fact. Anyway, here's the door so let's make sharpish like.'

Emma stepped inside, not a little afraid of her new surroundings. Two women in stiff uniforms sat behind a desk. On a shelf behind them numerous bottles were stored. One looked up on Emma's arrival.

'Have you an infirmary order?' she asked the girl.

Emma produced it and was told to wait with the two lines of other folks who were sitting on benches at one end of the long room. Emma shyly made her way to the queue and a large black-clad woman shifted to make room for the newcomer.

'Now sit yourself down, you're looking a bit peaky,' she said. Emma smiled her thanks, not wanting to put herself forward. She was feeling very strange. The benefit of the fresh air was wearing off and dizziness was once more encasing her mind. With an effort she managed to remain upright, forcing herself to stay alert by listening to the conversations going on around her.

'They say he's abroad around these parts,' said the black-clad woman.

'That's two now he's murdered they do say!' said her neighbour.

'He's a black-minded villain and that's a fact, but I wish the coppers would catch him,' said the original speaker.

'Charles Peace indeed. We'll have no peace in these parts until he's caught and hanged you mark my words,' re-joined her neighbour.

Emma pricked up her ears, there was that name again. So Charles Peace wasn't a Father Christmas figure after all. He was a real man and a murderer to boot. She shivered under her thin dress and worn shawl. Maybe there were worse things than being in the mill. Her thoughts leaped immediately to her friend. She hoped Susie was alright. Maybe she'd already been caught, she thought, perhaps a little hopefully. Another snippet of conversation reached her ears. Two farm wives were discussing spring lambing:

'It'll be late this year my man says…nowhere to hide the great beast had chased her around until she was exhausted, dropped her dead lamb there…too early you see a crying shame…need more help with rogue dogs, the boys are too

41

busy getting ready for spring harrowing and that good for nothing beadle is never around when you need him. That's the third we've lost already this year and very lucky my man came by or we'd've lost the sheep an all.'

Just then one of the women was called for her turn with the doctor so Emma heard no more of the rogue dog. She had never heard of a dog being a rogue before. She knew little of the society around her and not much more about the mill either, she realised. Emma was beginning to recover from her dizzy spell, thanks to the rest on the seat and she was able to take an interest in her surroundings.

'You're looking a bit better,' the kindly woman next to her spoke for the first time, 'and what brings you to the infirmary?' Emma explained her dislocated shoulder but didn't mention how she'd received it.

'Ah well-a-day,' replied her neighbour. 'These things do happen. Will you have a bite to eat?' She offered, holding out one of her paper bags.

Emma took a roll out of the bag gratefully with her thanks.

'Oh, it's nothing luv, you looked so peaky, a bitty food might do you good. Well, as I was saying about my Jeannie, I mind when she pulled her shoulder out, what a time we had with her. Couldn't dress her sel' or go to the privy. I had my hands fairly full with her I can tell you. But why didn't somebody come with you dear? You're too young to be out alone.'

Emma hung her head low, how could she explain her circumstances to this gossipy woman. She was spared a reply however, because the woman was called in to see the doctor, and saying her goodbyes she hastily gathered up all her bundles and shopping bags and forgot to wait for Emma's answer.

...

It had been a long day in the mill and the workers were in low spirits as they trudged up to their garret room. Neither Susie nor Emma had returned and as the women prepared for rest, they discussed the situation. It had been a day to remember, one that they had never seen the likes of before.

Tom Burly had threatened them over again but as none of them knew where Susie had gone, he had finally been forced to give in and allow them a scanty supper. Over the few minutes whilst they were stopped to eat, they huddled together questioning each other on a plan of action.

42

'We should go out and search for her,' said Bill, and his brother was in agreement.

'She ought never to have gone out like that herself, it's her own fault if anything happens to her, but I think we should help her just the same.'

'She's but a young un' and might come to some harm,' said Bill.

'But how are we to look for her?' questioned Meg. 'You know as well as I do that we're not allowed out a' t' mill.' They pondered the problem until Ned had the idea of talking to Tom Burly about their worries.

'Tom'll not listen to us, he's that mad with her for running out.'

''appen he is but it's worth a try, t' least he can do is send for the constabulary.'

They decided on Ben as their spokesman because he was the oldest worker. Anxiously they had awaited his return from talking to the overseer but as his bent head appeared, they were all sorry to see that he held no joy for them.

'Burly won't hear of it,' he said.

'What'll we do next?' asked the women.

'There's nothing we can do, except trust in the Lord, we've no say in these matters as you all know very well,' Bill replied gloomily.

'I'm not really a grumpy fellow but I feel that the masters take on too much,' he said. 'In the case of Susie for instance we all feel guilty but, how can we do anything for her when we're not allowed out? Susie should be our business, she's one of us.'

As they all discussed the happenings of the day, they heard the great bell ring on the outer door.

'That bell never rings at this time of the night,' said one of them, 'I wonder what it can mean.'

'Quiet your chatter and let's listen,' said Ben. But the walls were too thick and they heard nothing.

Chapter Seven
The Search Party

Tom Burly crossed the yard to answer the summons. He knew who was ringing the bell for he had felt apprehension growing within him the whole long day. Ben's appeal had not fallen on deaf ears, in fact, it had been the last nudge he needed to do something about the missing girl. But he wasn't going to lose face by admitting his mistake to Ben. Tom was the boss under Mr Brierly and he had to show his worth by being a hard taskmaster. He had his job to do and Susie was part of the mill machinery which had gone missing. It was his responsibility to find her as he would any other missing parts. So he'd sent Johnny Biggs to summon the constabulary and Tom was sure that the ringing bell was the answer to his summons. As the bell jangled for a second time, Burly slid the great iron bar back and provided entry for Johnny Biggs and the policeman.

'Now, what's all this, Tom Burly?' spoke up the law. 'It'd better be good getting me out at this time of night.'

Tom would not allow himself to be servile to one who, to his mind, was lower as to class, but on the other hand he didn't want to antagonise him either, so he held his peace and invited the constable into the inner room of the mill. It was a small place where purchasing transactions were made.

'Come in, come in and sit you down. Will you have a glass of ale?' he asked the policeman hospitably.

'Well, I'll sit down with you with pleasure, but I'll forgo the drink if you don't mind. Now, let's get down to business. Johnny Biggs here tells me that one of your mill girls has gone missing.'

'That's a fact,' answered Tom. 'We none of us saw her go, so we don't know how long she's been out.'

'Is that a fact?' asked Constable Blunt.

''Tis,' Tom replied archly.

'Well, now, I've been hearing a thing or two as goes on in this mill and let me check,' he looked into his note book, 'it seems that Mrs Murgatroyd was called here last night to see to a girl's shoulder and there was talk then that the other one was missing. How come it's taken twenty-four hours to report this to the local constabulary?' Tom Burly began to squirm and bluster.

'If the nurse knew of her disappearance, she should have reported it then, I didn't find out until this morning.'

'This morning you say?' slowly spoke up Blunt, purposefully removing his pocket watch and checking the time on it with the big clock on the wall of the mill.

'I thought she'd come back of her own volition. How was I to know that the little minx had gotten so uppity that she thought she could get along without help from her benefactor?' said Burly.

Constable Blunt was slow of speech and action, and he kept his eyes on Burly, who lost his bravado in the face of such concentration.

'Well, this is getting us nowhere. I didn't call you here to be blamed for her behaviour,' said Burly. ''Tisn't my fault she ran away,' he wheedled.

'I was just thinking of the girl in calling for you.'

'I'm just trying to set a timeline. In twenty-four hours, she could have gotten anywhere,' Blunt replied.

'Oh, I see, as to that, the women can tell you better than me. I don't go up there of a night. All I know is that a loud caterwauling started about 9 o'clock. I went up to see what was the matter and my life hasn't been the same since with girl's missing and dislocated shoulders, infirmary orders and police visits.'

'As to the mill goings-on, we'll leave that for the moment,' said the policeman, 'but first let's look into the missing girl. How many workers can you find to make up a search party? At this short notice, it won't be easy to find many in the village though I'll try.'

Tom's attitude changed with this turnabout and he agreed to find twenty or thirty of his residents.

'Right, I'll go down to the village and get a party and you muster yours. You take Mill Bottom and we'll come around Top Road to meet you. That way we'll head her off if she's running, but we'll cover all ground if she's hurt or been molested in any way,' said the constable.

Tom was only too happy to agree. This interview had not gone as he'd planned it all the time. For the second night in a row, the garret residents were disturbed. Tom turned the key in the lock, discreetly leaving the candle unlit as he called the workers. They were not sleeping and it was an easy task for them to rise.

They were so relieved that something was being done for Susie that they dressed quickly and gathered in the mill yard. Tom Burly counted them. Twelve women and ten men were assembled from inside the mill and just then the outside workers began to appear also. Johnny Biggs spoke as he arrived with them:

'I've got Sam and Ed and Caleb's gone down to the pub to summon more. Jimmy's at his mother's place and his missus will send him on 'at' after with her brother Fred.'

'Well, that's enough to get started,' said Tom Burly. 'I've a number of lanterns here and maybe them at the ends will take one and pick out the stones on the rough part. They can also make sure they check all the ground and alleyways. In case Susie is hiding, we'll be sure to search all the hidden corners of the streets.'

The search party began to straggle out of the mill yard. Their clogs made a clatter on the clinkers down the hill and the women gathered their shawls around them in the damp night air.

'Spring it might be, but I'd not like to be out sleeping i' this damp for a second night on the run,' said Bess.

'Maybe she's not out in it,' sniffed Madge. 'She's a pretty little thing with that auburn hair and she'll probably soon be taken in by somebody.'

'Oh, don't be so awful about her,' said the gentle Sally.

'She's more likely to be doing the taking in,' said the cantankerous Jessie Burns. 'That hair might be pretty, but any man worth his salt will think twice about the temper that's like to go with it.'

Sally was thoughtful. 'You know, she didn't even take her clogs with her. She must be freezing and sore-footed by now,' she said.

'Serves her right,' said Jessie spitefully.

'I'm surprised you've come out looking for her if you dislike her that much, Jessie.'

'You don't think I'd miss the chance of an outing at night, do you?' she retorted. 'I didn't get chosen to go to the fair and I'm certainly not being done out a second time. Besides, I always said that those two girls were too young to go gallivanting and now I've been proved right.' She sniffed, thinking because she'd had the last word that she'd won the argument.

But the quiet Sally just smiled to herself. The party with its few lanterns dotted here and there among the searchers moved down the brew to Mill Bottom. It was easier to walk on the level and all marched along briskly.

'What'll Tom do when he finds her, I wonder?' said Bob from the mill.

'I don't rightly know the story,' said Asa. 'Did she just run away, or what?'

Bob was quick to enlighten Asa and all the other villagers who'd come to join in the search.

'You mean,' spoke up Ed, 'that he locks you all in of a night?'

At a quiet nod from Bob and an 'aye, that he does' from Bill and Ben, the villagers were stunned.

'That's not right,' they finally agreed. 'You might be mill workers, but you shouldn't be treated as slaves. Anyone should have the right of choice.'

'Yes, but look what happens when the door is open,' said one of the older women. 'A young girl gets out and doesn't know what to do with herself.'

'That's because she's never been taught by being abroad in the world,' said Asa, punctuating his words with a pointed finger. 'The world is a very hard place to get along in if you haven't had the chance to find out about it from childhood.'

'What's that noise?'

They all listened and, in the distance, they could hear the clip-clop of horses' hooves. Through the darkness came a faint light, moving in like a Will o' the Wisp. As it drew closer, they could make out the shape of the delivery farm cart. And there was Emma, sitting up beside the driver, her left arm strapped tightly across her body as she held on to safety with the other one.

'Whoa, there!' The driver brought his cart to a halt alongside the crew of people.

'Did you think she was lost all this time? You might have known I'd bring her back safely without sending out a search party for her.'

The leaders of the group set him straight, explaining that it was Susie they were looking for and that, to their embarrassment, they'd forgotten all about Emma in the anxiety about her friend.

'Shame on you, but never mind, I'll turn the cart round and join you. You might need a conveyance.'

He didn't say what for, but Emma shivered at the implication. Her dear friend Susie reduced to a thing that needed a conveyance was the last image she needed that night and she went sick at the thought. All she needed was a soft bed, but her hard-straw pallet would be very welcome.

...

Constable Blunt made his way to the village square. He'd try the Black Swan, he thought. There'd be plenty of men there on a Friday night. Opening the door, he was in time to see John Blacklock strike a bullseye in the darts match that was in fine Progress.

'Good lad, John,' called his team members, 'that'll put us in fine fettle against 'the George' at Sparrow Pit.'

John made to raise his arm for a second shot, but sensing a newcomer, he lowered it for a moment.

'Why, Constable, what brings you here? It must be business, for you're in uniform, I see.'

Blunt explained his mission and was greeted with enthusiastic cries of proffered help from all sides. Young girl shouldn't be out alone of a night; they all agreed and hastily packed up their game for later. Darts could wait. Human life in danger couldn't. The small group joined Constable Blunt and began to search the village.

Blunt, realising the need for a lantern or two, returned to the constabulary. Sitting at his desk was his sergeant, Edwin Robinson.

'Now, what's afoot, Constable? Is all quiet in t' village?' he asked.

''fraid not sir, a mill girl's gone missing, and we're a two-tier search party in operation. I've just returned for some lanterns for my group, the mill party has its own. I've arranged to take my lot up Top Lane while the group from the mill takes Mill Bottom.'

'Good thinking, Constable, I think I'll join you, I'm just about finished here. The rest can wait until morning.'

So saying he rose, donned his helmet and, taking down his truncheon from its place on the wall, he followed the younger man. By the time they returned with the lanterns, the darts club and villagers were eagerly going about their task. They had divided into small groups and were just beginning to search the graveyard by the side of the church. The small beam that the lanterns gave off added a ghostly glow to the faces of the searchers who carried them, making the event take on a supernatural air. A large willow tree stood by the ancient gate, its feathery fronds blowing in the light breeze with a promise of better weather to come. But this night, the breeze was too light to disperse the heavy dampness that had settled on the village.

'Not a good night to be out in alone,' John remarked to his brother, and Matt agreed.

'You know, John, I've got a dismal feeling about this missing girl. What did they say her name was?'

'I don't rightly recall hearing it, but wait while I ask Caleb.'

He trudged off to find the nearest couple and, hearing Susie's name as the very girl they were searching for, he returned to his brother with a fast-beating heart.

'Matt, lad, I don't want you to take on too much, but I know you had a fancy for that girl Susie we met at the fair. Well, it's her 'as has gone missing.'

Matt stared in silence at his brother. He couldn't make an answer to John's words, but heavy dread was eating at him and he resolved to find her if any man could. He strode around the tombstones searching under overgrown grass and trailing ivy. All the searchers were steadily and methodically working their way around the roughly kept graves. After about an hour of the tedious work, Constable Blunt called a halt and suggested they move along.

Black night had fallen and it was beginning to rain quite heavily, but the search party was ready to move on and climb Top Road. As they strode uphill, Matt and John leading, they looked into the ditches along the roadside and the hollows underneath the rough stone walls. The rain was now beating down on the valiant crew and eerie night noises seemed to be following them from the graveyard. As they approached the crown of the hill, a creaking grew steadily louder. There at the top stood the gibbeting rock, with the hanging tree silhouetted against the night sky. As a flash of lightning suddenly brought it into prominence, John shivered convulsively hoping that this was not (as his mother would insist) an omen that boded no good. The creaking sound came from one of the heavy branches that was being blown by the wind, now part of a full-fledged storm. On the party climbed until everyone was standing together in this grim place.

'I hope the other half of the group is having more luck,' said Edwin Robinson.

The other searchers made no return. They were cold and tired and needed encouragement.

'Well, shall we get along?' Matt requested impatiently. He was still having visions of Susie hurt or worse lying where they would never find her and all his bubbles in the air would be burst on this one terrible night. He'd thought of her often and wondered what had become of her since the night of the fair. Now he had a lead and he didn't mean to stop until he'd found her again.

On Mill Bottom the searchers were having no more success than their counterparts. Rain dripped in a steady splish splash from the pony's tail. Emma, tired out from her long day had fallen asleep from the soporific noise. The wet band huddled as close as it could to the cart and not much conversation could be heard. They were all feeling the gloom that had descended on them since the rain had started, remembering that they were not the only ones abroad on this dismal night.

They plodded along dolefully trying as best they could to dodge the fast-growing puddles in the cart track, holding high their lanterns they looked into any alcove that was large enough to shelter even a small animal let alone a young woman. But they had little joy of their search. They had now reached the end of the lane known as Mill Bottom. At this point it forked into a track across country leading into a ginnel behind a row of pigsties. Stopping the cart, the driver began to pull loose sacks from inside.

'Here, put these over your heads, they'll keep off a bit of the rain and we can search these farm buildings.'

The group gladly took the proffered covering and the extra warmth the sacks afforded put them in better spirits. In twos and threes, they began to search the smelly buildings, though each of them felt in his or her own way that to shelter in such a fetid place one would have to be desperate indeed. The search took only a short time and brought no success and the group were calling it a day.

'After all,' spoke up Bess, 'if Susie is still alive, she'd be daft not to shelter in this storm, and if she's a corpse, she can wait a bit longer to be found.'

Sally was horrified at this callous attitude and the others were grouped somewhere in between. Emma, slightly refreshed after her rest, now joined in the discussion.

'I don't know how any of you feel about Susie, but she's been all I have in the world for all the life I remember, and I for one am not leaving her to rot until I've done something about it.'

The majority of the workers agreed and so the point was settled. Tom Burly felt that they should search the track down to the river bank and the dilapidated sheds that were dotted along their not-too-picturesque part of the village. So it was settled and Jessie, muttering under her breath, crept along with them. Though not happy to go, she had already made it patently obvious that she hated to miss out on anything exciting. Once again they split up into small groups to search the sheds. Though these were ramshackle, they at least afforded some shelter from the driving rain and for a little they began to feel warmer.

Emma was with Bill and Ben. She, with her injured shoulder, was not able to move any of the mouldering implements in the shed they'd chosen, but she held the lantern high while the two men removed the heavy iron ware. Suddenly they were startled as a rat jumped out from under the board Ben was lifting, and scuttled to safety in a dark corner. Bill stumbled against Emma and she dropped her lantern, which quickly lost its light.

'Oh confound it; now we can't see anything.' said Bill.

Emma kneeling down felt around the floor for the lantern. Her hand touched something cold and she drew it back in surprise.

'What is it?' Ben asked at her gasp.

'I'm not sure, I wish we had a light.' Emma knelt down again and this time she was able to put her hand on the lantern.

'Wait a minute,' striking a match Bill lit the unbroken lantern again and the thin light gave them back their sight. Emma looked down again for the cold object on the floor. It was a large brass button, one of the types worn by the military.

'Why would that be in this dirty shed?' she asked in wonderment.

'Well, I'd say it doesn't belong to anyone here and you should take it with you for good luck,' said Ben.

Not needing to be told again, Emma thrust it into her pocket, secretly delighting in its rich, solid coldness against her fingers. It seemed so set apart from the world she lived in and to symbolise this most unusual day that she had lived through. But it was not yet over and, having finished the shed, they made their way back to the rest of the group.

The sheds had not provided any answer to the riddle of Susie's disappearance, so now the party made its way onward towards the gushing river. This same river was fed by a fresh mountain stream where, if they'd only known it, Susie had drunk that very morning, which in turn was used to drive the mill race that kept the mechanism turning in Cressbrook mill. And further on it ran into that very canal the two had sailed along, and from where the girls had been delivered to begin their lives of slavery.

This was not uppermost in Emma's mind that night, though Susie was in her thoughts. The late rains had swollen the river, which in summer could get quite low and cause great anxiety for the mill managers. Now it caused anxiety of another kind. The searchers gazed out at the rushing river, the same thought in each of their minds. If Susie had been unlucky enough to fall into this torrent, she would never have been able to get out again.

'What's that in the water?' suddenly called out Ben.

'Probably a tree stump,' Bob Gavin replied.

'Are you sure it's not a body?' The women ran to look.

Jessie, always wanting to be important, spoke up loudly. 'I can see a hand waving. Do you think it's her?'

'Where? Where?' The onlookers wanted to know.

All the workers by now were clustered around the place where the bank curved. Sedge and weeds were caught in the sludge which had found its home at the bank of the river.

'I don't see how you could possibly see anything human in that filthy mess, let alone a hand waving on this dark night,' said Madge.

'You always want to be interesting Jess, but don't make up stories. We can't take any more tonight, and Emma is all in.'

'I could see something,' denied the obstinate Jessie. 'See, there it goes again.'

'It looks like a tree branch to me, waving in the wind,' said Madge.

'I saw it! I saw it!' Jessie was beginning to scream, and some others on the outskirts of the group took up her cry. As the town party approached the river from Top Lane, they could hear the cries and began to run. Constable Blunt was leading the group, but Matt and John soon overtook him. As they reached the bank of the river, the mill workers stood aside to let the constable through, but Matt was there first and it was all his brother could do to restrain him from jumping into the swollen river.

'Hold on lad we don't know yet if there's anything there.'

Matt swallowed hard. John was right. He must try to keep calm and then he'd be more use to Susie. Edwin Robinson came puffing up at that moment.

'Now what's all the excitement about? Have you seen something?'

Jessie pushed forward importantly. 'I seen a hand waving over there, sir.'

'Did you now? And how could you see a hand in this mire?'

'I did! I did!' screamed Jessie. 'There's a body over there caught in the reeds and sedge.'

Emma tried to see, but was unable to in the dark. As she moved forward, John caught sight of her.

'Why, Emma!' he cried. 'Where've you been hiding yourself? We've looked for you many a Friday night and thought we'd never meet again. And you're hurt. Whatever happened to your arm?'

'I'll not go into all that now, John, we've enough to think of with Susie being gone.'

'You're right, Lass, and no mistake. But don't go running off before you've told me how I can get in touch with you again.'

Emma didn't know what to say. How could she admit to belonging to Mr Brierly, not just working in the Mill? She hung her head and moved a short way from him. Many of the other workers had caught Jess's hysteria and were demanding that the sergeant do something about the body. Sergeant Robinson was a big man but he wouldn't send one of his men to do anything that he wouldn't do himself. Moving to the edge, he climbed over the bank and began to lower his bulk down into the water.

'Wait a minute, sir,' called the constable. 'You'll get swept away, I'll get the rope from off the cart.'

Running to get this, he quickly regained the river bank and flung the end of the rope to his superior. The sergeant slowly moved to the centre of the fast-flowing water, arriving at the place where Jessie thought she'd seen the waving arm. It was difficult to catch his words. The wind was hurling them in the opposite direction. Matt stood tensely on the bank beside Blunt. He never let his eyes stray from the sergeant. He was ready to jump into the fray at the slightest suggestion from anyone. There seemed to be a kind of island because, as the officer reached it, he was gaining height. He was clambering on to an object which was not easy to see in the dark. Facing them from his vantage point, he called to the watchers.

'I've found the body,' he called. The waiting audience gathered itself as one, every nerve strained to hear the news.

'It's only a dog!' The sigh of relief was tangible for a brief moment and then the sceptics in the crowd demanded proof.

'Show us! Show us!' they cried. The big man bent down to lift the object out of the water, but it was too heavy for him and as he straightened himself his

53

buttons burst from his over-tight trousers, causing an explosion of laughter as, by the light of the flickering lanterns, his corpulent frame was exposed. This comic relief helped lighten the tense atmosphere, and mirth reigned for many minutes.

Meanwhile Blunt, giving the rope into the capable hands of Matt, had lowered himself into the water to help his embarrassed sergeant to redeem his dignity. The two men were able to raise the dog high enough to clear the obstructions and, dragging it to the bank, proved to the watchers that it was indeed a canine corpse and not that of a woman. *Maybe that rogue dog has met its end,* thought Emma, not wanting to believe that a good creature had been drowned in the river. As the two officers climbed on to the bank, eager hands were ready to help them up on to almost dry land.

'I think we'll call it a night, folks,' said Robinson. 'My constable and I are in need of some dry clothes and I know the rest of you are pretty sodden as well. If Susie's still conscious, I'm sure she'll have sheltered before this time. We'll resume our search tomorrow.'

Chapter Eight
The Search for Susie

Emma woke with a start. She tried to shake off the phantoms in her dreams which were a mixture of terror and hope. She shook her head to release the night terrors, realising that her nightmares had probably been brought on by the stressful twenty-four hours she had lived through. A day that had begun in sickness and misery had had its small joy at the end. John Blacklock had insisted on accompanying her back to the mill and there he'd had a few words with overseer Burly.

As was his wont, Burly's cowardice was now protecting Emma from new onslaught, for John had made it quite plain that Emma was not alone in the world and that he, John Blacklock, was her champion. The delicious feeling came over Emma as she stretched on her pallet of new beginnings. If only Susie were safe, she thought to herself, today would be the most perfect day in living memory. But they had no way of knowing if Susie was safe. The chill returned as with dread she rose from her pallet and prepared for the day. This task took much longer than usual because of her injury. But at least she no longer felt sick every time she moved it. She joined the others in the refectory to eat her breakfast. For once the porridge was good, neither burnt nor raw and more oats seemed to have been used in the preparation.

'Glory be,' Meg Ogden remarked, 'wonders will never cease.'

'Susie would have had her wish today,' said Emma sadly. 'She always dreamed of tasty porridge.'

The tired workers spoke quietly together discussing the happenings of the previous night. Some were exasperated with Susie and some were angry, but the feeling that prevailed was one of foreboding and dread.

'The police sergeant said we'd resume our search today in the better light, but with last night's rain I can't see the light being any better and I'm sure we can't be spared from t' mill this whole day,' said Bill glumly.

The others silently agreed with him but hoped that he was wrong.

They didn't have long to wonder. Constable Blunt soon arrived and asked for volunteers to search in the morning while the light was better and make up their lost time in the mill by working an extra half hour each day until they'd made up for lost time. Though some of them grumbled about the extra time no one was missing when they assembled once again in the mill yard. And no grumbling was heard when the constable led them outside into a fine raw morning.

'We're making for t' river bank again,' said Blunt, 'because that's where we left off last night, and hopefully the other part of the searchers will meet us there.'

...

Susie woke with a start. What was that awful noise? She soon saw that it was coming from her companion of the previous night. Still laying there the sheep was in obvious distress. Susie, though not a farm girl, had often seen the new lambs with their mothers and realised what was about to happen very soon. She didn't know what to do to help the poor animal but she began talking to it soothingly. In time nature took its course and a tiny lamb was born, followed very quickly by a second one. Susie gazed in rapture as the mother, seeming to know exactly what to do for her new family, cleaned and butted her twins until they stood fresh and sturdily on their spindly legs.

The lambs, as knowingly as their mother had been in performing her new duties, butted her until they had found nourishment. The new arrivals had shown Susie a source of sustenance for herself. She would not starve, not while milk was in plentiful supply. She continued to watch the little family marvelling at their innate knowledge of survival and becoming very aware that she could learn much from the natural world. She had grown up with fear being instilled into her by the violence inflicted for wrongdoing in the mill but now she realised, watching the tiny lambs, that she should learn to trust her instincts.

...

The man in the sodden great coat dragged his weary way along the muddy road. Where would it all end, he wondered. For many days he'd taken shelter since the last one but he was tired, tired to death and he wanted in part to be caught despite constantly striving to survive. He wished for death, but the road he had travelled in recent years would not lead to a peaceful or glorious one but one of ignominy. He knew in his lucid moments that he had done wrong and deserved punishment but of late his lucid moments were few and far between. So he continued to drag his feet along a road well-travelled taking copious refreshment from the green bottle in his left hand. Finally, his mind or his feet gave out and he fell in a drunken stupor by the roadside to sleep it off.

…

Leaving the swollen river, the search party made its way once again past the derelict sheds and into a more pleasant part of the village. Progressing along the country lane between rough stone walls where in parts the Hawthorn branches, not yet in bloom, hung sharply over the hedges, the mill workers gathered the fresh scent into their unaccustomed nostrils. All enjoyed, though somewhat guiltily, the delicious freshness after the rain of the previous evening. As the path climbed adjacent to the pasture, they followed it in a straggling band.

'Give us a song, Caleb, it will lighten our hearts and help us to keep in step.' Caleb's fine baritone voice soon rang out, his friends from the pub joining in the chorus. Jessie was soon heard to grumble that they should all be remembering why they were searching and think of the poor missing girl, but the other women knew Jess well and were disinclined to take heed of her grumpy voice.

'She's always opposite to everyone else,' Madge said, beginning to join in with the songsters. 'What a contrary woman.'

Susie, sitting with her new playmates, heard the voices. At first she felt an urge to join the human company, but not knowing who they were, she cautiously took up her place of hiding in the sheep fold. There was something very familiar about their leader as the small band climbed up the hill towards her.

She peered out through the woven fencing recognising, as he drew close, her dance partner from the fair. One moment she was about to run out and join him, but the next she saw that he was accompanied by mill workers, and was that Tom Burly? Indeed she was right to remain hidden as she scrambled down the bank and hid behind a Hawthorn tree, the fold only offering scanty covering. Her thoughts were tumultuous as she saw Emma walking by with John Blacklock and all the friends of a lifetime following in the search for their missing companion. Susie found it hard to catch her breath as she felt the surge of different emotions running through her frame simultaneously. A mixture of love, regret, fear, but the one uppermost was ambition for a better life. It was this that forced her to escape from the mill and now to watch quietly as her search party gradually disappeared over the brow of the hill. They were following a road that led out of the village and down to Miller's Dale. Overcome with emotion and loneliness Susie dissolved into loud sobs shaking onto her knees in the cool grass.

As the search party moved out of Susie's sight they had no idea how close they had come to their lost friend but Emma looking shyly at John suddenly said:

'You know I don't think Susie wants us to find her. She took a huge chance in breaking out of the mill. She could easily have come home the morning after if she'd wanted to and taken her punishment. She's made her choice. Whether it's for the better only time will tell, and I'm going to miss her so much, but she's always been braver than me and she deserves her chance of a better life. I for one say that we should give up the search if she's not found soon.'

On Emma's words a ghostly pallor had come over Matt's face but he didn't speak. Although John was hesitant, he finally agreed with Emma.

'None of us can imagine what it's like to be a mill slave,' he said, 'and Susie must have come to the conclusion that she had to make a run soon or be there forever; but it's a rum situation and the authorities should do something about it for all of you.'

Emma hung her head. She'd had her chance too but her sense of duty or fear had forced her to return to the mill. And as things had occurred, maybe she'd made the right choice also. Only time would tell for her too, but for the time being she was content to walk by John's side on this spring day that was gradually becoming quite warm as noon approached.

The pleasure was short lived however; as noon arrived Tom Burly seemed to pull himself up short. Maybe he'd remembered that Susie had already used up in her colleagues' hours more than she was worth in the production of cotton. He blew a whistle and announced that the search was over for the mill workers at least.

'Damn fool girl has got herself into this and she can get herself out. I'm not troubling myself further,' he shouted.

Edwin Robinson turned to protest, but he was only the law after all. He didn't have mercantile money backing him, as did Tom Burly. So the search was called off and the mill workers were organised into double file and marched back to the mill. John tried to make a date to see Emma later but was pushed aside by the overseer.

'We might as well walk on to Miller's Dale,' John said to Matt. 'We'll be in time for the late shift at the pit. No point trying to get any sleep. I'm past it myself.'

Matt agreed and the two brothers set off willingly continuing to look about for signs of Susie for they, especially Matt, were not convinced that Susie wouldn't like to come back.

They were two strong healthy men and they strode along making good progress. John suddenly stopped and motioned Matt to take note of what appeared to be a bundle of clothes on the ground. As they drew closer, they became aware that the clothes were being worn by a man. Stertorous breathing came from the bundle and they looked at each other wondering if they should do something.

'He's only an old tramp sleeping off a skinful, let's leave him alone,' said John.

Just then the bundle seemed to come to and beady eyes surveyed his watchers. With more agility than the brothers would have believed possible, the tramp sprang up and with a loping gait moved off across the field and disappeared into a copse of trees.

'Well, I'll be jiggered,' said John, 'who'd a thought he could have moved so fast. You'd think the devil was after him.'

'Maybe so,' returned Matt, 'I've never seen the likes of him before. There's some rum 'uns working over where they've opened up the old quarry, but he can't be in work or he wouldn't be sluiced in the middle of the day. Oh well, we'd better be about our business or we won't be in work either.'

...

Susie sat pondering what she would do now. The sheep fold could obviously not be her permanent abode. *For the moment I can enjoy the idyll but in wet weather I'll need somewhere else to shelter*, she thought. The sheep were fun to watch as they frisked about especially the little lambs. She enjoyed playing with the little creatures chasing them as they ran in circles around the pasture and then back up to the fold. It was lovely to be in the open air and smell the fresh verdant grass. But the nights were different. Another night in the open air and as she wakened stiff and damp from the early morning dew, Susie realised that she would have to make some decisions regarding her future. She pondered what to do. The only job she knew was one she never wanted to do again.

'I love the outdoors too much to ever go back into a mill even if I was paid. I need some kind of sign,' said Susie to her woolly companion. The silent sheep continued to munch the fresh grass. The animal seemed to be used to her and made no move to frisk away like the other ones did. Susie pulled the pendant from around her neck where it hung on a chain. This was her lucky medallion, she'd rubbed it the evening she'd got home from the fair and it had brought her the courage to make a run for it. Now she hoped it would bring her the sign she needed. But as the day lost its warmth, it took Susie's usual buoyant nature with it. She became morose as she began to think of her friends in the mill, especially Emma. As the search party had passed by her hiding place, she'd noticed Emma's damaged arm and understood why Emma had cried out when she herself was making her escape. This knowledge left her even more subdued knowing that her friend's pain had been caused by her own bid for freedom. As midday approached, she decided to take a walk to stretch her stiff limbs.

I'd better stay near the hedge so that I'm not so conspicuous, she thought, as she cautiously began exploring the outer edge of the field. Some early wild sorrel was growing in a patch and she munched on it gladly. It made a delicious contrast to her three-day diet of milk and barley kernels that she'd managed to forage for herself. *What to do now.* Moving into the peak district would make sense. *That way,* she thought, *I'd not bump into any of the villagers who've probably been alerted to my disappearance, but how can I without footwear. Even this short walk has taken its toll.*

'Oh, come on Susie don'na be so nesh,' she said to herself, stepping off the pasture and onto the rough pathway to match her words. She saw a small copse of trees ahead and decided to move towards it. As she approached, she heard a noise coming from around the bend of the road. Uncertain what it was she ducked back into the copse to see what happened.

Chapter Nine
Susie Makes a Decision

From her hiding place she saw two horses being ridden by a couple of wild-looking fellows. They were followed closely by a red and yellow gypsy caravan and another one painted blue and green. Well, maybe this was the sign she needed. The cavalcade would provide her with cover, transport and perhaps protection, if she played her cards right. On this thought she darted from the copse and waved to the driver of yet another caravan (this time pink and blue). He hesitated for a moment then returned her salute pulling up his horse as he did so.

'I was wondering if you could give me a ride?' spoke up Susie. 'I've lost my way and am making towards a big town.'

'What big town would that be, Missy?' the driver answered, giving her a sideways look. 'There bain't any big town afore Buxton and we're no' planning to be there in a hurry.'

'Oh, anywhere will do,' said Susie, 'it doesn't really matter so long as I get somewhere before dark.'

The man looked her up and down, taking in the sorry state of her clothing, her threadbare shawl (mill worker's uniform) and her shoeless state. He also noticed her dirty though vibrant auburn hair, her slim waist and her merry eyes, and making an instant decision he stopped the caravan and helped her aboard. Susie could not believe her good luck in getting transport almost immediately and realised with a pang that she hadn't bidden farewell to her companion of the last three nights. She bit her lip resignedly and told herself not to be so daft about a sheep for after all she hadn't said a proper good-bye to Emma either.

'Where are you from?' the gypsy asked.

'Oh here away,' Susie answered vaguely.

'You running away from your mam and dad?'

'Oh no.' At least this wasn't a lie, she thought.

'A pretty girl like you shouldn't be roaming the countryside on her own.'

'Oh, as to that,' and she tossed her head, 'I can take care of myself.'

They rode on in silence, he feeling that maybe he'd said too much. She was probably a bit of a wild cat and he'd taken a chance picking her up. Their silence became companionable and Susie became drowsy with the rolling motion and the clackity clack of the wheels. She started suddenly when the carriage came to an abrupt halt. The driver was looking at her carefully, wondering if he should tell her they were at the end of the line or invite her to stay. Maybe she was a likely lass. Cleaned up she would be a looker and maybe she'd be a goer too. His intense scrutiny disturbed Susie and she began to feel a vague sense of unease. She wasn't used to being in mixed company. This man was much pleasanter than Tom Burly but there was something about him that she didn't quite like. So when he asked her if she'd like to stay with the circus, although this had been her original plan, she was not so sure how to answer. She was thinking that maybe she'd stay for a bit and see what it was like, after all what harm could come to her. At last she replied:

'Would the circus have some honest work for me to do?'

'I'm not sure, we'd have to see the ringmaster, I'm not in charge but he's usually in need of help with the setup of the tents. The animals need cleaning also, though their trainers are a bit fussy about who they'll let near the lions.'

'Lions!' Susie squeaked. 'I'll not feed the lions.'

She'd heard about lions, how ferocious they were, but she was not going to show her ignorance to this man by saying she'd not even seen a picture of one. Susie was an adventurous girl and she felt the excitement welling in her body.

'Can't you hear them calling, it's getting time for their feed,' he said. 'But if they take you on in the circus, you'll not want to be choosy.'

She bit her lip. She hadn't meant to give that impression but she didn't want to admit to being scared either. Now she understood; the strange noises she'd heard were probably animal noises in the distance.

'Well, I wanted to see some'at a life now it seems I'll be getting a good chunk of it,' she said naively.

Her new companion made no answer but there was a knowing glint in his eye. She saw her horizon broadening. A lovely day, a brighter future and maybe her driver wasn't bad. She'd stay and be happy, after all what else could she do?

'I suppose I'd better know your name?' she said.

'Jack, honest Jack,' he replied and he laughed into his jowls, a sound that sent a chill through her body.

'And what can I call you, my pretty?'

'Susie will do,' she replied.

'Susie what?'

'Just Susie.'

'Ah well I'll maybe call you Susie Just.' And he laughed his menacing jowly laugh once more as she wondered apprehensively what she had done.

The cavalcade had arrived at a large field outside Eyam.

Susie hastily jumped down from her perch and looked around the barren landscape. She saw bare fields surrounded by leafless poplar trees, but then in the distance she noticed a friendly old thatch peeping out behind the hay stack.

'Don't just stand there, girl, look lively!' a short bad tempered man yelled at her.

Obedient to his command she looked around to see what she could do. A chain of circus folk were unloading what looked to Susie's expert eyes like a large roll of canvas. She jumped into line and added her small strength to that of her neighbours.

Working diligently a couple of hours had passed before the big top took its shape in the centre of the field. She was amazed when she looked around, to see scurrying hither and thither like so many busy ants, the circus folk. Though not dressed in their performing clothes, they still looked different from anyone she'd seen before. Standing next to her was a short woman with muscular arms who told Susie she was a trapeze artist who worked with Louis.

'Where is Louis?' Susie enquired.

'Oh he's unloading our swings and trapezes and ropes to make sure everything is in order,' Carmel told her.

The twins followed, they were midgets, then came Big Joe, the elephant trainer. A bevy of clowns were next in line, though they weren't very funny when they worked, Susie felt wary of their bad tempers. Carmel explained that moving day was always a bit tense, so much to do in a short time because time was money, explained her new friend. Well, she'd heard that many times before in the mill so she realised that her new life would have some similarities with her old one.

Move-in day was exhausting. Everything the whole menagerie would need in the next four days had to be unpacked and stowed away so that it would be easily found when needed. Each separate act had its own storage drum which was placed in a pile alongside the ring. The side shows were something else. As they began to take shape Susie recognised some from the night they'd been allowed out and it struck her forcibly that this was the same fair she'd helped to build before. Her lucky charm had obviously done its work and she was back in familiar territory. A group of labourers had been hired for the half day, some of these were tramps or odd jobbers who had tramped far to earn a few pence. Like Susie, they were hoping to be set on for a few days whilst the fair was in Eyam.

Once the tent was erected, Susie was told to follow Big Joe and help with watering the animals. Nothing surprised her more than the elephants. They had been released from their travelling cage and were walking across the ground trunk to tail. Their slow cumbersome movements made her laugh but she was terrified of getting too close. Joe told her to water the dogs. That seemed easier and she went willingly to carry the pails to the little yapping creatures. There were six in all and they stood on hind legs as she moved towards them. She became aware that she was being watched and turned to look.

An old tramp was gazing across the field in her direction. Susie felt a shiver attack her spine. She was not used to being stared at by strangers and this one was swaying from side to side as though he wasn't quite right in the head. Not knowing how to escape his notice she turned back to the dogs and gave them more of the water out of her can. Looking out of the corner of her eye in the tramps' direction, she was relieved to see that he'd moved away. She scampered back happily to the man in charge and asked for another job. Happy Jack was waiting in line and decided that he could find her something to do.

'Come with me Susie Just,' he said, and though she wasn't too happy with the idea, she could think of no excuse not to follow him.

'Now my girl, it's time I got something back for the help I've given you.'

'But you have had something back,' said Susie, 'I've worked hard for you all day in the circus.'

Jack, ignoring her naïve remark, managed to push her into a small nook behind the cages and, tearing her blouse to the waist, he now proceeded to loom over her as he fondled her roughly. She caught her breath in fright trying to struggle herself free. But his strong arms would not let go and as his head dipped, his sensual lips bore down on hers. She smelled his fetid breath on her face. Using all her strength, she tried to push him away but she was caught between the steel girder, which held it, and the tent.

'Not so quick, my pretty, you'll not get away from me like that.'

'Oh please Jack I'm a good girl and I don't know what you're doing,' said the now terrified girl.

'Just stop your struggling and give me a good time, I deserve it for all I've done driving you here and helping you run away from whatever it was you were escaping from.'

His large body had moulded itself to Susie's slight one, his heavy breathing and the smell of him made her feel sick. He released his hold of her with one hand as he tried to unfasten his clothing. Sensing that this was her last chance to escape him, she wasted no time in thought, but quick as light she brought her sharp knee upwards. It found its target in his swollen member as she was only too aware from the bellow of pain which escaped from his throat. She didn't wait to find out if he was alright. Quickly she rushed out of her prison and leaped fleetly to the home of Carmel. Susie felt relief flow over her as she realised that the caravan was empty. Now she had some time to calm herself and she drew the heavy bolt across to secure the door.

When her breathing had become more normal, she had little time to gather herself before a light tapping was heard on the door and Carmel's voice was heard requesting to know why in heaven's name the door was locked. Susie had not time to consider a lie so she told her new friend how Jack had forced himself upon her and how frightened she'd been. The more worldly-wise woman drew the young girl to her, letting Susie sob out her fear and humiliation on her slender bosom.

'There now,' she said comfortingly, 'I know the circus is a very different place than you've been used to before and I should tell you that some of the more aggressive circus males feel they own any or all of the young women, and that Jack is notorious for his lechery. I thought you were his new woman when you arrived with him and so did most of the circus folk. But if you want protecting from him, I'll go get Rosie, the fortune teller, and her son Dan and she'll know what to do. Tonight you can stay here but 'at after' you had better stay with Rosie; you'll be safer.'

'Oh thank you, thank you,' Susie breathed her relief. But she now realised that the slight misgivings she'd had since arriving at the circus could be explained by the foreboding of imminent danger from people she'd thought she could trust. This life was going to be very different from the mill where all they'd wanted from her was to drive her each day to produce calico. She had not been aware that there was another more insidious danger that threatened her very self.

Carmel arrived back with Rosie, a large, smelly, woman, though friendly enough. Her gap-toothed smile was considerate as she looked the young girl up and down.

'Now what's this I hear of Happy Jack?' she questioned. Susie hung her head in embarrassment.

'I thought you wanted him, but now I see you're but a young un' and not used to men. You can stay with Dan and me after tonight. Carmel says you can stay one night with her but then Louis will want to be back, so get your things and bring them to my caravan.'

'I've only got the few things Carmel gave me,' Susie said sadly. Carmel would not meet Susie's eyes. She couldn't explain to the young girl the facts of life especially those in the circus world, and she couldn't refuse Louis.

'I'll see you around tonight and for breakfast. I'm not going anywhere,' Carmel said.

'Right,' said Susie, but she couldn't help feeling very sad, and her day had become one where the lightness had dissipated somewhat as she pottered behind the plodding woman to a shabby caravan on the outskirts of the park.

…

A lone figure was watching Susie's slow progress across the caravan site. Rheumy eyes ever watchful, though clouded, peered out showing his haunted spirit. She was the kind of creature that brought life back into his sluggish veins, she was just like his lost Jane though no, no-one was like Jane, now long gone.

She'd been carried off by the consumption. It hadn't been his fault she'd become sick. He'd been sent away to fight in the wars and she'd not heard from him, nor him from her. Starving herself and trying to eke out the few pence she'd earned digging turnips, for the child to eat as well, she'd been forced to take the path of other women in her situation and had ended on the streets. After the bairn died, she'd lost all will to live, the racking cough weakening her at every step in a miserable life. The consumption had carried her off quickly a year before he returned from the wars.

He wouldn't let any other young beautiful women end her way. In his mad state he was ridding the world of poor unhappy women. They'd not end on the streets. They'd have a peaceful sleep instead. This was where he became more fuddled. Sometimes they struggled, they didn't seem to have a mind that he was trying to save them, and at times their end was anything but peaceful. But that wasn't his fault either. Silly bitches shouldn't struggle. Meanwhile the girl with her companions had disappeared from sight into a caravan on the outside edge of the regular circle. He would watch out for her and see if she needed his help.

…

Susie soon got used to the change of pace from her former employment. The circus performers were very proud of their skills and were happy to share their knowledge with this energetic, vibrant girl whose auburn hair glowed with a new radiance and her green eyes sparkled as she began to enjoy her life of liberty. The trainer of the horseback riders saw her one day watching as they circled the ring. He noticed how entranced she was by the bare-back riders and becoming aware of her supple lithesome shape he suggested that he could teach her to become one of them. As she watched two horses come together with the riders standing on their bare backs and seeming to fly up into the air and change mounts while galloping round the ring, she was hesitant.

'How long has it taken to learn to do this?' Susie wanted to know.

'It's not the time exactly, but the perseverance and wish to succeed,' he told her.

She moved on to the animal cages there, to help with the feeding and watering of the animals in the menagerie. This was more her speed, but who knew what the future would hold? Such strange beasts she saw. Her life had been so sheltered! She knew nothing of wild beasts. Even farm animals were a luxury. In the mill, cats were in profusion to keep down the colonies of mice that seemed to appear from nowhere, and small dogs were used as rat catchers before the vermin damaged the cotton that was the livelihood of too many people. But here Susie was entranced to see wild animals which had been imported from warmer climes. This was a very small circus and an even smaller menagerie but people would come miles to see it and spend their money.

After dinner on her first night with the circus, she left Carmel and Louis to stroll around and find her bearings. The freedom was intoxicating. She passed the small gaily striped tent where the fortune teller plied her trade making a mental note to visit that lady in her professional capacity at some later time.

Rosie was standing in front of it as her son climbed a ladder to fix some ribbons to the pointed top. The wind played with them and set them to a merry dance as Dan tried his utmost to fasten them firmly.

'We're in for a storm tonight,' the large woman called to Susie, 'we're tying everything down before it arrives.'

'What's the laughter I hear?' said Susie.

'Oh it's the fun house,' Rosie returned. 'It's part of the carousel and the organ is just being installed.'

Turning down the pathway behind the tent she saw a wagon pulled up by horses and on the side, a large misshapen face. Outside the wagon a group of men were unloading something large from a flat-bed farm truck. The maestro was organising the unloading and assembling of the Wurlitzer organ, and next to this more people were putting the final touches to the carousel. Susie stopped to watch for a while and then continued her walk past the tent where the magic show would be performed.

The magician looked very ordinary in his everyday working clothes and peered at her as she strolled past. A dark-skinned man was squatting on the ground talking softly to the large basket beside him. He took no notice of her. His eyes were kind of milky and she wondered if he was blind. Red liquid dripped from his mouth. He appeared to be bleeding, but he seemed so calm that she left him and walked on to the shed marked Museum.

The shed was a permanent structure, a small almost derelict barn that was used for storage by the farmer when the circus wasn't needing it. When she took a look inside, she found a few jars holding strange objects. Seeing a body shaped parcel propped up in a corner she went closer to feel the wrapping fabric in finger and thumb. *Fine linen*, she whispered to herself, *how strange!*

'Now what's all this?' A voice arrested her thoughts.

'I meant no harm, all this is so new and different to me, I've never seen the like before,' she gasped.

'Maybe, if you'd like, I can give you a private peep at the museum, and tell you what all the exhibits are.' The man was well-spoken and refined looking, and she decided to take him at his word.

'If you wouldn't mind sir, I've a liking for old things and I'm especially interested in stuffs.'

'Stuffs?'

'Yes, like linen on that dummy in the corner.'

'Ah, you've met my prized possession, that's an Egyptian mummy.'

'A mummy, sir, what's that?'

'It's actually a corpse. It's how the ancient Egyptians prepared their dead for the afterlife. I was lucky enough to purchase this one as I was on my travels around the world.'

'You've been away from England then? How exciting,' said Susie. 'Are you really rich?'

'Not so very rich at the moment, this circus and side-shows are costing me a great deal of money. I'm Professor Richards, by the way, I was an archaeologist but things have changed.'

'Do you own the circus then?' Susie's eyes were the size of saucers.

'Not really, it's more complicated than that, but I won't go into it right now. Come, I'll show you around and you can tell me what you're doing here, then I'll show you back to your shelter for the night. My little show is one that is themed around the afterlife. My specimens on this shelf are freaks of nature. Here for example, is a two headed Guinea pig, and there a tailless cat.'

'Why are they in jars?' asked Susie.

'They are in a special solution to preserve them,' said the professor. 'In the living freak show, you'll see bear lady and the Siamese twins and others who need some cosmetics to make them as weird as the booth owners make them out to be. I think you'll probably like Mr and Mrs Lilliput best. They dance a reel to the smusic played by a fiddling pig. But we also have a sheep with three udders if you prefer something a little obscene.'

'How can that be?' said Susie.

'Well, you'll have to judge for yourself when you see them,' said the professor.

'The next exhibit is a group of tombstones from different parts of the world. This one's Roman and the one in the corner is from Greece, with a few I've picked up around the British Isles. Flanking them we have burial urns from Greece and Mesopotamia.'

'What are burial urns?' Susie inquired.

'In some countries parts of the body are removed after death and interred separately from the body. That's why the urns are of different size to accommodate the organs. On this wall we have natural science, animals have been stuffed in the position of their death to demonstrate their death throes, and here daguerreotypes of murder victims with their murderer's death masks next to them.'

'This is a very gruesome subject sir, I don't think I like it,' said Susie.

'Well, we'll pass on to something a bit more pleasant if you like. Here are souvenirs of my trips abroad. This is a replica of the Taj Mahal in India. Here we have a model of the pyramids along the Nile in Egypt, thought to house the body of the Pharaoh inside a sarcophagus.'

'What are these jewels?' asked Susie, to try to turn his mind to brighter things.

'They are statuettes of Egyptian gods, and jewellery meant as gifts to appease the gods and pay for the passing to Nirvana.'

'Where's that?' she asked.

'Similar to our heaven,' said the professor.

'You do seem to be in a different place,' said Susie. 'I've never spoken to anyone before who knew so much about unusual things. I think I'd better be getting back to Carmel's tent, she said I could stay with her tonight.'

'Very well,' said the professor. 'I'll walk you back.'

Susie felt comfortable with this man even though he was so far above her, he didn't make her feel small. As she turned towards the door, an egg-shaped object caught her eye.

'What's that?' she asked.

'It's a Fabergé egg and this one is most unusual because it's musical. It comes from Russia,' he said, as he turned a tiny key in the base of the plinth it was standing on. The tinkly sound began to play and Susie caught her breath, the sound seemed to speak to her in feelings she couldn't describe.

'Where did it come from, sir?'

'It came from Russia with a few other items. The egg symbolises the rolled away tomb of our saviour and the music box inside it plays a Russian tune from the orthodox church. I brought it back for my sister, but when she died it just came to form part of my collection.'

Susie listened to the tune which she found oddly disturbing. She thought it was maybe because it had a strange eastern lilt to it.

'I'd better be getting back to Carmel, sir, she'll wonder what's become of me, but thank you for your kindness in showing me round the museum.'

'I'll come with you and make sure you're alright now it's becoming dusk,' said her new acquaintance.

The fortune teller's prophecy was coming true. The clouds had turned into a full-blown storm, rain sluiced down and they could see lightning over the hill tops. Low rumbles could be heard as the thunder started to get stronger. Susie pulled her shawl over her head and began to run.

'We should shelter,' said Professor Richards, but she couldn't see the point.

'The caravan's only ten minutes away,' said Susie. 'You go back if you like.' The professor wouldn't hear of it, however, and jogged along at her side. The night was cold and dark with only the occasional flashes to lighten their way.

'I'm glad we're camped in a field,' said the professor, 'and not on any heath, or the ground might not be as level and we'd chance having an accident with mole holes.'

She agreed. They soon came upon Carmel's caravan. She was watching out for Susie and was happy to see someone had seen her home, but surprised when she saw who it was. She thanked him politely as he raised his hat to her.

'Now you're safe, Susie, I'll leave you with your friend and say goodnight. I hope we'll meet again sometime,' said the professor.

'Oh, yes sir, so do I,' Susie replied, 'for the visit to the museum was most interesting.' As they entered the caravan, Carmel wanted to hear all about it. She had never, she said, spoken to the professor and was a bit intimidated by one so high up.

'I thought the same,' said Susie, 'but he's really nice to talk to.'

Next morning the storm had passed and watery sunbeams were trying to push themselves through the haze.

'Here's breakfast for you,' said Carmel, 'better hurry and eat it. We've a lot of hard work to do this morning and the first matinee is this afternoon.'

Susie ate the hard-boiled egg and toast with relish. Fresh food tasted really good and was even better because Carmel served it to her with a smile. Then she enjoyed a cup of hot strong tea. Delicious. Just then Louis arrived to eat with them. Susie was a bit nervous of this muscular man with stern eyebrows. Carmel seemed to take him in her stride, joking with him, as he came up behind her and gave her a love pat on her bottom. Quick as a flash she had spun out of his grasp and pinned him to the floor.

'You'll not get me that quickly!' she laughingly taunted him. Susie joined in the laughter, enjoying the shared joke.

Everything was quickly coming to life as they made their way to the main tent. The animals were calling in their different sounds knowing that food would soon be on the way. Susie said goodbye to Carmel and made her way to the animal menagerie. Big Joe kept her running to obey his commands and the morning was soon underway. Once they were fed the animal trainers appeared to start last minute training sessions and grooming before the afternoon performance. Susie helped with the dogs, holding them still as they were brushed to a glossy or fluffy state depending on their coats. The_little dogs sometimes struggled and then she needed to watch out for their sharp teeth, but all in all it was great fun to help even as a small cog in the wheel of the whole splendid circus.

Chapter Ten
Let the Show Begin

The 1-o-clock performance was preceded by a grand parade of all the acts. The colour and gloss of the parade and the noise and confusion as all lined up in readiness was breath-taking. The audience members had spent their time in the side shows before the 'circus spectacular' and now were sitting eagerly waiting for the main event to begin. A clown playing a one-man band began to walk forward as the ring-master gave the sign to advance, and the whole glorious cacophony of spectacle moved forward. The audience were ecstatic.

Susie was perched on a high stool by the entrance, to be handy if the need arose. She was not sure what need might arise but that was where she'd been put and she had a good vantage point. She saw her little dogs going by and clapped wildly. Carmel and Louis were entering now and they gave her a special hand wave, and here were the horses and riders trotting forward with great majesty, heads held high. As Big Joe led the elephant forward the crowd went wild. The slow lumbering beast seemed to be enjoying himself as he flung back his head and trumpeted to add to the noise. Tumbling clowns followed and then a cart full of dwarves, made up to look like babies in frilly caps and pinafores with feeding bottles stuck in their mouths. Their antics brought the house down, the crowd wondering what they would do next for fun and games when the show actually began. This was only a preview after all.

They were soon to know. As the circle emptied, the ring-master once again took his place and announced that the show would begin. One of the star acts came first, to whet the appetite of the audience. The horses and trick riders made their entrance. First they circled the ring in immaculate array, trotting to the music that came from the Wurlitzer organ. After one revolution they divided in the middle and proceeded to dance in pairs, the riders standing on their backs. On the second revolution the act that Susie had witnessed being rehearsed earlier, was performed, and the second and fourth riders somersaulted and changed mounts in mid-air.

Oh, I could never do that, thought Susie. How the audience clapped and cheered as the act finished and Susie learned what her place was.

'Hurry up, girl,' shouted a roustabout. 'Get the shovel.'

Susie realised she was on clean up duty and hurriedly jumped off her stool and raced with her shovel to clean up after the horses before the cart with the dressed-up babies made its entrance. Now what was she to do with the manure? The trouble was most people had been working here many months and forgot to tell the new girl what she was to do.

'Use the bucket and don't forget to empty it after the show!' shouted the roustabout.

Now where was the bucket?

She was back on her high stool as the baby act came to its climax. One of the little people ran off with another one's bottle and then threw it to a partner. A seeming impromptu game of rugby began to take place, the original baby leaping for a swing as he once again grabbed the bottle and swung off over the heads of the audience on his borrowed trapeze.

Again Susie was called to duty. As the act ended, she was called to rake the sawdust covering the ground, before Carmel and Louis entered the ring to perform on their trapezes. Louis was red with fury as he and Carmel stood waiting. The clown had utilised Louis's trapeze for his own act and Louis was not sure now if the ropes were correctly tied. He prided himself on not using a safety net but now it would be expedient to make use of this equipment that was usually in place to protect Carmel. He caught sight of the perpetrator and ran after him in a fury.

The little man doubled back, still wearing his baby outfit. As he ran into the ring chased by Louis, the crowd roared with laughter thinking this had been planned. Louis was dark with enraged passion. The baby once again made use of the trapeze and Louis quick as a flash grabbed the stabilising rope, and taking it into his big hands he began to spin the trapeze with the baby round and round, faster and faster until the dizzy baby man could no longer hold on and made a leap for the safety net where he lay winded and crying.

The crowd laughed and cheered this wonderful act. And as he limped out of the ring the applause was deafening. But Louis left the little man, with no uncertainty that he'd better watch out, as he snarled 'you'll be sorry' into his face.

After this the well-rehearsed act of Louis and Carmel seemed like an anti-climax which made Louis even angrier and his fury was directed at anyone in his way. He was seen to trip the conjuror who followed them into the ring. The conjuror seemed not to notice and began with a few tricks that wowed the audience. He made coins disappear, brought silk scarves out of his top hat by the yard and exhibited sleight of hand with his card tricks. Then as he got into the live stuff, a white rabbit and a brace of pigeons appeared as if by magic. As the crowd clapped and waved a woman in a spangled costume made her entrance, and Susie gasped. This girl had long red hair and if she'd been dressed in cheap mill clothes, she'd be the spitting image of Susie. A contraption was brought onto the stage and the girl backed up to it, leaning slightly as she did so.

Susie held her breath as the drums began to roll and the conjurer braced himself and exhibited a handful of knives.

'He's never going to throw them at her,' an audience member said out loud, but that was just what he meant to do. The drum roll stopped and the first knife left his hand and whistled towards the girl making its landing on her right side. This was quickly followed by a second, and a third, to other parts on her body. Then a fourth, which should have gone to her ankle, flew wide, and all gasped as the knife point landed with a sharp splintering sound in the wooden strut over Louis' head, where he was lounging to watch the act. The conjuror didn't seem to respond to the accident, he just went on throwing the fifth knife to pin the girl's headdress to the back board.

Susie let out her breath as the audience, not realising the mistake, clapped its appreciation. Susie watched as the conjuror and Louis squared up to each other in the entrance and was glad to see Carmel smoothing the ruffled feathers of both performers. Susie breathed a sigh of relief as her little dogs ran on again jumping through hoops and riding on top of balls that they rolled across the floor. Their final act was a pyramid as they balanced on top of each other. Hooray, and they'd finished.

Clowns performed again and Susie did her clean-up job in preparation for Big Joe and the elephant. This was the last act inside and then the audience were invited to enjoy the sideshows and the outside displays.

The menagerie had come to life since last night and she quickly finished her clean-up job and followed the audience outside to enjoy the fun and games.

'Roll up, roll up to the shooting gallery!' a familiar voice sounded.

Susie spun around, thrown back in time to the night she'd met John and Matt. She was lost in reverie thinking back to that evening, when the same stall holder had done John out of his winnings, thus throwing Emma in his way. The same evening that had given Susie the incentive to escape from the mill.

Shaking her head to free it from memories, she moved with the audience to the cage of the lions. The wild lions did not take part in the actual show. They were exhibited in the menagerie and as the spectators walked around, the lion tamer entered their cage. To fearful cries from the onlookers he took the beasts through their performance. There were just three of them but he still had to have eyes in the back of his head, for they were fast acting animals and would seize their chance whenever they could. As he cracked his whip, they snarled at him and waffled their noses, raising on their hind legs to threaten him with their long claws.

His usual act came to an end, but today he was trying something new for his grand finale. He lured the large lion into the centre of the cage, separating him from the others. They were led through a wire tunnel to a second cage where food had been laid out for them. The door was then slammed down and the tamer was left with his star for their final act.

As he cracked his whip twice, the lion cautiously rolled over and opened his mouth in a large roar. The crowd were silent as the tamer quickly placed a stick to hold the jaws open and then, to enhance the exciting moment, one of the little clowns played a drum roll on a kettle drum, as the tamer knelt down next to his prize performer and placed his head in the lion's mouth. Before he could move to safety, there was a commotion and the 'clown drummer' seemed to hover in the air before slipping through the bars and into the lion's cage. The tamer quickly removed his head and the stick and leapt out of the cage, dragging the **clown** with him. The watchers thought that the accident had been part of the act and applauded loudly. But among the circus people consternation broke out. Who could be responsible for such a dangerous piece of horse play they all wondered?

Susie was wandering about the side shows remembering those that the professor had mentioned, and decided she'd take a look around the outside stalls. The booths were quite small and it was difficult to find room as the crowd jostled her past them in a noisy crush. She found herself next to a sideshow that described itself as the Wonders of the World, and once again her thoughts returned to the night the man in the tiger skin had offered them a place in his tent.

Just then she saw him as he came out into the open, selling tickets to his show, and she quickly ducked down behind a family so that he wouldn't see her. He was wearing the same tiger skin and looking just as greasy as he had last time. Susie melted into the crowd as they jostled her past this seedy individual.

The crowd suddenly veered to the left and Susie was swept with it into a tent where a small audience were waiting for the side show to begin. Quickly she gained a seat wondering expectantly what excitement would be in store. She didn't have long to wait. A character dressed as a pig snorted on-to the stage. He was carrying a fiddle. *Ah,* thought Susie, *this is one of the acts the professor told me about, but even I can see that the pig is a dressed-up person not an animal.*

The audience were murmuring to the same effect and some were even calling for their money to be returned.

'Let's give 'em a chance,' a farmer called, 'we haven't seen anything yet.'

The pig bowed low and began to play his instrument. This was the cue for the dancers to appear and Susie thought she recognised them, as a tiny couple ran on to the stage and took their partners to dance a jig. They were not children, they had the features of adults but were so tiny that they were not much bigger than babies. They danced delicately together. After the jig they began a more stately dance and as it ended, they moved on to country dances. Each delicate step followed the other and the audience were entranced with the miniature size of the couple, who were obviously real people this time and not a trick. Susie was relieved that the audience had settled down for she didn't want any harm to come to the delicate pair. Now she knew where she'd seen them before. They were the couple who'd been next to her at the tent raising.

The next act was billed as 'bear lady' and she wondered if she should stay or not. The title suggested a lewd kind of show, not one for a young girl to watch, and Susie now noticed that the audience was weighted on the masculine side. She rose to her feet but hadn't time to leave before the music for the next act began. The lights had been dimmed to prepare for the entrance of a strange phenomenon. A short creature shuffled on to the stage. It was wearing a scanty dress of leopard skin but it was difficult to tell if it was male or female. Its legs were bowed and covered in hair and its shoulders were hairy too. Its face was quite clear of hair but it had the features of a bear. The audience were now spellbound. Was this an animal or a human, and was it going to be wild and dangerous, they wondered.

As it moved downstage and squinted into the lights, a shiver went through the audience. The animal suddenly rose up on its hind legs and let out a kind of roaring grunt, turned a somersault and landed on an upturned stool. What now? The audience didn't have much time to wait. The creature began to speak in a gruff voice. She, for it was indeed a woman, began to tell her tale. When she had finished, the audience left the tent marvelling at such a strange tale, and wondering if she had told the truth or if it was just a scam to get more money out of them.

'I think the part about her mother being frightened by a bear when she was pregnant was true,' said a man, 'otherwise how could she possibly be such a strange creature?'

'Oh, I don't know,' spoke up a woman, 'my friend is a midwife and she's told me so many strange stories about misshapen babies being born. She told me of one who was born with two heads, and its mother had not been frightened by a two-headed monster!'

'My cow gave birth to a two-headed calf once and the vet said it should have been two calves that didn't separate properly,' said a farmer in their midst, 'so something similar could have happened to bear lady.'

'I think the whole thing is a scam,' said one loud mouthed fellow. 'I think they got us in under false pretences calling her bear lady!'

'Well, what did you expect,' said his wife, 'a naked woman? You never could spell so now you've paid for it.'

Susie was feeling embarrassed with herself for she had not paid attention to learning her letters either and she felt sorry for the blustery man. She was able to separate herself from the crowd and she went into a reverie wondering herself what had happened to cause such a strange misshapen woman. She pondered on how weird the world was and the circus she saw, had more than its share of misfits. It was obviously the right place for her where no one would find her out of place, or ask too many questions.

Chapter Eleven
Emma and John See More of Each Other

Without Susie the mill was a lonely place for Emma. The walls seemed to shrink, compressing all the life that was left to her within them. There were other women but she and Susie had always been together sharing their inner thoughts and hopes. Each day began and ended in darkness which Emma hadn't noticed so much before she lost her friend.

Meg seemed to be aware of Emma's suffering and made a point of being kind to the younger woman and Emma began, gratefully, to appreciate her company. The days went slowly by and soon it was a few months since Emma had seen John at Susie's search party. She stopped thinking of him constantly, though she still thought longingly about him as she lay on her cold pallet at night. One particularly dismal morning as she tended her loom Bill came into the carding room in search of her.

'Look sharp, Emma, there's that chap from the pub come to deliver coal and he's looking for you!' he said.

'How can I go?' said Emma. 'Tom Burly will punish me if I leave my loom.'

'He's out in the storeroom with the master, if you make haste you can be there and back before he returns,' said Bill.

'Then would you tend my loom please?' Emma spoke breathlessly.

'Go, go,' said Bill.

Emma ran down the stairs as quickly as she could. She knew where the coal bunker was in the cellar and fast as light she was down the stairs and into the dark cavern.

'I thought you'd never come,' John whispered into her ear as blinkingly her eyes got used to the dark. 'I've missed you so much,' he said, as his lips met hers falteringly.

Emma almost swooned with joy at his touch.

'I'm sorry to be so forward,' said John, 'but it's almost impossible to see you and I'm not giving up, so I intend to court you in all seriousness, but you'll have to tell me how I can go about it.'

'I don't know, John, I only know I can't live without you,' said the tearful Emma.

'If I can get put on the coal delivery route every Wednesday, can you come to the cellar and meet me here?'

'I'll try John with my heart in my mouth. Although I can't always rely on Tom Burly being out of the way, I'll do my best.'

John swept her lovingly into a warm embrace and Emma returned his kiss fondly.

'Now I'll have to go before I'm caught,' and so saying, she turned away from him tearfully and rushed back to her loom.

She thought no one had seen her departure but that night in the garret, Meg asked her where she'd been. Emma couldn't risk giving away her secret so she said she'd gone to the privy as it was closer than going up to the garret and she'd desperately needed to relieve herself. Meg seemed to believe her answer and Emma breathed a sigh of relief. Maybe she'd tell Meg later; in fact she might need help from the older woman if she was willing to give it.

And so the courtship began. At first Emma was terrified she'd get caught but as the weeks went by and John arrived as if by clockwork on Wednesday mornings, she began to feel more relaxed. She'd enlisted Bill's help because it was easier for a man, especially an old one, to wander around the mill and not get caught.

Then as summer grew heavy with its heady perfumes, John asked Emma to marry him. Her heart skipped a beat as she looked into those loving eyes.

'But are you sure, John?'

'As sure as I'll ever be,' he replied.

'But what'll your mother say?'

'She'll say she's as happy as I am. And I want you to come to tea on Sunday so that she can meet you herself,' said John.

Emma knew it would be difficult to get out on a Sunday afternoon. This was the one day they didn't work, and the old habit of washing their few small garments was still carried out after Sunday morning church. And in the afternoon, she had to help the other women to clean their room and the great room where all their other activities happened. Nonetheless, she replied in the affirmative, 'I'll try for you,' and was rewarded with a big hug from her delighted companion.

Sunday was a beautiful day and Emma tidied herself as best she could for her unexpected outing. She decided to tell Meg where she was going and Meg insisted on lending Emma her shawl which was a bit better than the girl's own garment. Having brought Meg somewhat into her secret, she now enlisted her help in getting out through the coal bunker and though it made her a bit dusty, she was grateful that she'd managed to slip away. Once outside the smell of the air in contrast to the acrid smell of the coal-hole lifted Emma's spirits and she stooped impulsively to pick some wild flowers from the roadside before continuing to skip joyously to John's home.

Mrs Blacklock opened the door to Emma's timid knock. She looked uncertainly at her floral offering, finally grabbing it from her with a distasteful sniff.

'Yes, well, our John would 'av' met you hi' self but I asked him to go an errand for me,' said the upright old woman.

'Oh, as to that, he didn't need to come and get me,' Emma replied.

'Well, let's go in the parlour and have a bit of a chat before he gets home,' John's mother said stiffly. Emma followed her into a spotlessly clean front room wondering why Mrs Blacklock seemed to be wishing to make an impression on her.

'Won't you sit down,' she said motioning to one of the straight-backed chairs, as she took the other one herself.

She didn't waste any time, as they sat down she began to speak. 'Since my husband died, John and Matt have been everything to me. They've helped me raise my three girls and I don't know what I'd do without them. I realise they're getting to an age to want wives but quite frankly, I'd hoped they'd marry someone of their own sort.'

Emma hung her head. She couldn't blame Mrs Blacklock because this had been her own first thought.

The older woman continued a little petulantly. 'John tells me you're a mill orphan and in my day those sort of folks didn't marry and set up house, they stayed were they'd been put by their betters.'

Emma didn't know what urged her, but suddenly Susie's words came to her. 'We'll not be mill slaves all us lives, we weren't born to it and we'll not stay where some bad men have put us.' She suddenly spoke up to Mrs Blacklock,

'Missus! I have been made to live as a slave but it's not how I was born. Because I was kidnapped by evil people when I was little more than a bairn, I have been made to work in the mill but it wasn't what I was born to be. Many of us are in the same plight and if, and if it hadn't been for a very dear brave friend, we'd not have had courage to change things.' She tearfully choked.

'What's the matter?' John had suddenly entered the doorway and saw that Emma was upset. His mother looked a bit subdued.

'I'm sorry, our John, as how I've upset your young woman. I'm only thinking of your welfare.'

'My welfare, mother? I'll thank you to leave my welfare to me. I know what's good for me, and it's Emma. She is the dearest, most gentle but brave creature I've ever met and I thought you'd have had sense to keep your tongue between your teeth until you'd had time to know her for yourself.'

'There's gossip in t' village our John and I don't want you to be harmed by it.'

'Gossip never did anyone any good and I thought you'd have been above the sort of folk that spread it. I'm obviously wrong, so I'll say good day to you and take Emma where she's made welcome. Come on Emma we'll go and visit Aunty Ann. She'll give you a welcome and no mistake and 'appen that's where I'll stay and take my wages from now on.'

At that moment someone else arrived and gave Emma a pleasant 'Ow do.' Matt entered the low vestibule dipping his head as he did so.

'You're not going, are you, Emma? I thought you were coming for tea.'

'I'm afraid we must our Matt,' said John. 'Mum's not made Emma welcome and we're going to Aunty Ann's farm. Will you join us?'

This put Matt into an extremely difficult position that he didn't want to be part of. But making a decision he finally spoke up.

'Well, mother, what's our John to do. He wants Emma and you'd better accept her or you'll lose both of us.'

Mrs Blacklock hesitated, she liked to have her own way, and she also wanted to have her hand on her son's wages.

'Well,' she said coldly, 'you'd better stay and I'll make a pot of tea.' John opened his mouth to object but Emma laid a light hand on his arm.

'Hush John, give her a chance, it's hard for people like her to accept something different from their neighbours.'

'Emma, you've got a good heart and I hope you'll teach my women folk a bit of your goodness as you get to know them and they learn to love you.'

The sniff his mother made suggested that this would happen over her dead body, but she didn't make any comment, and John hoped she'd change with time.

That Sunday tea was the first of many that Emma shared. She had never been invited into a home before and though the cottage was small, it seemed like a palace to Emma. A bright fire burned in the grate glinting on the newly black leaded surround, the Staffordshire dogs sat smartly on the mantelpiece reflected in the brightly polished hob. She felt a warmth and lightness coming over her despite Mrs Blacklock's chilly exterior. She loved being with John and hoped that in time she could bring his mother around to accepting her, for she knew that she couldn't accept John as a husband without his mother's blessing.

The first time Emma visited for tea there were just four people there, but later, two of John's sisters also made an appearance. Maggie and Sally were the older ones and took after their mother. The little one, Clarice, John told her looked exactly like him. That was maybe why they took to each other so happily once they became acquainted. Clarice was sixteen, and in service with the Brierly family. Emma's lack of social life had left her young for her age and the girls seemed to form a bond from the very start. Clarice became a small replacement for Susie, who Emma still missed desperately.

The rigours of mill life went on as usual, but Emma's new-found joy in the love of John and getting to know his extended family raised her thoughts above the stale, dank atmosphere and squalid conditions. Her spirits lifted, the young girl's happiness rose to heights she would never have believed possible. She looked forward to Wednesday and Sunday as she laboured long hours over her weaving. The other women marvelled at the glow in her eyes and the slight pink that radiated on her thin pale face. The change in her otherwise quiet demeanour caused jealousy in some of the meaner women and they gossiped and whispered behind her back, but Emma didn't care. She'd found her own way to freedom.

As her fingers deftly wove the fine fabric her thoughts leapt ahead with surprising speed spinning a fantastic life that was about to begin. Her mind was free, released from the drudgery of the past. Perhaps it was because of this new found confidence that she became a bit careless in her weekly meetings with John, or maybe the feel of Autumn in the air made her realise how time was marching on, but one day as she made her joyful way to the cellar, she was accosted by Tom Burly coming around the corner towards her.

'And where do you think you're going?' he said coldly. Emma stopped in her tracks wide eyed. She had no idea what to say. Finally, she spoke up.

'I was going to the privy and I didn't see you to ask permission and I'm desperate so please let me go,' she said clutching her belly.

'Go this once but you've not heard the last of this,' he retaliated.

Thankfully, she ran into the backyard and down the path towards the offensive smell. John had overheard her conversation and quickly followed after her. He was not going to miss their tryst. He gathered her shaking body into his arms, soothing her with words of love.

'Oh John I was that scared I'm sure he'll watch me from now on and I won't be able to see you again.' She sobbed.

'Calm yourself, love, I'll get you out of here by one way or other you just see if I don't.'

As Emma made her way through the fuggy air back to her loom, she was conscious of being watched and noticed Jessie Burns' eyes on her. Jessie had always had it in for Emma and she wondered if it was her who'd given her away to Tom Burly. She'd have to be a lot more careful, she thought, or Jess might give her away. Meg glanced at her as she resumed her work and Emma made a decision to take her into her full confidence. As Emma finished her story, Meg looked at her concerned.

'It's not as though I'll give you away,' she said. 'I've been watching out for you ever since I helped you out of the coal hole, but you know what they'll do if they find out?'

'You've known all along?' said Emma quietly.

'Yes,' said Meg, 'and if I know, you can bet I'm not the only one, so be careful, I'm on your side.'

'Oh Meg, John's asked me to marry him and I want to so badly but how am I going to manage that when I'm nearly always locked up in't mill?' sobbed the distraught girl.

'I don't know, lass. You and Susie have always been different from the rest of us. You seem to have more spirit somehow. I'm sure if you just keep listening to your heart, all will pan out eventually and you'll get your John one way or the other. I don't say it will be easy and I don't know of anyone who's been able to marry out of the foundlings before but I also don't know anyone who's got away from t' mill either and Susie has, so there's hope for you. Just keep on doing and hoping, that's my advice.'

Emma gave the older woman a hug.

'Meg, you've become such a comfort to me in so many ways. I'll never forget it,' she said.

Emma and John had other supporters also in family members. When John had threatened to move to Aunty Ann's home, his mother had known that she had to be careful. Her sister Ann had always adored her nephews and neither of them could do any wrong in Ann's eyes. John had taken Emma to the farm 'Foolo' to meet his aunt early on in their courtship. She and Uncle George had no children of their own so the Blacklock family were very close to them.

On one of their Sunday visits, Emma and John were surprised to see a little pony and trap drawn up by the cart road.

'Your aunt has many visitors but I've never seen this get up before,' said Emma.

'Oh that's Mam's cousin,' John replied, 'we call her Aunt Peg. She's a lovely woman, but a bit strange in looks. She works in a circus and helps with the sideshows, but don't mention it. Everyone knows but it's not talked about.'

Emma was intrigued and wondered what she was going to meet. As they entered the low porch, Aunty Ann called out to them to go through into the big farm kitchen, and there enjoying a nice cup of tea was a little hunched up person with a big smile on her face.

'Nice to meet you,' she said to Emma, 'I've heard about you via the grape vine.'

Emma looked at her quizzingly. She'd never heard this term before.

'Oh she means the family talk a lot, but mean no harm,' John reassured her.

'Sit down do both of you, and I'll get you some tea,' said Aunty Ann.

As Emma sat down next to Aunt Peg, she noticed her long red nails and the heavy make-up on her face. She tried not to be judgemental of the cheery woman but Emma's narrow life gave her few options. Her opinions had been formed by others and from a Biblical standpoint Aunt Peg looked like a Jezebel. Emma wondered what this pleasant woman did at the circus. The talk was all about the farm and the horses which Aunt Peg seemed to know plenty about. Maybe she was a show rider, thought Emma. She was gossipy and wanted to know all about Emma and the mill on which subject she seemed to be well-informed.

Emma relaxed in her pleasant company though she was not too keen to share her innermost thoughts. John, sensing Emma's reluctance to talk about herself too much, turned the conversation. 'And how are Sarah Annie and Fanny?' he asked.

'I haven't seen them in many a while,' said Aunt Peg, 'they have no way of visiting me, so we only meet when we visit your mam, John.'

John turned to Emma. 'They're some more cousins, Dad's this time, and they work in the mill at Ancoats, hemming handkerchiefs.'

'Ancoats is a long way, isn't it?' said Emma.

'Yes, it's near Manchester. All the big textile mills have opened up there since machinery took over from the cottage industry that used to abound in these parts. The only way they can visit is by horse and carriage or by the barges that sail along the canal,' said Aunt Peg.

Emma went very quiet, John wasn't sure what was the matter with her but he knew something was. Emma had not told John how her kidnap had been accomplished. She didn't really want it to be public gossip. She made towards the door and John followed her.

'It's alright,' she said, 'I'm just going for a short walk to get my thoughts in order, no need for you to come.'

'There may not be need for me to come but I'd like to,' said John giving her a small hug. 'Aren't we talking of getting married, eh, and I feel that married people should love each other through and through and share everything even their…especially their troubles.'

'Oh, John, I'll never deserve you. I haven't had a home and a loving family like yours. I've had very little privacy in t' mill and being able to go outside and think my own thoughts is a luxury I've never had. I'm grateful that you want to come with me and support me in my quiet times and I have to admit that Aunt Peg brought back a memory that I'd rather forget. And I was thinking of how I was kidnapped and brought to Derbyshire in a rickety barge along the canal.'

'I didn't know you were kidnapped!' said John in a shocked voice. 'However could that happen in such a quiet little spot as this?'

'I don't know, John, I was too little to understand but horrible things happen to children that most of the world doesn't know about, or even care about, if the truth could be told. I do remember having a nurse to take care of me and she's the only person I have a shadowy recollection of, but John please don't tell anyone about this. I'd rather forget it if I could. No good could come of telling anyone my story now. Too many years have passed by and I'm just a poor mill labourer, whatever sphere of life I was born into.'

'Well, lass if that's what you want, I'll back you up but I'm not saying it's right and every nerve in my body screams the injustice.'

'Let's go back inside. Your aunts will wonder what's happened to us.' And so saying, Emma dashed back into the comfortable home.

'And where did the two of you disappear to?' Aunt Ann smilingly called to them with a knowing look on her face. Emma put her hand on John's arm to remind him of his promise.

'Just getting a breath of air,' said John, 'as you know, both of us work in stifling surroundings and the good fresh air is a treat indeed.'

Aunt Ann had the grace to look ashamed of her thoughtless comment. 'Come away in then and have something to eat,' she said.

'How delicious this cake is,' said Emma. 'I'm not used to eating anything so good.'

'You've been brought up plain then, have you?' said Aunt Peg.

Emma could have bitten out her tongue. She now realised that she had made an opening for the family to ask questions of her.

John intervened quickly. 'Emma's a good worker and a plain liver, none better,' he said with a slight frown at Aunt Peg who knew Emma's story in part but was fishing for more.

Not to be deterred however Aunt Peg kept up the subject.

'You'd better ask John's mother to teach you to cook if you're unable. She's a good cook and you'll need to be able to make a meal for your man if you're planning to marry him.' She'd gone too far, even, for Aunty Ann.

'I think Peg, we'd better leave that subject alone. It's too soon to be talking of marriage yet,' she said.

Emma flashed a grateful smile at Aunty Ann but inside she was thinking that here was another thing she was unable to do and wondering what the use was of continuing with John. It was good to be welcomed by some of the family but it was never unconditional, she realised. In the mill she was safe and she only had to do as she was told, she didn't have to make any decisions.

Luckily for Emma John made the next decision for her. As they were walking on the pleasant lanes one Sunday, John once again asked her to marry him.

'Nothing has changed, John, your mother still doesn't accept me and I have to agree with her that I'm not good enough for you.'

'What absolute nonsense, you're thinking in terms of mercantile good, not in the goodness of humanity. I'm not interested in money worth or family background. I'm interested in your own sweet self and in that way you couldn't be better if you were a millionaire or your father owned the mill.'

Emma's delight in this speech showed in her pink cheeks and sparkling eyes.

'But what will we do about your mother, John?'

'She'll have to come round and I'm going to see your owner and try to get you out of that mill the first day I'm free from the pit.'

Chapter Twelve
John Visits Mr Brierly

It was now six months since John and Emma had been seeing each other regularly twice each week. John decided it was time to take matters into his own hands and he took a morning off work and dressed very carefully. He wore his best suit and a clean shirt with the collar carefully ironed by his adoring mother. He was off to see Mr Brierly and he wanted to make a good impression. It was a lovely day. The birds were singing as he walked from the village and arrived at bottom lane. He'd had to leave home early because he didn't want his family to see him dressed in his best clothes. Better to fight one battle at a time. That was how it felt as he strode nervously down the clinker brew. He wondered where Emma was at this moment. He couldn't know that she was just eating her meagre breakfast before being herded downstairs to start her long working day. He hadn't told her that he was visiting Mr Brierly today, the outcome of which would decide the rest of her life. Better to wait until he had good news.

It suddenly struck him that Emma would have nothing to do once he got her out of the mill. What would she do with herself, she was only trained as a weaver? This was the first time he'd thought about it. Once they were married, things would settle down, he knew, but she would need something to do in the meantime. His mother was not being any help but he knew that Aunty Ann would find her a home if the need arose.

Arriving in the mill yard, he stepped up smartly and pulled on the rope which rang the big doorbell. Usually the door was open but it was a bit too early yet. The clanging seemed to waken the place up and the overseer opened the door asking what all the noise was about so early in the morning. John stated his request to see Mr Brierly and was told in no uncertain way that the owner did not do any business until after 8-o-clock. John was nonplussed but asked if he may wait until a more convenient time.

'And how could a poor miner afford to waste time?' he was asked but John had made up his mind and was not going to be put off by anyone especially this man who had caused Emma so much difficulty in the past.

'That's not something I'm prepared to share with you,' he answered.

'I don't like your tone, young man, you'd better keep a civil tongue in your mouth if you know what's good for you,' said Burly.

Shaking his head to free it from making another retort, John swept away and seated himself on a hard stool at the back of the room. Better not to take a plush chair or he would add insult to injury. Burly, not being able to find any more to criticise, left him to while away some time and John was left alone with his thoughts.

Eventually Mr Brierly entered the room, a small frown on his rugged face. He grunted a good morning to John but made no attempt to put him at his ease. As John stood, the master allowed him to remain standing while he himself took the easy chair.

'And what brings you here so early?' he inquired. 'You might have known that I don't begin work until after I've had my breakfast.' John looked at the big clock on the wall and reckoned that he'd broken his fast two and a half hours earlier. If he'd spoken at once his irritation would have shown. So he waited cautiously wanting to make a good impression. When he spoke he chose his words carefully.

'I've been walking out with Emma Brierly for some months now and the time has come, sir, for me to ask for her hand in marriage.' The owner was completely stunned and began to bluster.

'These girls don't marry. They are part of the large scheme of the working mill. We don't sell our slaves any more than we sell our machinery.'

'Sell her!' yelled John, losing his calm completely. 'She is not an animal or a machine, she's a beautiful and grand woman, and I was not asking to buy her but for you to give her her freedom. However, if it's the only way to set her free from the likes of you, I'll buy her indeed, just name your price.'

'You must have been doing something with her that you shouldn't,' said Mr Brierly, 'or you wouldn't be so quick to give your money away.' Then slowly he lit a cigar. 'Have you got her in the family way?'

John was so angry that he didn't know what to say but his white face and clenched fists said it all. Mr Brierly realised that he'd gone too far for this proud young miner and changed his tune somewhat. Rising he spoke more calmly.

'Emma is too young yet to marry,' he said, removing a bit of tobacco from his tooth, 'come back again when she's older, if you're still of the same mind, and I'll think about it then.'

As he was about to sweep out of the room, John stopped him with, 'You think you'll put me off with your insults, but Emma and I have just as much right to find love as swanky folks who've made their money out of other people's misery. I will marry Emma, and if you think you'll put her price up by making me wait until she's of legal age, we'll see what the law has to say about it. Now I'll bid you good day,' and so saying he swept out of the room.

Mr Brierly was gobsmacked. He had never been spoken to like this in his life and he was not pleased with the outcome of the interview. He prided himself on Christian values and to have seen the hatred in another man's eyes made his halo feel as though it were slipping. He didn't like this feeling and inside he began to bluster, to rationalise his actions. The young miner had said he'd been walking out with Emma for some months. How had he managed that, Mr Brierly wondered? The slaves were locked in when they were not working, and he assumed they were safe, but now he saw that here was something to look into. If Emma had escaped from the mill to be able to have a courtship, someone else must have known about it. He determined to have words with his overseer as soon as possible.

John in the meantime felt strong and justified. He strode out on his way home marvelling at his own temerity. The feeling was short lived however, for he'd have to face his family with an explanation of where he'd been in his best clothes. His mother immediately jumped to the wrong conclusion. She could see no other reason for his dressed-up state than a marriage.

'Where is she then?' she screamed at him. 'I thought you'd at least have had the sense to be married at week's end rather than wasting a working day for such a paltry reason.'

John had never considered this aspect of the case but he wasn't going to be brow beaten by his mother especially when she'd got the wrong end of the stick. Ignoring her nagging screams of 'Our John what have you been and done?' he left her abruptly and went to his room to change into his working clothes. He didn't want to deal with her temper now so he climbed out of the window and down the thick ivy which clung to the back of the house. Gaining solid ground, he was off like a hare in the direction of the pit. He'd be in time for the second shift and work late so that he didn't need to waste any money or hear his mother's criticism.

After a long hard shift at the coal face, John was not in the mood to listen to his family's concerns about his future. As he approached his home, which should have been in darkness at that time of night, he was surprised to see all the lights still burning and even more unusual the glow of a coal fire in the grate, midweek. Apprehensively he entered a rather full house place. His mother was holding forth as only she could, but in addition to two of his sisters he was surprised to see his father's cousins, Sarah Anna, and Fanny sitting upright on the horse-hair sofa.

'Well ow do,' said John, 'whatever brings you here at such a late hour?'

'What does he say?' asked Fanny, her ear trumpet held aloft.

'He wants to know why we're here,' sniffed Sarah Anna.

'Well of all the nerve when we've come a long way to help his poor mother in her misery,' yelled Fanny.

John was totally befuddled.

'What misery are you talking about?' he said.

The deaf Aunt was not to be silenced.

'Our poor Bob,' she said, 'what would he say if he knew his eldest had gone off with a little tramp like that.'

'Hey hold on a bit,' Matt had now joined the fray.

'What are you talking about and why are you here so late at night?' John was completely bewildered and had missed the slight to Emma in the general hubbub.

'Mother suppose you tell everyone what's going on, so that tired workers can get to their beds.'

'John how can you take that attitude with me when you know what you did this morning, going off in your best suit and getting married without telling anyone. Then when I asked you to explain yourself, you took off through a bedroom window and ran away from home.'

His mother's face had flushed and she was breathing heavily. John looked as his family gazed at him, waiting for an answer. The long day had cooled his temper somewhat and all he wanted to do was sleep, but he couldn't believe that his mother would make such a fuss before she knew all the details, even going so far as to send for his father's cousins. At last he tried to say something in reply that would bring some lucidity into the conversation.

'I don't know why you jumped to the conclusion that I was getting married just because I was wearing my best suit,' he finally said, 'and I didn't have time for an argument because I'd been kept from my work, so I decided the quickest way out was down the ivy.'

'That's alright our John but why the best suit?' Maggie said.

If it had been anyone else, they would probably have received a candid answer but Maggie was not John's favourite sibling and she had irritated him by asking something that he felt was not her business. His answer was curt and he turned on his heel and went upstairs to bed, leaving them all none the wiser. *Let them stew*, he thought, *serves them right*. Shortly he heard Matt creeping upstairs to share his room. His brother had always been his companion and he decided that Matt should be told the truth about his day. When he had finished his story, Matt was quiet for a few minutes.

'You know our John,' he finally said, 'what we need to do is get mother on your side, and it won't be done by antagonising her. You've already said that Emma won't have you if mother isn't willing and Mr Brierly won't let Emma go til she's older. That gives you some time to bring mother round.'

John could see the sense in this but couldn't see how to do it.

'How'll it be,' Matt said, 'if Emma were to ask mother to help her learn how to cook. It would also be a good skill for her to learn. If she's going to leave the mill, she'll need some sort of livelihood to keep her going until such time as you can afford to keep her.'

'You talk sense, Matt. Aunt Peg had also mentioned this idea, I'll do it. But what about the present situation, and how did Sarah Anna and Fanny come to be here?'

'They happened to be visiting some friends in the area and just popped in. They brought mother some of their handkies and were all ears to hear wrong about Emma. You know what snobs they are and bad gossips into the bargain.'

'I don't much like my private life being bandied about to all and sundry but I suppose I'd better make some kind of a statement of intention or they'll get the wrong end of the stick again.'

So saying he looked longingly at his bed, the patchwork quilt turned down invitingly at one corner, and sighing deeply he returned to the discussion taking place about him downstairs. All eyes were on him as he entered the parlour.

'Well our John,' said his mother.

'Very well, Mother,' he replied, then catching a slight frown on his brother's face, he saw that this was not the way to build bridges and swallowed before he was tempted to make any more caustic remarks. As he explained the situation to all of his family, they at least kept quiet and let him finish before anyone spoke. Ending with a request to all of them to help him be patient while like knights of old he strove to do what it took to win his lady. Then they all spoke at once, each thinking that theirs was the only right answer.

'Let me speak!' roared John. 'You are all thinking of this as your own personal problem. It's not about you, any one of you, it's about me and Emma. The only problem I see is the fact that Mr Brierly won't let Emma go until she's of legal age. As our Matt has said to me, we need to use the time to her advantage by helping her to learn a craft that will give her a livelihood when she leaves the mill. Matt has also suggested that Mam might teach her to cook because who could teach her better than the best cook in Derbyshire.'

Mrs Blacklock was pleased by this praise but wasn't to be totally bamboozled.

Sarah Hanna added her bit at this moment, 'Who's talking about cooking? I thought we'd decided between us that she wasn't good enough for poor Bob's son?'

'What's that?' yelled Fanny waving her ear trumpet around threateningly.

'He wasn't poor. He was very well looked after by a good wife and I'll thank you to mind your own business where my lads are concerned,' said Mrs Blacklock.

'Oh well, I know when I'm not wanted,' bristled Sarah Anna, 'come on Fanny, we're going.'

'What's that?' yelled her sister.

'Now just a minute,' spoke up Matt, 'you can't leave at this time o' night. Let's all calm down and get some sleep. John and me's got to work in t' morning and you won't find a farm cart to take you tonight. You and Fanny are welcome to spend the night in mine and John's room and we'll kip down here if you'll all leave and let us get on with it.'

This seemed like a good plan and was, if truth be told, what Sarah Anna had had in mind. She nonetheless swept out of the room sniffing disdainfully, followed by Fanny who despite her deafness had got the gist of the idea. The girls followed in their wake disappointed that no more was being discussed tonight. When John and Matt had their mother alone, John once again broached the subject of his future. 'I'll not change my mind, Mother, so are you with me or against me.'

'John you're all I have, you and Matt,' she began to wheedle.

'If you play your cards right you'll not lose a son you'll gain a daughter,' said Matt. 'Emma has no one in the world, so you'll not have to deal with any in-law problems as most families have. If you treat her right, she'll love you till the day she dies.'

Mrs Blacklock realised she was bested and gave her consent to teaching Emma housewifely duties, but said she would not go further than that tonight. With that resolve she went her way up the stairs leaving the two brothers alone at last.

'Well that's that lad, I hope things carry on much smoother for you now we've settled, Mother, and you'll see the year'll go fast enough.'

Chapter Thirteen

Repercussions of the Visit

Lady Day was fast approaching and John decided to enlist his favourite sister's help. Clarice was in service and enjoyed two days each year with her family. One of these was Lady Day. Emma knew nothing of John's plan. He thought the invitation to learn cooking would be best to come from his mother, and Clarice's would be the gentle voice that would persuade her to accept the offer. Emma was invited to tea and the family waited as Clarice walked the two miles from the big house down into the village. Clarice hadn't been home since Christmas. She wondered how her family were getting on as she tripped along the country lanes. She had heard some whispers about her brother's visit to Mr Brierly, but being one of the lowliest workers, all talk had stopped when she entered the servant's kitchen. Service was a hard life but her mother had insisted that she should not work in the cotton mill and her brothers had agreed, noting the death rate of mill operatives and the long hours of work in addition to the dangerous conditions. They felt that the baby of the family would be safe living in the big house with the Brierlys.

Clarice carried her Simnel cake that she had made for her mother in a canvas bag, proudly. Cook had praised her efforts this year. She was careful not to jostle it too much as she wanted it to be as near perfect as possible. Her mother was a perfectionist and Clarice didn't want to be criticised when her gift was displayed. She had wrapped it in brown paper to save it from the disaster of last year. Being in service for a few years had given her a bit more confidence and she no longer felt like the baby of the family, though she knew that being the youngest she would always hold that position.

John and Matt had decided to meet up with their little sister to put her in the picture. She saw them approaching and felt such joy, as on reaching her, each brother wrapped her in a warm embrace. She agreed to do all she could to help the situation with Emma, promising to be a go between with the two women.

The three siblings entered the house place joyfully but it was short lived. A mill worker was standing there. John recognised her but couldn't remember how until she reminded him that she'd been at the fair that long-ago night when all had begun. Meg spoke up.

'Emma asked me to come and tell you that she doesn't want to see you anymore.'

'What happened to her?' John felt a cold hand grab his heart. 'Speak up woman, what happened to her?'

'She was found out, someone told on her, and she was shamed publicly.'

'What do you mean?' John was panting his voice gruff.

'She was stripped naked and beaten and then her hair was shorn to the very skin.' John went cold but he was sweating.

'Who did this?' he panted. 'Tell me or I swear I'll drag it out of you.'

'No need to frighten the poor woman, John. She came here to do Emma's bidding and will probably be punished too if she's found out,' said Matt.

John collapsed onto a chair his head in his hands.

'I'm sorry lass I meant you no harm, but I'm all fired up,' he said.

'How is Emma?' asked the quiet Clarice.

'She refuses to eat and just lies on her pallet when she's not working,' said Meg. 'I'm a' feared for her sanity.'

'What can we do, Matt?' said his distraught brother.

'Well, first we should send a message to Emma by way of this good woman, telling her you'll not let her go and urging her not to lose hope. Then we should let Meg get back before she's missed. At' after we'll put our thinking caps on and see how best to handle the situation,' replied Matt.

'First of all, you'll have the good tea I've prepared for you and 'appen Meg will join us,' said his mother.

'I'm not hungry,' said John. 'I blame myself for what they've done to Emma. She was scared to death and I didn't believe her that they could be that brutal.'

'Don't blame yourself, the only people to blame are the ones who shamed her,' said Mrs Blacklock. 'Now have some tea to keep your strength up and we'll talk about what we can do.'

John looked at his mother and saw that she was in earnest. *Well,* he thought, *if any good can come out of this, it's Mother's change of attitude.*

Meg thanked them for the offer but said she had to go.

'Then I'll put up a parcel for you to eat on your way,' said Mrs Blacklock kindly.

They talked well into the night but had made no plans when they finally went to bed. John was all for racing to the mill and releasing Emma, but as his family pointed out, he wouldn't be allowed in and his journey would be pointless.

'Better to save your strength until we have a plan,' Matt said.

The week progressed as usual but when John went to deliver his coal on Wednesday, he found the bunker padlocked and however much he pounded on the door it was not opened to him. He had to return to the mine with his delivery intact. This caused some problems for John and he had to answer to the manager for not leaving the coal as he'd been ordered. He felt his uselessness very deeply. He was not the kind of man who sat around twiddling his thumbs, but that is what he did until weekend.

On Friday night Matt asked him to go to the pub as they usually did but John could not bring himself to go 'swilling ale' as he told his brother and Matt left on his own for his social evening. After his brother had gone, however, John found he could not settle to anything and about an hour later he jumped up restlessly and grabbing his jacket from its peg, told his mother not to wait up for him.

As he rounded the hill at the top of the clinker brew and looked towards the mill, he noticed a strange orange glow in one of the windows. There could be no other explanation for it than that. The mill was on fire. John started to run. No one else seemed to be about. As he gained the street, he saw the beadle coming towards him in a leisurely way.

'Quick,' called John, 'alert the brigade. The mill's on fire.'

The beadle rang his bell and began to proclaim the news as loudly as he could. John kept on running. Emma was asleep in that mill and he was going to save her. Soon the Friday night revellers were alerted by the beadle's call and more men came running to help but John had a start on them. He banged on the door and rang the bell but no one came to answer his summons.

He searched the mill yard and finding a small tree trunk he began to force the door. His brother was now at his side with many other friends and they heaved the log together. Finally it gave way and he was into the burning building. They tried to hold him back but he would hear none of it. Quickly he ran to the door which led into the mill proper, from under which dense smoke was billowing.

He banged on the hot door scorching his knuckles and finally a sleepy Tom Burly appeared, wanting to know what all the noise was about.

'Can't you see man,' John screamed, 'the mill's on fire!'

'Oh bloody hell!' Burly exclaimed. 'Now we're in fir it.' John hadn't time to comment.

'Where are the keys to the garret?' he said.

'I'll go and get them,' said Burly.

'Hurry up man, people are going to die,' said John.

'I've got to save the raw cotton,' said Burly.

'Bugger the cotton,' John swore. 'The whole mill will go up soon.' But Burly still argued.

'Where are the keys to the garret?' John stormed, twisting Burly's arm in a vice-like grip.

'Geroff me,' Burly squealed and twisting free he tried to escape by running for the stairs.

'Give me the keys,' barked John as he jerked the squirming man to the floor.

His friends tried to intervene but when the keys fell out of Burly's pocket, John could contain himself no longer and planted a sharp punch to the man's chin sending him sprawling over the rail and into the stairwell. As he bent to retrieve the bunch of keys that would give Emma her freedom, he did not see the figure hiding in the shadows.

Now the smoke was so thick that John had to close his eyes. He wrapped a scarf around his mouth and tried to make his way up the narrow stairs to the garret room. He could hear shouting, crying and wailing. Then he heard a noise that could only be the large bell booming to alert the residents to their danger, and finally a banging on the garret door.

Thank God, he thought, *at least they're awake, and hopefully will be able to get down under their own steam.* His friends were coming up behind him to help save the mill occupants. John bent to unlock the door just as a burning beam fell above his head. He would have been injured by it if Matt had not pushed him aside at that moment. But in saving him, Matt had sent the flaming beam closer to the door and the flames rose and scorched into the wood.

'Stand back, stand back!' yelled John to the garret dwellers. 'The door's burning.'

Frantic screams could be heard on the other side, then suddenly the door burst open from the pressure on its other side and the terrified residents poured out, pushing their rescuers into danger.

'Slowly now,' said John regaining his balance. 'We'll help you down, wrap some cloth from that bin around your faces to stop the smoke choking you.' He searched the faces as they went by but didn't see Emma.

'Where is she?' he said. 'Where's Emma?'

No one knew. In the confusion to get out it was every one for herself. As the last woman was helped to safety, John recognised Meg.

'Where's Emma?' he asked.

'I don't know,' said Meg, 'she was not on her pallet when I woke up and checked her and now the air's so thick it's hard to see the nose on your face in there.'

John plunged into the room followed by Matt. It was now so full of thick dank smoke he could see what Meg had meant for; he truly couldn't see in front of his nose. The brigade had arrived and outside crowds of onlookers had formed to see the spectacle. This noise added to the crackling of the flames and was reminiscent of what Hell might be like, John thought. He was used to darkness and stale air in the pit, but this was a whole new experience. He forced his way through the confusion to the high window, discovering a beam that had split and fallen, and there underneath it was a woman. He turned into ice inside the fiery room as he knelt on the floor beside the body when he realised it was her.

'Have you found her?' asked Matt as John felt the weak pulse.

'Yes! And she's still alive!' answered John thankfully.

'Let's get her out before it's too late for any of us,' said his brother.

They had to lift the smouldering beam to release her as the flames crackled above them singeing both of their heads and making her release painful for all of them. Finally they had her free, and carefully carried her between them down the treacherously narrow stairway and into the evening air. As they reached the outside door, a cheer went up from the onlookers, who placed blankets on the grass to shield her from the evils of the damp night air, as they laid her gently down.

'She's still not coming round,' said John worriedly.

The brigade had done its best but the fire was completely out of control now and it was obvious that the mill couldn't be saved.

'Now what's going to happen?' said one fellow.

'We'll have to go back to the workhouse,' said another, 'there'll be no work here for many a year.'

'From one Hell to another,' spoke up the first man. 'Maybe we'd have been better to let the flames take us and put an end to our misery,' he said bitterly.

John realised that his prayers had been answered though he would not have wished this outcome on anyone. But at least Emma was out of the mill and all he had to do now was bring her round. He felt sure that she wouldn't need to go in the workhouse but her Hell would be of a different kind played out in her own mind. Just then the firemen were bringing another body out.

'How is he?' the crowd shouted.

'Not so good,' came the answer. 'He's not breathing.'

They laid him down on the ground next to Emma and as the fireman worked on him, John saw his face and with mixed emotions saw that it was Tom Burly. The fellow who had given Emma such a difficult life was here next to her breathing his last. John couldn't be glad, this was a fellow human being, but he couldn't be sad either, for he was certain it was Tom who'd given Emma her shaming. That terrible experience, John was sure, was the reason behind her stupor now.

Under the bruises on her face and head, her colour was deathly pale.

There were many cuts on her bald head and John could have wept when he thought of her gentle nature, and was still ashamed of himself for helping to cause all this pain to one he loved more than life itself. As he gazed at her, she began to stir. Emma slowly opened her eyes staring around her but with no understanding in the gaze.

'She's coming round!' Matt said, 'appen she'll do.'

But John was looking at her empty eyes and his heart was heavy even though she was alive. A policeman came by to see the casualties. He was making a list and spent time with the onlookers who knew the mill workers.

'So you say this is Tom Burly, the overseer?' he said, his pencil poised over the notebook he was carrying.

'That's a fact,' returned the onlooker. 'I know him well, nice chap.'

John couldn't believe his ears and wondered how well the onlooker knew Burly and if he was just trying to make himself important. When the constable moved over to Emma, John pondered how much he should tell of her treatment in the mill. Especially when the constable bent over Emma and remarked on her bruises.

'Those are some bad bruises, and did she have lice or something as her hairs all been taken off?'

John couldn't contain himself any longer. 'She didn't have lice, she was publicly shamed and had her head shaved by the *nice chap* as is lying there on the ground next to her,' he said.

'And who are you?' the constable asked, licking his pencil in readiness for the answer.

'I'm proud to say I'm this young woman's intended. My name's John Blacklock and I'm a miner,' he answered.

'And does this young woman work in the mill?' the constable questioned.

'She did,' John replied, 'but thank God she won't be working there again.'

'You seem to know a lot about things, where were you when the fire started?'

'As to that I don't know when it started exactly but I do know that when I turned the point in the road where I could see the mill windows, I saw an orange glow that could only be a fire, so I called the alarm to the beadle.'

'Thank you for your information, I'd better have your address, I'll be wanting to talk to you again,' said the constable.

'Our John, do you think that was wise?' said Matt.

'I don't know if it was wise but it was the truth and someone should know what's going on in that mill,' John answered. 'Now we should try to get Emma home. Could you go and find a cart? We'll 'av trouble carrying her down the brew at else.'

As the little parade approached the cottage, Mrs Blacklock heard them and came to the door.

'What in the world's happened?' she wanted to know.

'We'll tell you after Mam, now we've got to get Emma inside in the warm. I hope we've got a fire in the room.'

'We soon will have,' his mother replied as she bustled off to see to this. They laid Emma on the sofa. She still did not respond and lay limply during all their ministrations gazing ahead of her blindly.

'Poor lamb,' his mother remarked. John didn't reply but felt some warmth of gratitude for her change of heart.

At this point Maggie and Sally entered the room wakened by the bustling that had gone on.

'What's to do our John?' Maggie said.

'Emma's been hurt in a mill fire,' Matt responded for his brother.

'She doesn't look all there,' Sally said bluntly.

'Hush, hush, watch what you say, she was under a beam and the shock would make anyone glazed for a while,' said Matt.

John himself was in shock. How could his sister be so unthinking?

His mother was thinking of practical things.

'Where will we put her, she should have a bed to lie on peacefully?'

'She can have our room,' said Matt, and we'll sleep on the sofa for a while.

Mrs Blacklock scurried upstairs to get the bed ready for their surprise guest. She had been totally shaken by Emma's appearance. The girl, she thought, looked close to death. She remembered Meg's words, 'We're afeared for her sanity,' and she decided that if anyone could do anything to help Emma back to earth, she was going to have a good try.

'The shock to Emma's system occasioned by the happenings of the last week has put her into a stupor,' said Mrs Blacklock, as the womenfolk were helping her into a borrowed nightdress. Emma paid no heed to their actions, continuing to gaze ahead with glassy eyes. They laid her down under the patchwork quilt hoping to warm her freezing body.

'I'll stay with her awhile,' said Mrs Blacklock, 'I don't want her feeling strange in a room she doesn't know, if she comes to.'

The sisters left her, thankfully going to their bed. Nothing else could be gleaned tonight and they had to work in the morning. John crept in quietly as he gathered his night clothes.

'What do you think, Mother?' he questioned.

'Well, I'd say she's had more shock than a body can stand and it will be a matter of time how she does, but I'll nurse her for you and if good food will bring her back, she'll get as much as she needs.'

'Bless you, Mother, I knew you'd love her once you had the chance.'

So saying, after a desperate look at the wraith-like figure before him, John tearfully left the room, knowing his mother would do all in her power to help the sick girl.

As the night wore on, a change came over her patient, and Mrs Blacklock looked on Emma with fear. She had not wanted her son to marry so much beneath himself but she could not stand to see the poor bald head with its scabs and grazes without feeling absolute compassion for one used so badly. Emma was burning up with fever and started to toss and turn writhing around the bed in delirium. Her squeaky voice rang out.

'You'll not strip me bare, Tom Burly, I'm a good girl, I'm a good girl, no, no you're hurting me, stop it stop it. You'd not do this if I had a father to fight for me. You took him away from me...me from him...' and finally a piercing scream of...SUSIE...echoed around the still house and John came running upstairs to see what had happened with Matt close behind him.

'She's delirious,' said their Mother. 'She's making little sense; talking about being taken from her father, and is Susie the friend who ran away?'

John nodded. He didn't know what it all meant either but he was inclined to listen, knowing about Emma and Susie having been kidnapped.

'Should I bring a doctor?' said John.

'We'll wait a bit,' his mother replied, 'it's always worse in the small hours for someone in a fever. I'll sponge her down a bit and it'll 'appen make her feel cooler.'

So the night progressed but at 4. A.M. John could stand the feverish voice no longer and grabbing his coat, he raced off down the street to summon the doctor. That worthy citizen was not happy to be wakened at such an early hour, but when he saw the patient, he was a bit more understanding. He gave her a thorough examination exclaiming at the extent of her injuries.

'These have not all been caused by having a beam fall on her,' he said, after questioning them about the fire. 'I'd say she's been beaten pretty badly sometime before.'

John, hanging his head in misery, told the doctor about Emma's shaming at the hands of the mill overseer.

The doctor was aghast. 'I'd heard that some strange things were going on in that mill but I'd hardly have credited it if I hadn't seen this with my own eyes,' he said. 'If you want an eye witness anytime, you may call on me,' and he gave John his card. 'In the meantime,' spoke up the doctor, 'try to keep the patient cool, but guard against the shivers. She will suffer both heat and cold and it will be a very difficult task keeping her comfortable.'

'But will she do?' John asked fearfully.

'Time will tell,' replied the doctor. 'We'll know better once the fever breaks. I'll come again later in the morning. In the meantime, try to keep your spirits up, she has a good nurse in your mother.'

It was more than a few weeks before Emma began to gain her strength again. The fever had finally broken later in the day that the doctor had first seen her and as he crept into her bedroom, he noticed a change in her breathing. Her breaths were coming deeper and her face was a more healthy colour.

'What do you think, Doctor?' asked Mrs Blacklock.

'I think she's going to come round,' the doctor answered. 'She'll be weak for many a day but she'll come to herself eventually. This is where she'll need gentle care and nourishing food if she's going to thrive.'

'An'll she'll get it if it's the last thing I do,' answered John's mother. 'John,' she called to her son, 'go now and bring me a calf's foot and two pig hocks from Mr Hancock's shop and I'll make her a nourishing jelly.'

That was the beginning of Mrs Blacklock's tender care and she was true to her word and Emma slowly began to regain her strength. She was not yet herself but the delirium had gone and she was able to have some normal conversation with John and his family. John blessed the day that his mother had decided to forget her chagrin at his choice. She had truly cared for Emma during her long illness as though she were her own child. And then as the patient got stronger, she helped her sit by the bed each day and strengthen her muscles gradually.

The day that the doctor gave Emma permission to brave the stairs and eat with all the family was a joyous one indeed. As Emma entered the house place, she gazed around her, seeing the comfortable room with delight. Once again a bright fire twinkled in the grate and she looked with joy at all the familiar things she'd missed whilst she was ill. Then as her eye caught on the simple bunch of flowers in the centre of the prettily set table, tears glistened on her lashes and escaped, running down her cheeks. Mrs Blacklock caught her glance and smiled. Emma was more talkative that night than she had been for a long time, giving everyone the incentive to laugh and enjoy the delicious local meal that Mrs Blacklock had prepared. They had barely finished eating a dish of boiled beef in ale with turnips and carrots and a lovely egg glazed pie of blackberries and apples when a knock came at the door.

'Who can that be at this hour?' said Matt as he rose from the table and opened the door. On the step stood Sergeant Robinson with a policeman standing behind him.

'Ow do,' said Matt, remembering the pleasant sergeant from the night they'd searched for Susie.

'Is John Blacklock inside?' said the sergeant, not replying to Matt's cheery greeting.

'He is, won't you step up,' Matt answered, 'we're just celebrating Emma's return to health.'

'I'd sooner not come in,' said Robinson, 'I'd like to speak to him here.'

John had heard the conversation and appeared behind his brother not wanting the womenfolk to be bothered. 'What's to do?' he asked.

'I need to ask you some questions regarding the death of one Tom Burly,' said the sergeant. 'Could you come with me to the station?'

'Can't you ask me here?' said John. 'I'd as life not leave Emma when she's just getting a bit better.'

'I'm sorry, you need to come with me now,' said the law. John without another word, got his jacket from its peg and followed the two policemen out of the door.

Matt was left standing on the doorstep in a bewildered way. Should he accompany his brother? He grabbed his jacket and ran after the party, but he was told in no uncertain way by the policeman that his company wouldn't be needed. He returned to the house feeling totally forlorn. He had better buck up, he told himself, for his womenfolk would need him.

They were all as surprised as the two men. Well, at least Matt thought that John would be surprised. They hadn't had time for any conversation. The whole occurrence had put a damper on the evening and quietly they set to cleaning up and going about their preparations for getting Emma back to bed. She didn't want to go until John came back, but his mother soothed her fears and persuaded her to get her rest in case there were a lot of people to see at the station, for as she said, this would take a lot of time. Emma saw the sense in this and agreed to get her sleep.

The two girls also went to bed, but Matt and his mother stayed up until the wee small hours waiting, watching, for something that didn't happen. Finally as the clock struck three they both went their weary way to bed, in great fear of what the morning would bring. Matt should have been going to the pit but as he told his mother, he couldn't spend a whole day 'under' if he had no news of his brother, and after eating a scanty breakfast he set off in a hurry to the police station.

Gaining that building he was asked to wait while the duty officer could find out what had happened to John. He was kept waiting for over an hour, all the time hoping that John would appear and say a mistake had been made. But Matt had a premonition of bad news to come. He'd seen his brother strike Tom Burly

106

but had not thought that it was a bad blow and he hoped that John had not caused all the man's injuries.

Finally, Sergeant Edward Robinson arrived and beckoned Matt aside. He spoke quietly to him and seemed sorry to have to impart such news. Matt couldn't take it in and had to be told twice; that his brother had been arrested for arson and causing unlawful death to another man.'

'How can this be?' he begged. 'John was with me most of the time, and it was him who alerted the beadle to call the fire brigade.'

'Then you'd better keep your mouth shut if you don't want to be taken as well.'

'What's going to happen now?' Matt asked desperately.

'He'll be taken to Buxton for the assizes next month but you'd better get him a good barrister if you know what's good for him.'

'Can we see him before he goes?' said Matt.

'As to that he's already been taken,' said the officer, scanning his sheet of papers, 'last night in the Black Maria.'

Matt sank down on the hard seat, how could he tell his mother and Emma that John was a felon? After all she'd gone through, he was afraid that this would kill Emma. His mother was made of sterner stuff.

Chapter Fourteen
Circus Life for Susie

Something was always happening in the circus and it became second nature for Susie to accept her strange surroundings. She had been taken on as a girl of all work learning all the menial sides of the trade. She was not a performer or a trainer which set her in a different social position from those who were. One day she was really surprised to be approached by the conjurer's assistant, a semi performer, usually a bit possessive about her position. Melinda, for that was the girl's name, came around the corner suddenly as Susie was just finishing mucking out the stables. Susie startled, jumped sideways and almost knocked the girl over.

'Watch out, you'll have me on the ground,' said the girl.

'I'm so sorry,' Susie replied, 'I didn't see you behind me.'

'Never mind that,' said Melinda, 'I want to talk to you privately.'

Susie was intrigued and followed the girl into the corner of the stable where no one would hear them at this time of day. Melinda began quietly.

'I'm sure you've noticed how alike we are in looks?' she said.

Susie had, but didn't want to make much of it in case the other girl was uncomfortable looking like a menial worker.

'Er, yes I suppose we are,' she replied, 'but I haven't really thought about it.'

'Well, think about it now,' said Melinda shortly, 'because I want you to impersonate me tomorrow night.'

Susie gasped. 'How can I do that?' she choked. 'I'm not a performer and I never want to be one.'

'Oh don't be so soft, there's really nothing to it,' said Melinda.

'How can you possibly say that when you have to stand still and have knives thrown at you?' said the scared girl.

'I tell you it's nothing, you just close your eyes and pretend you're not there. Look I'll show you,' and so saying, Melinda closed her eyes and went into a kind of trance. She rocked slowly onto her toes and then her heels and made a kind of low murmur in her throat. Susie spoke to her but she didn't reply. The murmuring carried on until Susie began to feel a bit dizzy herself and her fear subsided. Melinda opened her eyes and laughed.

'See,' she said, 'easy as falling on your backside, now you try it.'

Susie was drawn in by the super confident performer and saw that she wasn't going to get out of this in a hurry so she closed her eyes and tried to make the humming noise herself. Melinda went into gales of laughter.

'I was just shamming you,' she said, 'of course you can't put yourself out or you might get pronged by the knives.'

Susie was very relieved thinking she'd got out of it but Melinda was adamant.

'You'll do this for me,' she said, 'because I've no one else to turn to and I'm desperate.'

'Where are you going as you need someone to take your place?' Susie asked.

'I think it'd be better if I didn't tell you right now,' said Melinda, 'we have very little time and I have to teach you the act before I leave tomorrow. Now I'll show you a few tricks of the trade,' and so saying, she took Susie's hand and dragged her to the circus tent.

The board was out ready for Melinda to coach her. Positioning herself in the exact place was crucial to her safety and that was what the performer taught Susie. After an exacting hour, Melinda decided that she was trained well enough to take her place for the one night.

'After all,' she said laughingly, 'I don't want you so good that Marcello will want to replace me.' So saying she left abruptly.

Susie went to her bed worrying sharply about the morrow. She woke with a pain of fear in her stomach but had to spend the day doing her usual tasks. Her nerves were on edge, not only with the thought of the act itself but also because she'd been told not to let on to anyone else that she was replacing Melinda. At six-o-clock, Susie knocked on the door of Melinda's caravan. She was shaking as the other girl helped her dress in the costume she usually wore herself. Melinda produced a disguise in the shape of an eye mask which was to cover half of her face.

'I've told Marcello I've got a cold,' said Melinda, 'and I don't want people to see my red eyes.'

'You mean,' said Susie, 'that you haven't told him I'm replacing you for tonight?'

'What the 'ed don't know, the 'eart don't grieve over,' replied Melinda.

'Oh, I don't like this one bit,' said Susie. 'You've only told me half a story and I don't see how Marcello is going to be bamboozled. He'll obviously realise I'm not you.'

'Don't worry,' said the now exasperated girl, 'he'll not notice the difference because he's usually drunk when he performs.'

'What? he's going to throw knives at me when he's drunk?'

'Don't take on so. He's never hit me yet,' said Melinda, 'at least not with his knives.' And so saying she turned on her heel and skipped jubilantly away.

Susie, left to herself, knew she had to make her way to the parade with the other performers. Some of them looked strangely at her mask but when she gestured to her throat, they seemed to understand that she had laryngitis and they soon left her alone. Circus people are a bit fatalistic when it comes to illness. Though strung up with nerves and tingling with excitement, Susie still waited in anticipation for her debut. Marcello arrived and took a swift look at her covered face.

'Whass a matter wid you?' he barked.

Susie was nervous of this strange but attractive man so she decided to take it slowly and pointing to her throat she gestured her pain. Marcello wasn't going to chance catching anything so he backed away from her but his expression still showed disapproval of the face cover.

'You'd better take dat off before de act. It will put me off my stroke,' he grunted.

Susie nodded her agreement but privately decided she wouldn't remove it until the act itself, that way fewer people would see her. She'd deal with Marcello later, perhaps as she walked with him in the parade.

Soon the excitement grew tangible as the last stragglers took their places and at a sign from the ring master, the performers began to move forward. Susie, moving with the cavalcade, could feel the blood pumping in her veins. *This would take some beating*, she thought. She copied the other performers as they prepared for the show. They straightened their backs, threw their heads back and seemed to flex their muscles. This was showmanship, thought Susie as she became one with the wonderful procession. When the parade was over, all the animals were taken back to their holding pens and Susie stood waiting with

Marcello for their act to begin. When would be a good time to remove her mask, she wondered? It couldn't be too soon or she would be found out. Carmel and Louis were waiting close by and Carmel gave her a strange look, but Susie moved away nonchalantly. She couldn't let Carmel know that she'd replaced Melinda tonight. She'd tell her the whole story tomorrow. The act before theirs was just beginning and Marcello moved towards her gesturing for Susie to remove her mask, she pretended not to understand him. This was going to be difficult. She moved around the performers hiding herself casually within the bevy of clowns but Marcello strode across to her reaching over to rip the mask from her face.

'Was da matter wid you?' he hissed.

'I can't do it yet,' Susie breathed, 'you'll understand when you see.' He recoiled as he heard her voice.

'You're no' Melinda,' he gasped.

'Shush, no I'm not,' said Susie.

'Well, I wan' to know wha's happened,' Marcello grunted, 'but there's no' time now we're abou' to go on. Do you know wha' to do?'

'Yes, I think so, Melinda trained me yesterday.'

'Well, don't screw up or the knife might end somewhere you don' want it to.'

Susie was dithering with nerves but at least her worries about Marcello were over. He knew there'd been a change and he didn't appear to be drunk, so far so good. Marcello began his act and it was going well. The audience were very attentive. Then the contraption that was part of her scene was taken into the ring and Susie walked, rhythmically, as Melinda had taught her, seeming to dance as she sashayed around the ring ending up at the piece of equipment; with her heart in her throat she climbed into place, and removing her mask she dropped it onto the sawdust.

The first knife whistled through the air and landed in place, followed by the second, third, and fourth. As Marcello bent to pick up his fifth and final knife a hush had come over the audience. Susie was spellbound waiting for the last chance for anything to go wrong. The knife hurtled towards her and landed in her headdress as it was supposed to do, and she was able to breathe a long sigh of relief.

'Alright, you're finished, take your bow,' Marcello hissed at her, 'but don' overdo it, this is my scene.'

'I can't move,' said Susie. 'You've pinned my hair to the board.' Quickly and not too gently Marcello freed her and she was able to take her bow.

'Now, young lady, you'll tell me who you are and what's going on,' said Marcello.

'I'm happy to tell you my name, it's Susie, and I'm staying with Rosie but as to what's going on, I'm as much in the dark as you are,' she answered. 'I'm to meet Melinda by the back gate at midnight and then we'll change clothes and places again. I told Rosie I was going to be late up tonight, so she and Dan will not wait up for me,' she replied hurriedly.

She knew Melinda had warned her not to tell Marcello anything but what else could she do when she had been found out? Marcello wouldn't let Susie out of his sight. He was afraid she'd disappear on him as well. At midnight they made their way to the place of rendezvous and waited expectantly for Melinda to arrive. They heard the clock in the church steeple mark the witching hour but Melinda did not arrive. They waited for three more hours to chime and still she did not come. They were both showing their fear but in different ways. He was angry, she was scared. What was she to do?

'I'd better get back to Rosie's van,' she told him.

'You'll do no such thing,' said Marcello. 'Until she arrives back, you're taking her place in my act and as I don't want you disappearing, you'll stay with me.'

'But I can't stay with you, I'll be glad to work with you on your act until Melinda returns, but I have to let Rosie and Carmel know I'm alright,' Susie said reasonably.

'You'll stay with me!' said the angry man. 'I'll have no more of your lip,' and so saying he swung her easily onto his shoulder. Susie struggled and kicked him in his back. He put her down to gain more leverage and struck her a heavy blow which rendered her unconscious.

When she came to, she was alone in a caravan she hadn't seen before. She tried to remember what had happened to her but her head was aching so badly that she couldn't muster her thoughts clearly and she went painfully back to sleep.

Next morning Rosie saw Carmel as she went about her daily tasks and the two women discussed Susie's sudden absence. Carmel was worried about her friend but Rosie was inclined to think that Susie had run away.

'She's a young flibbertigibbet in my opinion,' said Rosie. 'We none of us learned where she'd come from and now she's had enough of us and has moved on somewhere else. Maybe she's decided the work's too hard or 'appen she's found a man to take her in.'

Carmel's opinion of Susie was very different. She had taken to the young girl right from the start and she was worried about her. But she knew that Rosie's opinion was coloured by her fear that her son Dan was getting romantic notions about the pretty girl. She sought help from Louis, but he also seemed unperturbed by Susie's absence. And so Carmel was left alone with her worries and the day wore on.

That night Marcello's act did not include his prize performance. When asked why, he said that Melinda had a worse sore throat and he'd given her a night off. He returned to his caravan following the show and found a sorry-looking Susie.

'You should not have kicked me,' he told her, 'I have a strong temper so you'd better be a good girl from now on.'

'I want to go back to my friends,' said Susie plaintively. 'Have you found Melinda yet?'

'There is no sign of her and I have been out searching for her most of the day. You cannot go back to your friends until she is found. Now don't anger me by asking stupid things,' he said. 'Tomorrow you must appear with me in the show, so get a good rest tonight. I will bring you some food if you would like it.'

'I'm not very hungry,' said Susie, 'I have a very bad headache.'

'Well, suit yourself and behave yourself in the future,' he retaliated.

The next day was dismal. Rain clouds gathered in the sky and low rumblings could be heard in the distance. Susie woke early and ate a little of the breakfast that Marcello had prepared for her. She remained silent, seeing no point in antagonising him. She didn't mind taking the other girl's place, actually it had been fun being a performer instead of a worker in the circus. She was just worried about where Melinda had gone to. That night she performed her part as she'd been taught to do and everything went to plan. She was a bit nervous about taking off the mask, but no one seemed to notice that she was not Melinda. Wearing the other girl's clothes, she looked identical. The heavy rain was falling as they made their way to the van and Susie was soaked to the skin when they arrived at their sleeping quarters.

'When I'm changed, I'd like to go back to Rosie's,' Susie tried plaintively. 'I'm sure they're missing me and they'll be asking questions before long.'

'I've already to'd you that you're not leaving me for a second until Melinda comes back,' said the stubborn man. 'If you wan' life to be easy, do as you're told.' As he prepared some food for them in the galley kitchen, Susie made a dash for the door, but she wasn't quick enough and he caught her and brought her down with a rugby tackle. 'When will you learn, now you're 'urt again and it's your own fault,' he said. He purposefully locked the door and removed the key from the lock.

'Now you can't escape,' he told her, 'so why don't you settle down and be comfortable. I'm not a bad man and we could have some fun together, just like I had with Melinda.'

Susie went cold all over, she was reminded of happy Jack on her first day, and saying nothing in reply, she moved quickly to her bunk bed and wrapped the covers around her tightly.

'All right all right, I see what you're doing, and I can be patient,' said her tormentor, but don' expect to get out of here until I say so.'

In the still night, just as the clock had struck three a loud banging was heard on their door. Susie woke with a start but Marcello was already up and opening it.

'Wha's da noise all about?' he cried.

The roustabout who was outside started to explain his errand but Marcello was impatient with him. 'Jus say it quickly,' he said.

'We're moving on at once,' the man replied.

'In the middle of the night when we're all sleeping. What's happened?' said Marcello.

'I was about to tell you but you wanted the short version,' replied the messenger.

'Don mess wid me!' Marcello stormed.

'I don't know the full story but the police were around asking questions and the ring master decided we'd better go. You know that a lot of the circus people have big fears where the police are concerned.'

Now Susie spoke up, 'Do you know why?' she asked. 'I have a particular reason for asking and it concerns the rest of my life.'

Marcello frowned at her but he also wanted information so he kept quiet. The roustabout said he knew nothing else but they'd better look sharpish or they'd be left behind. As they quickly began to dress and collect their things, they spoke in hushed tones.

'Do you think it's anything to do with Melinda?'

'I don' know but we better move out quickly until we find out.'

A massive exodus was taking place outside everyone seemed to be running, but the silence was uncanny given all the scale of movement. It was obvious to Susie that this kind of emergency had happened in the past for all seemed to have a shared purpose to get away before the police took them in for questioning. Quietly people talked about the situation and Susie tried to glean what she could from their talk. It seemed that a body had been found and once again Susie heard that same name, Charles Peace.

Marcelo came up behind her, 'Don' you be talking they'll see you're not her,' he said.

Susie wondered what to do, this would be a good opportunity to get away while all was confusion but she didn't know where to go.

'Marcello they're talking about a murder that's just happened. Do you think it's Melinda? Should we go and tell the police she's missing?'

'No you don'. We'll get away from here as quickly as we can, we don' want any truck with the law an' you'll stay with me and take her place, that way no one will suspect it's me,' he answered.

'But I don't understand, you're nothing to do with the murder, you were here with me all the time.'

'Police, they get some strange ideas and I'm not going to give 'em chance so you just do as I say.'

'All right I'll do as you say but only on condition you leave me alone when we're not performing,' said Susie. Marcello didn't reply, he wasn't used to being spoken to like that, he frowned his annoyance but let it go until later.

The circus folk had formed a long line. Their caravans were now beginning to move forward at a steady pace, the animal carriages following behind. The quiet had been disturbed by all the activity that was necessary to move such a large cavalcade. At least the night was dry, not like last night, thought Susie but what would happen to Melinda if she came back to the circus and found that it had moved on.

Melinda was not likely to return. She had no intention of returning to the circus now she'd found Susie. Her last attempt to escape had been thwarted by Marcello but today she felt that luck was with her. She'd met a nice young man and she'd persuaded Susie to replace her. Her spirits were high and she began to whistle a merry tune as she tripped lightly along the country lane. She had been walking for about an hour and was getting close to the mill where she was to meet Sam when she heard a footstep close behind her. Spinning around she was confronted by an old tramp who was wearing an army greatcoat.

'Now what can I do for you, Missy?' he said.

'Nothing,' replied Melinda, 'I'm just out for an evening stroll.'

'Will you have a drink with me?' he said, producing a green bottle out of his greatcoat.

'No thank you, I have to get along, my boyfriend will be looking out for me, and he'll wonder where I am if I'm much longer,' Melinda replied.

'Is he a good man, or does he knock you around?' asked the tramp. Melinda felt uncomfortable with these strange questions. She wanted to get away from him but he stood in her way.

'He's a very good man and he'll be out looking for me, so I'll bid you good night,' she said.

'Not so fast. I just want to help you,' said the tramp swaying slightly on to his heels. Melinda noticed his unsteady gait and hoped that if she gave him a push he'd fall over and she could be on her way. She moved quickly to put her plan into action, but he moved quicker and with a strength she hadn't expected, he grabbed her around the neck and with a quick twist he had ended her short life.

Now he was confused. He hadn't expected it to be over so quickly. He looked around cautiously. Seeing no one about, his eyes searched for a place to hide her so that the body wouldn't be discovered. *For if it is,* he thought, *the trail might lead them to me.* Lifting her onto his shoulder he discovered that she was heavier than she looked. stumbling now under the added weight, he rounded the bend and saw a group of trees stretching upwards, their leaves shading the ground. *What better place to hide a corpse? This would be a fine green resting place for her,* and he'd saved yet another soul before she could be ruined.

Chapter Fifteen
The Circus Moves On

The circus managers decided they'd better move further afield. The goings on the last few days were not comfortable for those with a price on their heads and many of them had just that. Prof Richards agreed to stay behind and come to terms with the police. He was the only one who had the courage to do this. He was not a circus person and had only fallen into that kind of work by accident. He was packing up his small museum the next day when constable Blunt appeared in the doorway of the old barn. At first Prof Richards didn't notice him intent as he was on wrapping up his treasures. Then taking out his notebook he approached the professor.

'Good day to you, Sir, may I have a word.'

The professor indicated that this would be fine with him.

'I'm trying to ascertain the movements of a young woman we found a couple of miles from here night before last,' said the policeman.

'I notice all the circus folk have moved on very quickly, you might even say they've done a moonlight flit. I wonder, as you're the only one left, if you could shine some light on their disappearance and the appearance of the body I spoke of, that of a young woman.'

Professor Richards picked his words very carefully.

'Circus people come and go. They can only stay for a short while in any place. The locals can't deal with their presence and that of their animals for long. As to the girl, I've not heard that any circus girls are missing, but then again we take on extra help every time we make camp and they move on after the work is done.'

'What would your work be in the circus, you don't seem to be the usual type of performer?' the constable asked curiously.

'I'm not,' replied the professor affably, 'I fell into this work by accident and have stayed because the circus folks are friendly and ask no questions.'

'So will you be joining them when you've packed up?' said Blunt.

'I'll probably join them at some point but I'm not sure when, is that everything now because I have to get on with my packing?'

'I'll leave it for now but don't move from the village without reporting in to the station,' said Blunt.

So saying he snapped his notebook shut and as he left the barn, his eyes could be seen darting along the shelves taking in all that was still to be observed.

The professor watched him leave, a quizzical look on his face. Being with the circus certainly brought him into some strange situations. He wondered why the performers had left so suddenly and if the murdered girl was one of their own. He could not look into the situation now but consideration would have to be given to it in the near future if the trail was not to go cold. He continued to wrap and pack his precious objects, his mind far away thinking of times past and people who had moved on in this life.

His sister was one of these people. Although twenty years had gone by since her death, he still missed her. He thought of her often and also of her child who had suddenly gone missing shortly after her death. He dwelt now on things past feeling guilty that at the time he hadn't thought of anyone else's grief but his own. When his sister's husband had left town and the child had gone too, the family assumed that he had taken her with him. It was some years later when they crossed paths again that the other man asked after his daughter and Professor Richards realised that the child was missing. Both men had formed an intensive search but too much time had gone by and the child had left no trace. This, in addition to all the deaths in his life, had formed the professor's rather morbid mindset and his interest in the afterlife that Susie had been aware of on their short encounter.

Chapter Sixteen
Matt Goes Home Without John

When Matt arrived home, his mother and Emma looked up expectantly as he entered the house place both sets of eyes searching his face.

'What is it, Matt?' his mother questioned for both of them.

'I don't know how to break it to you,' he said.

'Tell us, tell us,' they both spoke together, 'we can't bear not to know.'

'Our John has been arrested for wilful damage causing death,' said Matt.

'He never, it can't be,' said Mrs Blacklock. 'He was here with me after you went out to the pub and I'll swear to his innocence.'

'It's not just setting the fire he's been accused of, he was also seen fighting with and striking Tom Burly which caused him to fall down stairs at the mill.'

'Who says that? Who saw him?' said his mother. 'Our John wouldn't hurt a fly, they must be lying.'

'I saw him hit the overseer, Mother, and maybe someone else did as well but we have to prove his innocence in a court of law. We'd better get him a good lawyer who'll defend him.'

'How are we to afford that,' his mother retorted, 'when you've both missed many shifts these last two weeks and we're down at rock bottom. I didn't like to mention it as we've had so much to think of recently.'

Emma hung her head in shame feeling responsible, and though not guilty she still felt somewhat to blame.

'Then I'd better get back to work as soon as I can and try to work extra shifts to make up for it,' said Matt.

'Couldn't I try to get work,' Emma asked.

'You're not well enough yet, and you're still disfigured from the beating you got, people will talk even more than they do now,' said Mrs Blacklock.

She knew her neighbours and their gossip. Emma desperately wanted to give something back for all the help they'd given her.

'Couldn't I at least learn to cook so that I can help in the house?' Emma begged. 'I need to do something to keep busy or I'll go mad sitting around waiting.'

Mrs Blacklock saw the sense in this. Emma was a working woman after all and she needed something to occupy her.

'We'll ask the doctor,' she said, 'if he decides you're ready, I'll teach you what my mother taught me to look after my man.'

'Oh thank you for being so good to me,' said Emma. 'I feel so bad about John's being taken up and I thank you from the bottom of my heart for not blaming me for him becoming involved in the mill troubles.' Emma wept.

'There, there someone is to blame, but it's not you,' said Mrs Blacklock sweeping Emma to her ample bosom.

'Well, I'll leave you women folk to your tears,' said Matt, 'but our John would be rejoicing if he'd seen what I've just witnessed.'

So saying he went quickly through the door and on his way to the pit before he wept himself. Emma bethought her of something she could ask Mrs Blacklock to teach her.

'I have a brass button that I found in one of the sheds when we were searching for Susie,' she said. 'Would you teach me how to sew it to my dress, it's very bright and it will cheer us all up as it glints in the sun.'

'I will with pleasure, lass. Can you go and get it and fetch my sewing box too?'

The women whiled away a happy hour with Emma's first lesson into housewifery, chatting about this and that which finally led to Mrs Blacklock praising Emma's efforts at button sewing.

'You'll be able to get work in the button factory one of these days,' she said.

Emma, though pleased to have done well with her first task, didn't much relish working in another factory.

'Where is the button factory?' she enquired.

'Why it's at Ancoats near the hanky factory where Sarah Anna and Fanny work.'

'I don't think I could get there very easily, do you?'

'As to that,' replied Mrs Blacklock, 'you'd have to lodge somewhere about and come home at weekends in the cart or the barge.'

Emma felt her cheeks blush at the acknowledgement from Mrs Blacklock that she had a home with them. But now she had a place where she was happy, she didn't want to lodge out with some stranger and work long hours again in a factory where she knew no one. She didn't know how to react. And was very thankful when the other woman said,

'Well, never mind now, let's get you well before we start talking of work.'

The mill fire had caused much hardship in and around the village. The inmates who had been housed in the mill were taken to the workhouse in Miller's Dale but the independent workers had no way of making money. Hard times were upon the people of Derbyshire bringing with them a blight that was easy to see in their pinched faces and haunted eyes. Aunty Ann visiting the Blacklock home one day to see how Emma did and to hear any news of John brought the plight of the mill folk to her sister's attention.

'They have no bread, no coal, and definitely nothing to make a good soup with,' she said. 'It's a crying shame, the masters make use of everyone when they need work doing but there's no-one to help them in times of trouble.'

'I'm ashamed to say,' replied her sister, 'that I've been pulled down with my own worries to the degree that I've thought of no one else. What do you think we could do for the poor souls?'

'Well, I've been thinking of something on the grounds of a soup kitchen,' she answered, 'but I've no idea how to start one with little money or anyone to help me.'

Emma suddenly sat upright. 'I could help,' she said, 'I've nothing to do while I get better and John's mam is going to teach me how to cook.'

'We could ask the minister at the church to lend us a room as we're trying to do good works and 'appen Mr Hancock at the shop where the girls work would give us some soup bones,' Mrs Blacklock added.

'This will stop us from brooding over our John,' said Mrs Blacklock, 'and we'll try to get other folks involved as well.'

'So you have no news on that score?' said her sister and Mrs Blacklock shook her head.

'No nor likely to until we get closer to the assizes,' she said. 'This idea of yours will help us while away the time.'

The women decided that sooner is better than later and without more ado they put on their hats and coats and set off to the church to see the vicar Rev. Ambrose Higgins. The pleasant faced corpulent man welcomed the women. His shaggy eyebrows shot up into his white curly hair as he heard the plan to feed his flock.

'It's just what we need to brighten everyone up,' he said. 'I'd been wondering how I could get my parish involved and now you've all done it for me, bless you.'

The soup kitchen project turned out to be very successful. Emma was able to get over her usual shyness with her new purpose in life. And she toured the village asking for help for her work mates. Mrs Blacklock found her a cap to cover her damaged scalp so anyone who seemed interested in her scars assumed that she had received them at the time of the fire. Some people were hesitant and shifty eyed, not wanting to admit they had nothing themselves. They were proud people and would have helped if they could. But many were only too happy to help with donations of vegetables and meat bones and the like. Mrs Blacklock was true to her word and she taught Emma how to make a fine, rich stock as a base for the soup. Soon Emma was peeling and paring different kinds of vegetable matter and learning what the more unusual ones were. It was a multi learning experience for the eager girl and Mrs Blacklock was very pleased to see how well and quickly she picked things up.

The day for the soup kitchen had been set for Tuesday each week and as the first one arrived, the excited Emma transported her pans of soup to the church hall. It was a heavy task for the convalescent girl but she soon gained strength as her enthusiasm increased. The village women set to and the wonderful aromas of the different soups wafted around the hall and into the adjoining church. Rev. Higgins appeared to ask a blessing on this wonderful endeavour and then, slowly at first, the recipients of the cooking began to arrive.

'You'd not think they were the better off workers, would you?' said Aunty Ann.

'It only takes a few weeks without work to reduce them all to scarecrows,' said Mrs Blacklock.

They came in helplessly, wishing that they were the ones who could help their neighbours in times of need, rather than the recipients of that help. But they were deeply grateful for all that and they dipped the fresh hunks of bread Emma had made into the proffered bowls and ate slowly and thankfully. Emma worked with a will ladling out bowls of nourishing soup and she felt stronger than she had for many a while. Her thoughts strayed to John wishing he was by her side or in the pit.

Just then a strange man came through the door. The women all stopped to watch him. He was unsteady in his gait and wore an army greatcoat. As he reached the line, he gazed at the hot soup as though he couldn't believe his eyes, then muttering something unintelligible about his starving Jane, he rushed for the door and was gone. But not before Emma had noticed that the buttons on his coat resembled the one she'd sewn to her dress and that one was missing.

Now she was in a quandary, should she go home for the button and return it to him, or should she keep to her task? There were many people to serve so she decided to stick to her task and look for him to return it later. They had been serving for an hour or more and the soup was about finished when they had another disturbance. It was constable Blunt coming in to ask some questions.

'Now listen up all of you,' he said, 'how many of you worked in the mill that burned down.' Most of the men raised their hands and some of the women also. 'I'd like to ask you some questions about a mill girl who went missing a while ago.'

Emma went cold, why were they asking about Susie now, she wondered. None of the mill workers knew Susie because they'd worked in a different part of the mill. Emma didn't know what to do. Obviously she knew Susie very well, in fact better than anyone. But she wanted to know what this was about before she admitted it. Thankfully she wasn't the only one present who'd known Susie. Rev. Higgins spoke up.

'I knew her a little because the mill workers attended my church and Sunday school on Sunday mornings,' he said.

'Will you come with me sir,' said the constable. 'I need someone to identify a body we've found.'

Emma didn't remember anything else as she fell to the floor in a dead faint striking her head on the corner of the table. 'What a nasty end to such a good day,' the people were whispering. Emma had come round though she had a nasty gash on her head and the ghostly paler had returned to her cheeks. Mrs Blacklock and Aunty Ann were fussing around her.

'Now, now what's to do, why did you go and faint like that.'

'Susie is my best friend in all the world and hearing that a body had been found was such a shock to my system that I suppose I just fell down,' said Emma.

Both older women were quiet thinking similar thoughts but not wanting to share them.

'We'd better get you home,' said Mrs Blacklock. 'Can you manage to walk?'

'Yes, get her home, me and the other women will clear up here,' said Aunty Ann.

'I'll try to walk, the cold air will 'appen do me good,' said Emma.

'That's the ticket and maybe Matt will be home when we get there and he'll cheer us up,' said Mrs Blacklock. Emma didn't think so, not when he heard the news anyway.

She decided that she wasn't going to lose heart until it had been proved that the body was that of Susie. After all it was a long time since her friend had gone missing and it made little sense that she was still in these parts. Emma cheered herself with the thought that Susie would have moved far away and with this idea foremost in her mind she could comfort Matt when he returned from the pit. Mrs Blacklock was watching the girl out of the corner of her eye and she saw a change for the better in her countenance.

'Shall I make us a cup of tea luv,' she questioned. Emma was very thankful for the older woman's obvious concern and replied in the affirmative.

'This is a trying time for all of us but I'm not going to make it worse by believing something before it's 'appened,' she said. When Matt arrived home, he was happy to see the two women sitting in companionable silence sipping tea. The way they'd taken to each other since Emma's illness made one less thing for him to worry about.

'How did you get on?' he said, and they were able to share with him the happier part of the day. He had enough to think about and why tell him about an unknown girl, thought his mother. Emma knew differently but she wasn't going to discuss his private feelings with his mother just yet.

It was not to be expected that news of a murder could be kept quiet from the gossips and very soon it filtered through to Matt that Rev. Higgins had identified the body as that of Susie. She had been wearing Susie's mill clothes and though her shoes were different, everything else spoke the terrible truth. The face had been disfigured and this seemed to be a calling card from Charles Peace but the hair was hers and the slightness of form and there seemed to be no doubt about it. Matt was beside himself with grief. Now he had to admit his feelings to his mother.

She could not believe that both her sons in one night had fallen head over heels in love at first sight. Her senses were reeling. Her life seemed to be tossing in a little boat on a storm ravaged sea. But she must go on for John's sake as well as Matt's. Matt could not bear to live on gossip, he had to know the truth and rushing out of the door he made his way to the police station to ask about the happenings of the last week.

'I'm glad you've popped in,' said Edward Robinson, 'I was going to have to visit you about your brother's trial, I have to present you with this subpoena as a witness for the prosecution.'

Matt didn't understand. 'Could you explain it to me, I think subpoena means I have to go to the trial, which I was doing anyway, you just try to stop me. But, 'the prosecution' how can I be a witness against my brother?'

'The lawyer will explain it to you when you have your pre-trial meeting with him. Now what was it you wanted today?' Matt had become so upset he hadn't remembered why he'd come.

'Oh, I wanted to know straight from the law who that murdered girl is, we've heard lots of rumours but I need to know the truth,' said Matt.

'How are you involved with that case?'

'I'm not involved with the case but the missing mill girl was someone I met at the Whitsun fair and when she went missing, I couldn't get her out of my mind,' said Matt breathlessly.

The inspector looked at the young man thoughtfully.

'We have had a positive identification,' he said, 'but I'm not really at liberty to divulge the information yet.'

'I think I'll go mad if I don't know,' said Matt.

'Well, all I can tell you is, you'll not like the answer,' said the inspector.

Matt left the station in a trance. Two pieces of bad news in a matter of minutes, he wondered how he could go on living. He let his steps lead him away from the village and slowly walked soulfully uphill. He could not face those at home just yet. He didn't see the man in front of him until he was almost on top of him. It was twilight and the dusk was the excuse he gave himself for bumping into the other person. The man lurched sideways letting out an uncouth oath as he stumbled over the rough terrain. Matt went to give him a helping hand but the fellow brushed his hand away roughly slurring some profanity between gritted teeth.

'Alright then, alright,' said Matt. 'I was only trying to help you, suit yourself if you'd rather fall down,' and with that he turned on his heel and continued his journey. But as he walked something in the man's face jogged his memory and he puzzled over it, trying to remember when he had last seen it. Then it came to him, it was when he and John were walking into Miller's Dale after they'd stopped searching for Susie. Oh if only we hadn't given up so soon she'd probably still be alive today, he thought falling to his knees, loud sobs racking his body.

On the bleak hillside where no one could see him he had a chance to release his feelings. Presently all tears spent he rose up from the ground and retraced his footsteps towards the comfort of home. The tramp had disappeared as he had the previous time. The coincidence of him seeing the phantom figure today as he had on the search day sent chills down his spine and though he was not normally moribund, he felt that this was a bad omen. His mother noticed the difference in his walk as he entered the house. She looked up seeing at once the waxen expression on his face.

'Ee lad donna tell me it's confirmed,' she said. Matt couldn't answer but his quiet nod said it all as he sat down at the back of the room and Emma felt a lead weight attach itself to her heart.

Chapter Seventeen
The Subpoenas

Not much sleep was had in the cottage that night. Each of the inhabitants dealt with the terrible news in his or her own way. The three main grievers were still numb with the news and the sisters were not really involved with the dead girl except through their family. Maggie and Sally were young and flighty and didn't want their lives to be affected by someone they had not known. They couldn't see why their mother had taken Emma in to live with them, they had never understood her change of heart. When Emma produced black armbands for all of them to wear the next day Sally was irate.

'I'm not wearing mourning for someone I didn't know and someone who is no better than she ought to be,' she stormed slamming the door as she left for work. Matt went purple as he gazed on the elder sister.

'Oh, I'll wear one for you,' said Maggie quickly not wanting to antagonise her brother.

Matt had not yet told his family about his subpoena. His brain had gone numb with the other shock he'd received. Now he bethought himself and filled them in on the conversation he'd had with Constable Blunt the night before. At this point he decided to forgo telling them that he was a witness for the prosecution. He couldn't understand it and thought that a mistake had been made which would all sort itself out when he met with the lawyer.

Time moved faster than that, however, and before he had left for his shift in the pit, they received an early morning visitor in the person of the beadle. Mrs Blacklock was beginning to wonder what next. She had never had a visit from that worthy in her life. He stepped into the house importantly when Matt opened the door. He was carrying many buff envelopes. He presented one to John's mother and one to Emma with the time and place of the trial. Then importantly announced the information that they would be summonsed as accessories if they failed to comply with the instructions.

'You don't need to take on so we've no intention of not coming to our lad's trial,' said Mrs Blacklock.

'You'll be a witness for the defence,' said the beadle, 'but Emma Brierly and Matt Blacklock will both speak for the prosecution.'

The outcry at that information was deafening; both witnesses demanding to know why they had been called to witness for the prosecution. The Beadle officiously said he was not at liberty to inform them.

'They would,' he said, 'be interviewed by the crown lawyer who would enlighten them in due course.'

'Oh I can't take any more bad news, I'll just die.' Emma wept.

'Keep up your courage, lass, remember we'll be there with you and I'm called for the prosecution as well,' said Matt comfortingly.

'It'll perhaps be just to tell the story of what we know and we can 'appen put them straight with being for the prosecution, for I know that John isn't guilty. I haven't shared a bed with him all our lives and not known him as well as I know myself. Now we have a lot to do before this 'ere date but we also have to get on with everyday living and I'm off to' t pit to earn some money for our John's defence and I think you two have soup to make.'

So saying he donned his cap and purposefully walked out the door.

The women pulled themselves together and began to prepare the soup for the following day. They couldn't let the poor starve because of their heavy hearts. An official looking letter had arrived by the mail when they returned home the next day. Mrs Blacklock seized it up and tore it open briskly. It was only after she'd done this that she noticed the address and recognised it was for Matt.

'Oh dear I hope he doesn't mind me seeing it,' she said, 'for I'm going to read it for all that. I can't bear to wait 'til he comes home. I'm all a jangle with nerves.'

So saying she proved her words by pulling out the letter and reading the formal writing. It was from the lawyer for the prosecution, inviting Matt to meet with him at his law office in Buxton on Wednesday next, to discuss the case.

'What about me,' said Emma, 'have I to go too?'

'It doesn't mention you, maybe you'll get your own letter another day.'

'Oh I wish it was all over,' said Emma, 'what if I say something that incriminates John, I'll never forgive myself but I don't understand and I might say something without knowing.'

'Now my girl you just speak the truth and if those lawyers try to twist your words, I'll set them down with one of my looks,' said the older woman matching her demeanour to her words.

Emma had to smile, Mrs Blacklock looked so ferocious, and she remembered when she was not in the woman's good books and how uncomfortable it had been. She almost felt sorry for the lawyer in advance. The next day sure enough Emma's letter arrived and at least the good news was that she and Matt were to see the lawyer the same morning. So far the defence had not contacted Mrs Blacklock.

The next Wednesday they were able to cadge a lift into Buxton with a farm cart. A 9-o-clock appointment for Matt meant he had to miss work again. Emma was not called until 10 A.M.

'We'll be wasting a lot of time, won't we?' asked Emma.

'Yes but let's see how much we can pick up by keeping our ears open,' Matt replied.

'If we see anyone we know, we'd better keep quiet; we don't want to be giving anything away.'

Just then Matt was called in and Emma was left alone with her reverie. The big clock, ticking loudly on the wall, was keeping beat with her racing heart demanding she listen and observe each passing minute. Just then the outside door opened. Emma went hot and then cold as she recognised the man who had entered. It was Mr Brierly.

She shrank into the corner of her seat and averted her eyes hoping he wouldn't notice her. Either she had her wish or he was as uncomfortable as she was herself. Taking a newspaper out of his inner pocket, he shook it out and began to read shielding his face from view as he did so. Emma was left alone with her thoughts, of course Mr Brierly would be called for a witness. He was the one who'd lost his mill in the fire, and would be many months if not years in being able to trade again. Matt came out of the office at this point and Emma gestured with her head to stop him saying anything to her that they wouldn't want Mr Brierly to hear. He beckoned her outside and they left together. Before they had time for any conversation, a wagon drew up and out stepped Jessie Burns.

'Well, who'd 'a thought you'd turn up here,' she said malevolently.

'I don't know what you mean,' Emma returned quietly.

'Well, you've a nerve after your so-called boyfriend killed Mr Burly and set fire to the mill so none of us have any work,' Jessie spoke indignantly.

Emma was completely dumbstruck, she opened her mouth to retaliate but Matt was too quick and he led her briskly away saying quietly, 'Least said soonest mended.'

'But what can I do,' Emma begged. 'I have my appointment at 10.'

Matt took his pride and joy out of his pocket, a watch that had belonged to his grandfather. 'It's only half past nine,' he said, 'maybe she'll be gone by the time you have to go back in there. Let's go in the church where we can talk quietly.'

Emma was relieved at this plan she was really quite shaken by Jessie's outburst. They walked quickly to the church Matt telling her that he'd decided not to leave her in Buxton alone after the reception she'd just had from Jessie Burns.

'What did the lawyer say,' she wanted to know.

'He just wanted me to repeat what I'd already told the policeman the night of the fire. I told him that I'd been with our John after I heard the crier calling the fire, and ran out of the pub to help with the buckets. Then I'd seen my brother trying to break into the locked mill to save the souls inside. At that point I went to help him and never left his side again except when I went to find a cart to convey you home, but as I told him Burly was already dead and lying on the ground next to you.'

'I wonder what they'll want to know from me,' said Emma. 'If it's about John and me walking out, it might not look good for him especially about my shaming. He was that mad.'

'Well, I can see it not looking so good but you just tell the truth and the law will be on your side,' said Matt hopefully.

Emma was of a different frame of mind, she hadn't been treated very well by authority figures in the past. It was now time to go back to the lawyer's office and she was relieved that Jessie was nowhere to be seen. Mr Brierly, however, was just leaving and though she kept her head down, she felt his eyes boring into her forehead.

The lawyer was civil with her but not particularly warm. How could he be, Emma thought, he had to get a conviction and she shuddered convulsively. He

130

asked the usual questions about name and abode and seemed surprised that she was living with the Blacklock family. He wanted to know her connection to them and she had to admit that she was being courted by John. Had he already known, she wondered, but she had to tell the truth hadn't she or it would look worse for John when it came out? This was a more difficult ordeal than she had anticipated and she shuddered to think what the actual trial would be like. Finally his questions were over and he dismissed her until later saying he had enough evidence to go on. When she told Matt this, he didn't answer but looked a bit glum. The cart arrived to take them home and they travelled in silence each with private thoughts to while away the journey.

Mrs Blacklock was the next to hear from her lawyer, the defence lawyer Mr Pargitter. He requested her to come to his lodgings on Spring Terrace, Buxton on Friday next. Aunty Ann had not been called as a witness but she offered to accompany her sister on the day in question and Uncle George drove the two of them in his pony and trap so that they could keep their own schedule. The little pony trotted along and the cart bounced and jostled in the pot holes on the country lanes, the hawthorn boughs without their foliage now that summer was over, framed the rough stone walls at the edge of the roadway. The starkness of the scene and the unusual outing weighed heavily on the minds of the two sisters. Aunty Ann made a hesitant attempt at conversation. 'Did Mr Pargitter tell you anything in his letter?'

'Not really,' was the reply. 'He only said I was to come today and be prepared to answer questions about the day of the fire. Though I don't know what I can tell him except that my lad is innocent through and through. There's not a cruel bone in his body and I've thought and thought as how anyone can be that wrong as to take an honest chap up for killing another when all he was doing was saving poor souls from a fire. You know him yourself, can you believe he could have done something so wicked as kill another man?'

'No I can't,' said Ann, 'though it must have been hard for John to see Emma so badly beaten up, he could have hit Burly in a flash of temper.'

'I'll never believe it,' said his mother, 'and you mustn't say so either or you'll not be my sister anymore.'

Mrs Blacklock drew away from her sister and into herself leaving no room for misunderstanding her meaning. Ann was silent, she realised she'd made a mistake in expressing her feelings. The rest of the journey passed in absolute silence though there was much to see as the road got busier with all kinds of traffic as they drew nearer to the city. Carts and wagons were in profusion but when a cavalcade of gypsy caravans came into sight, even Mrs Blacklock came back to earth and took notice of all their bright colours. Don't let's fight, I'm on your side and John's,' said Aunty Ann. The two sisters embraced tenderly.

Mr Pargitter sat pensively slightly rocking in his chair his fingertips together almost in a position of prayer He'd asked her the obvious questions name, address, relationship to the plaintiff and so forth, but now he didn't seem to be able to get to the point. Mrs Blacklock began to squirm in the straight-backed chair he'd invited her to sit in when she'd arrived at his stark domain. The walls were washed in a gruesome green, the only rest for the eyes coming from the rows and rows of leather-bound books that adorned the shelving. Finally he spoke:

'I need to get some idea of the relationship between your son and the injured girl but as she has been called as a witness for the prosecution, I am treading on thin ice if I ask this question in court,' he said.

'I don't know what I'm allowed to say as I have no experience of this kind,' replied Mrs Blacklock.

'No of course you don't,' he spoke kindly, 'but if you were to let slip a comment without thinking about it, I could form my own opinion you see.' He stroked his neat beard as he looked up at her winningly.

'You mean like Emma living with us now?' his witness queried.

'Yes, the very thing. Has it been a long duration?' He gave the same disarming look and once again stroked that immaculate beard.

'Well, it's been since she was hurt at the mill and in the fire,' returned Mrs Blacklock.

'You say at the mill and in the fire, were these then two different instances,' asked the lawyer.

'Yes sir that they were, a week or so before the fire Emma was publicly shamed and beaten raw because of her friendship with my son.' Mr Pargitter hastily brought the interview to a close remarking on her choice of the word 'friendship' as he expertly handed Mrs Blacklock out of her chair and gently guided her to the door.

'Good day and watch what you say to the opposing side,' he warned her.

'You could have knocked me down with a feather him as 'ad encouraged me to talk now telling me not to do. As though I would speak like that to the prosecution,' she indignantly told her sister on the way home.

'It just shows what power they have over us poor folk,' retorted Aunty Ann. 'We none of us know which way the wind's blowing, they can obviously wrap us around their little fingers and then change their minds in an eye blink. And this was the defence lawyer, think what's going to happen with the prosecution,' said her sister.

Mr Pargitter was pleased to obtain this information from his witness. It was not exactly ethical but he now knew how the prosecution would act. He had to find a way to discredit that other worthy's evidence. At this point he didn't know what tack to take but he would think about it and try by fair means or foul to win his case. That it was also to prove the innocence of John Blacklock was not uppermost in his mind.

The party left Buxton behind still discussing the trick that had been played by the lawyer. Uncle George had had enough and seeing up ahead one of the brightly coloured caravans, he thought to distract the women from their grumbles.

'See the circus is ahead,' he said, 'shall us stop and have some fun?'

'I'll have no more fun 'til my lad's free,' said his sister-in-law.

'Aw come on, it won't do you any harm to stretch your legs awhile.'

'Well, you go if you want, I'm stopping here,' said Mrs Blacklock determinedly. Uncle George pulled on the pony's reigns shouting 'woa there' rather more loudly than he needed to. His wife was left in a difficult situation she wanted a change but felt that she should support her sister.

'You know Libby,' she said a little cunningly, 'our Peg might be in this circus, we could pay her a visit.'

Both sisters had wondered what Peg did in the circus but they knew it was frowned on to ask questions. Libby Blacklock stared at her sister unable to believe her words but wanting to solve this family mystery for all time. Her sister could see the conflicting emotions in the other woman's face and felt sorry for her but finally Libby made up her mind and proceeded to climb down from the trap. The circus was not open yet but some of the side shows and the menagerie were ready. The three paid their entrance fee and proceeded to walk around the interesting fair ground. They were mesmerised by the larger animals especially the lions and the elephant.

'This is something like,' said Uncle George, 'I've always wanted to see an elephant and now I have. I don't need to see it do tricks, I'm happy with its raw state.' Mrs Blacklock laughed as she watched the monkeys in their cage.

133

'Ee I'm glad we stopped, it's taking my mind off our troubles,' she said gladly.

'But I wish John was here to win me another gift from the shooting stall instead of languishing in jail.'

'Now, now, he'll be back with you in no time, the trial won't be very long happening.' They spent a happy hour wandering around the menagerie and side shows but were sorry to miss Aunt Peg of whom there was no sign.

'Appen it's a different circus she's in,' said Uncle George, 'there are others.'

He was not to know that the reason they hadn't seen Aunt Peg was that she'd seen them first. In astonishment she had taken hiding in one of the caravans, not wanting her family to be aware of her other life until she was ready to share it with them.

'Well, never mind,' said Mrs Blacklock, 'it's been a nice change anyway and has got my mind away from my troubles. Now we must get back to Emma, she'll be missing us.'

Emma had decided to take a walk. It was a pleasant day and there would not be many more before the winter was upon them. She took the path out of the village which led to Miller's Dale. She had never taken this path alone before, but knew it slightly from the day they had searched for Susie. She was in pensive mood as she began to climb the gentle incline of the hill, but watching the sheep gambling around and butting each other in playful fashion lightened her thoughts somewhat.

She laughed lightly thinking how lovely it was to be away from the mill. *I can't believe how lucky I am to be living in such a place when poor Susie is dead and gone*, she worried. Not having been able to enjoy nature in her early days, Emma was now revelling in the beauty all around her. The rough stone walls and the fields of every hue which reminded her of the beautiful quilt Mrs Blacklock had put on her bed telling Emma that she'd made it herself many years ago when her husband was still alive. Emma was hoping that someday she herself would have the skill to make one for her own home when she and John were at last married. When would that be, she wondered. So much had happened to her recently but much more was to happen before they could be joined together for life.

She reached the brow of the hill and looked down on the beautiful gentle valley, below she could see someone walking there he looked very tiny so must be a long way off. She saw no one else. *Maybe they're all at tea*, she thought, *I haven't had mine yet so 'appen I'll go back and see if they're home yet.* The figure she'd seen was now clearer and she realised that he was coming closer. There was something oddly familiar about him, the way he walked. He was weaving about from side to side and she could see now that he was wearing a long garment possibly an overcoat. She stared into the distance trying to establish where she had seen the man before. Then it came to her he was the one who'd left the soup kitchen so suddenly, the one with the missing button. This would be an opportunity to tell him she'd found it and offer it back at some point.

She sat down to rest on the rough stone wall. Biding her time. Not yet having completely regained her energy she began to snooze. Suddenly she was startled awake by a rough hand shaking her.

'Young woman,' spoke the owner of the hand, 'this is no place to sleep, wake up and walk with me.'

Emma tried to shake the sleep away so that she could be in control of what was happening to her. It was the man in the great coat. She smiled hesitantly, 'Oh it's you,' she said, 'I've been waiting for you to tell you I've found your lost button,' she gestured to his coat. 'I haven't got it with me but if you'd like to call at Mrs Blacklock's house where I'm staying, I'd be glad to sew it on for you.'

'Why do you make soup for poor folk?' he questioned her.

'Because I would be poor too if a kind lady hadn't taken me in,' said Emma.

'You're different from t' others,' he said looking her straight in the eye. 'I'll 'appen come and visit your kind lady myself.'

With his head on one side as he studied her, he reminded her of a little sparrow, but just then he seemed to make a decision and turning purposefully he loped off down the path. *Strange man,* thought Emma, *I'd better get that button ready in case he comes for it.*

The weather that had been so unseasonably warm suddenly turned with a vengeance and black clouds were the harbingers of the rain that began to sluice down on the little town. Rivers of silt ran down the clinker brew and it became almost impossible to traverse these with the heavy pots of soup for the kitchen. Aunty Ann began to call on the other two women to give them a hand carrying the pans and between the three of them they were able not to disappoint the starving people who still turned up in their droves for the only good meal of the week.

The year was now into November bringing with it a cold snap as well as the rain. This was not the worst of the month, however, November would also bring the Assize court to Buxton and the little family looked forward with fearful anticipation wishing that it would soon be over and hoping with all their hearts to bring John back home.

Working one day in the soup kitchen Emma was surprised to see the strange man entering the door. He looked around for her hesitantly and seeing her at last he made a beeline to her side.

'I've come for me button,' he told her roughly.

'I'll be glad to get it for you after I've finished here,' said Emma, 'but as you see we're very busy. Why don't you sit a while and have some soup?'

'I don't need food, I'm living on my own anger,' he answered. Mrs Blacklock looked across at Emma to see if everything was alright. Emma shook her head slightly and the older woman came over to see what she could do.

'I'm trying to persuade our friend to have something to eat but he thinks he doesn't need food,' Emma began to say but he cut her off rudely,

'Friend, friend, I've no friends on this earth. And the one I had has been sent to that other place too soon thanks to the likes of thee. Why didn't you give her soup well, well,' and his voice began to rise angrily before it cracked and the man rushed once more out of the door.

'Well, that's a strange one,' said Mrs Blacklock.

'I feel very sorry for him but I can't like him,' Emma replied.

'Well, we'd better get on with our serving, we're almost done for today. I don't know how we're going to continue at this rate, we need more people to donate ingredients if we're going to continue with our soup kitchen,' and she shook her head sadly.

Their return journey was even more hazardous than it had been in the morning, the road was awash with the heavy rain and the women slid and stumbled as they made their slow way down the brew to their home.

'We'll not make it by ourselves,' said Mrs Blacklock. 'If I stay here sheltering under this tree with our pots and pans could you go on ahead, our Matt should be home by now and he could 'appen give us a hand.'

Emma was only too glad to help and she left the other woman sheltering from the rain. It was a dark creepy night not one she liked to be out in alone. She shivered convulsively hoping Matt would be home to help them. Just then a figure jumped out in front of her from around the corner. Emma started. Then recognising who it was her panic subsided a little.

'Oh, it's you,' she said. 'Have you come for your button?'

He swayed from side to side and she didn't like the look of him as he drank from his green bottle so she stepped back a bit. He began to speak but it was so slurred that she couldn't understand him. She began to feel very scared but couldn't decide what to do. He was strange but he also looked as though he would be strong and living out in the open, he could probably run well.

As she was wondering what to do he made a sudden lurch for her hand and she instinctively stepped sideways. He stumbled into the wall and she seized her chance running as if her life depended on it. He lumbered after her clumsily, shouting something unintelligible. She ran on panting for breath. Just as she reached the corner of their street, she almost bumped into a man coming from the opposite direction and she realised with great relief that it was Matt coming to look for them.

'Oh thank you, thank you,' she gasped.

'Whatever is the matter?' He wanted to know.

'I was being chased by a strange man,' she said breathing hard.

'Well, that won't do we'll go and look for him.'

'First we need to help your mother with the soup pans before he chases her too,' said Emma. 'Quickly before anything happens to her.'

Matt didn't need telling twice, and hurriedly they started back up the hill but they saw no sign of the tramp. Mrs Blacklock was still where Emma had left her leaning against the wet wall.

'You look as though you've seen the devil,' she greeted them.

''Appen Emma has,' said Matt.

'Whatever do you mean?' she wanted to know, so Matt told her haltingly about Emma's ordeal.

'Oh I should never have left you to go by yourself,' Mrs Blacklock spoke guiltily.

'Nay, it's not your fault,' said Emma. 'It was that strange man from the soup kitchen again. I think we should go to the police station and tell them about him. I'll cut his button off my dress and take it to the police. It'll 'appen be a clue to his identity.'

'We should have a bite to eat first. I've got some pikelets, our Matt must be starving,' said his mother.

After they had eaten, they all set off for the police station. Emma had carefully cut the button from her dress. It was a pity but she didn't want anything from such a strange person and it had been useful as a learning device. The duty sergeant was surprised to see them all on such a bad night. He'd been hoping to finish work early and get off home before the storm got any worse.

'What can I do for you,' he asked a bit belligerently.

Matt spoke up first. 'Emma was just chased on her way home from the soup kitchen,' he said.

'What time was that?' asked the sergeant.

'It would be about 6-0-clock,' said Emma.

'You said just now,' he turned to Matt, 'It's now 7-0-clock.'

'Yes,' spoke up Mrs Blacklock, 'but we all needed our tea. We've been working hard all day.'

'Well, if it can wait an hour it can also wait till morning. I need my tea and I'm about to go home.'

So saying he ushered them to the door and bade them a curt good night.

'Well, I never, did you ever hear the likes of that,' Mrs Blacklock spoke indignantly.

'I suppose he did have a point,' said Matt, 'police need to eat as well. Maybe the two of you can come down here in the morning. I'll have to be going to my work in the pit.'

So it was decided and they made their wet way home again.

Chapter Eighteen
A Visit to the Police Station

Next morning the rain had stopped but it was still very dark and dismal as the two women made their way back to the police station. Sergeant Edwin Robinson was on duty today and though they found it hard to deal with him after his connection to John, they at least knew he would listen to them about the night before. Emma told her tale, not leaving out anything about the button and where she'd found it. Sergeant Robinson was very interested in the story and the whereabouts of the greatcoat it had come from.

'Now when did you say you were accosted by this man,' he said.

Emma didn't want to get anyone in trouble so she hesitated but Mrs Blacklock was not so 'nice'.

'It was last night at 6-0-clock,' she said, 'as Emma was on her way home from serving soup all day to the poor. And we came here to report it at 7, but your duty sergeant hadn't time to listen to us, he was in such a hurry to get home to his tea.'

Sergeant Robinson said nothing but he thought a lot. He was pretty sure this was the man they'd been looking for for some time and he was wondering what punishment he'd mete out to his sergeant for once again letting the blackguard slip through their fingers. He took their statements and told them to be aware they might be needed again if he could be found and brought to trial.

Edwin Robinson studied the button carefully. It was definitely from an army greatcoat and was of an old style not now used. The embossed picture had been updated in more modern times so it might be easier to trace the man wearing the coat. Then there was the possibility that the coat was not with the original owner. A retired soldier could have given it to an old tramp. He scratched his chin thoughtfully. This was the first possible lead they'd had to the murderer. They knew the man's name and Charles Peace had been in the army and had fought in

139

the Napoleonic wars. It seemed more than likely that he was the owner of the button and the man who had accosted Emma Brierly. He would have to form a search party with the few men he had available. Going in to the back part of the station where the cells were, he alerted his constables to his need. Luckily no prisoners were housed there at the moment and his two constables were whiling away the time playing cards.

'We don't pay you to sit around,' said Robinson, 'look sharp and do something useful.'

The men grumbled but slowly came to listen to their orders.

'We need to make inquiries in the village as someone has spotted our possible murderer,' he said beginning to fill his men in with all the details of the case. They were now alert realising that an important part of their job was about to begin.

'We'll start with mill bottom as that's where the girl was chased, then we'll make our way around and end up at Top Lane calling at all the houses in between. Make sure you have your whistles handy to summon one another and if nothing un-towards happens, we'll meet back here at 3-o-clock, right?'

It was a dismal morning to be out but the men knew it was very important that this man was caught before any more young women lost their lives.

They began their search for clues. First house.

''ello Mrs, have you seen anything of a strange looking man in an army greatcoat?' shake of the head, slamming of the door. Next house the same and so on right along the street. Nobby Barns began to become a bit dejected. Coming to the cottage at the end, which was different from the others with remnants of roses around the door, and stalks of Brussels sprouts and Winter cabbage in the garden he met a different response to his question.

'Ay that I have I were out walking yesterday, though a wet miserable day it were to be out in. I come across this fellow he were weaving in his walk and drinking out of a green bottle as he went. I giv' him the time o' day and he never said a dicky bird. He were obviously not from around here, we're civil with people in these parts. I thought it were very strange.'

'Could you tell me which way he was going?'

'As to that he were weaving so badly but I think he were making for t' Castleton road.'

'Thank you, you've been most helpful, can we call on you again if we need to verify his identity?'

'Ay that you can I'm al'us happy to help the law,' said the old man. The day wore on and soon the constable was knocking on the door of the Blacklock home. Emma answered the summons. She had been sitting by the fire trying to be useful by doing some mending. She bade the policeman enter. He gingerly removed his helmet and cautiously set it on his knee as he sat down in the proffered chair.

'Now you've given a statement about the incident when you were chased by a man in an army greatcoat,' he said. 'Have you anything to add at this time?'

'Not really,' Emma replied. 'I had been waiting for him you see to return a button that I thought was his.'

'What made you think it was his?' asked the constable.

'Well, I noticed that he had one missing when he visited our soup kitchen last week,' Emma said.

'Did you know this man then?'

'No,' Emma replied, 'I've seen him four times in all. The other time was earlier that week. Late afternoon I'd gone out for a walk and I saw him in the distance.'

'Where was that,' asked the constable.

'It was on the road to Miller's Dale, I saw him in the distance and recognising his strange gait, I waited for him, to return his button. He was quite pleasant that time but he said something strange about me not being like the others. Then he turned up at the soup kitchen again and when I offered him soup, he got quite angry with me and said he didn't need food, he was living on his own anger.'

'When was this last time?' the constable wanted to know.

'It was early afternoon on the day he chased me,' said Emma.

The constable rose from his chair thanking her for her information and doffing his helmet he said goodbye and left. It was almost three and he made his way back to the police station. The three men compared notes. Another witness had seen the man making towards the Castleton road so this seemed to be the way to follow their suspect. All witnesses remarked on his strange gait and the fact that he took copious refreshment from a green bottle.

'It shouldn't be difficult to find him,' said Robinson, 'there can't be many about who fit the description but we'll need more men to help, he might be dangerous. Coates, could you go down to the pub and see how many special constables are there, and rally them to us.'

'Righto,' said his constable.

It was four-o'clock and the night had dropped early when they started out on their dark journey walking quickly to keep themselves warm. It would be a long night. The suspect had a good start on them and though he would probably be walking more slowly it was at least three hours since he'd been seen setting out. There were eight men in all, including the five specials who had turned up to help. At first they walked briskly but as the cloud of night fell darkly among them their steps became slower and it was obvious to Robinson that they were not going to reach Castleton until the early morning.

'Let's stop up a bit,' he called, 'we'll 'appen be able to get a cart and horse to carry us a bit quicker.'

They were coming to a farm isolated on the moorland and they heard dogs barking as they approached it.

'Coates, go up and see if they can find us a conveyance,' said Sergeant Robinson.

No sooner said than done his constable stepped smartly up to the door and when it was opened by a bent old man Coates made his request. The fellow was slow to understand and even slower to harness the young colt so the party lost valuable time, but at last they were off across the moors. The colt was fresh, he had already had his portion of oats and Sergeant Robinson found it hard to control the overloaded wagon. They were making very good time however, so he tried not to reign in their power system. The small lamp hanging on the whippletree gave off very little light but it was better than none. They could see a few yards in front of them and all the men searched the gloom for a sign of their quarry. At length after a couple of hours, they were approaching a small village. There were now a few gas lights in the village square and they were able to see much more clearly but still no sign of the man they were searching for.

'We'll stop at the pub and ask if he's been seen,' said the sergeant.

So saying he pulled on the reigns and brought the wagon to a standstill. The thirsty men tumbled gladly into the warm interior. Not many locals were out in the dismal night so the barman was glad of the unusual custom. They all took a glass of ale as they chatted pleasantly with the few locals who had ventured out.

'A man in an army greatcoat you say you're searching for,' said an old fellow in the corner, 'ai I've seen him on many a night, he's a bit strange doesn't talk much.'

'But he always gets a fill up of his precious green bottle,' added the barman.

'Has he been in tonight?' asked Robinson.

'No not yet, but it's early for him, he usually comes in close to closing time.'

'That's 10-o-clock, is it,' asked the sergeant.

'That it is and not a moment later,' said the barman hurriedly.

'Is he a regular?' asked Robinson, wondering if they should risk wasting time or if they should press on.

'No, he's not that, I've seen him maybe half a dozen times in the last year.'

'Is he always on his way to Castleton?' asked the sergeant.

'That I couldn't tell you but maybe Joe would know.'

'What's that?' called the corner dweller holding his hand behind his ear. The sergeant went over to the old man so he'd be able to converse more easily seeing that the old fellow had a hearing problem.

'Could you tell me anything more about the traveller in the greatcoat, where he goes when he leaves the pub, or where he stays in these parts?' he said.

Old Joe scratched his head in a perplexed kind of way.

'I don't rightly know, but once he did let slip that he'd fought in foreign parts,' he said, 'and he had a sister somewhere about but I don't rightly know where.'

'Thank you, you've been most helpful, now sup up lads,' he called over his shoulder, 'we've a way to go tonight.'

Following on the information they'd just received they made their way to the Castleton road. The rain was falling more heavily as they left the small village. Away from the cheerful lights the night seemed even darker than it had before. As they approached the small town of Castleton, a dark mass loomed out at them leading one of the specials to jump backwards and almost upset the cart.

'Be wary men,' said the sergeant.

'It be only Peveril Castle,' spoke up another.

'It's a ruin from Norman times,' said Edwin Robinson. 'But it would make a good place to hide, we'll stop here awhile,' and so saying he made good his word by pulling in the pony. The searchers divided off into twos and threes. The castle was a ruin so there were not so many rooms to search but it was in three storeys the top most one crumbling around the ramparts. The second one was more or less intact and under it was a store room which had been used to dump rubbish. This was piled high in places and the men found it hard to go about their task with any success. Two men searched each room and the final two climbed up to where the ramparts had been. Only a small portion of the original walkway was left now and it was crumbling away in places. They searched diligently but it

143

was soon obvious that no man was hiding here. Coates and his partner, who had been delegated to search the storeroom were soon panting and out of breath as they moved piles and piles of rubble.

'There's not room here for more than a rat to hide,' said his partner. Coates agreed and just then to prove their point a rat scuttled from its hiding place and ran along the outside wall looking for freedom. The men saw it disappear into the corner.

'Where's that varmint gone,' said Coates curiously.

'Well, there's one way to find out,' the other man answered and so saying he took his pickaxe and began to dig in the pile of debris releasing a stench that had been covered over for many years by the smell of it. It took some time but by and by a large hole was discovered in the corner under the rubble.

'This is obviously were our friend the rat went,' said Coates, 'let's dig around a bit to enlarge it before we tell the sergeant what we've found.'

So saying both men set to and soon they had a hole big enough for one of them to climb into.

'We'll need a lantern to see what's below us,' said Coates. 'Could you go and find one from off the cart and some tinder to light it.'

The other man scurried off not wanting to miss the discovery of anything exciting. As he left Coates continued to poke around in the hole they'd discovered. It began to get easier as the under-soil softened up a bit and soon he could poke his head down. He found his own tinder box in his pocket and managed to make a light trying to see what was below him. Not seeing much, he called out to anyone below. His voice came back eerily proving that the place was hollow. Sergeant Robinson had heard him calling out and came to see what had happened just as the special arrived back with the lantern. The three men looked into the opening, shining the light into the hollow and were very surprised to see a flight of metal steps little bigger that a step ladder let into the rock face just below them. 'Well, who wants to go first?' said the sergeant.

'I'll volunteer sir, if you want to follow me, and the special can hold up the lantern so as we can see,' Coates replied, trying to get in the sergeant's good books after having annoyed him the previous evening.

So saying he scrambled into the hole and made his way gingerly to the flight of steps. He slowly felt his way down the steep rock face the sergeant climbing not far behind him. He was about half way down as far as he could tell when the steps suddenly stopped.

'Why've you stopped?' said Robinson.

'There's no more steps, Sir, I can't get any further,' Coates replied. 'You'd better go back up.'

'We'll not give in that easily, be a man,' said Robinson.

Coates gritted his teeth, he could not answer back but he was wishing he hadn't been so quick to volunteer. The sergeant would be more careful with what he said to a special. And they'd see how much of a man he was when his foot was dangling in thin air. He began slowly to sweep his foot around the rock feeling with all his might for some opening where he could get leverage, for steps there were none. He had almost decided to brave the sergeant's wrath again when his toe suddenly caught hold of something tangible. It was a small hole in the rock where he could get a foothold. He cautiously shifted his weight to the right allowing his right foot to take it. Now he moved his left foot to try for another foothold. 'What are you doing?' barked the sergeant, and just then Coates didn't need to answer for a chunk of the rock that was holding his foot came loose and he fell away into space with his sergeant's voice anxiously drifting eerily away into the distance. A ledge of rock broke his fall. He could still hear muffled noise coming from above him and knew that it was Robinson who had scrambled as quickly as his portly frame allowed up the steps to try to get help.

He lay still, bruised and shaken. He could not tell if any bones were broken but he was in considerable pain. He must have passed out for time went by and when he woke, he couldn't decide where he was. It was actually only a few minutes and Robinson had made good use of the time. He was very quick to act in an emergency and luckily for Coates he was in the process of mustering all the men and had brought rope from the wagon in the hope of rescuing the injured constable.

Some of the specials were rock climbers and they formed a human chain to climb down to the injured man. They saw how the steps had come away from the wall at the bottom and realised that no one should have ventured out on them. Sergeant Robinson was very subdued when he saw the damage. He hoped that no permanent injury had occurred to the man under his charge. The rescue party slowly began to climb down the rock face using their coiled ropes when needed. It took about half an hour to safely reach Coates where he lay. The sergeant felt his legs and arms for breakages and was relieved not to find any obvious ones. They had formed a sling and now they placed the injured man into it, two of the others carrying him between them. Slowly they made their way back up the rock face feeling very relieved when they reached the steps. One climbed the steps and helped the second one who in turn dragged the sling which a third guided from underneath. With great thankfulness they arrived at the opening where their journey had originally begun.

'Bring more light,' said the sergeant, 'I want to have a better look at him.'

'I'm alright, Sir,' said a somewhat groggy Coates.

'Well, let's get you back to base while some of us plan our search more cautiously.'

'I think I'm able to stand, Sir,' and so saying he made good his word. 'I don't need to go back I can keep on helping with the search party.'

'Well, if you're sure, we don't want any more mishaps,' said the relieved sergeant.

Turning to the rest of the men, he requested to know if anyone knew where they were. One of the specials, Peter Parker, spoke up, 'I be a mountain climber in these parts and I think the cave underneath the castle is the one known as *Devil's Arse Canyon*. It divides from *Peake Cavern* up ahead. There's many caverns in these parts and a very labyrinth of passageways. If our quarry has got into them, we'll have a difficult job on hand finding him. They even lead into some of the *Blue John* mines a ways further up.'

'Right,' said Robinson, 'we'll go back into the fresh air for a while and see what we can see. We now know that this is a fine place for anyone hiding from the law to find shelter. We don't know, however, if he's cottoned on that we're on to him so he might get careless.'

So saying he led his little band outside into the dark wet night and more than one of his men was wishing they were still in the dank cave. They took the walk up to Man Tor though it was treacherous at this time of year especially on such a dark night. It was an open stretch of land and the wind and rain beat down on them as they battled against it.

'I can't believe any fugitive would be daft enough to stay out in this weather,' said Coates.

Robinson was about to make a retort before he remembered what his short temper had caused last time and bit his lip. His constable maybe had a point, why were they searching this high ground on the off chance that their quarry had come this route?

'What do you think, Peter Porter,' asked the sergeant, 'where ahead would be a good place to digress from this route?'

'We'd have to turn back, up ahead it only gets more bleak and the climb down into Peake Cavern is a tortuous and difficult decent even for expert climbers. We'd be better going back to the castle and taking the path by the stream. Which I would suspect the soldier has done. For why would he make it more difficult for himself if he doesn't know he's being followed?'

This made sense to Robinson so he about turned the search party and took Peter's advice. The night was now far advanced and the party of eight slithered its way along the wet river bank. The pony had not been able to navigate the narrow path so they'd left it with the cart tied to a railing for later. At that time, they might need its help, hopefully to carry the murderer back with them and into custody. Edwin Robinson was feeling low spirited, though the last thing he would do was to let his men know of his feelings. He braced himself against the weather as the light in the lantern suddenly went out and he was left floundering blindly for it was too dark to see anything.

The men gathered around him to give shelter as he struggled to relight his lantern. On the third attempt it caught and once more they could see a little in front of them. Robinson kicked something with his foot and on closer scrutiny he was surprised to find a green bottle there on the ground.

'Here's a clue at last chaps,' he jubilantly called, 'see here's the green bottle.'

They all clambered around to see. 'But it could be another green bottle not the one belonging to our murderer,' said Coates.

'Why are you always contrary?' retaliated Robinson.

'I didn't mean to be, Sir, but we should be sure before we get all excited, near a pub there are always lots of bottles thrown out and many of them are green,' returned Coates.

Once again Robinson was forced to see the other man's logic and bending down he lifted the bottle for closer inspection. He observed the name embossed on the side as he cleaned off the grime with the flat side of his thumb.

'Hold the lantern high,' he told one of the specials, 'so I can read the writing.'

Embossed into the glass was the name of the brewery. 'Friendship Farm, Somerset, where the cider apples grow.'

'I think that's all the proof we need, I've never seen the likes of this bottle before,' he said.

The going was much easier on the river path and they made good progress. Sergeant Robinson felt his spirits rising as they moved expectantly forward to the small town of Castleton. They had arrived at last and once again visited the local this time 'The Bull's Head'. Asking their usual questions about their quarry, they were pleased to gain a positive reply on his whereabouts.

'He were here earlier this night,' the barman said, 'and he left because he had a bit of a scuffle with that fellow over there.'

'Which fellow, the one in the window?' said the sergeant.

'Ai that's right, Sam Fellows is his name.'

'Could I have a word with you, Sam Fellows?' Sergeant Robinson said as he joined the man at the window.

'That you can. I'm always willing to oblige,' Sam answered.

'Well, I hear you had a bit of bother tonight and I'd appreciate knowing more about the fellow who gave it to you,' Robinson began.

'That I did, obnoxious brute of a fellow, said this was his seat, he always sat here and bade me remove myself in no uncertain terms.'

'And was this true, was he a local to this pub?'

'I haven't clapped eyes on him before, I don't know where he thought he was but it wasn't here.'

'Did you learn anything about him, where he was going for instance?'

'He said he'd been thrown out of better pubs than this one and he'd go over the hills where he was wanted.'

'Do you remember if he had a green bottle with him?'

'He did yes. It were a strange shape, not like the ones they sell here aways.'

'Was it maybe this one?' the sergeant asked, producing it out of his uniform pocket.

'It looks very like it, yes.'

'Thank you very much, you've been most helpful,' said Robinson.

'So men, we'll be on our way back along the stream path, he obviously dropped his bottle after the pub which means he's going in the opposite direction,' said the sergeant.

They once again retraced their steps going back to Peveril Castle. When outside the bulk of this edifice they attended to the pony taking him out of the shafts for a while to rest him. The sergeant spoke to Peter Parker as the man who knew the terrain.

'We need to make a plan of action, we don't know where he went but we know it's somewhere in this direction. It's only a few hours ago so we should be able to head him off if only we knew where he went after the pub.'

'Could it be he went back to the other pub do you think?' asked Coates.

'I shouldn't think he'd do that, why would he do you think?'

'Well, he lost his bottle he might try to buy another one!'

'That's right,' one of the specials spoke up, 'he didn't seem to be able to do without it.'

Sergeant Robinson had to agree with this logic though somewhat hesitantly.

'Right let's harness the colt again and go back to the first pub,' he said.

As they approached the pub they could see from a distance that something was up. A small crowd of people were surging around an object lying in the yard. As they drew closer it was obvious that it was a body. The sergeant drew up hurriedly and jumping down he rushed into the fray.

'It be the barmaid from the local, Molly be her name,' said an old fellow. The still corpse was little more than a child, her golden curls sitting damply on her shoulders. She was still warm. This could only have happened in the last short while.

'If only we'd stayed here instead of going on a wild goose chase,' said Coates.

'I've had just about enough of you tonight,' said the sergeant. 'You always want to find someone to blame and if it's your superior officer you'd better keep stum.'

Coates looked his anger but had the sense to hold his tongue this time.

'We'll have to split up now,' said Robinson, 'Coates you take one of the specials with you and the pony cart and find out all you can in the pub then load up the cart and take this poor creature back home to her family. At after you'd better get home for some rest for I feel your accident has upset you more than a bit. The rest of the men follow me, we'll try to find this villain before the trail goes cold.'

So saying he lost no time in questioning the locals about where the murderer had gone. One of them had seen the man making good his escape into the tunnel that led to the Peake Tavern and that is where the search party followed him.

At first the going was good but within a half hour the tunnel began to narrow and the men were forced to walk in single file. The path began to rise in front of them and they were soon labouring to climb the steep slope. The rock climbers were used to this and were very fit but Sergeant Robinson didn't have the right physique and soon began puffing and panting trying to keep up with his more active men. Luckily the cave was very dark and the others could not see how purple his face had become. He didn't want his men to be concerned for his welfare. Adding itself to the steepness, the walls were dripping with condensation which in turn made the rough-hewn steps they were climbing slippery and difficult to negotiate. The more athletic began to help the others and though Sergeant Robinson tried to prove his worth, he finally had to accept help from his constable Nobby Barns.

He was glad he'd sent Coates back, he felt that this would have been too difficult for the injured man. They laboured uphill doggedly.

'I'd never have thought how much land there were under us,' he said.

'Oh it goes on for many a mile,' said Peter.

After a turn in the path it suddenly veered sideways and started to go steeply downhill. This was almost worse than the uphill climb and the men began to slither and slide their way down. The leading man was suddenly startled by a large rat and his feet shot from under him as with an oath he landed awkwardly on the hard floor his lamp crashing down beside him. Now they couldn't see. The treacherous path they were on left them no possibility of feeling their way in the darkness. Robinson contained his frustration seeing that anyone could have dropped the light in that situation and mustering his limited amount of patience he spoke slowly.

'Let's all stay still and quiet,' he said to the muttering men, 'and 'appen Barns can feel around for the lantern for we can't do anything without some light. Are you in a position to do that Nobby?'

'Ay, Sir, I'll try,' came back the hollow voice.

A scrabbling could be heard lower down as Barns tried to make good his word. Finally he found the lantern and then a tinder box had to be handed from Robinson through the men so he could light it. This mishap had lost them some time and the sergeant was finding it harder to contain his frustration, but eventually the light came eerily along the dark corridor and the search party could once again be on its way.

They came to a place where the rock above them narrowed in the cavern and they had to bend their necks hen like to avoid the stalactites that were forming on the roof. They had reached the very lowest part of the canyon and now were approaching the lead mine which at this time of year had some flooding problems. The miners had finished work and downed tools for the day, some of which were left lying on the spar of rock which formed a ledge higher on the wall. 'What was that, quiet men, I heard something strange.'

A kind of whooshing sound came. More of the men could hear it now and they all stayed quiet to see if they could detect where the sound was coming from.

'It sounds like water running,' one of the men remarked.

'And it's getting louder,' said the sergeant.

'Look lively ahead there and see what you can find?'

The ones at the head of the column turned a sharp corner taking the light with them and leaving the others in deep darkness once again. The light of the lantern played on a very waterfall as it cascaded out of the rock face. Parker clinging to the side called a warning to the ones bringing up the rear or all would have been swept away with the force of it.

The light, though weak, showed up a large obstacle that was caught on a small spar of rock. The other searchers were able to catch up and crowded around the pool of water that had formed around the object. It was difficult to get a good hold on the side so as to pull it free so Robinson sent one of the specials for a tool from the ledge. Delving deeply under the obstruction they were able to free it and bring it to shore.

The excitement of the watchers grew and a cheer rang out as their find turned out to be an army greatcoat. They were on the right track for their quarry. This find gave them new energy and they surged onward with vigour. It was very difficult to negotiate the path as it narrowed to less than a one-man width, but valiantly they progressed even though the going was slow. By now the water was flowing so fast that it had become a steady stream and the searchers had to be extra careful not to fall off the ledge.

'If it gets any worse, we're going to need a boat,' called the sergeant, 'and I wonder why he took his coat off.'

'He was maybe too hot, or it was encumbering him so he couldn't walk fast enough,' came the answer.

His men seemed to be thinking on their feet, thought Robinson, this made a nice change.

'What's that ahead,' one of the searchers called as he lifted the lantern higher. It was a shadow and looked like the outline of a man. The searchers began to run sideways on the ledge and as they did so the shadow moved away more quickly. But suddenly the figure knelt down and took aim. A shot rang out.

'Woa, he's sporting a gun,' called Robinson, 'take care.'

Another shot rang out and one of the specials cried out in pain.

'He's winged me.' This was one of the worst spots it could have been to apprehend their quarry, thought Robinson, how were they going to catch him now they knew he had a gun? The injured man dropped back in the search party not wanting to hold up his friends from doing their job. The rest pressed on bravely. Should they extinguish their light, thought Robinson. It was hard to tell, if they couldn't see, it would be more dangerous but if they could see the man could see them better to shoot at them. He decided to call the man's bluff.

'You're surrounded, Peace,' he called. 'Better give yourself up we've got you covered.'

The man answered with another shot, which went wide of its target. Uncanny laughter rang out at this point, the eerie noise bringing goosebumps to the skin of the searchers. Robinson was trying to calculate how long between shots they had to apprehend the man. The gun he was using was probably one he'd had in the army and the sergeant knew that the ones used by the entire British Army were the Enfield Pattern Model. In this enclosed space the man would be facing the same problems as his search party and would not be able to reload within five minutes of discharging his rifle.

He whispered his plan to his men and they passed it along the line.

Soon the shot rang out, and he timed the space he had before the next one. The front men crept along the floor cautiously towards the sound of the shot. There was the man once again lining up his quarry. They surged forward hoping to catch him off guard, but once again the shot rang out. This time more men were ready to grab him before he could reload his firearm. The sergeant's plan had worked but not without another casualty. One of the first responders had been shot in the leg.

All was suddenly pandemonium. Two of the constabulary grabbed the quarry, but he writhed around and managed to break free, now two of the specials were able to jump him, one from behind. He wrenched one arm free but not the other one, and a third pinioned his arms behind him as Sergeant Robinson read him his rights. This was all punctuated with the screams of Nobby Barns in the background. Parker was able to tie a tourniquet around the injured leg thus giving Barns some relief and finally the arrest accomplished they all began to make their way back slowly. Parker helped the injured man and they brought up the rear. Arriving at the cavern, Robinson was surprised to find Coates waiting for them with the cart.

'I thought I told you to get some rest,' he growled.

'I was alright, Sergeant, and I thought you'd need a conveyance for your prisoner,' Coates answered smugly.

Chapter Nineteen
The Trial Assizes

The morning of the trial dawned at last. The whole Blacklock household was up early. The fact was that most of them had not slept much. Emma could not bring herself to concentrate on a future that might not include John and now in addition she had been called as a witness in the trial of Susie's murderer Charles Peace. It was to take place on this self same day. And thinking of this brought back her grief in the loss of Susie. She was all a quake when Mrs Blacklock called her down to breakfast.

'I can't eat a single thing,' she said.

'Come along deary you need something inside you, have a nice cup of tea to warm you and a piece of butty.'

Emma could not refuse the kind woman and found that the small repast made her feel stronger. Uncle George was going to take them to Buxton in his pony trap in time for the 9-o'clock start.

Buxton was a busy place that morning. Uncle George decided to let the travellers down before finding somewhere to park the trap and see to the pony. Walking gingerly into the law court Emma was not able to take an account of the building. Its grandeur was more than she had ever seen before. This splendour did not help her to calm herself and she began to shiver with fear that soon all the people in the court would be staring at her. Mrs Blacklock was not feeling much brighter but she tried to be her usual confident self for Emma's sake. The mood of the two other girls was tangible. They were not called as witnesses and although they had plead their wish to be there for their brother's sake it was obvious to their mother that it was merely because they didn't want to miss anything that they had begged to come. Mrs Blacklock felt betrayed by them as she frowningly looked in their direction, wishing with all her heart that she had refused Sally and Maggie's request to be part of the family party.

'Bear up, Mother, we'll not let our John down with sour looks,' said Matt.

Mrs Blacklock bit her lip, she'd have to take control of her feelings and not let anyone else know what she was thinking. But inside her stomach felt like jelly and she couldn't rid herself of the thought that her darling would soon be gone from her forever. Just then Mr Pargitter saw her and made his way across.

'Madame, you shouldn't be in here,' he said, 'there's a special room for defence witnesses.'

'Where should Emma go then?' asked his witness.

'All the prosecution witnesses are to go on the other side of the building in the room by the door,' he answered.

'Oh please don't leave me,' begged Emma.

'Don't worry, Emma, I'll be with you,' said Matt.

Emma had to be grateful for his concern but she dearly wanted the motherly woman who had taken her in, and though she nodded her head to him in gratitude, she wept as the kind woman was led away.

At 9-o-clock the proceedings began. The courtroom was full as the prisoner was led into the dock.

'Look there's our John,' Sally squealed out to her sister.

'He looks a might pale and scruffy, he could have cleaned himself up a bit,' Maggie responded. Sally was thoughtful.

''appen they don't give 'em much water,' she replied.

This comment chastened both girls as thoughtfully they waited for the trial to begin.

'All rise for his worship the judge,' and the court rose as of one man.

'Look at them robes, they're costing someone a pretty penny,' whispered Maggie.

'Shush,' hissed the woman sitting behind them, 'do you want to get the court cleared?'

Maggie tossed her head, she didn't like being told what to do. The trial began. 'Call the first witness for the prosecution. Call Ben Brierly.' Ben entered the courtroom slowly. He raised his arm to salute Emma as he left the waiting room. As all the witnesses had been told not to speak to each other, they were still in the dark as to why they had been summoned. Ben made his slow way into the court. He didn't want to be here. He was not the kind of man who was comfortable out of the mill. Since the fire however, he had nowhere to go except the workhouse and now he had been subpoenaed to the trial.

'State your name,' the lawyer demanded of him.

'Ben Brierly, sir,' he answered.

'And is it true that until the fire at Cressbrook mill you resided there?'

'Yes, sir.'

'What did you do in the mill?'

'I was a tenter, sir.'

'Now we've got rid of the obvious questions, I want to ask you some more personal ones. Do you know the plaintiff, John Blacklock?' Ben paused, he didn't know how to answer this question honestly, he'd seen John but had never spoken to him and he didn't want to say anything about him that would go badly for him in the trial.

'Well, man, answer the question it's not too difficult do you or don't you know him?' Ben quaked in his boots finally he opened his mouth and a little squeak came out.

'Er...I don't rightly know sir if I knows him or not,' he said.

'Good God,' the lawyer hissed to his clerk, 'we've only just started and we've already met a stumbling block or should I say a block head.'

The lawyer tried to keep calm, he smiled pleasantly as he thought, but Ben was by this time so muddled in his mind that he knew not what to say and all he saw on the face of the lawyer was a grimace.

'Shall we begin again,' said that worthy, 'have you ever seen John Blacklock?'

This was much easier for Ben, a straight question at last. 'Yes Sir,' he said thankfully.

'When did you see him?' asked the lawyer.

'I seen him delivering coal at the mill.'

The lawyer wiped his brow, this was better.

'When did you last see him?'

'Last time I see'd him was after the fire when he was sitting on the grass next to Emma's body as I thought was dead, but she come back to life at after.'

'Did you see John Blacklock strike Tom Burly on the night of the fire?'

'No, sir, I wouldn't say strike sir.'

'Well, then what did you see?'

'I seen smoke and the man in question broke down the door to get into the mill to save the souls inside.'

'Where were you?'

'I were hiding sir so they'd not see I wasn't locked in my side of the garret.'

'What did you see?'

'I don't rightly know sir the smoke were too thick.'

Ben was almost choking by this time he was so upset with the questioning. The lawyer seemed to realise that he'd get nowhere with this witness so he let him go.

'You may step down, no more questions at this point but I may call you back later,' he said.

Ben stumbled down and had to be helped out of the court shaking.

'Call the beadle.' The beadle came into court answering his call. He was a swaggering man and his sense of importance in being called as a star witness gave him even more confidence.

'State your name and occupation.'

'My names Joe Higgins and I'm beadle in the parishes to the west of here.'

'On the night in question did you see the plaintiff, John Blacklock?'

'That I did sir he were coming up aways from the clinker brew and he drew my attention to the glow in the factory windows which I my lord ascertained to be a mill fire and I alerted the brigade.'

'Could the plaintiff have visited the mill before he climbed the clinker brew do you think?'

'I don't rightly know sir. It would have been a good way round!'

'Where did the plaintiff go after you had spoken to him.'

'Well, sir he ran like the devil towards the mill saying something about not letting the bastard do his worst to her and saving his own true love.'

A gasp went round the court at his strong language but he was only repeating the words of the prisoner so the court was not cleared. John hung his head; if only he'd been more cautious, he thought. He remembered saying the very words that had been attributed to him. 'So sir after the brigade arrived, did you see the plaintiff again?'

'Yes sir I saw him after he'd rescued a woman and he was sitting with her on the grass, and then at after they brought out a corpse and laid it next to her.'

'Thank you, you may step down.' The next witness was called it was Jessie Burns. Once again the preliminary questions were asked and Jessie was able to show off her importance in being called as witness.

'Yes, I'm Jessie Burns and I was working in Cressbrook Mill until the time of the fire. Now I have nowhere to go, it's my home and my welfare I've lost in one horrible night thanks to the likes of him,' she gestured at John with a sweeping motion of her arm.

'Yes, thank you, just answer the questions without colouring the facts if you can,' said the council.

Jessie showed her displeasure in her sulking face, she didn't like being told off especially when this was her moment of glory.

'Now do you know the plaintiff, John Blacklock.'

'Oh yes sir, I know him ever so well.'

'How do you know him?'

'I've know'd him ever since he started delivering coal to the mill and skulking around the cellar with Emma Brierly.'

At this information Maggie and Sally raised their eyebrows at each other. They hadn't known how their brother had got caught up in the affairs at the mill. This was getting interesting.

'Next question, Miss Burns. On the night of the fire did you see John Blacklock?'

'Yes, he hit Tom Burly on the stairs and Tom fell down and banged his head.' Jessie looked around her importantly.

'Now Miss Burns where were you when the fire got started?'

'Why sir I were locked up in the garret with the rest of them.'

'I see, so how did you escape from a locked room and go to your safety?'

'It were him who opened the door an' let us out,' Jessie said grudgingly.

'So how do you know that John Blacklock hit Tom Burly causing him to fall down the stairs if indeed you were locked in the garret?'

A hush had come on the court. Sally held her breath for the answer and Maggie gripped her sister's fingers hard.

'I 'er don't know,' Jessie floundered.

'Come woman you have made a statement and now you need to back it up with facts. That is how a law court works and if you are found to be lying for any reason, you could be convicted of perjury. Now how do you know that John Blacklock hit the overseer?'

The livid scar on Jessie's face stood out glaringly against her pale skin as she went hot and then cold. This was not how she'd envisioned a court of law to be. She wished that she'd stayed out of it, but it was too late, and she squirmed around in her mind trying to find some lies that would get her out of this predicament.

158

'I know I shouldn't have done sir but I was listening in to a private conversation of two people in the workhouse where I'm now obliged to live. One of them was saying that he'd seen John Blacklock strike Tom Burly.'

'Now, Miss Burns, remember that you are under oath, who were these two people, may the court have their names?'

'I didn't know one of them but the other was Ben Brierly,' she answered in a scared tone of voice. Now she'd done it what would happen to her when Ben found out.

'You may step down,' said the council for the prosecution. 'Call the next witness.'

Matt was next called into court. He strode with a purpose, straight of back and gaze. He looked at the jury who would be the ones on whose decision his brother's future depended, he was determined to do all he could to make a good impression and so exonerate John from the charge. The usual questions were asked of him. Name, abode, job, relationship to the plaintiff etc.

'Now on the night in question, where were you?'

'I ate at home with my family and then decided to meet some friends in *The Black Swan*.'

'You say you ate with your family was your brother part of that gathering?'

'Yes sir.'

'And did he also accompany you to *The Black Swan*?'

'No, sir, he decided to bide awhile at home.'

'Are you close to your brother?'

'I am sir we've been everything to each other all our lives especially since Dad died.'

'Did your brother often join you in *The Black Swan*?'

'He did, every Friday night we'd go to play darts.'

'What was so different on the Friday night in question?'

'Nothing really, he just decided not to come with me,' Matt replied hesitantly. The lawyer had seen the hesitation and decided to probe deeper.

'Had something happened to make it abhorrent for your brother to drink with you that night?'

Matt thought back to the night and remembered John's words. What could he tell the lawyer without alerting that worthy to John's feelings?

'I think sir,' he said, 'that my brother was in rather pensive mood and needed time to himself.'

'But then why did he change that mood and later appear at the mill at a very opportune time, in fact just as the mill was about to burn down?'

'I don't know sir you'd better ask him.'

'I intend to do so but that does not allow you to be impertinent, you'd better watch your mouth or you'll be charged with contempt.'

Matt bit his lip, after all his castigation to himself on his behaviour, he'd let John down already.

'You may step down but don't go anywhere, we'll reserve the right to call you back.'

'Call Emma Brierly.' Emma jumped with a start when Matt returned to the room.

'How was it lad,' she said.

'Oh it was alright,' Matt said trying to put a brave face on it, 'I didn't tell them about you and John being courting, but I'm sure someone else will so you'd better tell them yourself.'

'No talking among the witnesses,' said the clerk of court as he came in to call Emma. Emma was so scared that she thought she wouldn't be able to make it to the courtroom. Her legs were of the same jelly like consistency as Mrs Blacklock's and she wobbled forward slowly. Then she saw John and realised if she didn't buck up, she might be the cause of his death warrant and that gave her heart. When Emma stated her place of abode, the lawyer paused her and asked the question she'd anticipated.

'You say you are living with the Blacklock family?'

'Yes sir.'

'Is this then since the time of the fire?'

'Yes sir.'

'Why then would the Blacklock family take you in?'

'Sir I was very badly hurt in the fire and I collapsed and lost my senses for some weeks and Mrs Blacklock was kind enough to say I could stay.'

'What is your relationship with the plaintiff?'

Emma stood upright and her gaze was steady as she looked straight at John.

'He is my intended husband, my lord.'

A murmuring spread throughout the court room. 'Silence,' said the clerk of court.

'How long has this connection been going on?' said the lawyer.

'For eighteen months, Sir, since John and I met at the Whitsun fair when it was in Eyam way.'

The lawyer turned to his clerk.

'This puts a different light on the situation. It could mean we have found a motive,' he said quietly.

'Now let me put it to you, miss, when you were injured in the fire, did Tom Burly have anything to do with you being locked in the garret room?'

Emma thought for a minute, she could see that this was not looking well for John.

'He had no other thing to do with us that night than he had any other,' she answered. 'It was always his job to lock us in the garret and had been every night for as long as I can remember.' A shocked gasp ran around the court.

'Do you mean to tell me that you were always locked in?'

'Yes Sir.'

'Did John Blacklock know this?'

'Yes Sir.'

'I think we'd better hear from the plaintiff but we will reserve the right to call you back so don't go far,' he said to Emma.

She was led out of the court. She wished with all her heart that she could stay and hear John's testimony but it wasn't allowed.

'Call John Blacklock.' And he was released from his ankle chain so as to be able to move out of the dock and into the witness box.

'Now will you state your name for the record.'

'I'm John Blacklock and I live in Litton, close by Cressbrook Mill.'

'Am I right in thinking that you work in the mines at Miller's Dale?'

'You are that sir.'

'Now, you've heard Emma Brierly's statement, have you anything else to add to it?'

'Before all this happened,' he said, 'we were walking out together on Sundays.'

'And when did you stop *walking out* together?'

John paused again, he was going to incriminate himself whatever he said so he may as well tell it as it was, but he'd try and leave out Emma's shaming.

'Come man we haven't got all day,' said the prosecution lawyer.

'I was just trying to get it right in my head sir so as I'd not make any mistakes,' John replied. 'So here goes. Emma and I met at the Whitsun Fair as she said and at after she seemed to disappear from the face of the earth, then when I thought I'd never see her again, she turned up in the search party for her friend Susie. I vowed I wouldn't lose her again and asked her to tea so she could meet my mother. It was difficult for her to get out of the mill because all the slaves were locked in. I was asked by the pit to deliver the coal to the mill and I was able to see her for a few minutes each time I made my delivery.'

'And you call this walking out with her?' The lawyer sneered.

'It was the only way available to us,' said John simply.

'So I put it to you the burning of the mill and killing of the overseer Tom Burly was to your advantage in furthering your courtship of the said young woman.'

'I know it looks like that but I didn't burn down the mill,' said John, 'and I had no intention of killing Tom Burly but I admit striking him when he refused to give me the keys to the garret.'

A low murmur went around the court and the bailiff had to threaten to clear the court before all the noise was suppressed.

'You may stand down and return to the dock.'

The next witness was called and it was the mill owner. Mr Brierly stumbled into court and John could see how he'd aged in a few months. John felt he could almost be sorry for him if it hadn't been for his treatment of Emma. Mr Brierly, being the mill owner, was treated with great respect.

'Thank you for coming today to give evidence in a trial that must put you in great distress,' said the magistrate. 'Could you in your own words describe the happenings in your mill leading up to the night of the fire Sir.'

Mr Brierly began slowly in a quiet voice, 'Owning a mill is a great responsibility. The mercantile process is not an easy one. The master of a mill has the charge not only for the building, the machinery, trade and commerce but also for the wherewith-all of his work people. Most of these are as children in their minds and must be taken care of, fed, housed, and watched over for their own good. They are not worldly and have no aptitude for the working world except their own piece of the process. Known as hands because it is their hands that we prize and not their simple minds. I have thought a lot about the months leading up to the fire since it happened and I have to say that maybe I was responsible in some little way.

'At Whitsuntide I released six of my workers to help with the erection of the fair stalls. They worked hard and long and I gave them a treat as compensation.

This was to allow them a night at the fair, not a sin in its simplicity, but leading to two girls being allowed to get above their station. The one Susie, ran away and now we have heard of her murder. The other one Emma, I learned from Tom Burly, was sneaking out of the mill to meet her lover. The same John Blacklock you see before you today, accused of killing Burly and setting fire to my mill. I had met John Blacklock some months ago myself when he had the temerity to call on me and ask for Emma's hand in marriage. When I refused him on grounds of her youth, he left with an oath saying he'd make me sorry, or words to that effect.'

'That is a bare-faced lie,' yelled John and the court exploded into uproar.

'Silence in court,' called the bailiff.

'John Blacklock, sit down, any more outbursts of that kind and you will be sent to the cells and not be allowed to plead,' the lawyer challenged.

Mr Brierly's face had become the colour of beetroot and the lawyer was afraid he'd have a fit.

'Now sir could we return to your point,' said the lawyer. 'I think your point was that the people who work in your mill have not the intellect to deal with worldly affairs and must be taken care of like little children. Am I correct?'

'To some degree I would answer yes,' Mr Brierly said.

'Is that then your reason for locking them in the garret when they are not dealing with the heavy machinery in the mill?'

A murmuring was once again to be heard among the onlookers. Mr Brierly flushed an angry red and he spoke up to defend himself. 'This is what I mean,' he said. 'I am called Master for that very reason because I am the master of all things and they are all my responsibility.'

The lawyer thought maybe he'd gone too far with this point of questioning and decided to leave off as the case was becoming more intense.

Emma had been taken back to the waiting room but it wasn't long before the bailiff came to escort her to another courtroom. There she was to give witness in yet another murder trial. As she was being sworn in, she looked across to the dock and there saw the man who had worn the army greatcoat, Charles Peace. The man who stood accused of ending Susie's short life and leaving her bereft without her friend. The intensity of his blue eyes seemed to pierce into her mind as he stood staring ahead. And she hoped that he could read her thoughts thus seeing the torture he had caused her by removing one who was so dear. She had never understood until she'd lost Susie how emptiness caused by death could feel so very permanent. She dragged her thoughts back to the present preparing herself to witness for the prosecution in this case as well, for though it was easier than John's trial, she still felt very shaky as the lawyer prepared to questioned her.

'Now Miss Brierly you have made a statement that you have seen the prisoner only four times in your life. Is this the case?'

'Yes sir.'

'And tell us in your own words how you came to be connected with him?'

And Emma told the tale of her connection with Charles Peace ending with his warning to her to 'be careful, that there were some rum'uns about.'

'Thank you; you may step down.'

Emma went back to the witness room and as she did so she saw Mrs Blacklock moving towards the courtroom, so this must mean that the prosecution was over and now the defence had begun. Emma wished desperately that she could go in and listen to the defence but it wasn't allowed. So she moved slowly back to her place to wait for the outcome.

Aunty Ann and Uncle George, sitting quietly in their seats were alerted by the announcement of the next witness's name.

'Here she is, oh doesn't she look scared,' said Ann.

'She does that,' George replied.

'I wish I could go and speak for her,' said her sister.

The usual questions were asked and when the onlookers realised that this was the mother of the accused, they seemed to observe more quietly than usual, because they perhaps understood what an ordeal this was going to be for her, and all held their breath in anticipation.

'Now Mrs Blacklock on the night in question we have heard that your two sons ate tea with you and then Matt decided to meet with his friends in 'the Black Swan' as was his wont on Friday nights. Is that correct?'

'Yes Sir.'

'Now, Matt has given evidence that his brother John chose not to accompany him that night and instead decided to stay home with you, is that what happened?'

'Yes Sir.'

'Could you enlighten us further as to John's reason for his decision.'

Mrs Blacklock thought back to that night and fear clutched its cold hand around her heart, what should she say in answer, she knew if she told the truth it would look bad for John, but she was under oath so she had to speak.

'I don't recall his exact words, Sir, but it was something about not being able to swill beer when he didn't know how Emma did,' she replied.

Mr Pargitter looked surprised he had not expected that reply and seemed to wish he could take the question back, but it was too late. He finally spoke, 'I see, but this was before the fire, what then was his worry about Emma?'

'Sir, one of Emma's friends had visited to tell us that Emma had been punished for walking out with our John and she didn't want to see him again out of fear.'

A gasp went around the court and John hung his head in desperation. Now he knew that it would go badly for him. And what could be seen of Mrs Blacklock's demeanour matched that of her son for beneath the hanging heads they had both gone deathly pale. The lawyer for the defence hesitated, he needed time to gather his ideas together.

'Could we take a short recess, M'lord?' he inquired of the judge.

It was granted and Mrs Blacklock was relieved to stand down, but John just had to stay there and await the court's pleasure. The next twenty minutes seemed like an eternity to him but finally the recess was over and the proceedings continued with the next witness being called. Mr Pargitter decided to change his original plan of action. The short break had given him time to pull his thoughts together so he had Ben Brierly recalled.

Ben was still shaking from his previous visit to the witness box and now hearing his name called he went into a hot sweat as he was led back into court. Mr Pargitter spoke kindly to Ben trying to allay his fears and get some sense out of him.

'Now Ben I've recalled you for the defence because I don't believe that you had a fair chance to give your evidence last time, is that correct?' Ben nodded his head too scared to speak.

'Now Ben I know you're scared but you have to speak up to give evidence,' said the lawyer as he gazed expectantly at the witness. Ben gathered his racing thoughts and finally rasped out,

'Yes sir.'

'That's better, now on the night in question you have given evidence that you were hiding, so that Tom Burly would not know that you were not locked in your garret room, is that correct?'

'Yes sir.'

'Now I ask you was there any reason that you didn't want to be locked in that night that was different from any other?'

Ben was silent he had a huge secret that he did not want to divulge but if he didn't, John would probably be found guilty. People began to murmur and the bailiff called quiet in court. Mr Pargitter sensed the hesitancy in Ben and suspected that he knew something about the case, and was not just keeping quiet out of fear of being in court. He became sharper with the old man.

'Ben Brierly, if you have any evidence you must speak out or you will be put in prison for perjury,' he said crisply.

Ben began to shake in his shoes and finally sense of the outcome for himself won and he spoke up in a quivery voice.

'I had heard someone plotting to fire the mill earlier in the day and I thought I could stop them if I was there,' he said.

Pandemonium had broken out and the clerk of court shouted loudly, 'Silence in court or I'll clear it.'

At the admonishment, quiet prevailed and Mr Pargitter was able to continue his questioning.

'Now Ben I will ask you a very important question.' All waited with baited breath. 'Was the person you heard plotting John Blacklock?'

'No sir,' Ben replied.

'Who then was it?'

'I can't rightly say, sir.'

'Come on man do you want an innocent to hang?' Ben took a deep breath and hurriedly gasped out his evidence:

'It were my own brother Bill, he didn't want to do it sir but it were Tom Burly who had something on him and he couldn't refuse.'

The court had broken out in loud whispers everyone was amazed at Ben's evidence but a brother wouldn't lie about his own kin they said. Mr Pargitter asked one more question.

'Did John Blacklock have anything to do with the happenings at the mill on that fateful evening?'

'No sir, he did not.'

'No more questions.'

'Call Mr Brierly.' Mr Pargitter turned to his clerk. 'We need to get to the bottom of this,' he said, 'before we can move on.'

Mr Brierly once again entered the court.

'Now sir remember you are still under oath. Now cast your mind back to the week before the fire. Do you recall what happened after Tom Burly had 'let on to you' that Emma was, in your own words, sneaking out of the mill to meet her lover.'

'Yes I remember very well she was punished in front of her contemporaries to be a lesson to anyone who decided to take the same route. We can't have young girls running off into the wilderness alone where they are at liberty to be molested by anyone. As indeed was the case with Susie.'

'Do you consider that the punishment meted out to Emma was an unusually harsh one in view of Susie's disappearance?'

'No, I do not, we have to have some sense of order.'

'Thank you, sir, you may step down. Call Doctor Roberts.' The doctor took the oath and answered the preliminary questions.

'Now Dr Roberts you have been called as a witness to speak about your opinion as a medical man following the happenings in Cressbrook mill. After which I shall ascertain whether they had any bearing on a later mill fire that occurred that same month, do you understand?'

'Indeed I do.'

'On the night in question, following the fire, were you called to the home of Mrs Blacklock to attend to one Emma Brierly who had been injured in the fire?'

'Yes, I was.'

'What were your findings on that fateful evening?'

'I examined the young woman and found her in a state of stupor. She had been badly injured in the fire after a beam fell on her but these were not the only injuries I discovered. She had bruises to more than half of her body, her hair had been shorn to her head and there were many cuts around her scalp.'

'Did you question what had caused them?'

'Yes, I questioned John Blacklock, who was the man who summoned me to take a look at her.'

'And what was his reply?'

'He said that Emma had been shamed, a practice that occurs in the mill to control wayward employees. This shaming is done by the foreman and is in front of all the workers male and female. She was stripped of her clothes, beaten unmercifully, then held down by two men, while another shaved her head, not too gently in my opinion.'

A gasp had gone out around the onlookers, but what would this evidence do for the man in the dock, even though Ben Brierly's evidence had seemed to exonerate him from the charge.

'What was your reaction to the news?'

'I said that I would be glad to give evidence against the brutality that goes on in the production of cotton.'

'Thank you, sir, you may step down.'

It had been a long first day of the Assizes and at this point the judge decided that he would call it a day and the court was bidden to 'all rise' as he swept out of the courtroom and went to his chambers.

John's family hastily made their way to the exit, there to wait for the ones who had given evidence. Those who were bearing witness had had to swear that they would not discuss the case with anyone. So they were silent as they made their way home in Uncle George's pony trap.

Chapter Twenty
Day Two of the Trial

Day two of the trial began the same as the first day. Once again the Blacklock family were up with the lark and deposited in Buxton by Uncle George and his pony trap. Although they were able to take the proceedings a little more calmly on the surface, inside each one was tingling at what the day could bring.

Mr Pargitter once again led the questioning for the defence and chose to call the foreman from the Miller's Dale mine where John and Matt worked. He corroborated John's evidence of delivering coal at the mill on Wednesdays and when asked to stand as a character witness, he was very glad to do so.

'John Blacklock is one of my best workers and this case has not only brought character defamation to him and his family, but has deprived me of two of my best workers in him and his brother.'

'Thank you, you may step down. Now I'm taking the unusual step of bringing in another witness who was not called yesterday. Call Bill Brierly.'

Bill came into the court hanging his head. He looked even more scared than his brother had, if that was possible.

'Now Bill Brierly,' said Mr Pargitter after he'd asked the usual questions, 'I want to be clear about what happened in the week leading up to the fire at Cressbrook mill.'

'Yes Sir,' said Bill, 'I'll try to answer your questions honestly even if it means me having no place to live, for I've already lost my place of work just like all these other chaps.'

'Now Bill we've heard about how your brother listened in to your conversation with Tom Burly but we'd like to hear it again in your own words.'

Bill coughed hesitantly and hung his head. He didn't know how to begin telling his awful tale that had ended in death and might bring more blood-shed before this day was finished.

'Come Bill we haven't all day to waste,' said the lawyer.

'Well, sir it was like this,' Bill began hesitantly, 'I'd been doing a bit of grubbing around to see what I could pick up like, as things in t' mill were scarce and I have a big belly to feed, and Tom Burly come sneaking up on me and said he'd tell the master if I didn't do something to help him.'

'So what did he want you to do to help him?' Asked the lawyer.

'He told me where a can of oil was and said I had to soak the cotton bolts in it so they'd go up fast. I telled him I wasn't going to have any truck with it. I knew all the slaves were going to be locked in the garret, mi own brother and all. Burly said if I didn't, I'd be laid off and I'd have no place to go because the work house wouldn't have me if I didn't do as I was told by my betters. I didn't know what to do sir. I were in a sorry plight, I can tell you.'

'But why did the overseer want to fire the mill man, it doesn't make sense,' said Mr Pargitter.

'I don't rightly know, but Tom Burly said the mill had been going through some hard times and they didn't have enough work for everyone and the masters were trying to recoup their losses. I don't understand it sir, I'm only one of the hands and I don't get anything except my whittles. I don't cost anyone much.'

'You may step down Bill. Thank you for filling us in on how things are in the mill. I think we'll call Mr Brierly back in court.'

The atmosphere had become decidedly chilly as the master of the mill made his reappearance. He, of course, had not heard Bill's testimony and it is hard to say whether or not he felt the chill but his face was as sour as it had been previously.

Mr Pargitter took his time with this witness. He knew that he had to be careful with one of the mercantile gentry. He smiled pleasantly at the older man.

'Now sir would you say that you are a respected man in these parts?'

'Indeed I am, my mill is known throughout the West Riding.'

'And you sir, are you considered honest by your contemporaries.'

'I don't know where you're going with these questions but I find you extremely impertinent. You'd better watch what you are implying.'

'I have not implied anything yet but I'd suggest that you be careful what you say, I'd hazard a guess that you don't want to be tried for perjury.'

Mr Brierly went purple in the cheeks and then white and he suddenly sat down, reaching for the flagon of water that was by his side. The clerk of court was quickly by his side helping him to loosen his neck tie. A murmur went

170

around the court, each one picking up a few more words as it reached them. No one knew what would happen next and it seemed that only Mr Pargitter had control of the situation.

'Now sir are you suitably rested? If you are, we'll continue. What do you know about your overseer Tom Burly blackmailing one of your slaves to set fire to the mill?'

Mr Brierly had just gained some of his colour back but now his face was once again ashen.

'How dare you ask me such questions, I know nothing about this unfortunate happening!' he retaliated.

'That sir, is not good enough. We have heard in this very court how your overseer told one of your poor hands that he would be turned out in the cold if he refused to oil the cotton, so causing the fire that burned down your mill.'

'But I didn't have anything to do with it!' Mr Brierly exclaimed. 'Why would I set fire to my very livelihood, I ask you?'

'That is a question indeed,' said the lawyer. 'If we believe the 'hand' we will believe that you did it to recoup some of your losses from a poor year, using your insurance scheme.'

Mr Brierly fainted and fell to the ground. All was absolute confusion. The clerk of court ran to assist the afflicted man and one of the clerks of session appealed to the court to help.

It just happened that Mrs Murgatroyd was in the courtroom. She had been very interested in the case and felt that she wanted to know how John did, for Emma's sake. She came forward with her bag of first aid equipment and taking some feathers out of the case she proceeded to set fire to them under the patient's nose. Mr Brierly began to come round, coughing with the rank smell of the burning feathers.

'Get away from me woman,' he said in a bad-tempered way.

'Well, now I'll be glad to, once I know you're not going to faint again. I take no pleasure in being shouted at when I'm doing my best,' said the nurse.

Mr Brierly calmed down and had the grace to apologise to her.

'Right,' said Mr Pargitter, 'can we now continue with the trial?'

Mr Brierly was given a sip of water and he nodded his head in agreement that he was ready to continue.

'If you know nothing about this allegation about yourself, could you help us to shed any light on the situation? Do you in fact know any other who could have done this deed?'

A look of uncertainty had come over Mr Brierly's face but he finally rallied himself and spoke firmly.

'I am completely in the dark about this whole thing,' he said. 'Until you questioned me today, I had not thought it could have been anyone but John Blacklock who fired my mill, and I am still not convinced otherwise.'

'You may step down. I'll recall Bill Brierly.' Bill was brought back into court looking slightly less upset than he had the first time.

'Now Bill Brierly, remember you are still under oath. I want to ask you some more questions about the night the mill burnt down. Were you there when it happened?'

'No sir, I didn't set fire to the mill, I couldn't do it sir, not with all my friends in the garret, and my brother, as I thought. I went and hid from Tom Burly in the outhouse for I knew it would be safe there if he set the fire himself. Ben found me there and we had a good chinwag but we couldn't go back into the mill knowing what we knew.'

'Did Tom Burly give you any idea who was responsible for the order to fire the mill?'

'Objection!' (this from the prosecution). 'It has yet to be established that any order was given by a third party.'

'Overruled,' this from the judge.

'So,' said Mr Pargitter, 'when Tom Burly tried to blackmail you into firing the mill, did he tell you who had given the order that it should be done?'

'No sir. He said it were none o' my business, I were just a hand and not paid to think. But I ask you sir, if I'm found guilty will it be my hands that are hanged, no damn it, I'll be taken from this place and hung by the neck until I'm dead.'

This speech caused murmuring in the court, most agreeing with the witness, but the clerk of court had the last word.

'Silence or the court will be cleared!' he yelled.

'You may stand down, but we will have to get to the bottom of this,' said Mr Pargitter.

'May I approach the bench m'lord?' This being allowed the two lawyers approached the judge.

Mr Pargitter began, 'M'lord it is obvious that some double dealing has been going on with these mill folks, but how to get to the bottom of it I do not know. We are not here to solve this problem but to decide on the guilt or innocence of John Blacklock. And I am not sure how to proceed.'

The judge gave his opinion that the proceedings should go ahead in the trial of John Blacklock and that another court should try the case of the firing of the mill and the inquiry into the nefarious deeds of the mill owner. A small recess was granted to allow all involved to gather themselves and then the case could proceed.

Just as the lawyers were getting started again, a disturbance occurred at the back of the court. A banging could be heard on the solid oak door that had been barred to anyone not allowed in, to the proceedings.

The clerk of sessions went to find out the reason for the commotion and as he opened it, a small figure was propelled into the hall. She had been using her entire strength to try to open the door and when it was opened from inside, she almost flew into the place. Everyone was curious to know the cause of the disturbance.

But the Blacklock family gasped with one breath, the girl who had entered was no other than Clarice. She picked herself up from where she had fallen and stared in awe at her surroundings. The judge gained his composure and demanded to know the reason for the disturbance. The clerk of court tried to find out by whispering a series of questions to the newcomer.

'M'Lord,' he finally said, 'the young woman has some evidence that she says is vital to the progress of this case. She is in service at 'the big house' that is sir, the home of Mr Brierly, and she has come to report an incident that she feels will answer all questions about the fire in the mill. Will you hear her sir or is that part of the case closed for another sessions?'

'In light of the fact that she has already come a long way and anything that will help provide clarity of purpose in this complex case should be considered, I think we will hear her evidence now,' said the judge.

'Call the young woman into the witness box.'

'Very good M'lord. Call Clarice Blacklock.'

'What name did you use?' said the startled judge.

'Clarice Blacklock, M'lord for she is the sister of the accused.'

'Oh very well, I suppose we'd better hear her anyway but it's most unusual to bring in a family member as witness at this stage.'

Clarice climbed into the witness box, thankful that she was going to be heard after her long and difficult journey to get to the assizes. The butler had refused to give his permission for her to attend her brother's trial. So she had had to climb out the window the night before and make her difficult way to Buxton. She knew that once she had given her evidence, she wouldn't have a job but she couldn't think of that when her brother's life depended on what she knew. Mr Pargitter took the floor.

'Now Miss Clarice I don't know what evidence you can give so I'll ask you in your own words to tell us what you are doing here today and how you can move this trial forward?'

Sally and Maggie gaped as their little sister was applied to for information, for neither one of them considered her old enough to know what she was doing.

Clarice took a deep breath and began to speak, 'Well, sir, I am in service at the home of Mr Brierly and his family. I have worked with them for about five years. In that time, I've risen from maid of all work to a bedroom maid. I've also got to know the family although we are not supposed to repeat the things we hear in private. I've thought and thought about whether or not I should break my confidence with the family, even though it means keeping quiet when my own brother is accused of setting fire to the mill. You see I know he didn't do it, because I know who did.'

The courtroom was suddenly in an uproar.

'Silence in court!' called the clerk of sessions, but no one took the least bit of notice, so the judge had to add his voice to the confusion.

'If the noise does not abate instantly I will have to clear the court,' he bellowed, and finally the chatter stopped.

Sally and Maggie and Aunty Ann and Uncle George held their breaths as one person, as they did not wish to be excluded at this important moment.

'Well, young woman you'd better go on with your tale,' said the judge. 'We are already making history with this case, and it will have to be recorded in the annals of court procedure, for a more mixed up piece I have never come across.'

Clarice took another breath and the court was now hushed, taking its breath with hers.

'One day, a week before the fire, I was asked to clean the smoking room because the downstairs maid was ill. And in the process, I had got myself into the corner of the fireplace to attack some pesky cobwebs which wouldn't be removed. Just then the door opened and Mr Brierly came in with his nephew

174

Ned. They had come into the room for a smoke and I was nervous that they would see me because I was not supposed to be in the public rooms cleaning when the family needed to use them. I crouched down further in the corner between the chimney piece and the abutting wall and they continued to have a private conversation because they didn't know I was there. Ned said that they should do something to allay the cotton crisis and his uncle asked what he thought they should do.'

'What was his tone of voice as he made answer?' asked Mr Pargitter.

'Well, sir it was kind of sarcastic like, as though he thought Mr Ned was getting above himself.'

'So what happened next?' the barrister questioned.

'Mr Ned said he thought they should burn the mill and so gain the compensation given out by the authorities, and he said he knew just the man to do it. Mr Brierly was absolutely appalled, I thought he was going to have a stroke sir. He began to cough and choke and Mr Ned said he had only been joking, to calm him down like. But Mr Brierly didn't seem to think it was a joke sir. He used some shocking language which I won't repeat for ah'm a good girl sir, and have been brought up properly.'

'Did Mr Ned happen to mention the name of the person they might call on to fire the mill?'

'Oh yes sir, he said Tom Burly.'

Now the court should be emptied because none of the onlookers would be silenced. But how to do that was a task no one could manage. The onlookers left their seats and in one teeming mass they swarmed the front of the court-room, taking the clerks and lawyers with them until they reached John Blacklock and demanded that his shackles be unlocked so that once again he could be a free man. The judge raised his voice and somehow was able to command attention.

'If we do not attain some kind of order in this courtroom the case cannot be finished and the prisoner will once again be locked up!' he said.

That pronouncement led to a kind of half calm and the judge was able to proceed.

But what of John's thoughts in this about turn, with the evidence his sister had brought to bear on the case? His hopes had soared. He had begun this day with deep foreboding of it probably being his last, and now his little sister had braved everything to come to his rescue, and his feelings were reeling. He would have loved a drink of water but there was no way given for obtaining one. His family, as they observed, were equally in a kaleidoscope of mixed emotion.

Aunty Ann whispered to her husband, 'Oh George, tell me it's true, for I can't rightly believe our little Clarice has saved the day for our John.'

'It seems to be true but let's not hope too soon or we'll fall harder if the judge makes a different decision.'

Sally and Maggie had mixed emotions. Maggie felt that Clarice should have remembered her station but as Sally said, if she had, John might even now be facing his doom.

'And who's to say he isn't, for the judge has still to make his pronouncement on his verdict,' retorted Maggie.

This new evidence had caused consternation among the officials. The judge called the lawyers to approach his bench.

'I think we will have to have another recess,' he said, 'whilst Ned Brierly is brought to court. In fact he should be arrested.'

Edwin Robinson was surprised when the clerk of court approached him in the witness room. And as that worthy entered, all heads turned to watch him as they tried to ascertain this new occurrence. Emma and Mrs Blacklock especially were interested in the outcome. The clerk realised this and carefully escorted Sergeant Robinson outside before he spoke.

'New evidence has been brought up and we need you to arrest Ned Brierly,' he said.

'Ned Brierly? Why he's the nephew of the mill owner,' Robinson said.

'Yes, that's right, but you need to do it quickly before he gets wind of it and escapes before we've had time to question him.'

'I need to have some idea of what he's being charged with before I can arrest him,' said Robinson, reasonably.

'Well, you'd better come in and speak to his lordship but make it snappy he's waiting for you.'

The court was still full, given the new evidence the judge had deemed it imprudent to allow the onlookers to leave before the new witness had been apprehended.

As Sergeant Robinson approached the bench, the judge spoke to him quickly.

'We need to arrest Ned Brierly on a charge of conspiracy, as quickly as you can before he hears the way the trial has gone today.'

'Yes sir, I'll be on to it now,' and so saying, he turned on his heel and left the court.

Emma was waiting to hear what was going on, but she suddenly heard loud cheering from the other court-room. She moved quickly to the door to see what had happened. A man leaving told her that the trial of Susie's slayer was over and that Charles Peace had been found guilty of murder and sentenced to death by hanging.

Emma felt sick. She had known what the outcome would be, but she still felt sorry for a fellow human being and dreaded hearing the same ending in John's trial. She went back into the waiting room, feeling Mrs Blacklock's eyes on her all the time. She sat quietly by the other woman's side and reassured her that so far all was well with John and the noise was from the other court.

…

Ned Brierly was sitting quietly in the smoking room, making use of that place to enjoy an expensive cigar. His uncle wouldn't be in for some time, for Ned knew that that gentleman had been called as a witness in the trial of the miner who was accused of burning down the mill. He was feeling somewhat bored. Never in his most dismal dreams did he imagine that his life would have taken on the drudgery that it had. Whilst he had been up at Oxford it had been one long round of parties and routes, but since returning to the North his social life had ebbed somewhat.

His uncle, who had once been generous to a fault, had become something of a skin-flint and his usual cheerful countenance had recently taken on a pinched expression that comes in later life. He appeared to have the woes of the world resting on his face. Ned felt he could have cheered him up if only the older man had listened to him. The outcome had been a bit of a shambles, but at least it had all turned out to the mill owner's advantage if he could only have seen it that way.

Now it was too late, the mill had gone, but at least there'd be handsome compensation. Ned was uncertain what line to take with his uncle. Should he admit his part in the firing of the mill or leave it to the scapegoat they'd found? As he sat in his own reverie, he heard the clanging of the doorbell. Then it went again. Why didn't the servants answer it? He wondered. Finally he heard footsteps approaching and one of the footmen entered, ushering in two men who could only have been law officers.

'Mr Plods,' thought Ned rudely, but he was sensible enough to hold his tongue.

The larger of the two spoke, 'Are you Ned Brierly?'

As he'd just been addressed as Mr Ned by the footman, he saw no point in denying this fact, so spoke up in the affirmative.

'I'd like you to come along with me to the assize court sir if you'd be so kind,' said the larger policeman.

'Whatever for?' Ned retaliated.

'We'd like you to answer some questions regarding the firing of Cressbrook mill,' said Sergeant Robinson.

'That's preposterous!' Ned blustered. 'And what if I refuse?'

'I was hoping to save you this route sir, but if you refuse, I will arrest you on a charge of conspiracy to cause wilful damage and possibly a greater one of murder.'

Ned went white and grabbed for his smouldering cigar. Taking a deep drag into the comfort of his tobacco, he calmed himself somewhat and agreed to accompany the constable and the sergeant on their business. It would have been hard for the two men of law to ascertain how fast his brain was moving through the expression of those reptilian eyes. Ned was playing a waiting game and realised that he must not let anyone know how his heart was beating in this unexpected turn of events.

The carriage bowled along the dark country lanes, no stars lighting their way as they made good speed to Buxton. Ned knew that Burly had died and decided it would be expedient to pin the fire on him rather than on John Blacklock who it seemed had some kind of defence or why would he himself have been arrested? His half-closed eyes took in everything that was happening with his two companions. They were sitting opposite to him and he missed nothing. He wondered what kind of a case they had against him. He was sure his uncle would find him a good lawyer, for he wouldn't want the shame of one of his family being found guilty in a criminal court of law.

As they drew up to the Assize court, for a fleeting minute Ned wondered whether to make a run for it, but decided this was imprudent if he was planning to plead his innocence and wrongful arrest.

The three figures walked into the packed court. Three very different men indeed. The one young, seemingly calm and obviously affluent, the other two officers of the law one middle aged and overweight, the other much younger but shabby and unkempt. A whisper could be heard from all the onlookers. It was a time when looks mattered a great deal and no one observing what was taking place would have convicted one who looked as smart as Mr Ned.

Luckily for John Blacklock, Mr Pargitter wasn't interested in how things looked. He was only concerned with the truth of a situation and he was determined to get to the bottom of this one.

Ned was sworn in and requested that he have a private lawyer. This was not the way Mr Pargitter or the judge saw it. They had seen other well healed prisoners slide away from justice because they were rich, but any prisoner was entitled to a fair trial. Ned Brierly was called as a witness, in the trial of John Blacklock and was not on trial himself, so Mr Pargitter was careful in his manner of questioning and treatment. It would not do to antagonise the mill owner's nephew just yet. So the preliminary questions were asked and Ned admitted to his name, place of abode and work-place, also his relationship to Mr Brierly.

'Now Mr Ned Brierly, could you tell the court your connection with the mill? We have heard that you have some kind of part to play in the mercantile process but we need to have an understanding of what you do there on a day to day basis.'

'Since coming down from Oxford where I gained a first,' he drawled, 'I am now one of the under managers in my uncle's mill.'

'And what does that involve?' said Mr Pargitter thinking in his mind what a twit, born with a silver spoon in his mouth.

'I am part of a very large mercantile process that organises and arranges for purchase and delivery of raw cotton to be delivered to the mill so as to continue the production of superior material,' said Ned.

'And what has been your place since the burning of the mill?' Mr Pargitter questioned.

'There has been little to do since that event,' Ned Brierly returned briskly.

'Just so, just so,' said the lawyer. 'Have you then had more time on your hands to enjoy your unexpected holiday?'

'I don't know what you think you are getting at. If you must know, the fire has incommoded me a vast deal. It is my job to deal with all our suppliers who have been inconvenienced, and also with the representatives of the board of compensation,' said Ned.

'Compensation you say. I suppose you'll be getting a tidy sum?' said Mr Pargitter.

'We are not sure yet, all losses have to be taken into consideration before a final figure can be ascertained,' said Ned.

'Tell me,' said Mr Pargitter, 'will you have more compensation this year than if the same thing had happened say two or three years ago?'

'No,' Ned replied, 'we are only compensated for the goods we own.'

'Has this then been a lean year in the mill?' enquired the lawyer.

'All business, not just the cotton industry, has been lean these last few years because of the wars that have been raging overseas.'

'I see, no more questions for the moment. You may step down, but don't go anywhere, I may want to call you back. I think I'll call John Blacklock again.'

John moved into the witness box once more. He was beginning to wonder where this would end, but his thoughts were a bit brighter. Mr Pargitter must have some ideas if he'd called Mr Ned.

Outside the courtroom, Emma was surprised when Mr Ned appeared in the doorway of the witness room, she couldn't begin to understand how he had become a witness for the defence. He eyed his companions warily and sat down as far away from them as he could.

Meanwhile in the courtroom Mr Pargitter resumed his questioning of John.

'Now Mr Blacklock can you cast your mind back once more to the point in the evening when you and a group of men bashed your way into the mill using a small tree as a weapon?'

'Yes sir,' said John. 'We were about five men and it was difficult to break the door, it being a very stout one, but we managed it at last.'

'And when you reached the inside of the mill, would you tell us again what you saw.'

'We had not broken into the part of the mill where the production of cotton takes place. We had gained access through the main gate and front door. It is where the business affairs are transacted and where the main stair-case leads to the upper floor, which in turn leads to the garret where the slaves are housed. At this point, although the fire started in the mill proper, smoke was already seeping into the main room and it was difficult to see. I saw a man creeping stealthily through the door from the mill and into the main lobby where I was standing. I ran to him, and discovering that it was Tom Burly, I held on to his arm and asked him for the keys to the garret room so that I could rescue the workers. He wrenched himself free and ran off up the stairs with me following quickly. I knew that Emma was locked in and I couldn't understand why he was being so obstinate.'

'So what happened when you caught up to him?'

'We struggled and finally I hit him on the chin and the keys fell out of his pocket as he fell down the stairs,' said John.

'Did you try to help him in any way?' the lawyer asked.

'No sir, the smoke was becoming too dense and I could hardly see him. I knew I only had a small opportunity to help the garret sleepers and I thought that Burly could help himself.'

'Where were the other men who had broken in with you?'

'They caught up with me as I made for the upstairs and we formed a human chain to help the injured of whom there were a few.'

'Did you see Tom Burly after that?'

'Not until the firemen had arrived and carried him out of the burning building and lay him down on the ground next to Emma.'

'Now tell me John, this is very important, did you mean to kill Tom Burly?'

'No sir, I wouldn't harm anyone intentionally, but there were extenuating circumstances and I was only thinking of saving the souls in the garret.'

'Thank you, you may stand down again.'

At this point the judge called the lawyers to approach the bench.

'I think we've heard enough evidence,' he said. 'This has been an exceedingly long trial. We'll have the summing up now. Mr Pargitter you will go first as defence attorney.'

Mr Pargitter recounted the evidence paying special attention to John's heroism in saving many people from a fiery death, which had been started by vandalism of the worst kind. He skirted over the fact of who had set the fire because that was a case for another trial he felt. He concentrated on John's action in the injury of Tom Burly expressing his belief that the defendant had acted out of chivalry and not malice aforethought when he struck the obstacle to saving the prisoners in the garret. He closed by saying that he felt a miscarriage of justice had been played out in imprisoning John Blacklock in the first place and hoped that it would be put right with the decision of a wise jury.

The prosecution could have been biased against John but chose to show his leniency. Little Clarice had done her bit in bringing truth to the situation and another day would tell of the trial of Ned Brierly.

The jury huddled together discussing the case and soon announced their verdict of not guilty in the case of firing the mill. But they advised an open verdict in the death of Tom Burly.

John, they said, should be released, but bound over to keep the peace.

The courtroom went wild. Soon it would be difficult for John to effect his escape. Everyone within distance of the prisoner's box wanted to shake his hand. His family who were present in the courtroom tried to push their way through to him. It was well-nigh impossible. Mr Pargitter and the clerk of sessions came to his assistance, and two other clerks of the court helped them to get John safely away to the third witness room, where his family were finally able to show their joy in what had transpired.

Uncle George pumped John's hand, not able to find words to express his emotions. Mrs Blacklock fell on his neck weeping unrestrainedly. His sisters wanted their moment of glory with the hero of the day and it was no use that John wished to have a quiet moment with Emma; they were all talking at once.

But of course the one who had won the day was little Clarice and John took her into his arms lovingly. She had always been his favourite sister and now he had reason to show her his affection without any of the others grudging her the attention.

Finally John espied Emma standing quietly at the back of the room. Just like her, thought John, not wanting to push in ahead of his family and he vowed that she should have her rightful place by his side as soon as he could arrange it.

He gently put Clarice aside and striding over to Emma, he took her into his arms and lovingly at first then building in passion he kissed her deeply on the lips so that none present could mistake the relationship between them.

All was quiet now except for Sally's hissed comment to her sister.

'He could have waited until he's at home,' but for once Maggie showed her disagreement by remaining silent.

'Well, this has been an emotional day!' said Uncle George.

And Aunty Ann agreed, saying to everyone, 'Let's get out of here if we can, and make our way home.'

As they sat in the little cottage that night drinking cocoa, they were all very quiet, each alone with their thoughts. It had been a terribly trying time and each of them had to get over it in his or her own way. Uncle George finally broke the silence wondering what the repercussions would be of John's open verdict.

'Mr Pargitter explained that it will mean nothing so long as I keep the peace,' said John. 'And I don't need to be reminded of that for I hope I never see the inside of one of those places again as long as I live.'

He and Emma were sitting together on the settle in front of a bright fire, his arm around her shoulders as if he would never let go of her. Clarice sat on the little cricket next to them. Her thoughts were pensive, her body weary for she hadn't slept for twenty-four hours. But though her eyes were heavy she couldn't think of sleep yet, her thoughts were too charged, wondering what the future would hold for her. Her bravery had paid off for her brother but what of her future?

Matt spoke up, realising that though this day was almost over, they would have to make plans for the morrow.

'So lad what do you plan to do now?' he said.

'I suppose I should get back to work as soon as I can,' John replied.

'But surely you'll not go tomorrow?' said his mother. 'You need to have at least twenty-four hours rest.'

'I'll go with Matt tomorrow just to see the foreman and I'll make plans to start the next available shift. We can't be nice about this mother, for we're all needing some brass after these weeks inside.' Matt agreed with him, but wanted to know what Emma would do.

'I was there at the trial of the murderer of Susie and though I can't think of anything worse than seeing a man hang, however bad he's been, I want to be there tomorrow for Susie's sake,' she answered.

No one else wanted to see any more of the law but Aunty Ann didn't feel that Emma should go to such a terrible place by herself so she offered to go with her.

'Well, I can't say I wouldn't be delighted to have company so if you're sure, I would love you to go with me,' said Emma.

John took Emma into his arms lovingly and gazed worriedly into her eyes. 'Are you sure you'll be alright love? I don't want you to be disturbed again after the time you've gone through.'

'I'll be alright John especially now that Aunty Ann is going with me,' Emma replied.

John kissed her gently on her full lips, delighting in their union. On these plans for the morrow the impromptu celebration party broke up and Uncle George promised to bring his wife over the next day early.

Chapter Twenty-One
The Hanging of Charles Peace

It was a bright unseasonably warm morning in November and the excitement in the air was tangible. All the people from around the area had set off early in the morning so as not to miss any of the excitement. Charles Peace, the notorious murderer, had been found guilty and was sentenced to be hanged on the tree outside the village that very day. As the droves of people hurried along not wishing to be late, others tried to enhance their meagre wages by selling their wares to the passers-by at the side of the road. Cries from the vendors could be heard, 'Sweet silk violets come and buy.'

'Pots and pans for sale or trade!'

'Will you buy my pies and pasties? Chestnuts hot.'

'It seems that the whole world has something to sell,' said Aunty Ann, 'and the day is turning into one of fun, food and frolic. Just listen to that cheeky trollop.'

'Hey mister would you like to come with me for a good time?'

'Good time indeed I'd like to give her a good smack I would and all,' said Ann.

But what of the man who waited in gloom for his death? He had been caught, and tried, for committing four murders. He'd thought he was helping them, but society had decided otherwise, and now he must pay the price. He knew he wasn't a bad man but he'd lost his way. Life had been hard on him. Both of his parents died when he was a young boy, through cholera or some such disease of the poor. He was lucky to survive, he'd been told by the authorities who'd taken him in.

Into the work house. He'd have been better left on the streets he thought, to make his way as best he could. He was forgetting in his befuddled state that he'd been less than five years old. He would probably have died. He was chosen as a soldier at sixteen and fought all over. Now he was to meet his maker and maybe the wife and child he'd lost while he was fighting for queen and country. He heard the noise outside his cell and wondered what it was. In his wildest dreams, he wouldn't have thought they'd all come to see him and if he had he would have wept a little, wishing someone had shown the same interest in his life before he went astray.

If one person had cared enough to protect him from the evil within, he would not, he thought, have come to this sorry pass. But no one had cared and now here he was facing the ultimate penalty. People are fickle and they wanted their pound of flesh, they were not to be done out of the spectacle of his cruel death by any do-gooders.

The crowd moved on, a mass of humanity bent on enjoyment. Perhaps the pleasure was that of experiencing pain second hand and maybe in so doing they could expunge their own iniquities, or perhaps get a sense of thrill from the horror about to be inflicted upon another human being.

The self-righteous believed they were doing God's will in destroying one who had destroyed. They made up a small quantity of people whose prayers and incense murmured on the toxic air.

The first villagers were approaching the tree by the gibbeting rock where the prisoner would be brought a little later. The first to arrive jostled for places wanting to be at the front of the circle so as to have a best view. Others arrived and took their places a pattern being drawn as each circle added to the previous one. Within an hour the place was so dense that scuffles began to break out and orderliness was a thing of the past.

'Hey you pushed me and now I've dropped me chestnuts.'

'Get over it then, what do you expect in this crush?'

'I expect you to show some manners you oaf.'

'Who are you calling an oaf?' And he dealt a sharp fist to the other's nose.

Not to be outdone, the first to be assaulted retaliated with a sharp right to the other's ear.

'You've rendered me deaf!' called his assailant and jumping on his back he brought the other down in the mud.

People scattered in all directions, in their turn causing other conflicts, and soon a wholesale riot had broken out in the orderly circles. At this point John Law's whistle blasted out and the villagers tried to look their innocence not wanting to be arrested and so miss the spectacle.

Emma and Ann were standing quietly some distance away. Emma abhorred violence in all its forms. But she was here to pay a last tribute to her friend by seeing with her own eyes the end of one who had destroyed the life of Susie, her dearest friend.

'Have you been able to discover the whole story of Susie's murder?' asked Aunty Ann.

'No, I've read a pamphlet on the subject but the facts were very scanty, and I'm hoping that maybe we'll learn more today. I don't know why I should think that but it's my last chance of finding out what happened to my friend.'

It was approaching 11-o'clock and the jailers were dragging a man forward as the crowd jeered and taunted him. The prisoner was to be exhibited to all in the gibbeting cage which swung from the tree. The felon was stripped of his clothes down to his loin-cloth and forced into the swinging cage, there to be poked and prodded by the feral crowd. Fathers lifted their little children up for a better view of a poor creature who had deviated from the path of righteousness thus teaching them an early lesson on the sins of the world. They were encouraged to throw rotting vegetable matter at the more sensitive parts of the man's anatomy, there to inflict the most discomfort as fetid matter ran into his eyes and mouth. Although he kept, silent it was obviously becoming more and more difficult for him to maintain this state, Emma noticed.

She could stand this wanton cruelty no longer and she moved away from the gibbet, linking arms with Aunty Ann, she moved the other woman backwards. As they did so, however, Emma tripped on a stone and would have fallen had not a veiled woman caught her into her arms. There was something familiar about the woman and her headgear and veil and Emma realised it was similar to the clothes often worn by Aunt Peg when she visited Aunty Ann or Mrs Blacklock. The young woman was watching Emma intently as though she was trying to make a decision.

'Let's move on Emma, it's not safe to be here,' said Aunty Ann.

But just then her decision seeming to be made, the strange woman lifted a corner of her veil and to Emma's complete stupefaction, she unveiled the face of the dead woman, her dearest friend Susie. It was too much for Emma after the weeks of torment she had already suffered, and she dropped to the ground in a dead faint.

She came around suddenly with the strong smelling salts getting up her nose. This caused her to cough violently and open her eyes. And she was left gazing into the deep green eyes of her dead friend. Slowly gaining full consciousness, she sat up and gathered Susie into her arms laughing and crying at the same time.

'Oh, I thought I'd never see you again. Where have you been and how did you come back to life when you were dead? You were murdered by this very man who sits in the gibbeting cage.'

'It's a long story,' said Susie, 'but quickly we must get away before I'm recognised.'

At this point Aunty Ann spoke up.

'Emma are you going to introduce me and tell me what's going on?'

Emma briefly shared her scant knowledge that this was indeed Susie who she'd thought was dead.

'But if Susie is alive, he isn't a murderer and he should be set free!' said Aunty Ann gesturing at the gibbet as she spoke.

'I'm not the only one he's killed,' said Susie. 'I changed places with another girl and she's the one who's dead along with three others. Now quickly let's get out of here before I'm recognised or I'll be caught and taken back. Oh by the way this is my friend Margaret, she's been helping me and even lent me her hat and veil for today so that I wouldn't be recognised.'

Emma turned to say hello and realised that underneath the hat with the oversized bunch of bobbing cherries, she was looking into the smiling face of Aunt Peg.

'Well, my goodness this is a turn up for the books! Our Peg as I live and breathe,' said Aunty Ann hugging the short woman as she spoke.

'How do you fit into all this?'

But Susie was obviously fidgety and would say no more until they'd moved away from the crowd. Unfortunately as they made to move away they were seen by someone who knew Emma. It was none other than that gossip Jessie Burns. She was there to glean all she could about the day, and seeing Emma she swooped upon her wanting to share memories and learn all the gossip.

'Well, this is a surprise,' she began, 'I'd heard tell how you'd got brain fever after the fire and weren't expected to live. I was surprised to see you in court t'other day and I ses to misel' she must of got over it like.'

'I was ill for a long time,' Emma replied, 'but I'm better again now.'

'An what about your boyfriend then? Do you think he'll swing for killing Mr Burly?'

Emma couldn't believe her ears, even from Jessie Burns this was totally unbelievable.

'I knew no good would come of you sneaking out to the coal bunker to meet him and now both of you are in a right pickle.'

'Excuse me, I must get on,' Emma said, trying to get past the other woman. She'd suspected Jess Burns had known more about her story than she would have liked but was shocked to hear her admission that she'd known all of it. Emma needed to get rid of her so she asked the other girl where she was staying. Jess was not happy to divulge her whereabouts but said she'd be in touch and so saying moved away from the group. Emma was pleased that she hadn't seemed to be suspicious of Susie and that she'd gone quickly.

But Emma had not reckoned with Jess's nosey slyness and would have been aghast if she'd seen Jess making her way to one of the guards of the convicted prisoner. She tugged on his sleeve, trying to get his attention.

'See here!' she shouted above the din, 'I've just seen one of the murdered girls. She's in disguise, it's true, but I'd swear it's her as sure as eggs is eggs.'

'Just a minute Miss, I've got enough to do here without looking for disguised girls. You go across the road and find one of the other policemen who are doing nothing,' he said. 'They'll just be sheltering in the copse in case of trouble.'

Jess swore, thinking her news worthy of more excitement. She would get some interest, she declared to herself and made her way over to the copse. There, sure enough she found two constables waiting for trouble and she once again told her story of the missing girl's reappearance. They could not ignore the information and one of them went with the triumphant woman to discover the truth of the matter.

Emma and her friends were moving away from the revellers and didn't notice Jess heading them off with the law in tow, until she suddenly appeared in front of Emma.

'What's all this?' the policeman asked. 'This woman has been telling me that one of you disguised women is the murdered mill girl. What have you got to say for yourself?'

Susie stopped dead in shock and the other two women stepped in front of her as Aunt Peg loped off along the diagonal country lane which today was congested with people still arriving to see the spectacle. Susie had come to her senses and putting on a drawl reminiscent of the circus people, she answered the policeman quickly.

'I dunno wha' she means guvnor, I ain't no ghost and I'm not in disguise, I be a flesh and blood circus performer.'

'I'm sorry you've been troubled,' said the law, 'but I wonder if you'd mind removing your veil so that we can see your face.'

Susie was reluctant but she was wearing heavy theatrical make-up and hoped that it would suffice to hide her true identity from Jessie Burns. She coquettishly lifted her veil staring slyly at Jess and daring the other woman to give her away. Jess gazed on the face of the other woman and wondered if she'd made a mistake. This woman resembled Susie in so many ways but in others was so different that she felt unsure. At this point Emma spoke up, 'This is my friend Mary and I'm sure I would know the difference. Besides, I do know this other woman, she's Jessie Burns, and I've worked with her for many years. She's always been known as a gossip and a liar.'

Jess had gone white. No one had ever spoken to her so bluntly before. Truth to tell, the mill folks had always been a bit afraid of her tongue. Now the mill was burned down however, there was nothing to be afraid of anymore. There were no overseers and Emma was at liberty to expose the cantankerous woman for what she was.

The constable didn't know what to do but in view of the busy day, he warned the women to keep the peace and moved back to his place of vigilance.

Emma turned on her heel and dragged 'Mary' out of Jess Burns' earshot. She was casting daggers at them out of her eyes but realised that she could do nothing else without proof as she wasn't sure of her own knowledge. The three women hurried after Aunt Peg.

'We'd better find somewhere to hide,' said Emma. 'You know what Jess Burns is like for poking her nose into things that don't concern her. I was appalled to see that she was a witness for the prosecution in John's trial. I don't know what she had to do with the whole case.'

'I'm sorry, I don't know what you're referring to,' said Susie.

'Oh of course I'm sorry, you probably don't know about the mill being burnt down, and John Blacklock being tried for doing it along with killing Tom Burly. But yesterday was a happy day after months of misery because John was found not guilty and allowed to go home. We have so much to catch up on, I don't even know where you've been hiding yourself!'

Susie had heard about the firing of the mill but she hadn't heard about John's court case.

'We'll talk when it's safe, but for the minute we'd better catch up with Peg and make ourselves scarce,' said Susie. They hadn't far to go.

Aunt Peg couldn't keep up much pace so they soon saw her in the distance and putting on a bit of a spurt they quickly caught up with her. They had much to talk about and Aunty Ann invited them to go home with her to the farm, which was not far away and would give them the safety they needed.

Chapter Twenty-Two
A Visit to Foolo

Uncle George was pleased and surprised to see all of them. 'How'd it go?' he wanted to know.

'As to that,' Emma told him, 'we were not able to see the end of him thank God. I could not have seen a fellow human being put to death however bad he'd been.'

'Not even when he killed your friend?' uncle George re-joined.

'Well,' said Emma, 'he didn't exactly kill my friend for here she is.'

And laughing and crying at the same time, Emma removed Susie's veil for her and displayed her playful face.

'Well, I never?' said Uncle George. 'And what are you doing in this story, our Peg, for now I see it's you standing in the shadow?' Aunt Peg came forward and pecked her cousin on the cheek.

'You'd never believe the last few weeks,' she said, 'even if I told you about them, but one thing I must impress on you is not to tell anyone yet of Susie being alive.'

'Well, come away in and we'll have a nice pot o' tea and 'appen a plate of ham and eggs.'

As the kettle sang on the hob and Uncle George toasted strips of ham on a toasting fork, Aunt Peg began her tale of life in the circus. She even went as far as telling her cousins of the sideshow she was attached to, and her sobriquet of Bear lady.

'Well, I never!' Aunt Ann said, breaking eggs into a pan on the fire. 'And how do you fit into all this?' she asked Susie.

'Mine is a long story,' Susie began. 'It starts many years ago when Emma and I were kidnapped from somewhere in the south and sailed along the canal system, to be sold into slavery in the mills of the north. The one in question being Cressbrook mill.'

'Emma, I didn't know you were kidnapped!' said Aunty Ann in a shocked tone.

'I haven't really spoke of it much, I don't see what good it will do now,' said Emma lightly.

'Well, I understand 'ow you feel,' said Aunty Ann. 'Why don't you set the table,' she added, to change the subject.

Not to be silenced, Susie spoke up again. 'But we should speak of it, we weren't born to be mill slaves, and we'd be in a different level of society if it hadn't been for those evil people taking us as infants.

'After I escaped from the mill, I spent three days in the open, living in a sheep bier. Later I was lucky enough to be picked up by a circus and that's where I met Peg. Then I had to escape from the circus because I'd impersonated the knife thrower's assistant, and when she didn't come back, he kept me prisoner so's he didn't lose me as well.'

'My goodness you have had an eventful life since Emma last saw you,' said Aunt Ann.

'And I suppose you don't want anyone to know where you are in case the knife thrower finds you again?'

'That's exactly right.'

'So was the girl who was murdered the one you were impersonating?' said Uncle George.

'Yes, the very one. She'd noticed how alike we were and that's how I became involved,' Susie answered him.

'You've had an exciting life since you left the mill, but so has Emma let's all sit down and she can tell you whilst we're eating,' said Aunty Ann.

'What's that?' said Susie taking her place at the table. For a couple of hours Emma hadn't thought of John, she remembered in shame, but now she was as eager to tell of the court case as the other women were to hear it. And with Ann adding her bits to the tale Emma began to recount her story as they all tucked in to the good food and ate hungrily. When she spoke of the search for her friend Susie added her part to the tale:

'I saw you looking for me from my place with the sheep.'

She said quietly. Emma blinked back tears remembering her grief in the loss of her friend, but she understood Susie's need to escape so she said nothing but laid her cutlery down, for it would have choked her to eat for a few minutes. It was after all Susie's courageous move that had led to Emma's own life reaching fulfilment. Emma continued her story about the fire, Tom Burly's death and the trial, ending with her love for John and their agreement.

'Well, that's wonderful news, you've not let the grass grow under your feet either,' said Susie laughingly.

'So where is John now?'

'He went to the mine with Matt to arrange their return to work,' Emma answered.

Susie went very quiet. She didn't want any questions about her future and she hadn't thought about Matt for a long time. She'd been living a completely different life for the past year and though it was lovely to see her old friend again, she knew she couldn't slip back into what she had been. The circus had shown her a new kind of freedom that she hadn't realised existed for someone in her sphere of society, and she regretted deeply her decision to stand in for Melinda. For if she'd refused, she would be her own free spirit and maybe Melinda would still be alive.

'You're very quiet,' said Aunt Peg. 'This is obviously a very happy day for my cousins and we shouldn't spoil it for them by thinking of our own troubles.'

'You're right,' Susie responded, 'and I wasn't unhappy, just thoughtful, for I have to decide where I am to live now that the circus isn't an option.'

'Is there no-one in the circus who could help you?' asked Aunt Ann. 'I'm sure you could tell her, Peg, for you've spent most of your adult life there and must have some ideas.'

'Ann you must think that I have some clout with the owners, which couldn't be further from the truth. I may have been there for a long time as an entertainer, but we're nothing, especially women who are as misshapen as me. And there you have it! Susie herself is likely to have more importance in a male world.'

'But only if I was willing to sell myself, and that isn't going to happen! I've escaped twice from ruthless men and I have a bit more gumption now, so I'm certainly not going to let it happen again. I was not born into this servitude and I'll not live in it one moment longer,' Susie answered.

'That's easy to say Susie, but where will you go and what will you do?' Emma showed her concern.

'If Aunty Ann would be kind enough to put me up for a while, I'll think of something, never fear,' said Susie. Emma was embarrassed that Susie should expect a perfect stranger to house and feed her but the new Susie didn't seem to find it cheeky. Aunt Peg also seemed to promote the idea.

'Well, that's settled then,' said Uncle George, 'but you'll 'appen 'elp our Ann, for she's a deal to do of a day?'

This being arranged Susie seemed quite happy with her new lot in life and Emma thought it was time to take her leave and get back to Mrs Blacklock and John. It was hard to leave her friend just as she'd found her again, but as Aunty Ann said, she'd be able to visit her regularly now she was staying at the farm.

After Susie had impressed upon her friend once again that no one must know of her return to life, not even John or Matt, the girls said a fond goodnight.

Chapter Twenty-Three
Plans to Be Made

Emma arrived back as Matt returned from his shift at the pit.

'How'd it go?' she asked him.

'Well, alright I suppose. They want our John back next week but there's been some complaints.'

'How can that be when he was found not guilty?'

'It seems gossip has gone there ahead of him and some of the miners are saying they won't work with a hot head. The overseer has decided to give it a try and see how things go.'

'Well, I can't see how people can be so bad. They must know how hard it's been for him and all of us and how he needs to get back to normal life now it's all over.'

'Well, lass, people only think of themselves in bad times and our John is a good fast worker and makes some of the skivers look weak. But how did things turn out at the hanging?'

Emma swallowed. Her conscience smote her as she answered him, 'I can't rightly talk of it, Matt. I couldn't watch a man put to death, however evil he is, so I didn't stay to the end.'

'Ay, I understand,' said Matt quietly.

Oh, how guilty she felt not telling him that Susie was alive. They both went into the cottage and were greeted with smiles. John stood up to embrace Emma and Mrs Blacklock bustled around getting them some tea. How lovely and warm the atmosphere was, thought Emma, even without a fire. How very lucky she was to be a small part of this family.

Clarice moved towards her and took her hand.

'We haven't had time to talk much, but I want you to know how glad I am that you're going to be my sister,' she said simply.

Tears glistened in Emma's eyes at this token of love from John's youngest sister and she spoke up through them, 'I will never forget what you did for him and me yesterday. It was a true act of sacrifice to speak truth whatever the cost, and I'll never forget it.'

'Here, here!' said John. 'But talking of never, we should think about the future. Has Matt told you I might be out of a job soon?'

'He mentioned it but it's early days yet. However, I should be thinking of getting some work. I can't expect you to keep me any longer now that I'm well, and perhaps I could get work at the pit in the cook shop. I know they want women in there and I've done a bit since your mother taught me for the soup kitchen. What do you think?'

They all thought it was a good idea to try, so Emma decided to walk with the brothers when they both went to the pit the next week. 'And what about Clarice?' asked Sally, peevishly.

'She needs work too now she's walked out of the big house.'

'She'll get something in time, and meanwhile she can help me with the soup kitchen,' said her mother. 'Rome wasn't built in a day as the saying goes.'

Sally sulked, but John was delighted to hear the change in his mother's attitude. He could hardly believe it but of course he'd been in prison a long time and had not been party to her gradual change. He welcomed it with an open heart.

'But we've never asked you how the day went Emma, was it dreadful?' asked Mrs Blacklock.

Matt answered for her.

'She doesn't want to talk of it,' he said.

'I will tell you about it some time when I've had chance to arrange my thoughts, but not just yet,' Emma replied.

'Ay, yes I understand,' said the kind woman, 'it must have been an ordeal after yesterday.

Emma bowed her head. None of them knew just how difficult it was for her to speak of yesterday and her mind was still in a turmoil. She felt such guilt not telling them of Susie's reincarnation but how could she give her friend away when she was in danger from the knife thrower.

She also suspected that Matt would be all for rushing to Foolo and declaring his love, and if Susie had wanted him, she would not have run away or at least she would have sent him a message by Emma. Emma knew she had to save him from the hurdy-gurdy of his own emotions for a little time at least.

The plans they'd made that night were put into practice and Emma was taken on to work in the canteen and Clarice took her place helping in the soup kitchen.

Both of the girls enjoyed their new jobs. Emma especially liked working in the canteen. She felt such pleasure in rising early and walking with the two men to the coal mine in Miller's Dale. It was heavy work but nothing like the cotton mill, with all the anxiety it entailed.

Nothing gave her greater joy than to share her pay packet with the rest of the family each weekend. She now felt truly one of them and it gave her great satisfaction. She also felt satisfied that Susie had settled down with Aunty Ann and Uncle George. Emma had had her original misgivings when Susie seemed to be pushing herself into the family at the farm but as they learned her worth, Emma realised it was a good fit for all of them. The circus had given her experience with animals and she was able to use this ability on the farm. One day as she finished slopping out the pigs, she became aware that she was being watched and as she turned her eye caught on her old friend Margaret.

'It's lovely to see you,' Susie said, 'but what brings you here mid-week? I hope nothing's wrong.'

'No nothing's wrong exactly, but the circus has nowhere to go and the ones of us who have no animals to feed have been given a few days off.'

'Well, come away in, do!' said Susie. Aunt Peg was quick to see the proprietary way Susie treated the farm house. This was good and bad, she thought. As they sat drinking tea, Aunt Peg brought up the reason she had come to visit. 'Not that I need a reason for I know that I'm always welcome,' she said.

'You are an all,' Uncle George agreed, 'but what can we do for you extra?'

'Well, it's like this, the circus has nowhere to go for a time. The people are jumpy because of the murder and it's no use telling them that he's caught and hanged and they can get on with their lives for they won't believe it. They're very superstitious. So knowing that I have family with farm land, the circus master asked me if I'd come and ask you if they can park on your land for a while until we get it together again?'

Uncle George sat on the settle thoughtfully stuffing tobacco into the bowl of his pipe.

'Well, Ann, what do you think?' he asked his wife.

'I don't know. It will make a lot of mess having all those animals around, and what about Susie and the knife thrower?'

Susie had been listening in to the conversation in surprise and fear and she was glad that Aunty Ann was also thinking about her problem with Marcello.

'How'd it be if I was to have a word with the professor?' said Aunt Peg.

'What could you say that would make it all right with the knife thrower?' her cousin answered.

'Susie's told us what a mean man he is and he's not likely to listen to anyone in authority. He thinks he's the bee's knees because he's daring and tough.'

'The point is he might be daring but Professor Richards is an educated man and doesn't need bluff to assert his authority.'

'We could always give it a try,' spoke up Uncle George.

Susie was of mixed feelings. She would like to have her enforced seclusion finished but she was also afraid that once her story was out in the open, she wouldn't have anywhere to hide from the wrath of Marcello.

'I'd be very discreet,' said Aunt Peg, 'and I'll have to find out if the professor is back at the circus again. I know he's been absent for some time.'

They all decided that it was a good plan, though on Susie's part, somewhat reluctantly, and Aunt Peg was able to return to the circus with good news.

Chapter Twenty-Four
The Circus Moves In

A few days later the cavalcade arrived at Foolo farm, and Aunty Ann watching out for them was amazed at the colourful spectacle they presented.

'Ee look at all them carriages and caravans. Whatever have we done George?'

'Oh don' na fush thy sel' woman, it'll be a nice change to farm work and they're paying us well for rent,' said her optimistic spouse.

The circus was very interesting Ann found as they settled in their carts and a few animals. She took a walk into the North meadow and watched as the bevy of unusual people heaved to and between them erected the big tent form the centre of the little community. It was all so colourful and gay, just as Susie had described it to her. And she enjoyed making the acquaintance of the circus folk. The animals were being fed and one by one their noises abated as each began to eat. This act taking their interest more than the change in their environment which had disturbed them earlier.

After this first evening Aunty Ann began to make it a ritual that she would take her evening stroll around the circus chatting to the people who soon got to accept her as one of them. They were simple folk quick to share their stories and equally quick to take offence if all was not right with them. So in this way Ann soon detected a change in the atmosphere. She couldn't quite put her finger on the cause of it but on the third evening she sensed a coldness around the usually friendly folks. She was about to ask Carmel but decided to talk it over with George first as was her wont in things of note. He was in his usual spot of a night sitting in the chimney corner smoking his pipe. Susie was drawn up on the other side of the chimney piece. All was quiet with them. As Ann entered, he lifted his head and gave her a nod.

'All right then?' he said.

'Ai awright,' she returned and took the other chair by the fireside. Sensing a tingling in the atmosphere, Susie rose to her feet and offered to make them a drink in the kitchen.

'Ai lass that'll be good, for I sense Ann has something to say to me,' said George.

'It's not much,' said Aunty Ann, 'but I've a sense something is not quite right in the circus.'

'What kind of not quite right?' George was all ears.

'Well, I can't rightly say, but there was an atmosphere tonight and when I went past the fortune teller's tent, she was arguing with someone and it wasn't her son. And the little people were sullen and wouldn't give me a smile. They're usually cavorting around and getting up to some kind of mischief but tonight they were all quiet and surly.'

'Well,' said Uncle George, 'I think we should bide a while and if things don't change you should have a word with our Peg or her friend Carmel.'

'Can I come in now,' Susie called, 'I've got us a mug of tea.'

'Ai come in an' welcome,' George returned, 'for tea is something I'm good and ready for.'

Next day was one of blustery rain and the farmers realised that the circus animals had sensed the winter weather coming on and with their heightened senses they had passed on their fears to their groomers. The owners of Foolo were not accustomed to living on the edge as were their lodgers. Circus people sensed the change in anything and everything, living in constant worry for their livelihood. This year had been a particularly bad one for them with the murder and hanging of one of their roustabouts. As Uncle George made his way to the barn for the milking, he saw a figure battling in the opposite direction against the wind. He had never met the professor so didn't realise who the man was but he raised an arm in greeting. The man finally approached him gasping out his name as he shook the other's hand.

'Let's go in the barn out of the weather,' said Uncle George kindly.

'I'm glad we've met, I need to talk to you,' said the professor. 'I'm sorry I wasn't here when the others moved in but I had plans to make and they were not doable without some visits. I know the circus people won't like some of the arrangements that I've made for them but they'll get used to them eventually. I was wondering if you and your good wife would be open to housing some of the stock for the winter season. I know it's a lot to ask of you but things are very difficult this year and I need to break up the whole circus and I'm trying to find the means to do this. Don't answer me now, speak to your wife about it first for it will mean a lot of extra work for both of you.'

'I'm glad you don't want an answer right away because I'm fare flummoxed as to what it would be. Well, I've got places for all the horses. I've booked them in to a Christmas show at the zoo with their keepers. I haven't told them yet so please keep it under your hat. The elephant and lion are the most difficult. I have nowhere for them yet. I'm hoping to get the camel a place in a live creche for Christmas time but it will only be for a couple of weeks so he'd need stabling as well. All the keepers will be going with their animals and I've got some of my people gigs over the holidays. The little people are going to a pantomime on Blackpool pier. Although I haven't checked it with them yet I've made arrangements for them to be in Snow White and the Seven Dwarves. I think they'll be pleased. They are very worried about their future.'

'You've been very busy, and so have we. Our Peg said I should talk to you about a problem we have.'

'Oh yes, please go on,' said the prof.

'Well, this is just between you and me?' Uncle George wondered how to put it, he didn't want to seem as though he was telling this important man his business.

'Yes, go on,' said the professor again.

'Well, sir before the circus came to live with us, we'd taken in someone else,' he glanced hesitantly in Professor Richard's direction. The professor was quiet and made no reply so George carried on.

'It seems sir she had been working for the circus and one night she was persuaded against her will to impersonate another performer.'

'Was she then a performer?' said the professor.

'No sir,' Uncle George continued as far as I know she was not a performer. In fact she had been looking after some of the animals and she is very good with them sir, such a help to Ann and me now.'

'So I don't understand the problem?' said the professor.

'Well, the girl she impersonated was murdered while out at night meeting her boyfriend and our girl was kept prisoner by the knife thrower in case she also disappeared.'

'Whew,' the professor drew in his breath. 'So she's afraid Marcello will see her and imprison her again?'

'That's the long and short of it,' said Uncle George.

'What was the name of this girl?' Professor Richards wanted to know.

'Her name is Susie, and she's had quite a checkered career so far. She was the girl who went missing from Cressbrook mill and when the body of the circus performer turned up the police thought they'd found the missing girl,' said Uncle George. The professor looked thoughtful.

'I met Susie one night about six months ago looking around the exhibitions,' he said. 'I wondered what had happened to her.'

'Well, you need wonder no more, she's living with us up at the farmhouse,' said Uncle George.

'Could I visit her do you think, then we'll think of something to do for her predicament.'

Uncle George was glad this had turned out so well and he hoped that Aunty Ann would be equally pleased. Susie was cleaning out the milk churns. She ducked down behind the wall as the two men walked by but uncle George leaned over the low wall and whispered to her.

'It's alright lass I've told the professor and he's going to sort things out for you. Finish what you're doing and then come up to the house to hear what he has to say.'

Susie's heart was beating fit to jump out of her chest. She hoped this would be the end of hiding from Marcello and she could live in peace at the farm.

Susie slowly entered the house place where the professor was sitting on the settle with Aunty Ann. Aunt Peg was also there squeezed into a straight-backed chair in the corner. She didn't know where she belonged now that the semi-gentry was present.

'Come away in do,' Aunt Ann spoke to Susie, 'we've been trying to find what's best to do about your situation.'

'We should say Ann as how we want her to stay with us,' said her husband, 'but we want what's best for her too.'

'Exactly, exactly,' said the professor. Susie hadn't seen him since the night he'd shown her around his exhibition, she didn't know if he recognised her now so much had happened in the interim period.

'I appreciate all you're doing for me and can't believe how kind you are actually considering my welfare as well as the circus needs,' said Susie.

The professor turned to her before he spoke, he hadn't been able to get her out of his mind and had worried about her more than a bit. Hearing of her murder had upset him and now his unhappiness was fast dissipating as he saw her alive and well. And he was having some difficulty containing his feelings. He was a quiet introverted man and had not cared for many people in his life. He had kept himself to himself until he joined the circus but these innocent needy people had begun to pierce his heart and he was becoming attached to all of them in a way he had not felt possible in his early years. He finally spoke to Susie.

'If you wish to stay here with these good people, I'll make sure that Marcello doesn't bother you,' he said. 'But I have another idea. The animals will be going to their winter quarters soon and I've been able to find places for some of the acts in theatres around the country. Although I've not told them about it yet I've secured work for the little people in a Christmas pantomime in Blackpool and I'm thinking you might like to go with them. The pantomime is Snow White and The Seven Dwarves and we need a Snow White?'

'Well, that sounds right champion,' said Uncle George. 'What do you think, Susie?'

She didn't know what to think. On one hand it would be a new challenge to be in theatre and she could also get away from her unhappy memories connected with Derbyshire. But on the other hand, she would be leaving her connection with Emma again just as she'd found her and also the people at Foolo and all her friends at the circus.

'I'd like to think about it for a bit and maybe speak to my friends before I make up my mind,' said Susie showing her gratitude in the way she said it.

'Yes of course,' said the professor. 'But I'll have to find another actress if you don't want the role so let's say one week to make up your mind.'

'Thank you, sir, you've been most kind,' said Susie.

As Uncle George showed the professor to the door, Susie whispered to Aunt Ann.

'I really need to see Emma but I don't know how I can arrange it,' she said.

'We could invite all the family round for tea on Sunday if you like,' Ann replied.

'But everyone except Emma thinks I'm dead,' said Susie.

'Well, how will it be if we just ask Emma and John?'

'I'm not sure, do you think he can keep my secret from his brother?' said Susie bluntly. Aunty Ann was startled.

'Why on earth would you not want Matt to know? Susie hung her head in shame.

'Oh I see,' said Aunty Ann. 'I didn't even know you'd met Matt. Do you have some kind of arrangement with him?'

'No, nothing like that,' re-joined Susie, 'but when all this started, I met Matt at the fair the same night Emma met John. I only saw him the once but I had the idea that he fancied me and when I saw him in my search party, even from a distance it was obvious that my disappearance had hit him hard.'

'Well, I never, how could that have happened so quickly?' said Ann.

'I think you're worrying unduly. We should see them all on Sunday and make known to them that you are indeed alive. Emma must be having a rare 'how de do' keeping it from the Blacklocks when she's living there.'

Susie wasn't sure, she saw that she was being selfish but she didn't want to hurt Matt and she didn't want to walk out with anybody just yet, her life was too mixed up. Finally, she agreed to have Emma and John invited and thus fixed, Uncle George drove his pony trap over with the message.

As Sunday dawned Susie was shaking with nerves. She hoped it would go well for she didn't want to run away again. She helped with the milking and tidying up the cottage and then Aunty Ann taught her to bake some scones for tea and the morning passed pleasantly enough.

When Emma received the letter in Aunty Ann's hand inviting them to tea, she didn't know what to think. Was Susie going to make herself known to John? And if so should she, Emma, tell him ahead of the visit? She was in a quandary. But she decided as Susie had obviously made some kind of decision, she would leave it like that.

On Sunday Emma and John set out to walk to Foolo but just as they were leaving Matt came around the corner. He'd been for his Sunday pint with the lads and seeing them going for a walk he asked where they were bound.

'Aunty Ann asked John and I to tea,' Emma replied.

'Oh, wait up a bit I'll come with you,' said Matt. Emma didn't know what to do she looked hopefully at John but of course he didn't see the problem. He and Matt had been used to going to Foolo all their lives and couldn't see a reason to stand on ceremony. In fact, he couldn't see the need for Ann to invite them this time. So Matt turned himself around and accompanied them. He was in merry mood having imbibed a fair amount of ale with his friends and he kept up a jolly repartee as they strolled along the lanes.

'I don't remember when I last felt so happy,' he shared with them, 'maybe my misery has passed at last.'

Poor Emma didn't know what to do, she knew he was soon in for a rude awakening and she couldn't think of a way to save him from it. John was happy to see his brother in such a light hearted mood and didn't understand Emma's seeming sullenness and so the three made their way to the farm.

Aunty Ann welcomed all of them and made no sign that Matt was not as welcome as the invited guests. He was very jolly and all were happy to see him in jovial mood after so long in misery. Emma was uncomfortable, for the note had been addressed to her and she felt guilty for bringing an extra guest. If she'd only known Ann had realised at once what had happened and decided to make the best of it.

Susie had immediately made her escape when Uncle George looking through the upstairs window, had seen the three coming along the lane and reported their extra visitor. Now Susie had to decide what to do. Should she take the bull by the horns and announce her presence or should she stay upstairs all the time the visitors were there and miss the opportunity. She must think. If she did go down, how was she to go about it? Truth to tell, she was scared of the outcome. She was supposed to be dead, so to suddenly appear to them was likely to cause a furore and she didn't want to be responsible for causing shock to anyone else. Just then she heard quiet footsteps coming upstairs and Aunty Ann appeared around the door jamb.

'What shall I do?' Susie begged her.

'If I were you, I'd tell them.'

'Yes, I've decided that but how?' answered Susie.

'I have a bit of a lace curtain here and you could do the veil thing again like you did at the hanging. If you want, I can tell them that I have a surprise for them but that they mustn't tell anyone about it. Did Matt ever make his feelings known to you?'

'Not in so many words but I could tell how he felt.'

'Well, the point is, he didn't speak out about it?'

'No, he didn't,' said Susie.

'Play it cool and pretend he means nothing to you and you didn't understand that he had feelings for you,' said Ann.

'I don't think I'm a good enough actress, I'll blush when I see him.'

'The point is you'll be covered until you get it together and then when you've cooled down, I'll help you unveil, how will that be?'

'It might work. I'd like this deception to be over with and now the professor knows it will be easier to protect myself, I'll do it.'

'Good girl, I'll find the veil and help you disguise yourself again.'

And so saying, she made good her word and rustling in the clothes chest she found the piece of light fabric and gave it to Susie.

'Right I'll go down now and you can come when I call you.' Susie felt hot and then cold she hoped that this would work out. Ann went downstairs.

'I wondered where you'd gone,' said her husband.

'I just had something to see to upstairs,' Ann re-joined, 'and now I have something to tell you. We have a friend staying with us who is trying not to be seen because of the harm that might be done to her if she is known to be here by a certain person. He is one of the circus performers and we've been keeping her safe but she feels that she should let you all into her secret because of past times.'

'My goodness, whatever is this secrecy?' Laughed John and Matt agreed saying he was glad he'd come along if there was going to be some fun.

'I've asked her to veil herself so that the shock she gives you won't be too great,' said Ann, 'for I don't want you big lads swooning on me.'

'What is this?' Matt replied. 'I've never swooned in my life and I don't intend to start now.'

'Alright, don't say I didn't warn you,' said Aunty Ann as she laughingly turned to the stairway and called, 'you can come down now.'

There was a hush of expectancy as the veiled lady entered the room. All eyes were upon her, even those who knew who she was, for Emma was as nervous as if she was the one wearing the veil. Maybe it was something in Susie's stance or her bearing but suddenly Matt went glassy eyed and let out a screech before he fell to the ground. It broke the spell as all gathered around him trying to bring him back. Aunty Ann went for her smelling salts and wafting them under his nose she talked calmly to the others saying to Susie, 'You'd better take it off luv before he comes round or he might go off again with the unveiling.' John gasped as Susie removed the veil.

'We thought you were dead.' She said nothing preferring to tell her tale when Matt came to. Emma squeezed John's arm.

'We couldn't tell you because of the man who'd kept her prisoner but oh I wanted to so much and now I'm that relieved.'

Matt's eyes slowly opened and he searched the room for the veiled lady who of course was not easily seen. Susie had drawn to the back of the room not wishing to cause any more upset. Matt struggled to his feet. 'Where is she?' he cried.

'I'm here, Matt,' said Susie quietly, 'but you must not take on so. I've been in hiding because my life was in danger, but now with help from the professor, I'm going to be able to resume my own identity and forge a new life for myself.'

Matt just gazed at her. He couldn't believe his eyes. He'd had his castles in the air squashed with the news of her death and now here she was telling him she was going to forge a new life. He shook his head to get his bearings. Of course he'd never told her how he felt and maybe her disappearance and subsequent death had made him romance a bit in his head. He would have to calm himself down before he spoke to her directly because now he realised that she didn't share the same feelings. If that was the case, why had she felt compelled to tell him of her reincarnation? He had forgotten that he had not been invited to hear the news today but had pushed in to the party with John and Emma. How could he have been so stupid? She obviously didn't care for him at all and he'd better be leaving, so thinking, he gathered himself up and made for the door.

'Just a minute, where do you think you're going,' asked Uncle George.

'I'm just away home,' said Matt, 'I wasn't invited, and I feel a fool.'

'Donna be hard on ye'rsel, you've received a shock and anyone could have fainted in this situation.'

Matt was grateful to his uncle for putting it like that and of course no one knew how he felt so he hurriedly sat down again and accepted a cup of tea from Emma's hand. Emma understood the situation, she also knew how Susie wanted more from life than most girls her age, none better.

Now Susie spoke up. 'Some of you know my story how I escaped from the mill and ran away with the circus. How I was happy there except for being easy prey for disreputable men until I helped a girl to leave the circus and get away from one of these men. She looked like me and was murdered. The man who thought he owned her thought he also owned me after she'd gone and I ended up being his prisoner until I could leg it and get away from him. Now before I decide to go anywhere else, I have to think my situation through for I don't want to be easy prey to any more men.

'The professor has offered me a part in a pantomime for Christmas and it sounds like fun but once again I'll be on my own with some of the male circus people and I'm not sure how safe I'm going to be.'

This was the first time that Matt had heard Susie's story and he found it hard to believe what had been going on under his nose. He realised that Susie had had a very difficult time of it in her life. He knew that she had been kidnapped in infancy and taken to work in the mill at an early age and he thought he understood her feelings about men but he had no idea how her early childhood had impacted her life as a young adult. How could he, his life had been relatively stable thanks to a good mother and family? Matt wanted to take care of Susie, buy her presents once he could afford them, and keep her safe from the world, but for Susie that was not enough, she had a fire in her being that went with her red hair and she would not be used, bought, or broken.

Susie intended to live life to the full on her own terms. Matt looked across at Emma and wished that Susie could be more like her. He felt guilty for this thought but could not control his feelings. He now shook his head saying to himself, *Don'na be so daft man she's alive, isn't that what counts most, for where there's life there's hope,* and suddenly his mouth split into a wide grin and taking her hand in his, he shook it warmly and congratulated her on her good fortune. His gaiety was infectious and soon the whole room was laughing and hugging joyously. They made plans to meet again soon and in the meantime they all agreed they'd think on the situation and hopefully come up with a perfect solution.

Chapter Twenty-Five
Off to Blackpool

Meanwhile that nosey Parker Jess Burns had returned to the workhouse with a feeling of frustration and anger. Her life had never been a happy one but she had enhanced it by seeing the faults in others and by trying to make herself important by reporting those faults to the people in authority. As each dismal day wound to its close and she retired to her hard flea-ridden pallet, her sordid mind became more resentful. She especially resented Emma who seemed to have made a happier future for herself. It all got too much for her one night. As she lay thinking back to the day Charles Peace had been hanged, she made a decision to go in search of the veiled lady. She convinced herself that by unveiling the woman as Susie, she would gain notoriety. She planned carefully saving a small amount of her meagre rations each day so she'd be able to eke out her existence until all was revealed to the authorities.

It was on a Wednesday night which was a little brighter than the earlier days of the week that she finally crept out of the dismal hulk that had become home since the fire and made her escape carrying her small bundle of food wrapped in a pocket handkerchief she'd stolen. She'd heard at the inquest that Emma was staying with the Blacklocks. This then she reasoned was the place to begin looking for her prey. The night was cold and she gathered her thin shawl tightly around her scrawny shoulders squeezing every ounce of warmth to her thin chest. She had a walk of just over three miles before she reached the little cottage where Emma now made her home. The workhouse was built away from the main thoroughfare so worthy citizens were not bothered by their less fortunate neighbours.

On arrival, Jess tucked herself into a corner of the end wall of the row of cottages. Here she was sheltered from the cold and damp. Her plans were to stay here for a while until she'd got some sense of the place where Emma was living.

It could, she realised, become a rather long camp out. She didn't have long to wait, however, before she heard life stirring within the cottages and Bill Briggs emerged from number five to use the back privy at the end of the row. This was useful knowledge, Jess thought, for she would have the same need before long. One of the Blacklock boys followed the neighbour and though Jess couldn't see if it was John or Matt, she recognised the family look and knew it was one of them. She made a mental note of which cottage they'd come from. She was elated to find her first quarry so easily for where John was there Emma would be.

Jess didn't want the three to see her when about half an hour later she heard the door click open. She watched stealthily as they left the cottage and made their way towards the clinker brew and so upwards towards the Miller's Dale road and the mine. There was plenty of bracken and dormant Hawthorne trees under the dry stone wall at the roadside and she scurried within this camouflage and followed the three unobtrusively.

Jess had not thought out her plan beyond her wish to find Emma and once they reached the mine, she didn't know what to do for the day. She used up a little time by breaking her fast with the first of her scanty meals, but now what, she wondered. Listening carefully, she heard something unusual in the distance. She saw smoke to the left of her and then heard the noise which turned out to be one of the new locomotives. She'd been told about these but had never seen them until now. She was mesmerised by the spectacle and a bit in awe of something that came along so fast. *I wonder if I could ride on it,* she thought. No sooner thought than she was scrambling down the brew that led to the railway cutting. Luckily for her the train seemed to be slowing down and she began to run downhill in the hope of riding on it. The goods train had reached the station to pick up coal from the mine and transport it to the black country and the kilns of Staffordshire. Jess didn't know this, of course, her mind was on herself and getting transport to somewhere for the day. From her hiding place she watched as the coal came through a chute and filled up each of the goods wagons. She saw her opportunity as the last wagon was filled and quickly ran up to the filling station and swung herself on to the chute, sliding down it and on to the top of the coal.

Now full, the train left the station and began to gather speed. The ride was not very comfortable for Jess as she was buffeted around on top of the coal. She couldn't help thinking of how the queen must have felt as she'd experienced the same kind of travel. Must be different on comfortable seats, she thought to herself. Then she really began to enjoy the ride as faster and faster it went seeming to fly past the livestock in the fields.

She had just begun to settle down when the train started to slow down as it approached another station. She saw carriages shunted off into a siding waiting to be coupled onto the train where she was hiding. The station sign told her they'd arrived in Buxton and it was much bigger than Miller's Dale. She had found a small round hole in the side of the wagon and she was able to peep through it and observe people boarding. They were not ordinary people. They were the size of children but they had the faces of adults. Jess stared at them in amazement. Accompanying them were also some normal sized adults but all were dressed in strange clothes.

For a minute Jess couldn't believe her eyes, then she remembered hearing about a circus and saw that the performers were getting on to her train. *Well,* she thought! *This certainly beats sewing mailbags.* Just then a young woman joined the throng and Jess's eyes almost popped out of her head for there was Susie and this time she wasn't wearing a veil or make up and it was definitely her. *Oh, what a stroke of luck*, thought Jess. *I don't think I'll be going back to the mine tonight. I'll stay with the circus till I see what I can find out.* After another bumpy ride the train once again began to slow down and Jess could see through her peep hole that the fields had given way to more urban scenery with rows of houses clustered around mill chimneys, which as they came nearer, she could see were topping the large mills they adorned. With excitement Jess saw that they'd reached Manchester for there was the name sign. Now came her problem. How was she to alight from the train without being seen? Even to leave the wagon without means would be difficult but without showing herself it would be impossible.

The train had stopped and the circus people were getting off. Yes, there was Susie again with an older gentleman giving her his arm as he raised his top hat. Jess felt her hackles rising in jealousy of the other girl. How had she managed to make contact with a gentleman who seemed to have taken a fancy to her and move her out of poverty. And all these other people as well, thought the envious girl. The cavalcade moved along the platform and was soon out of her sight. She looked desperately around not knowing what to do. Now the wagon she was in began to shake in preparation to move on again. The wagons were being shunted into a siding and she knew she'd missed her chance. She was filled with woe as they began to move once again away from the people she'd wished to follow.

The small band had now boarded another train that would take them to Blackpool. The seaside! The air was tangible in the circus coaches. None of them had ever seen the sea before and they were all terribly excited. Susie watched the little people with interest. They would be her companions for the next few weeks and she wanted them to like her. The professor was accompanying them to the play house and then he would leave again to carry out his rather, Susie thought, secret life. He was a quiet man and kept himself to himself but he seemed to have a liking for her and had spent some time in her company since arriving at Foolo.

'Snow White' the show they were all performing in would have a two-week intensive rehearsal schedule. Then it would open at the play house on the pier in time for Christmas. Susie was very excited about this prospect. She had never been to the theatre just as she had never been to the circus until circumstances had led her to join it. She rubbed the lucky medallion hanging on a chain around her neck just as she had when she ran away from the mill. *It will bring me luck,* she thought as it always has in the past. She put it carefully inside her shirt. *No one needs to see I have riches*, she thought to herself.

They were housed in a quaint hotel in the backstreets of the town a short walk from the pier. The circus performers settled down easily to their new life. Although the rehearsal schedule was tight and they rehearsed long hours, they were all used to hard work and found the change of scene invigorating. To live in solid structures instead of caravans was also a unique experience for most of them and they enjoyed the change. Walking briskly to the theatre one day the second week Susie was struck by the appearance of a woman loitering just ahead of her. She glanced away and the woman disappeared around the end piece of the street. *I must have been mistaken,* thought Susie, *but it did look like Jess Burns*. As the excitement of impending opening night approached, there was not much time to think of other things and Susie forgot about her imagined sighting of Jess. There was no reason for Jess to be in Blackpool so Susie shook off the idea as a figment of her imagination.

It was dress rehearsal and the atmosphere in the theatre was electric. Tonight the footlights would be lit for the first time to show the wonderful painted backdrops on the stage. This theatre was one of the newest and had its own 'fly tower' where the backdrops were stored and then dropped down at the appropriate point in the show. In 'Snow White' the first scene was the king's castle where Snow White was born, then the second was farm lands as she escaped her wicked stepmother, the third the mine where the dwarves worked and Snow White sheltered and finally back to the castle of the king where the evil spell was broken by the kiss of a handsome prince. It was a very romantic story and Susie who'd never heard of fairy tales was entranced by it.

Was there a handsome prince in her life? Who knew what the future would bring but for now she was happy with her new found career. Acting was giving her the excitement she craved for the present time.

Chapter Twenty-Six
Two Surprises

And what of Emma? She had been sorry to see Susie go again just as she'd found her but was also relieved that she'd be safe from the knife thrower. The little family in the cottage had settled down to some semblance of normal life. It was not so exciting as the one Susie was living but a lot more stable and one which suited her fine. Her work week was consistent seven until five. She liked being a cook and was praised often for her light pastry. At weekends she only worked Saturday mornings and in the evening, she went with John and Matt to play darts in the pub. Sunday they made a point of visiting Foolo after church and thus the pattern of their lives was stamped.

The Saturday before Christmas, John surprised Emma by handing her a present.

'What's this then?' she said. 'I've never had a gift before and it's not Christmas yet.'

'Open it and see,' John replied.

She opened the tiny box and gasped in surprise, sitting on black velvet was a ring with a tiny opal stone in it.

'How beautiful!' Emma exclaimed breathlessly. 'What does it mean?' she asked her heart racing.

'It means I want to make it official; I'm asking you to become my wife?' he said smiling gently at her. The world stopped for Emma who had never felt such delicious contentment.

'Say yes, please do,' said John.

'Oh yes with all my heart,' Emma replied.

He gathered her into his arms and kissing her lightly said, 'You'll be mine for ever and ever and no more evil will come close to you while I'm taking care of you.' Emma melted into the warmth of his embrace as Mrs Blacklock entered the house place.

'Now then you two what's going on with no lights on in here.' John lit a candle at the fire and turning from Emma but still with his arm around her he told his mother their good news.

'Well, lad I'm right glad for both of you,' his mother said, 'and 'appen tomorrow we'll walk over to Foolo to tell them the news if the weather's fit.'

The weather complying the whole family walked to Foolo the next afternoon. It was a merry band that set out across the fields and the professor who was taking a walk met them on the way.

'I'm glad to see all of you,' said Professor Richards. 'I'll walk with you to the farmhouse, I've something to ask you.'

'Is Susie alright,' Emma asked anxiously.

'She was when I left Blackpool a week ago,' said the professor. 'She's really enjoying her new career and getting to know the little people better as they work together.'

Aunty Ann and Uncle George were glad to see their family and bade them, 'Come in, come in.' They happily assembled around the big fire in the grate and Aunty Ann put the kettle on the hob. Aunt Peg was already there visiting them. She spent much of her time in the cheerful kitchen now that she was camped at the farm and liked feeling the warmth of her family around her. Emma helped Aunty Ann to make and serve the tea and some parkin she had made. As she did so her new ring caught the light and glinted on her finger.

'What's all this then?' Aunty Ann inquired smilingly. John wanted his to be the news so he put a finger on his lip to Emma and standing importantly he made a little speech, 'The best woman in the world has agreed to become my wife and I have given my dearest Emma this little ring as a token of my love.'

'Well, I never,' Aunty Ann replied giving John a smacking kiss on his cheek. 'When will the wedding be?'

'I'm hoping it will be as fast as we can get the bans read,' said John. 'I saw the parson this morning and he's going to sort it out for us in case Mr Brierly makes any trouble.'

'Why would he do that?' Prof Richards asked.

'Well, he thinks he owns Emma because she was a mill slave, Susie as well,' said John.

'That is outrageous,' said the professor. 'I had no idea. You say Susie was also a mill slave?'

Emma nodded her head shyly.

'What is your background, Emma, if you don't mind me asking?' said the professor.

'I don't like to speak of it sir because I don't see it doing any good. I like to put that side of my life behind me, but I'll tell you sir as you are interested, that Susie and I were kidnapped from London and sailed along the canal system to Cressbrook mill, there to become mill slaves,' replied Emma quietly.

The professor seemed startled. He had no idea that this kind of thing was going on but finally he asked, 'When would this be exactly?'

'Well, I'm not exactly sure,' replied Emma, 'but I think it was spring about fifteen years past.' The professor went quiet and as he seemed to be in a reverie of his own, the chatter about the wedding once again started up.

'Where'll you live?' Uncle George wanted to know.

'Well, that I'm not sure of yet,' John answered, not wanting to share his even greater news before he'd told Emma his idea. The truth of the matter was that he hadn't been happy in the mine since he left prison and he'd heard of a way to be free from criticism. He'd seen a notice wanting men and their families to emigrate to the New World and he only had to have Emma's approval and that of his family to take the opportunity. He was waiting for the right moment to break the news to all of them. The women gathered around Emma to see her simple ring exclaiming on the prettiness and milky light of the opal. Emma looked starry eyed at John knowing that never again could she feel this new bliss. The professor now spoke up to all the party.

'I'd almost forgotten why I wanted to see all of you,' he said. 'Because I found a cast for the show on Blackpool Pier, the organisers have given me some tickets for opening Saturday night which is a week from now, and I wondered if some of you would like to see your friend in the show?'

'Oh could we go John, but how'll we get there?' said Mrs Blacklock.

'There is a train from Miller's Dale early Saturday morning,' said the professor, 'and if you wish to go, I'll try to procure tickets for all of you and some of the circus people as well.'

'We'd better be careful who we tell about Susie, we don't want any harm to come to her,' said Aunty Ann.

'That's true,' said the professor, 'I'll be discreet you may have no fear of that.'

The next Saturday all were assembled to start the long trek to Miller's Dale station. In addition to the Blacklock family and those from Foolo the professor had invited Carmel and Louis to join Aunt Peg. with strictest instructions not to tell anyone of Susie's presence in the pantomime. As they entered the coaches there was an air of excitement as all gathered for their treat to Blackpool. For most of them it was the first time they'd experienced a treat of this magnitude.

And they were also to stay overnight in a small guest house. All as the professor's guests. They couldn't believe that anyone could be so generous, but he had his reasons. And though Sally and Maggie had tried to sneer at the whole thing especially John and Emma's engagement they still wanted their weekend of fun and would not stay at home for any price.

The train wheels clattered along seeming to sing a song with their rhythm and the people in the carriages were lulled to a sleepy contentment as they travelled along. After some time, the train began to slow down. Uncle George came to with a snort. 'We're stopping Ann, I think we're in Manchester,' he told her.

'I know we are, you soppy date, I've been watching all the time you've slept,' she answered.

'I've not been asleep. Just resting mi eyes,' he retorted.

The others in their carriage laughed to hear him. He'd snored most of the journey and they'd been a party to it. The train drew to a halt with a clanking of wheels and a screeching of brakes. Even these noises, new to the travellers, brought excitement to the group. 'We're here, we're here,' they sang together as they collected bags and baggage and prepared to alight.

Professor Richards met them in Manchester. He'd gone on a few days ahead to make sure all was ready for them and now he helped them to alight and find the correct platform to take them on the next leg of the journey.

'The pantomime actors are very excited that you're here for opening night,' he told them. Susie could hardly contain herself when she knew you were all coming to see the show as well as stay overnight.

They waited on the platform for the Blackpool train and soon it was pulling in and screeching to a halt. They all clambered aboard and took their seats for the final stage of the journey. They were into open fields again, now they'd left Manchester, though it was a rather dismal day and the fields were not green as they would be in summer. The travellers didn't mind one bit for this was an unexpected pleasure and a dismal day was not going to dampen their spirits. The train chugged on and presently the scenery changed and buildings could be seen in the far distance. The excitement grew in the carriages as they approached their destination. Slowly the train drew into the station and the people waiting for it stepped back so that they would not be sucked underneath it. Susie was one of the waiting people smiling joyfully as she greeted all her friends. As Carmel clapped eyes on Susie, she laughed and cried as she took the smiling girl into a warm embrace. Louis greeted her warmly and shook her hand saying, 'We thought we'd lost you, how happy I am to see you alive.'

Then the Blacklock family alighted and hugged her delightedly.

Emma couldn't wait to tell her friend her good news and she shyly showed Susie her pretty ring as she told her of their plans.

'John is hoping we'll marry soon, and I can't express to you how happy we both are.'

Susie showed her delight at the news by hugging her friend as she told her, 'Emma you deserve a good man after all your patience and mistreatment in our earlier days. I know you'll be happy; make the best of this time in your life.'

Emma and Susie walked together arm in arm through the small streets of the town refusing to be parted as they made their way to their guest house.

'We're lodged just in the next street,' said Susie, 'and I think Professor Richards has got you somewhere close by. We'll not be able to go in the boarding house until this afternoon so what do you want to do now?'

'We'd all like to see the Winter Gardens,' said John.

'Righto, no sooner said than done, it's this way,' said Susie, showing her pleasure that they were here in her pink cheeks and happy smile. The seaside town was not too busy at this time of year. If they'd been there at Whitsuntide it would have been crowded out with all kinds of people. The popularity of the place had turned it into a very Mecca and the country people were amazed by something new at every turn.

'Where do all these streets lead to?' said Uncle George.

'To the sea, where else?' Susie laughed.

'How'd it be if we took a look at the sea first,' said Aunty Ann.

'I've never seen the sea and we have all afternoon to see the gardens.'

They all agreed and set off down the main street which had a sign to the beach. The tide was in and the group from Derbyshire gazed in wonder as the waves swept over the beach and broke with a roar over the esplanade.

'Wow, did you see that?' cried Matt. 'I can hardly believe this is happening to us, whatever will we see next?'

'When the tide is out later in the afternoon,' said Susie, 'there are usually donkeys giving people rides, but it will depend on the weather. Let's walk along the promenade and get some whelks from the vendors there.'

A strong breeze was blowing as they strolled along the promenade with their little bundles of whelks and it whisked Uncle George's bowler hat off his head. Playing with it merrily, it seemed to have a human mind and kept the man running back and forth as he chased after it. The group made a happy sight to onlookers, except one. Jess was hiding in one of the bathing huts that graced the front. As it was winter and no sea bathing was happening, the flimsy building had made a shelter for her since she'd managed to break the lock and gain entrance. The sight of so much happiness stuck in her throat and made her more angry than usual. Jealous rage overtook her senses and after smashing the only plate that the hut possessed, she stomped off furiously along the beach only stopping when she reached the breakwater. Now a bit calmer, she began to think more lucidly. She must have a plan. She would get rid of Susie, for as Susie was thought by everyone to have been murdered, she would not be missed by anyone, Jess reasoned. But how? She went back to her little hide out to sit and think. Presently she was awakened by a strange scuffling sound and there, its beady eyes looking at her through the gloom, was a large rat. The scream she let out scared it away through a hole in the light frame of the hut. But it had given Jess an idea. She'd get some rat poison she thought and it would fulfil two objectives. The plan of where she would get rat poison was more difficult, until she remembered seeing a yellow substance sprinkled outside the back doors of public houses, to get rid of vermin. The very thing, she thought. I'll sweep some up and it will cost me nothing.

The revellers were having a wonderful day. After their walk along the promenade, where they'd stopped to buy postcards, because Mrs Blacklock couldn't miss this opportunity to send one to Sarah Anna and Fanny, they had made their way to the Winter Garden where a tea dance was in progress. 'How elegant,' said Aunty Ann and Mrs Blacklock agreed.

'Shall us get some tea and those little cakes?' she said.

The men, however, wanted something stronger than tea and Uncle George suggested that while the women folk were enjoying their tea and cakes, the men would go to the pub on the corner and check out the local ale. A game of darts was in progress when they arrived and once again John exhibited his skill in the game. The locals were impressed and invited the visitors to join them any time they were free in the next two days. Waving goodbye to their new friends, they went back to join the women in the Winter Garden and marvelled at the unusual plants in the greenhouses.

'I think this is a small version of the Crystal Palace I've heard so much about,' said Uncle George, 'but until I'm able to travel to London and see it, this will suffice for my enjoyment.' They all agreed being the first wonder of this type they'd ever seen.

Now it was time to check in to their respective guest houses. There were so many of them that three in a row had had to be procured. The landladies were very happy to have all these visitors in Winter and were very welcoming to the people from Derbyshire. They all liked to gossip and shared stories of their everyday lives with the older women being most interested to hear Aunty Peg's stories of the circus and Ann's of the farm life she lived. Not to be out done Mrs Blacklock shared her story of being the wife and mother of men in the mining community and the hardships in the area after the burning of Cressbrook mill.

'Well, I never,' said one of the landladies, tongue in cheek, 'you do seem to lead exciting lives in Derbyshire, we only have tides and shipwrecks to keep us busy.'

'Well-a-day,' Mrs Blacklock returned not understanding her sarcasm. 'We all have our crosses to bear in this life.'

'But we've so much to be thankful for,' said Aunty Ann. 'Look at this lovely weekend for a start, that we have to thank the professor for.'

'Yes, indeed,' the others agreed.

Chapter Twenty-Seven
Snow White and the Seven Dwarves

They made some small changes to their apparel as befitted theatre goers and then all met in the street and made their way to the pier for the main attraction of the evening. The play house was very grand. All new amenities had been added and the friends marvelled at the gas lights along the wall giving soft light to the beautiful paint work and draperies. In the niches along the walls matching statues of Gods and goddesses graced the sconces, and candles lit the faces of the statuary.

'Well, I never who would have thought we'd see a place as posh as this in our lifetime,' said Ann, and her sister agreed almost reverently.

'Doesn't it just show how things can change when someone changes the world order,' she finished.

'What do you mean by the world order?' Emma asked.

'Well, what I mean is, Susie running away from the mill and changing her position, just by that act. For its since that day that all has changed,' answered the older woman.

Thoughtfully Emma followed the group as they made their way to their seats and sat in comfort on the upholstered chairs.

'My, this is a bit of alright,' Uncle George remarked to no one in particular, but they were all thinking the same thing as they sat anticipating the show that was about to begin. A small orchestra was sitting in the pit. Soon they struck up a melody for the opening song, and without more ado the curtains opened on the first scene, that of the king's castle where Snow White was soon to be born. The people from the circus were used to spectacles but even they were entranced to see the story unfolding before their eyes. The villagers had never been to a performance of any kind and were totally enthralled by the story being played out for their entertainment.

When the grown-up Snow White made her appearance and Susie was seen by her friends to have an ability to act that none of them had imagined, they gazed in silence at the beautiful princess, who was being played by their friend. Professor Richards gasped as she made her entrance, gazing at her as though he had seen a ghost. Mrs Blacklock looked at him closely and he hurriedly changed his gasp into a cough. But she'd been alerted to something not being right in the professor's world and put it aside to think of later. The wicked stepmother now made her entrance and spoke into her mirror asking who was the fairest in the land. The story moved forward and the mirror said 'you oh queen.'

Maggie whispered to Sally, 'Knowing she's the fairest seems to make her more evil, I wonder why that is?'

'I don't know,' re-joined her sister, 'is it jealousy that makes you more evil sometimes?'

Maggie was about to retort but Matt shushed her loudly for he wanted to hear all the story especially when Susie was speaking. The little dancing girls now came on to the stage dressed as villagers with sounds of 'ooos' and 'aahaas' from the audience.

'The little ones certainly seem to be popular and you can see why,' said Aunt Peg.

'Aren't they lovely,' her cousin responded.

All agreed that they were. Now came the scene when the dwarves first made their entrance and delighted the audience with their tricks. Louis still hadn't forgiven them for ruining his act all those months ago. He felt that that had been the beginning of all the bad luck for the circus, so he refused to laugh at their antics and wouldn't applaud them in any way. Carmel was used to Louis's sulks but this time she was a bit short with him. 'Grow up,' she hissed. Then she was shushed by the others, as Snow White was banished from the castle by the wicked queen, because the mirror had chosen her, not her step mother as the fairest in the land.

An intermission was now going to take place while the audience bought refreshments and stretched their legs. Emma was just joining the others again when she noticed someone she thought she recognised out of the corner of her eye. *Surely I'm mistaken*, she thought, *Jess Burns can't possibly be here.* The person had now disappeared into the crowd of people waiting at the drinks stall and Emma shook the thought out of her head. She'd obviously been mistaken.

As the bell sounded just then to end the intermission, she forgot her worry and made her way back to her seat with the others.

The story now took on a much darker theme as Snow White travelled through woods and glades and finally into a deep dark forest. She had not been killed by a woodcutter. He had too much loyalty to her real mother, but she had to journey away from the evil at the palace. Here Snow White met up with the dwarves and their real purpose in the play was seen. They became her protectors from all things evil and she was shown to be happy with them in their tiny cottage by the underground mine. But once again evil raised its ugly head and the queen sought the wisdom of her mirror. She realised she'd been tricked and Snow White had not been killed. The audience felt tense as they knew that the wicked queen would harm Snow White. As the disguised queen sold apples to the unsuspecting Snow White, Uncle George had had enough and he proclaimed in a loud voice, 'Don't do it Snowy she's poisoned them the wicked creature.'

Aunty Ann was so embarrassed she clapped her hand over his mouth telling him to, 'Whist if he knew what was good for him.'

But the rest of the audience took it in good part and the actors had not been unsettled by his cry. Now the tension which had been lost by Uncle George revived again and Snow White went to bite the apple, but as she was doing it, Emma saw the dwarf playing Happy beckon her from the wings. Susie tried again. This was her finest acting moment and she didn't want it to be ruined, but just then the little man ran on, and grabbed the apple from her hand.

'What's going on,' she hissed at him.

'Just pretend to bite the apple,' he said, 'look at the yellow powder on the side of it, someone is trying to poison you in earnest.'

The audience began to feel restless, they couldn't hear but could see that something was not right. Just then a rope fell down from the fly tower and looking up Louis saw a slim figure disappearing over the top of the flies.

'I have to go Carmel,' he said, 'something is wrong in the tower.'

'Why you,' she retaliated.

'I am able to climb as you know,' he said quietly.

He left his seat cautiously, as the performance continued. Snow White had eaten the apple and sunk to the floor supposedly dead. The seven dwarves had lifted her into a glass coffin and all stood around her weeping. Meantime Louis, followed by the professor, had gone out of the theatre and around to the stage door. It was locked.

'What did you see?' asked the professor.

'Someone was climbing into the fly tower,' answered Louis, 'and they couldn't be up to any good.'

'What do you propose to do then?'

'I'll climb up after them if I can get into the theatre,' said Louis. 'See there's a window up above the entrance door, I'll try to climb the wall.'

Planting his toes into the small crevices between the brickwork he soon reached the window and levered himself over the sill.

'Don't wait for me,' called the professor, 'I'll go back in and try to watch you from the stalls where we're sitting.'

Louis disappeared into the theatre, and the professor returned to his seat, but as he counted the dwarves, who were keeping vigil over Snow White, he noticed that there were only six instead of the original seven. Just then he noticed a muscular arm as it appeared underneath the flies. He glanced around him, no one else seemed to be any the wiser. The arm disappeared but it was now followed by a small figure and the professor saw some members of the audience looking up. *Oh dear,* he thought. *They've seen it.*

Just then their attention was called back to the stage as the prince came galloping on riding what appeared to be a real horse. He leapt down and gave an impassioned speech about a beautiful maiden in a glass coffin who was to be his wife. He lifted the lid and kissed her lips.

Matt didn't like this, he knew Susie was acting, but the man had kissed her lips, and he found it difficult to keep his temper. Snow White was supposed to come back to life with the magic in the Prince's kiss, but something was not right, she still lay there not moving.

Professor Richards had had enough, he ran to the footlights and clambering over them he arrived on the stage. Now the audience began to grow more than restless telling him to sit down and let them see the rest of the show. He ignored them and going to Susie he felt for a pulse. By this time Matt had clambered on to the stage also. 'What's happening?' he said.

'She needs a doctor quickly,' said the professor. 'Is there a doctor in the house?' he asked the audience.

A small man with a ginger moustache began to push his way forward and Matt helped him climb onto the stage. The stage manager bethought him to bring down the curtain so that the audience were not a party to the doctor's ministrations. Now the audience knew that something was wrong, they had become very quiet waiting to be told that the girl was well, and hopefully it was only a faint she had suffered.

The doctor held Susie's wrist trying to feel for a pulse as the professor had. The doctor was more successful, he raised his finger for silence so that he could hear better.

'There's a slight flutter,' he said happily.

'Get the apple,' said the professor. 'We need to test it.'

'But she only pretended to bite it,' said Happy. 'I warned her that there was some yellow powder on the apple and not to bite it.'

'But who could have done it,' said the stage manager. 'I checked all the props myself and no one could have tampered with the apple.'

Professor Richards then filled them in on what he and Louis had been doing before Susie failed to wake up on stage.

'Louis noticed something strange in the flies and he and I tried to get into the building by way of the stage door, but it was locked,' he said.

'Someone could have tampered with the apple then climbed up into the fly tower. But they were seen.'

Just then a rope cascaded down with Grumpy leaping down with it.

'Quickly,' he called. 'Louis is chasing a girl up in the fly tower and he needs help.'

Carmel leapt into action. Removing her heavy outer clothes, she made use of the rope the little man had dropped, wrapping it around her foot she climbed her way to the top of it and swung into the flies. Most of the eyes were upon her every move except for the doctor and Matt who were concerned about the outcome of Susie's faint.

The professor also watched Susie carefully. Suddenly she coughed and, as in the fairy tale, a piece of apple flew out of her throat. She had not been poisoned, as she had taken note of the warning from her fellow actor, and had turned the apple around, so missing the yellow powder. A piece of the apple had stuck in her throat causing her to choke and faint. The professor rushed to ease her up and as he did so, he noticed the chain around her neck with her lucky pendant dangling there. Susie never removed her pendant even on stage. He gazed at it silently for a moment and then a warm glow came into his eyes.

'Susie my dear,' he said, 'how long have you had this pendant and where did it come from?'

'It's always been with me,' said Susie. 'I refused to take it off, but I've had some fights about it throughout my life I can tell you.'

'Susie, do you remember when I showed you my exhibition?' said Professor Richards. She nodded.

'Do you remember being struck by the musical Faberge egg?' She nodded again.

'Well,' said the professor, 'this lucky charm was the top of the metal work which decorated the egg, and it broke off whilst my sister owned it. She put the charm on a chain and hung it around her baby's neck.'

Susie suddenly became fully alert.

'Do you mean, Sir, that I am that baby?' she gasped.

'Yes, my dear, dear, niece, I thought I would never see you again and now here you are. When I first saw you, I was struck by how like my sister you were, but thought I was imagining it because I so much wanted it to be true. Now the pendant proves it after all these years.'

He helped her out of the glass coffin and embraced her lovingly as though he would never let her go again. Susie was completely staggered by the events of the evening but Emma was delighted for her friend. The two girls hugged each other as if they would never let go again and Emma danced her friend around happily reminding her as she did so, 'Susie you always said you wouldn't stay where bad men had put you. You always said you were born to greatness, and this night has proved you right.'

The eyes of the onlookers were on the happy act that was taking place smiling gently at the two girls, but suddenly something grabbed their attention in the flies and all looked upwards. They saw that Carmel had reached where Louis was sitting across the top beam and crouching in the corner of the roof truss was a young girl scowling at them.

'Who are you and what are you doing up in the flies, you're going to get hurt,' she exclaimed.

At first the girl was quiet and Carmel couldn't tell if she was scared or sulking. Then she let out an ear-splitting scream and raising her hands above her head she leapt at the acrobats as though she was part of their circus act and they were all in the big top.

'Look out,' yelled Louis and Carmel was able to get a better hold of the truss she was grasping. They thought at first that the girl would make it to a firmer hold but that wasn't to be. Her slight frame hurtled downwards gaining momentum as it fell and crashed into the sides of the glass coffin. This splintered into large fragments, on one of which she landed, impaling her through the heart.

Screams and consternation rang out among the watchers. The professor had swung Susie around to save her from the attack and she stood limply in his arms. The doctor quickly moved to the accident victim. It was obvious that she could not survive after her fall with its grizzly outcome, so he wasted no time on her pulse but quickly closed her staring eyes and covered the scene with a loose wing fly.

He turned to the others and suggested that they vacate the stage and that the stage manager call the police. The investigation would be long and arduous, the set was ruined and the cast were in no fit state to finish the play. So the theatre personnel had plenty to organise and went about the business of dispensing tickets so that the audience could enjoy the show another night.

The people from Derbyshire gathered together. They were all shaken by the events of the evening and talked quietly among themselves as the stage manager's voice bellowed in the background.

'This way, Sergeant, I'll lead you to the body on the stage, yes under the cover.'

Emma felt sick and snuggled up to John. This latest event had stunned them so much that even the wonderful news the professor had just imparted was difficult to take in.

'I don't understand it, 'said Uncle George despairingly. 'Why would that young girl want to harm Susie? Because it's pretty obvious to me that it was her poisoned the apple.'

'We can't know that yet George,' said his long-suffering spouse. 'You can't just go jumping to conclusions, leave it to the police and let's concentrate on Susie and the professor's news.'

They all crowded around Susie, and Emma hugged her friend warmly saying, 'Thank goodness you refused to part with your pendant for love nor money. Imagine you being the niece of a professor?'

The rest of the group were equally surprised and delighted that Susie had at last found the family she had been parted from all those years ago.

There was one of their number, however, who was not feeling so elated. Matt had been living a bitter sweet life ever since he learned of Susie's return from the dead and when he'd watched her in the glass coffin, he'd known his feelings for her were still very raw. Once again she'd been reincarnated and his joy had soared only to be dashed by the news that she was the niece of the professor and far above him socially. John understood his brother better than anyone else and was feeling pessimistic about the happenings of the day.

'Isn't it wonderful, John?' said Emma.

'Uh, Uh,' he returned noncommittally.

'What's with you?' she asked quietly.

'I don't know yet,' he returned, 'but I know that my brother will be disappointed so I can't really rejoice until I've talked to him. To see your friend joining the other side as it were of the social sphere makes me wonder if a fairy godfather is going to turn up for you. And if he did, if you'd leave me standing and toddle off to live a life of luxury?'

Emma was stunned. After her original rejection by his mother, background had not entered her thoughts. Emma loved John with all her heart and thought he felt the same, but if he didn't trust her to be true to him, how could he love as she did? They went very quiet, each with their own thoughts.

The police inspector now called for silence so that he could begin questioning each of them. The professor was the first to be questioned and he gave his statement about the door being locked and Louis climbing through the window to follow the intruder. Then Louis added his part. 'So,' said the policeman, 'do you think it was you climbing after her that caused her to slip and fall?'

'Indeed not,' said Louis, 'Grumpy was with me at the time and he can prove my alibi.' Grumpy spoke up then and told his part of the tale of how he'd climbed down for help when he saw the girl threatening Louis and how Carmel had climbed up to help.

'How come you're all such good climbers?' The inspector wanted to know.

'We're acrobats in a circus,' said Carmel, 'but I didn't recognise the girl who climbed into the fly tower.'

'Has anyone identified her?' said the inspector. The whole company shook their heads.

'None of us really saw her properly,' said Mrs Blacklock, and they all agreed.

'Do we know why she was climbing around the theatre?' the inspector asked the stage manager.

'No sir, but we'd had an incident in the show,' he replied.

'What incident?' asked the law.

'Well, sir during the show Snow White, played by Susie here, bites into a poisoned apple and she dies. The seven dwarves build her a glass coffin. She is displayed in it because her body fails to corrupt and she still maintains her beauty. The tale goes that one day a passing prince sees her and kisses her where upon she comes back to life.'

'Alright get on with it, I haven't got all night,' said the inspector.

'Yes sir, well tonight when the Prince kissed Susie, she didn't come back to life immediately because we think the apple had really been poisoned.'

'What makes you think that?' asked the inspector.

'Well, sir, there was some yellow powder on the side of the apple,' said the stage manager. Here Happy butted in with his two scents worth.

'When I saw it, I warned Susie but she still seemed to bite the apple on its other side and we thought she was a goner then she coughed and spat out a piece of the apple and sat up'

'What makes you think she'd really been poisoned?' said the questioner.

'It was the yellow powder sir, as is put down for rats,' said Happy.

'As it seems to have been an attack on the actress playing Snow White, I think we'd better ask you Susie if you'd mind taking a look at the body,' said the inspector.

'Oh no, I think that's a bit much to expect of her,' said the professor.

'I don't mind, Uncle,' said Susie, hesitating before she used the family name. We need to know what's going on!'

The professor gazed at her with pride in his eyes. This was the best day he'd had for a long time and he wanted to spare her more pain if he possibly could.

'All right my dear,' he said, 'if you think you're strong enough?'

Susie looked at him in wonder. Strength was definitely not what she was missing after the life she'd lived and the adventures she'd had in the last two years. Emma moved to her side.

'I'll come with you Susie as I've always been, and we'll discover this together if there's anything to discover,' she said. The two girls climbed back on stage with the inspector moving slowly to the shattered casket. The inspector lifted the covering and discovered to them the horrific scene. Both girls gasped, seeing again the horror that they'd only glimpsed briefly before, with the added shock of realising that they knew the victim. There, impaled on the spike of glass was the mangled corpse of Jessie Burns.

'Why, it's Jessie,' said Emma, 'poor thing.'

'However could she be a part of this tragedy,' said Susie.

'You know her then,' the inspector said. Both girls nodded gently.

'We both worked with her at Cressbrook mill until it burned down,' said Emma. 'Then she went in the workhouse.'

'When was the last time you saw her?' the inspector inquired.

'I think it was the day Charles Peace was supposed to be hanged,' said Emma slowly.

'I think I've seen her since,' said Susie, 'it was here in Blackpool last week, but I couldn't be sure it was her. Now it seems I was right.'

'She must have been stalking you,' said the inspector. 'Is there any reason why she should be?'

'Not that I can think of,' said Susie, 'she always was a jealous, trouble making type but that's no reason to follow me.'

'I'll need statements from both of you,' said the inspector, 'then you can go. Get some sleep, it's been a long night for all of you.'

A rather subdued group returned to their guest houses. Their landladies wanted to know if they'd enjoyed the show but they were all too mixed up emotionally to tell them properly. They just said yes, it was enjoyable and then went to their beds to sleep and hopefully dream of a better tomorrow. Susie joined Emma in the women's room, she was too excited to sleep. The professor had wished her a fond, 'goodnight sweet dreams my niece,' but her head was reeling. She knew she shouldn't dwell on the horrible spectacle she'd seen at the theatre but she couldn't help it. Jess had never been a friend to either of the girls but living in close proximity for so many years had given her a familiar feeling like a piece of old furniture or a snarled rug that caught your toe every time you got too close. Now Jess dead and in such a way while trying to harm her, left Susie unable to stop her beating heart. The 'if such and such and so and so' inevitably plagued her thoughts for many hours and she knew that Emma wasn't sleeping either. Finally both girls got up and went downstairs to the quiet living room of the house so as not to disturb the other women in the room.

'I don't know what I've ever done to cause such hatred in any one,' said Susie.

'I don't think she hated you exactly,' said Emma, 'I think it was more envy because you had the gumption to make changes in your life and she just didn't have the get up and go. She allowed her jealousy to poison her mind and finally it killed her. We must try to give her a decent funeral, and not let her go to a pauper's grave, with bones rattled over the cheap stuff box that serves as a coffin.'

'Yes,' agreed Susie, 'I have a little money put by from my wages at the theatre and I'm sure my new uncle will help us.'

'Your new uncle,' laughed Emma, 'who would have thought how it would all turn out.'

'I know, I can't believe it, I have to pinch myself as a reminder that it's not all part of the fairy tale,' said Susie.

'Now what of you, are you and John making plans for the future?'

Emma was hesitant she didn't really want to share John's doubts with anyone. She felt that once she and John had time to talk it over, all would be well with them. But her heart was heavy and she needed to lighten the load so she spoke to her lifelong friend as friends do.

'I think you finding your uncle was a bit of a blow for John. I don't think he'd ever considered that one of us could have connections to a higher walk of life. Although he's ambitious, he also believes in man staying in his own station.'

Now it was Susie's turn to be quiet. She hadn't had time to consider the change to her own circumstances as it would affect her friends and their beliefs. She didn't even know what the professor's plans were for her, she hadn't had time to give it a thought. As she answered her friend, she was cautious.

'I don't intend to change my lifestyle too drastically, 'she said. 'It's taken me too much time and effort to become independent from owners who are men. I think the professor is different but who can tell, it will all take time.'

'Yes,' agreed her friend. 'It's late, let's go back to bed. I think you have to work in the morning and I don't know what the rest of us will do now after the accident.' So saying, they took their candles and lit their way back upstairs.

Chapter Twenty-Eight
John Is Worried

A dreadful calm had settled on the visitors next day. Being Sunday not much was open but they weren't inclined for much activity anyway. The police soon arrived. The inspector had decided that he needed to conduct interviews before they took the afternoon train back to Manchester. He was sympathetic to all of them. 'What a dreadful thing to have happened,' he told them, as they gathered in the friendly drawing room of the guest house. He gave an overall view of his planned inquiry but said he felt that the ones who'd worked with Jess in the mill were the couple he'd need to question more thoroughly. John had expected this and he was feeling a bit glum this morning, his hopes for the trip to Blackpool had not materialised. Thinking once he had got everyone feeling comfortable and content, he would break the news of his plans to emigrate and invite as many of his friends and family to join them. Now everything seemed to have shattered again just like Snow White's glass coffin. John felt wretched. He knew he'd treated Emma badly. It hadn't been anything to do with her that Susie had found her uncle. But he had a tight feeling in his chest that someday that could happen and he would lose the woman he loved more than life itself. *How could I have been so daft*? he asked himself bitterly. *Emma has agreed to be my wife and I trust her. But am I being true to her when I'm planning to move to the other side of the world without telling her?* John tried to talk to his brother about his problems but Matt was not in the mood to hear his brother's worries, he had enough of his own.

With all this diversity of feeling, they assembled in the drawing room to hear the inspector. He wanted first to be apprised of the background of the inhabitants of Cressbrook Mill leading to Susie running away and joining the circus. Which she willingly told him about. Then John and Emma told the story of their courtship, the firing of the mill and Jessie's removal to the workhouse. And finally, it was the professor who filled in the last part of the puzzle how through the appearance of the broken piece of the Faberge egg he'd found his lost niece. As the professor finished his story, the inspector put away his pencil and scratched his head.

'It seems to me,' he said, 'that we have more mysteries here than we're ever going to solve in one day. Do any of you know if Jess Burns has any family at all?'

'She has a father,' said Emma, 'because she always bragged to us about knowing who her father was and keeping his name, whereas we mill orphans were named after the mill owner, Brierly.'

'I see,' said the inspector, 'but you said she went to the poor house when the mill burned down not to her father's house?'

'Yes sir, that's what I understood,' said Emma, 'though by then I was living with the Blacklock family so I didn't know all the details.'

'Well, thank you, you've all been most helpful and I should let you go now so that you don't miss your train. Susie, I understand that you will be staying in Blackpool to finish your contract with the theatre so maybe you'll find time to answer me a couple more questions in a few days' time.'

'Yes sir,' she answered only too pleased to get to the bottom of this horrid occurrence.

'Have you any questions?' he asked.

'Only when we can hold the funeral, Emma and I would like to give her a decent burial,' said Susie.

The assembled group were surprised at this generosity from ones who had been treated so badly, but as Susie said, 'No one knows what demon prompts us to behave badly, and maybe Jess had her reasons and I'd like to put an end to her sin.'

The professor looked kindly at his niece. 'You are so like your mother,' he said, 'that it warms my heart to hear her kind of spirit living on in you. Bless you, my dear.'

Susie bowed her head and smiled gently as she kissed his cheek.

'Thank you, Uncle, for saying that,' she replied.

John felt tears pricking his eyes and turning to Emma he whispered in her ear his apology for treating her with such contempt the previous night.

'How could I have been so selfish and doubted you or your friend?' he said. Emma looked up at him joyfully.

'Oh John,' she said, 'how could you possibly think anyone could take your place in my heart, either mother, father, sister, cousin, uncle, or aunt. If I found them, I'd be thankful, but they would only enhance a life I've found with you and your family already.'

He kissed her gently, his heart lightened by her words and he vowed to himself that he would never doubt her again. The question of where they'd live in the future he'd leave for another day, enough had happened already this weekend.

They made their preparations to leave and it was a tearful goodbye for Susie and Emma. There were so many loose ends. The visitors hadn't even seen the end of the pantomime but tickets had been issued for another performance so some of them hoped to see the end of the show at a later date. There would also be an inquiry into Jessie's death and some of them might be called back to speak at that. The professor had many legal issues regarding his niece and he vowed to contact his sister's widower to tell him the good news. The professor wasn't sure about a kidnapping charge against the owners of Cressbrook mill but he was considering it. None of this was imparted to Susie just yet. Let her get used to who she was first, thought the professor.

Chapter Twenty-Nine
The Professor Takes a Trip

Professor Richards was determined to get to the bottom of Susie's history. Her disappearance in early childhood had partly caused his melancholy life and now he'd found her again he couldn't wait to put his new energy into use. He felt that the first step to solving this mystery could be in the hands of his brother-in-law. It was many years since he had seen Max. He had not known him very well when his sister chose to marry him. The marriage had taken place whilst he himself was on his world travels. The joy he'd experienced in finding his niece again was soon followed by a wish to know how she'd gone missing. He was determined to make amends for all she had suffered in her short life. He was not a very emotional man but he had been close to his sister and since her death and the disappearance of her baby he had withdrawn into his grief.

He decided to visit London and go to Somerset House, there to see if he could trace Max Renford. Without more ado he set off taking a train to Piccadilly Station. He never thought to let Susie know what he was planning. He was so unused to having anyone dependent on him.

Susie missed her friends from Derbyshire and her new-found uncle.

But she knew he was constantly travelling and thought little about it.

The Pier show was closed for a week while the stage crew rebuilt the glass coffin and cleared the set of debris. They still had rehearsals and the actors were put to work helping prepare for the new opening. The little people were lots of fun especially Grumpy who'd made up his quarrel with Louis and now was much happier.

'You should play Happy instead of Grumpy,' Susie teased him.

So the week was whiled away one way and another with the show, and visits by the inspector. A post mortem was held on Jessie's body, and a verdict of death by misadventure was pronounced at the inquest; which Susie had had to attend with the others who'd been present on the night. Professor Richards was obvious by his absence and the magistrate noted this with a frown on his face.

Meanwhile the professor was spending his time in between the stacks of papers at Somerset House trying to find information about his brother-in-law and his infant niece. It took him two whole days and then towards the end of the second one he came across a dusty file sneezing loudly as he lifted down the information he was seeking.

Maximillian Renford's marriage to Suzanne Emeline Richards. He searched further in the file and found the birth record of a daughter Suzanne Mary Renford. So Susie had been named for her mother, he'd forgotten that but of course it made sense. He took note of all the addresses that were recorded especially the one for Max Renford before his marriage. This had been a good day, tomorrow he would visit Greenwich and the childhood home of Max.

The Blacklock family were settling down again in Tideswell but John was not happy at his job in the mine. His workmates had accepted him back and life was much as it had been before the fire, but John was restless. It was as though everything that had happened in the mill had destroyed something in his happy-go-lucky nature. He wanted to move on and make something of himself. As he and Emma walked home from the mine a few days later, he shared with her his restlessness and broke the news of his wish to leave England. She was silent for a while. John's news was a total shock to her.

'I'd no idea you were thinking of anything like that,' she finally said.

'Well, it's been in my mind since I was wrongly arrested,' said John. 'I wanted to think it through before I told you and all my family. I just think it will be good to have a complete break from all the bad things in our lives.'

'I thought you'd got over it, John, no country is going to be perfect and at least we know this one and have some idea how to go on. A new land will be so strange and it will be just the two of us,' said Emma.

'Oh, I'm not planning to go without Mother and Matt, and my three sisters will have to come too,' John spoke confidently.

'Well,' said Emma, 'if you can persuade all your family to join you, count me in.'

For secretly she was confident that at least some of them wouldn't want to sail across half of the world. John's face spread in a warm grin, he had the opposite opinion of his family and being the eldest and the man of the house, since his father died, he was quite confident that he could persuade them all.

236

...

The professor set out early next morning to call on whoever lived at the address in Greenwich. A parlour maid opened the door to him and asked him to wait in the drawing room while she summoned her master who, she said, was enjoying breakfast. Presently a jovial man entered the room. The professor didn't recognise him and his heart sank, he'd obviously got the wrong house, but he'd asked for Mr Renford and had been shown in?

'I'm sorry,' he spoke up, 'I think I've got the wrong family I'm looking for Mr Max Renford.'

'He's my younger brother,' said the jovial man, 'my name is Michael; how do you do.'

'I'm pleased to make your acquaintance. I'm Professor Thomas Richards, Max Renford's brother-in-law.'

They shook hands but a little hesitantly on Michael Renford's part.

'I didn't know Alison had a brother,' he said. 'I had understood that she was an only child.'

'Oh, I should have explained; my sister, Suzanne, died some twenty years ago and I lost touch with Max, but I need to get in contact with him again on a pressing matter that has just materialised.'

'I see, I see, well that explains it,' said Michael. 'I'm not in regular contact with Max and Alison. Her father's lands are in the North of Scotland and Max went up to live with her family when he married Alison some five or six years ago.'

'I see,' said Professor Richards, 'but I presume you have an address where I can contact him?'

'Well, yes I do,' said Michael hesitantly, 'but it's a bit difficult. You see my brother has specifically told me not to divulge this information to anyone unless he is first apprised of their wishes. I think I've already said too much to you. I would have to make contact with him, after I am satisfied that you have identified yourself adequately. I'm sorry about this but I made a promise to my brother.'

The professor was stunned he had not imagined he would have need of a birth certificate for himself, but after a pause he bethought him of the marriage certificate of his sister and Max that he'd taken the precaution of bringing with him. He produced it now but didn't show the birth certificate of his niece. After perusing the document for a while, Michael looked up and met the professor's eye. The professor was surprised to detect a glint of fear there, and could not think what the man had to be afraid of. Michael spoke hesitantly, 'I don't know what to say to you,' he pondered. 'I knew your sister, a delightful young woman. She was everything to Max and when she died, he went over the edge for a while. It was many years before he could live a normal life again. I'm afraid that if he hears from you, it might return him to his depression.'

The professor had not intended to bring Susie into this conversation but saw that he had no other choice, so hesitantly he began the story of her going missing, and his search for her ending quite recently and surprisingly in the very circus where he himself had taken refuge. Michael sat down heavily mopping his brow with his breakfast napkin. He could not speak for many minutes, he was obviously in shock, observed the other man. Finally, he gathered his breath and spoke.

'My brother, Max…when he told me of his wife's death also told me of the death of his infant daughter,' he said. 'I had no reason to doubt his tale so we grieved for both of them for a long while. Max seemed to fall deeper and deeper into depression until he sought help, and finally after many years, he began to improve and thanks to Alison today he is a new man.'

'I wonder why he would tell you this,' said the professor. 'When my sister died, Max and I met and he saw his child alive. I thought he'd taken her to live with relatives but some years later I met him by chance and he asked after my niece. It became apparent then that the baby had been taken, for each of us thought the other had charge of her. I have never forgiven myself for my tardiness in this and I made it my life's work to find her. Now I intend to find her father and get to the bottom of this mystery either with your help as a decent gentleman, or on my own, whichever it is, so be it.'

Michael went very pale, the ramifications of what he'd just been told could be endless, and might lead his brother and possibly himself to the wrong side of the law.

'If you'd wait a short while for me to make arrangements, I'll have my carriage made ready for us to visit Scotland,' he said. 'We'll have to break our journey somewhere in the north country and change horses there.'

The journey to Scotland was a long one. When they finally drew up at the metal gates preceding a long driveway, they were both dusty and travel worn. It had not been an easy journey for either of them. For guilt and self-righteous wrath do not make comfortable travelling companions.

Both were trying to keep open minds for the outcome, but it was obvious that all was not cricket, and the professor especially could smell a rat. He knew that he could not let his own guilty state about Susie cloud his judgement. He must give the other family the opportunity to defend their actions and tell their story, but his emotions were more than a little raw when he thought how his niece had been treated for most of her life.

Michael knew more than he had admitted. In Max's ravings during the worst years of his depression, he had suffered from terrible nightmares. At this time he'd been living in the family home with his brother, and Michael had been awakened many a night with his brother's ravings. Max had screamed out in his sleep for the wife he'd lost and the child who'd been abandoned.

'I couldn't stand to look at her, one who'd taken my Suzanne from me,' he'd raged at his brother.

Now, the time Michael had dreaded was coming to pass and as the carriage streaked onwards, the dread came ever closer until the journey ended and they reached Ballynifore Castle. The coachman blew his 'yard of tin' and the gatekeeper drew open the gates so that the carriage could sweep through. If this spectacle was meant to impress it didn't have that effect on the professor. The more he saw of the arrogance of these people, the more edgy became his mood until the final straw, when a footman, supposedly helping him down from the carriage, let him slip sprawling in the muddy road.

'Have a care, Graham,' said Sir Michael, but the act had already occurred and no amount of apology could sweeten the professor's reaction. He dragged the young person down to his level and tripped him into the mud also. This did not make a good beginning to the visit and Professor Richards wished with all his heart that he'd held his temper, but with this last indignity, he had finally snapped. Michael was at his most affable trying to smooth everyone's feathers as they entered the massive hallway.

The professor had put himself in the wrong and was now feeling very foolish especially as the critical eyes of about a dozen stags (the result of the local taxidermist's endeavours) gazed down on him reproachfully. The arrival of the two men had caused a stir in the bleak castle. Not many people just dropped in for a casual visit, they were too far from the beaten path.

The laird made his appearance walking down the formal oak staircase looking for all the world like one of the stuffed stags (thought the professor). On this thought he almost lost his assumed frostiness as a laugh threatened to gurgle out of him. He managed to repress it, however, and bowed politely over the hand that was offered to him. Michael explained their business in a need to speak to Max.

The laird had them shown into the drawing room while a footman was sent to alert Max to the appearance of his unexpected guests and a wish from the laird that he would make hast to greet them. In the meantime, they made small talk about the weather, the political situation and things that were going on in London at the time. The professor was interested to hear what was going on in the capital, he'd been absent in the provinces and with a travelling circus for so long that he'd lost touch with the wider world except by weekly reference to The Times.

The butler now entered bringing in refreshment in the form of coffee and pastries and a bowl of jam and clotted cream to sweeten the savoury. The professor felt uncomfortable accepting hospitality from these people, but he was so hungry that he tucked in voraciously, putting his conscience to the back of his mind. It was close to an hour later when the food had been cleared that Max finally showed his face.

He had changed, Professor Richards noted. His thin face had filled out somewhat and his previously dark hair was now almost entirely grey. His eyes held a haunted look, and though he tried to smile at his guests, he was obviously ill at ease. The professor, after the first pleasantries had been exchanged, determined to stay silent until there was something important to say, and sat back, leaving the conversation to Michael. The laird diplomatically left the room, saying he would appraise his wife and daughter of the visit, and hoped they'd have the pleasure of the guests' company at luncheon.

When they were left alone, Michael finally spoke getting rid of pleasantries quickly. 'Yes they were all well,' Max replied, 'but what brings you here today and why bring Professor Richards?'

Michael lost no more time he went straight to the point.

'Max,' he said, 'you had a daughter some twenty years ago named Suzanne after her mother and Mary after ours.'

Max went pale, he suspected what was coming.

'When you spent many years in my house following the death of your wife, you told me in no uncertain terms that the child had also died. Is that true?'

The silent cold of the room made itself felt. Although there was a small fire in the grate it hadn't made much difference to the overall atmosphere. Max cleared his throat. 'Yes,' he said, 'I did tell you that.'

'And was that information the truth?' Michael questioned him.

Max squirmed a little, not able to take his eyes off his brother-in-law. Finally, he answered. 'It was the truth as I believed it,' he said.

'What do you mean by that?' asked his brother.

Max looked towards the door his eyes showing hope of possible escape but the professor was in the way, placed between him and his egress.

'We haven't all day,' said Michael, 'you'd better tell us what you know.'

At this Max became hysterical. 'I didn't want to do it but how could I look after a small child without my darling Suzanne?' He sobbed playing on their mercy.

'What did you do that you didn't want to do to my niece?' finally spoke up the professor. 'Let's have less of the histrionics and more of the truth.'

Max had gone very white but he realised that he couldn't get away from confessing to the professor so he spoke at last.

'You and your family never offered to help me, and my family didn't want her, so I had no choice but to farm her out with a wet nurse for a few years,' he said.

'You gave her to a common slut of a wench and led us to believe she'd been kidnapped,' said the professor clenching his fists ominously.

'I had no choice,' whimpered Max pathetically.

'You keep saying you had no choice,' said his brother, 'but none of us knew you were looking for someone to take the baby, Mother would have been happy to care for her. She always wanted a girl.'

Max sobbed again, put on a spot as he had been, he would have to confess the truth.

'I couldn't stand to see her,' he said, 'not after she'd killed her mother and left me without my darling Suzanne, and I wasn't going to let her take my mother from me as well.'

The professor who'd stood up during the diatribe now sank into his chair in disbelief.

'I can't believe that a decent man would do that to his own child,' he said.

Just then there was a disturbance at the door and a dainty, dark haired woman entered the room. Max ran to her falling at her feet and begging her to save him from the tyrants who were trying to harm him. Professor Richards felt his disgust at this spectacle and was not able to cover his expression. The woman, who was introduced as Alison, Max's wife, frowned her displeasure at the visitors.

'You Michael, know of Max's tendency to depression and I can't believe you'd cause him such upset,' she said.

'Depression is obviously an excuse not to stand up and take his punishment like a man,' said Michael, 'considering what he did to his own daughter.'

'His daughter?' said Alison. 'I've never heard of a daughter, what's going on, Max?'

Now he had to admit the truth and falteringly it all came out, but he swore that once he had delivered the baby to the wet nurse, and paid her handsomely to raise the infant as her own, he hadn't heard from her again, and he thought that the matter was closed. Then he tried to play for sympathy again emphasising the nightmares and depression that had plagued him for many years. Both men were disgusted as was the laird who had joined them at his daughter's request because Max was so distraught.

'How can you think of your own feelings after what you did cold heartedly twenty years ago to your own flesh and blood,' said the professor, 'I have no sympathy with you, but possibly now that you've finally told the truth about your child, the nightmares might cease. And where is the woman now who was paid handsomely to raise you daughter, for she is obviously the missing piece in this jigsaw. Where might we find her?'

'She lived in Blackfriars,' said Max. 'She ran a home for unwanted small children and she said Susie might be adopted by good parents because she was very young and pretty.'

The professor could bear it no longer. 'I'll have her address, then I'll take my leave, for I can't stand another moment in your presence,' he told Max then he turned to Alison, 'God spare you from having children fathered by this sorry excuse for a human being.'

Then he turned on his heel and left them. Sitting on the outside settle, his body sank into his arms in despair. Never had he felt so dispirited by events. He had found Susie's father, but what a sorry specimen he was, and how could he tell his niece of her rejection from her own wealthy father? Presently Michael came out and joined him. He was not looking any happier than the professor felt. His usual jovial expression had gone. The two men sat silently, their thoughts similar but unshared. At last Michael spoke, 'Are you ready to depart for I see no reason to tarry here further. I've got the address in Blackfriars.'

With a nod of the head Professor Richards agreed to journey back to London and visit the wet nurse in Blackfriars.

The harrowing journey became even worse when the weather turned and gentle snowflakes began to fall.

'This could be quite pretty if we were travelling on better roads,' said Michael.

After a very long arduous journey, they finally approached Blackfriar's Bridge. The carriage swayed across it as it leaned heavily on its unsafe pylons. *This area of London is very run down and creepy,* observed the professor. It was many years since he'd been in the former haunts of the Dominican order who'd given this area of London its name and it was definitely less salubrious than it had been fifteen years ago. The lack of improvement gave the professor pause, where were they coming to? Having stopped to ask the way of a small waif who was mud larking along the shore of the muddy river, the coachman was able to deposit the two men at the door of a dismal, run down building which seemed to grow out of the very mud on which it was standing. They alighted from the carriage and Sir. Michael rapped on the door with his silver headed cane. Nothing happened for many minutes but just as he lifted his arm for a second rally, the door was opened by a tiny waif wearing filthy rags. Her dirty bare feet peeped out under the hessian pinafore which covered her other garments. The two men were taken aback as she addressed them in a very guttural voice. 'Whadya want,' she said rudely. Sir Michael was the first to recover and spoke more gently to her than he thought she deserved.

'My child, would you mind telling the person in charge of you that two gentlemen wish to speak to her?'

The girl looked suspiciously at them through half-closed eyes then she threw over her shoulder an expletive request, 'Two bloody fellas wan' to see you Ma?'

To say they were surprised was to put it mildly, her tone of voiced language belied her few years and they were shocked beyond belief. A large slatternly woman finally pushed her way to the door, a baby hanging precariously over one shoulder as she hastily fastened her gaping blouse. 'Yes,' she said without preamble. The professor spoke up now, he'd gained back a little of his composure and the anger within him was now beginning to manifest itself.

'Are we speaking to the owner of this establishment?' he asked sharply.

'Ho hoity toity, this establishment indeed.' The woman showed her black teeth as she laughed mirthlessly.

'I'm Mrs Burns if that's what you mean and I'm the one who does all the work, though I'm hardly the owner Owd. Reu. Sees to that.'

At the mention of her name the professor went quite pale and Sir Michael thought he was going to faint.

'Here let me help you,' he said, giving the other man his arm. Then he turned to Mrs Burns. 'You can see that my friend isn't well,' he said, 'may we come in and rest awhile.'

'Who do you think I am and what do you think this is, a snug?' her indignant response woke the baby and it began to squall. 'Now see what you've done, I'll have to put it down,' she said.

'Just a moment,' spoke up the professor, 'are you the mother of Jessie Burns?'

The woman slewed herself around. 'Who wants to know?' she said.

'I am Professor Richards and if you are she, I'm afraid I have some bad news for you.'

'Oh alright you'd better come in,' she replied.

The waif went ahead into the stinking apartment. Sir Michael wrinkled his nose but tried not to show it as they were enveloped in the odour of everything stale, cabbage, urine, onions, cat and that other all-pervading smell of dark disease which bespoke poverty. The woman hastily swept the contents of a wooden settle onto the floor with one of her beefy arms disturbing a yowling Tom cat in her wake. It flew sideways hissing its annoyance.

'You'd better sit down,' she said ungraciously.

'I think madame you'd better sit down yourself,' said Professor Richards, 'for the news I'm going to impart will not be easy for you.'

'Easy for me, easy for me? Nothing in life is easy for me Mr Professor,' she spat at him as she put the dirty infant down in a wooden drawer with one broken end, wrapping a ragged blanket around him with a semi-maternal gesture.

'Nonetheless we should talk,' said the professor gently. Reluctantly, Mrs Burns sat down opposite him negligently rocking the crying child as she did so.

'Now what's all this about,' she said, 'if you've come to tell me something has happened to Jessie, I'm not surprised. I haven't heard from her in well-nigh fifteen years. She disappeared with one of my best payers, God rot her hide.'

The professor looked up from the worn carpet he'd been studying, on her words, but said nothing. Mrs Burns seemed to go on in a sort of reverie, brought on by news of her missing child.

'She was my first,' she said, 'got knocked up by Owd. Rue. When I was little more than a child myself. He saw me as a way of making money for him and I became his beer and opium supplier. I can't remember how many children I've had since to take care of mine, and other women's but it'll soon stop and then what will become of me, gentlemen, what will become of me?'

On this plaintive note, she seemed to come back to the present her eyes getting a kind of knowing light in their expression.

'What will become of me, gentlemen?' she asked again.

Sir Michael now spoke up, the mood broken. 'How can we say, woman? We have come here to gather information of quite a different kind though we do commiserate with you on the death of your daughter.'

'Dead? She's dead?' screamed Mrs Burns suddenly wailing and beating her breast in theatrical style. It was so obviously fake that the professor spoke sharply.

'Mrs Burns,' he said, 'Jessie was killed in a tragic accident in Blackpool last week, we are sorry for your loss but want to know what she knew, or you can tell us, of a child you nursed some twenty years ago named Susie Renford?'

It was obvious from the look in her eye that Mrs Burns knew exactly what the professor was referring to but she put on a face of none comprehension and once again went into a paroxysm of grief.

'Oh my Jessie, my love my first born how could this have happened oh woe is me!'

Sir Michael spoke sharply, 'Woe will be you if you don't speak up and give us the information we need. And we haven't got all day.'

Mrs Burns got a canny look in her eye she knew that she had information these men wanted and she knew she had her daughter's death as a pawn, she also needed money badly to set her up for a life apart from Old Reu. And she was milking this to the hilt. She spoke up then.

'What I have I hold, until my dying day,' she said, 'and no man's going to get it from me. My little Jessie was taken from me and someone's going to suffer.'

The professor tried a different tack. 'The baby Susie had a pendant around her neck; what happened to it?' he said.

His bluntness brought an immediate reply, 'It was stolen from my dresser the very day my Jessie left with the baby.'

She bit her lip realising that she had been made to admit her involvement. She tried to take it back, 'I don't mean as I ever see'd it but her father as't me to put it safe by for her.'

'You met her father?' questioned the professor.

'I ain't saying nuffink else,' said Mrs Burns.

'Well, you've already told me enough to get you a prison sentence so you may as well share the rest to get your freedom,' said Professor Richards.

At this turn of events, Mrs Burns turned pale. She didn't like talk of being taken up by the law and she squirmed inside. So changing her tactics she began to wheedle.

'How say you give me two hundred gold sovereigns and I'll spill the beans on Owd. Reu?' she said.

'Two hundred gold sovereigns!' expostulated Sir Michael. 'Why, woman, that's a king's ransom. Let's make it twenty and we can start talking.' He was very firm so she tried not to push her luck too far.

'Alright,' she said, 'but let's make it Guinea gold shall we and then you have a deal?'

'Oh you drive a hard bargain, Mrs Burns, but I'll see what I can do for you,' he replied.

So Mrs Burns filled in the gaps between the information that the two men had already gleaned from various sources mainly from Max. He had brought his infant daughter here to Mrs Burns on the death of his wife. He'd given her twenty guineas and she hadn't seen him again. Professor Richards clenched his fists and wished he could make use of them on his brother-in-law. When the money ran out after a few years, Mrs Burns had been at her beam ends, she hadn't been able to sell the baby. No rich adoptive parents wanted a red head so she had to let Owd. Rue do as he did with unwanted children and sell them to the highest bidders. That year it happened to be a Northern gang who were working with the cotton industry. Owd. Rue had decided to sell his own daughter at the same time. And the two girls, one a few years older, had been barged to Derbyshire.

Jessie had been given instructions to watch out for the younger girl but they didn't know that once away, Jessie had looked out for herself. The pendant was a mystery. Mrs Burns swore she'd put it safe but it had disappeared with Jessie and the baby. Her story finished, Mrs Burns held out her hand for her payment.

'Not so fast,' said Sir Michael, 'where's Owd. Rue now?'

'I've no idea, Sir, he comes and goes as he pleases. It's about a month since I see'd him but if he's got wind of your visit, he'll be around soon I'd guess. I have to start packing and scarper before he gets back and takes my money.'

So saying she grabbed her hat and coat and ran out the front door, quick as lightning the little girl followed her. The two startled men were left alone with a squalling infant and two other small children who stared wide-eyed from make-shift cots at the back of the room.

'Well, what do we do now?' asked Sir Michael.

'If you'll stay here, I'll find a constable and alert the police to the situation,' said the professor. 'Sadly, these children will have to go to the workhouse but I'm more interested in finding Owd. Rue. And the constabulary can do both things.'

Sir Michael was not comfortable being left in these surroundings but he saw the need for one of them to stay so he agreed to the plan and he bade the professor to hurry up back to him. Luckily, as he was feeling that the smell would pervade his nostrils for the rest of his days and the cries of small children, the eldest of which was making constant pleas for sops, the professor arrived back with two policemen and a nurse in tow.

'Thank goodness,' said Sir Michael, 'that one's demanding food.'

He pointed out the older child. The nurse took command of the situation. She found four more children in a smaller room behind a curtain and clicked her tongue unhappily at the condition they were all in.

'The woman in charge of these infants should be locked up,' she said. 'Why did you let her go?'

'It wasn't our choice,' said the professor, 'she just ran out like lightning when we mentioned calling the law.'

'Did you give her money?' asked the nurse.

Guiltily Sir Michael admitted he had, but it was for information he told her.

'Ah well, you look a bit green, so I suppose you aren't used to the likes of her,' said the nurse.

'No indeed,' replied Sir Michael.

'Well, if you'd like to go, we'll see to the rest of this,' said the nurse. 'And the police will put a watch on the door for the man in charge of this operation. We've been on the lookout for him for quite a while but couldn't get information on this baby smuggling, now we have a line and hope we can end it. Though of course these people, though evil, are only providing a service to others more wealthy, to conceal their nasty secrets.'

Sir Michael was very quiet as they left the house. The nurse's words had sunk in and he could not forget his brother's ill-advised actions in leaving his little daughter in such a place. The professor's thoughts were running in a similar vein but he was also pleased to solve the mystery surrounding Jessie Burns' hatred of his niece.

He understood how a child could hold a grudge all her life for having been ill-treated herself. Now he would have to return to Susie and he decided she was old enough to hear the truth about her background and he determined to emphasise the love her mother's family had always felt for her and hope that she had not been permanently damaged by the neglect in her childhood.

The week leading up to Christmas was a hectic time for all of them. The people from Derbyshire paid another visit to Blackpool and this time they saw the pantomime all the way to the end. They all agreed that Susie was a beautiful Snow White and should try her luck on the London stage where they were sure she'd go far. The professor listened to their ideas with cold dread in his stomach. Although it was him who'd suggested the part of Snow White for Susie before he knew her identity, he now wanted a better life for his niece.

Another man who listened to the others making plans for her future with dread was Matt. Susie seemed to be moving ever further away from him as she discovered each new ability. In despair he realised he'd probably never be able to speak to her of his heart's wishes. On closing night after the curtain had come down for the final time (for the applause was deafening and they'd had six curtain calls) all the friends met together in a corner pub to celebrate their achievement. They all chatted in a convivial friendly way and the professor was able to get Susie alone for a while so that he could fill her in on his journeys. First to London, then Scotland and finally back to London he told her.

When he gently told her that he had found her father, he could not stand the look of joyful hope that came into her eyes. He felt an absolute cad for bursting her bubble of happiness but knew he had to tell her her own father's part in her disappearance. The joy that had lit her face was now switched off with this information. She was quiet for a while and he gave her this time of silence to accept the double blow he'd caused her by his words. Finally, she spoke up.

'Well, I should have known that if he was still alive, he obviously didn't want me or he would have come looking before today.'

Professor Richards wanted to reassure her but didn't see the point in lying to her. It would then take longer for her to brave the truth of the matter again. The professor spoke gently of her mother for whom she was named and when Susie learned her true identity, her eyes lit up again.

'You mean I have a real name and I was named for my mother?' she asked.

'Yes,' said the professor. 'Her name was Suzanne, Emeline and you were named Suzanne for her and Mary for your grandmother who was my mother.'

'Do I also have a surname instead of Brierly?' she asked breathlessly.

'You do, and it's a good name even though your father turned out weak for I met your uncle Michael and he's a decent chap. Your family name is Renford,' he told her. Susie was so excited that she called to all her friends.

'Listen up everyone,' she said. 'I want you to share my good news that my uncle has just told me. I have a name, its Suzanne Mary Renford and I have a good family that loves me.' And turning to the professor she begged him, 'When can I meet them all Sir I'm so excited?'

'Well, we'll have to see about that,' he replied hesitantly.

Emma now spoke up, 'Oh Susie now you can say, as Jessie Burns always did, that you also know who your father is.'

Susie's eyes clouded over with being reminded of Jessie's sad demise which had been brought about by hatred of herself. In addition to that she was reminded of the actions of her own father in destroying her young life.

'I'm sorry,' said Emma, 'I shouldn't have reminded you about Jessie, but I wonder why she was always so jealous of you, she didn't treat me so badly.'

The professor had not intended to tell Susie everything in one day but saw no reason to keep it quiet now that he had an opening.

'I think I have the answer to that,' he said quietly.

'Oh please go on tell me,' said Susie, 'I've racked my brains to know.'

'Well, after I'd visited your father in Scotland, I accepted a ride to London in your Uncle Michael's carriage. We had gleaned information of the woman who had charge of you for the early years of your life. We visited her in Blackfriars and she was none other than Mrs Burns.'

'You mean she was Jessie's mother?' said Emma incredulously.

'None other,' said the professor.

'But how did we both end up in a Derbyshire mill?' asked Susie.

The professor was hesitant to tell her but when she begged, he told her the whole story of both girls being sold to the mill as slaves.

'My goodness,' said Emma, 'she must have been the girl you were with on the barge, who reminded me of my monkey, and when we met her again, we didn't recognise her because of the accident which took half her face.'

'No wonder she hated me,' said Susie, 'it was bad enough selling an orphan under your care but to sell your own daughter was something else, poor Jessie, I understand her anger now and I'll forgive her for what she tried to do to me. Tomorrow when we bury her, we'll all remember her sad little life.'

'Amen to that,' said all her friends.

Chapter Thirty
Goodbye Jessie, Hello Future

It was a small group that turned up at the little cemetery to say a last goodbye to Jessie. Susie and Emma had done their best and the funeral was a respectable one. The minister was intoning the committal when the mourners were surprised to see a carriage with a crest on its side draw up in the lane way. The girls exchanged a surprised glance at each other in wonderment. Just then the footplate was let down on the carriage. Professor Richards was surprised to see Sir Michael step daintily down, between the puddles that had gathered, being careful not to muddy his boots. The burial was over and the mourners had sprinkled dirt on the coffin. Sir Michael moved forward and took the professor's outstretched hand.

'It's good to see you here but I didn't expect you,' he said.

'No,' Sir Michael returned, 'I didn't intend to come, but business in the North brought me within ten miles, and I decided to meet my niece before circumstances move her on again.'

'My goodness,' he exclaimed as he looked across at Susie. 'I would have known her anywhere, she's so like her mother.'

'Yes, isn't she,' replied the professor. 'She haunted me from our first meeting, but I had no way of pursuing a quest for her identity until I saw the pendant.'

'Have you solved that mystery yet,' asked Sir Michael.

'I think the older child must have stolen it from her mother's drawer,' said the professor, 'but I have no proof. Let me call my niece over to meet you. Susie, my dear there is someone here I wish you to meet.'

Susie's heart was beating fast, she wondered if it was her father but the professor soon corrected her on that point by introducing her other uncle Sir Michael.

'Well, my dear I was just saying to the professor here how like your mother you are.'

'Am I really?' said Susie. 'I should like very much to be like her for uncle has told me how beautiful she was,' she said naively.

'You are just as beautiful as your mother,' said Sir Michael, and Susie had to hide her blushes for she realised that she'd been a bit forward.

Sir Michael had not just journeyed to meet his niece, he had a proposition to impart to her from a very unlikely source. He'd heard from Alison, his brother's wife, he told them. That lady had been shocked and horrified to hear how her husband had treated his little daughter and she wanted to make amends.

She had discussed her plan with her father and then, when he'd agreed, she'd told her husband what he must do. Her plan was to offer Susie a home with them in Scotland living as a lady, as the granddaughter-in-law of the laird of the castle would demand. And in time, Alison had said, after being in the company of the aristocracy, Susie would make a good marriage for herself. For what else were ladies after? Her life would be made for her. Sir Michael had been approached to contact Susie and set the plan in motion.

'What of Max?' asked the professor when Sir Michael spoke to him about the plan for Susie's well-being.

'He is eating humble pie as far as I can see,' said Sir Michael.

'Personally, I don't like it,' said Professor Richards. 'But I have to question myself if it's just selfishness on my part or if I feel the plan is one that will not make Susie happy.'

'How can it not make her happy?' said Sir Michael. 'She'll be rich and well-placed in society.'

'Well, we'd better ask her what her plans are for she's a very independent young woman from what I've observed,' said Professor Richards.

Susie, when applied to, had very mixed feelings. The thought of wealth was definitely tempting and somewhere in the dark recesses of her mind, she would love to have a relationship with that ghostly figure who had fathered her, but he was also the person who had mixed up her life and now stirred her emotions somewhat unfavourably.

But she had made herself a pact. It was that she would never again be owned by anyone, however well-meaning they appeared to be. A stepmother was not what she wanted either. Snow White was still in her mind, and now knowing that she was beautiful, she saw that she might pose a threat to another woman. She didn't share any of these thoughts with her two uncles but thanked Sir Michael and asked for time to think about it.

That night she spoke to Emma of the offer her uncle had made. Emma was delighted that Susie's head had not been turned by all the good fortune that had suddenly come into her life.

'Don't be daft, Emma, I'm still myself,' she said laughingly, 'and we've shared too much in our lives for me not to ask your opinion about all these relatives who suddenly want me. They're maybe just being kind but I don't want to live my life as a charity case. I think the professor genuinely cares for me, but what about these others. They might have ulterior motives, though I can't think what they might be. I have to decide what to do with my life as you have yourself, but I'm not planning to jump into anything until I've thought about it. What about you. You'll marry John soon I presume?'

'Yes, that's the plan but John is feeling dissatisfied with England at the moment and though he hasn't told his mother or his family yet, he's got the wanderlust.'

'What do you mean,' said Susie. 'Where does he want to go?'

'He's not sure yet, he mentioned America or Australia, but I don't want to sail all that way on a convict ship. I mean would you?' Susie was quiet for a bit then she spoke.

'Maybe not a convict ship but somewhere else would settle my problems with too many relatives wanting me. What a turn up for the books, if only I'd had someone wanting me when I was little,' she said pensively.

'You wouldn't have been the same person, and you wouldn't have met me if your rich relatives had wanted you as a child,' said Emma thoughtfully.

'You're right, lass, and we have each other and what we have, let's hold on to.'

'I'm with you there, Susie, let's not be parted again, at least in spirit.' And the two girls hugged each other as they remembered everything they'd shared. How they'd supported each other through all the suffering as children, grieved over their necessary parting as teenagers, but now having grown into young women, they realised that their painful experiences had set them free. And with knowledge of that free choice, they lightly took hands and danced a kind of jig.

As they reeled around and around, Emma picked up on Susie's theme and chanted in time to the dance, 'To have and to hold from this day forward. For better for worse, for richer for poorer, in sickness and in health…and whatever life brings in the future, together we'll stand.'